MARY BALOGH, was born and raised in Swansea, South Wales. She moved to Saskatchewan, Canada, after graduating from college, and taught high school English for twenty years before retiring to write full-time. She currently enjoys a stress-free life at home with her husband, the youngest of her three children, the family dog, and her computer. She also enjoys her involvement with the Catholic church, most notably as an organist and cantor. She is the author of the Onyx historical romance, *Deceived.*

ANNE BARBOUR developed an affection for the Regency period while living in England. She now lives in the Black Hills of South Dakota with her husband, a retired lieutenant colonel. She is the mother of six children, all grown, and she loves to boast of her five grandchildren. Anne's latest Signet Regency is *Lady Liza's Luck.*

SANDRA HEATH, the daughter of an officer in the Royal Air Force, spent most of her early life traveling to various European posts. The author of numerous Signet Regencies, including *Cruel Lord Cranham* and *The Makeshift Marriage,* Sandra now resides in Gloucester, England, together with her husband and young daughter.

MELINDA McRAE holds a master's degree in European history and takes great delight in researching obscure details of the Regency period. She lives in Seattle, Washington, with her husband and daughter. Her latest Regency

ANITA MILLS, th.......................................al, *Autumn Rain,* resid......................................us-band Larry, eight c.......................................her of history and Eng......................................as-sion for both into a writing career.

FROM THE HEART

Five Regency Love Stories

by

Mary Balogh

Anne Barbour

Sandra Heath

Melinda McRae

Anita Mills

A SIGNET BOOK

SIGNET
Published by the Penguin Group
Penguin Books USA Inc., 375 Hudson Street,
New York, New York 10014, U.S.A.
Penguin Books Ltd, 27 Wrights Lane,
London W8 5TZ, England
Penguin Books Australia Ltd, Ringwood,
Victoria, Australia
Penguin Books Canada Ltd, 10 Alcorn Avenue,
Toronto, Ontario, Canada M4V 3B2
Penguin Books (N.Z.) Ltd, 182–190 Wairau Road,
Auckland 10, New Zealand

Penguin Books Ltd, Registered Offices:
Harmondsworth, Middlesex, England

First published by Signet, an imprint of Dutton Signet,
a division of Penguin Books USA Inc.

First Printing, January, 1994
10 9 8 7 6 5 4 3 2 1

Contents

The Anniversary

by Mary Balogh

SHE stood with her forehead pressed against the glass of the window, staring sightlessly downward, picturing in her mind how the day would be unfolding if she had accepted Hester Dryden's invitation—if she had been *allowed* to accept it. She would have left here in the morning. She would be arriving now if there had been no delays on the road. It was such a glorious mild sunny day that it was very unlikely there would have been delays. She would be arriving now, kissing Hester, turning her cheek for George Dryden's kiss, linking arms with Hester, and going inside to meet the other guests. Jane Mallory, her best friend along with Hester would be there, Edward Hinton, Charles Mantel ... She smiled bleakly. All her old beaux would be there, and numerous strangers, too.

There would have been tea and dinner, cards and gossip, conversation and laughter, to look forward to for the rest of the day. And Valentine's Day tomorrow with its day-long activities and ball in the evening. And then the return home the day after tomorrow. It would all have been quite harmless and very pleasant. Pleasant—it was a very bland word. But it would have been no more than pleasant. It never could be. And never had been. Valentine's Day had never been the time of sweet romance she had always dreamed of. She had lived in the country until two years before, and no one there had ever made anything special of the occasion. Her parents, she sometimes thought, did not have one romantic impulse between them. Two years ago, although they had been in town already, she had not been allowed to attend the Valentine's Ball that everyone else was attending because she had not yet been presented at court. Her parents were sticklers for what was socially correct. It was rather funny under the circumstances.

And then last year ... She closed her eyes and pressed her forehead more firmly against the glass. It was better not to think about last year.

He might have allowed her to go to Hester's, she thought, opening her eyes and turning from the window at last in order to wander across the room to her dressing table, where she idly lifted a brush and ran her hand over its bristles. She had thought it a mere formality when she had written to ask his permission. He had never withheld it before. But this time he had. She was to remain at Reardon Park, she had been instructed. He was to come there himself on the thirteenth. Today. There was no sign of his arrival yet.

She might have expected that he would be glad of her absence during his visit. The last time he had come, he had stayed for three weeks. But they had not once sat together in the same room or walked together or eaten a meal together. Except when they had had company, of course. They had not exchanged above a dozen words a day during those three weeks. If he felt duty-bound to come home in order to consult with his steward or show himself to his people, then he should have been relieved to know that she was planning to be at Hester's for a few days.

Or perhaps it was her very request that had prompted his decision to come home. Perhaps he was deliberately trying to spoil her enjoyment. Precious little enjoyment she ever had out of life these days. Though there was no point in feeling self-pity. She had brought it on herself. All of it. It was entirely her own fault that she was where she was now, living the life she was living.

She set the brush back on the dressing table and raised her eyes to her image in the glass. Amy Richmond, Countess of Reardon. Her eyes mocked herself. She was wearing her best and her favorite sprigged muslin, the one she had scarcely worn the year before. In February! It was true the weather felt like spring and the sun outside felt almost warm. But even so—muslin was not quite the fabric for February. And she wore the new blue kid slippers that matched the sash of her dress almost exactly. Jessie had spent half an hour on her hair before she was satisfied with the way it looked. Very often she did not even summon Jessie to do her hair. She combed it back smoothly herself and knotted it at her neck. But today there were waves and ringlets. Her hair looked almost blond this way.

She was looking her very best. As if for some special occasion. As if for someone special. Because he was coming home? A faithless husband, who had married her almost a year before and not bedded her on her wedding night or any night since, who had brought her here on her wedding day and left the same evening to return to London? Who had been home only once since ... for those three silent weeks? Who had now forbidden her attendance at the only Valentine's party of her life? Had she dressed like this for him?

She hated him.

She should be wearing one of the wool dresses she would normally be wearing. The brown one—the one she rarely wore because it seemed to sap her of both color and energy. She should have her hair in its usual knot. The fact that he was coming should be making not one iota of difference to the pattern of her day.

She stared at herself in indecision. But even as one hand reached for the brush and the other for the pins in her hair, she heard it—the unmistakable sound of an approaching vehicle. Her stomach somersaulted uncomfortably, and her hand returned the brush to the dressing table. She crossed to the window, careful to stay back from it so that she would not be seen to be looking out. A curricle. He had chosen to drive himself rather than come in state with all his baggage. That must be following along behind with his valet.

He was wearing a many-caped greatcoat and a beaver hat. He was dressed sensibly for winter. It would be very obvious to him that the muslin had been donned in his honor. She felt a wave of humiliation. And dread. Should she go down? Or should she stay in her own apartments and let him seek her out if he chose to do so? What if he chose not to? Then the situation would become unbearable. She would be afraid to venture from her rooms at all for fear of passing him on the stairs or walking into a room that he occupied. Better to go down now.

The dutiful, docile wife.

How she hated him.

She left her room and descended the stairs slowly. She entered the grand hall reluctantly, feeling small and cold in its marbled splendor as she always did. She was aware of Morse, the butler, who stood in the open doorway, and of several silent footmen, none of whom looked at her. What must they make of her marriage? she wondered. Did they laugh belowstairs at her humiliation? She clasped her hands loosely before her and raised her chin. She took several slow, deep breaths.

And then his voice outside was giving instructions to a groom and greeting Morse, who was bowing with the stiff dignity peculiar to butlers. There was the sound of his boots on the steps at the same time as Morse moved to one side. And then there he was, seeming to fill first the doorway and then the hall with his tall, solid presence. As sternly and darkly handsome as ever. His expression was as stony as ever, though she had the strange impression that he had been smiling before entering the hall.

His steps did not falter when he saw her standing there to greet him. He strode toward her, stopped a few feet away, and bowed to her. "My lady?" he said. "I trust I find you well?"

"Thank you, yes, my lord," she said, watching his eyes move down her body. She felt proud of the fact that she was as slim as ever, perhaps slimmer. Jessie said—not entirely with approval—that she was slimmer.

"And my son?" he asked.

She felt a flaring of anger at his assumption of singular possession. He had not set eyes on his son for two and a half months. "Well too," she said, "I thank you."

"You will take me to see him before I go to my room?" he said.

It was phrased as a question, but really it was a command. She was to take him to see his son. No matter what the household routine might be. The master had come home, and the master wished to see his son. She inclined her head and turned to lead the way to the stairs. Fortunately, she thought, she had turned away soon enough to make it seem likely that she had not seen his offered arm. She had no wish to take his arm. Since she did not take it, he paused for a few moments in order to remove his greatcoat and hand it to the butler before following her.

He was glad she had come down to greet him. God, he was glad of that. For the last several miles he had felt nothing but dread. If he had not written to warn her of his arrival—and he probably would not have done so if she had not first written to ask permission to attend Hester Dryden's Valentine's party—he feared that he would turn utterly craven and change his destination. Going back to Reardon was the hardest thing he had done in his life. Last time it had been hard enough, but at least then there had been a clear reason for going. He had gone home for the birth of her child. His child. Their child. It had been hard to believe, alone in London, that he had fathered a child. It had been even more difficult to believe when he had gone to Reardon to find her huge, ungainly, and startlingly beautiful that his seed had caused that bulk inside her.

He had stayed for the birth and the christening before fleeing back to London. He should have stayed then and worked something out with her. But how could one work something out with a stony-faced, tight-lipped, hard-eyed girl when one knew oneself responsible for ruining her life? The word *rape* had never been used—not even by her father that first day. Never by her. But it had hammered in his brain for almost a year. Very nearly almost a year. A year tomorrow. A valentine's wooing! A rape that no one else called rape except him. How could one work something out with the woman one had raped, impregnated, and forced into marriage? Guilt, which gnawed at him constantly, tore into him whenever he set eyes on her.

And now he was to set eyes on her again. And to work something out with her. Something that would make her life seem a little less like imprisonment in the country. Something that would make his own life a little more bearable—something that would give him just one good night's sleep again.

He was glad she had come downstairs and not hidden in her rooms as she had done during his last visit. He would not know how to handle that, just as he had not known then. Perhaps he would take his cue from her again: keep away from her and return to London after a week or two with nothing settled at all. With a wife like a millstone about his neck and a guilt as huge and painful as a cancer. And a son he ached for.

He had smiled at Davies, the elderly groom, and at Morse, pretending to both them and himself that he was delighted to be back home. He would smile at her, too, he had decided, if she had come down to greet him. And yet he knew the smile had faded even before he got inside the hall and saw her standing there, a slim and beautiful girl. Too slim. Beautiful, but lacking the sparkle of something—he had never discovered what, he had never had a chance to get to know her at all—that had made him fall reluctantly in love with her two years ago. He had caused the thinness. He had destroyed the sparkle.

"My lady?" he said to her. He had never called her Amy. She had never called him Hugh. "I trust I find you well?" What a strange way to address one's wife of less than a year after a two-and-a-half-month absence from her.

"Thank you, yes, my lord," she said.

He should have taken her hand and raised it to his lips. But he hesitated a second too long, and the moment when it might have been smoothly done passed.

"And my son?" He lay awake at nights wanting his son, longing for that tiny, warm, perfect little bundle of life that had aroused such an unexpected welling of love in him as he had watched it emerge wet and blood-smeared from his wife's body. Her son. She had carried him inside her for nine months and delivered him after an agony that had lasted longer than twenty-four hours. The child was more her son than his. And yet in London he longed for his son. And that was how he had referred to him now. He wished he could recall the words and ask how *their* son was.

"Well too, I thank you," she said coolly. There was that in her voice and in her eyes that told him she still hated him as much now as she had when she had summoned him to tell him that she had changed her mind about not marrying him because there was to be a child—his stomach could still lurch at the memory of those words. She probably hated him more now because now she had had time to realize that it was a life sentence she had taken on.

He could not wait for a more decent time, when he would have had the opportunity to change from his dusty clothes, to wash and to comb his hair. His son— their son—was three months old already. He had been two weeks old when they had parted. He would have changed.

"You will take me to see him before I go to my room?" In his effort not to sound abjectly pleading, he sounded just the opposite, he feared. The arrogant master come to see his heir. James. He rarely thought of the child by name. He thought of him as his son. He offered his arm too late. She had already turned from him without a word to take him to the nursery. He paused for a moment to remove his greatcoat before following her.

She was slender. Not exactly thin. She was as shapely as she had been before he had impregnated her. Her hips still swayed as she walked with a provocation he guessed was unconscious. He had never been able to bring himself to court her in the normal way, although he had been in love with her for almost a year before it happened. He had not wanted to be in love. He had not wanted to marry. He had earned and coveted his notoriety as one of London's most active rakes. She had been a bright little star beyond his reach because he had chosen to live his life in a different sphere from the one she moved in. And now, although she was his wife and the mother of his son, she was forever outside his sphere, or he was outside hers.

But something must be settled.

The child's nurse smiled at his wife and then, seeing him, curtsied deeply. "He has just woken up, my

lady," she said. "I have changed his nappy, but he is
rather cross." She flushed, darting him a look. The
baby was crying in his crib.

His wife bent over the crib while the nurse tactfully
withdrew. He watched her face in profile. It softened,
and she smiled—and he knew again that he had been
shut out of her life. Because she hated him.

And then his stomach lurched again. His son had
grown. He was no longer the tiny, red, and wrinkled
little bundle of ugliness and beauty with his shock of
dark hair. He was now all plump and cuddly beauty,
his hair still dark, but thinned out, sleek and shining.
He stopped crying at the sound of Amy's voice or at
the fact that she picked him up. He stared about him
with dark eyes. His son looked like him, the earl
thought. By what miracle had he been carried in his
mother's body and born of her, and yet looked like
his father?

He clasped his hands very tightly at his back. He
felt that rush of almost painful love again. He swallowed, afraid for one moment that he was going to
cry. "He looks like me," he said.

"Yes." Just the one word, curtly and coldly spoken.
He wondered if she loved the child, since it was what
had finally forced her hand. She had had the foolish
courage to refuse him when he had offered for her
the day after the—rape. She had recalled him five
weeks later when she had discovered that that single
drunken encounter—they had both been drunk—had
had consequences. The chances were that she would
hate the child as she hated him, especially since the
child resembled him. And yet one glance at her face
reassured him. She loved their son as he did.

"May I hold him?" Again his plea sounded more
like a command. He stepped forward and reached out
his arms before she had a chance to reply. She handed
him their son without looking at him. She was careful
not to touch him at all. She had touched him that

night. All over. With eager, seeking hands and mouth. She had been drunk, of course. He had known that and should have prevented what had happened even though he had been well into his cups himself. The point was that he was used to drinking and its consequences. He had not been by any means beyond all responsibility. He had known that it was the drink that made her bold and amorous. But he had taken advantage of it. He had done nothing to douse her eagerness. Just the opposite. He had used all his expertise on her. He had penetrated her body knowing full well what he did, knowing even what he must do the following morning. She had moaned with the pain, desire, and eagerness to be taken to the end of what she was experiencing. He remembered the shuddering spasms of her climax, the sobs of helpless joy, the clinging arms, the damp, fulfilled body. The smell of gin.

And then his son was in his arms, all soft, warm, sweet-smelling babyhood. He weighed so little that there was the instant fear of dropping him. The child's mouth found the bare skin above his cravat and was trying to suck. He turned and walked toward the window with the baby so that his wife would not see his agony—and his ecstasy. He touched one of his son's hands and spread the little, clinging fingers over one of his own. Perfection even down to the cuticles of the nails. How could one look at a baby's hands, he wondered, and not believe in God? It was a thought that took him completely by surprise. He was whispering to the baby. He did not know what words he spoke. The baby began to cry.

"He is hungry." The lack of emotion in the voice that came from behind him jarred him.

"Then he must be fed." He turned away from the window. "You have done well with him, my lady. He looks well cared for."

"Of course," she said, reaching out to take the baby from him. "I am his mother."

The baby rubbed his face against her shoulder, seeking food. He let them know his dissatisfaction at not finding what he sought. She flushed. The earl wanted more than anything to watch her set the child to her breast. He wondered what she would do if he did not leave or if he instructed her to feed his son. But he had no right to witness such intimacy. He had given her the protection of his name because he had taken her honor and her reputation and because his child was in her. He was her husband in the strictly legal sense. That doubtless gave him the right to any intimacy he chose to claim. But he had chosen to claim nothing. He was neither her friend nor her lover. He had no right to watch her set their son to her breast.

He made her a stiff bow. "I would be honored, my lady," he said, "if you would dine with me this evening." He would be damned if he would live with her as he had lived for the week before the birth of their son and the two weeks after. Surely they could spend a few days together in civil courtesy. And something must be settled. He was aware that he had come on the spur of the moment because he had not wanted her at a Valentine's party without him, perhaps flirting with other men, perhaps falling in love with another man, perhaps beginning an affair now that she had performed the duty of presenting her husband with a son and heir. He would not be able to blame her for such behavior—she had nothing from him. He just could not bear the thought of it. He had come without really planning to do so, but having decided to come, he was very aware of the occasion. Saint Valentine's Day tomorrow. The day on which he had raped her—though only he had ever used that word. It would be a bitter anniversary. Something must be done. Something . . .

"Of course, my lord," she said. He could scarcely

hear her voice above the angry wailing of his hungry son.

He turned and left the room. He wondered what they would talk about, seated alone together at the dining room table. Perhaps it would have been as well to dine in their separate apartments as they had done during his previous visit.

God, he loved her still, he thought, coming to an abrupt halt at the top of the stairs that led down to his apartments. He was shaken by the unexpected realization. Shaken by his meeting with her now that he had been away from her again. So slender and lovely—and so cold and joyless. He wondered how she would have responded to him if he had chosen to court her. London's worst rake and society's freshest blossom. Perhaps he might have brought her to love him. He had no experience with innocence, but he had had plenty of other experience with women. Had he chosen to make the effort, he could surely have adapted that experience to the wooing of innocence.

Perhaps she would have been his wife now, the ornament and the love of his life. Perhaps that look she had always had—that look of eagerness, mischief, whatever it had been—would still have been there. Perhaps she would have looked at him that way. Perhaps she would have loved him. Perhaps he could have added another dimension to her life instead of destroying all that was worth living in it.

A pointless thought. He shook it from him as he descended the stairs. And yet something had to be done. He had made an empty shell of her life. He had made his own scarcely worth the trouble of living. Was it too late to woo the woman one had ruined and married and incarcerated on one's country estate and heartily ignored for almost a year? Too woo her on Valentine's Day? It sounded like the appropriate day on which to try. Except that for them it would be the worst of all possible days. He had wooed her exactly a year before, wooed her away from a party she had had no business attending right into the bed in which he had taken his pleasure with countless courtesans and mistresses. It was too late this year to try to set the clock back, to try to do it right.

Far too late.

Wasn't it?

Was it?

Was there any way he could go back and do things as they should have been done? How should they have been done? How would he go about wooing her if she were not already his wife and did not already hate him? He knew only how to lure women into his bed. He was an expert at that. How would he woo Amy if she were still a young virgin and he the man eager to win her as his wife?

He shrugged as he opened the door into his dressing room and saw in some relief that his valet had arrived and was already making his rooms look lived-in. He did not have any idea how he would go about it. But perhaps, he thought, he should get some ideas before the next day dawned. Somehow, he thought suddenly, if anything was going to be set right, it was tomorrow that it must be done. The memories of last year needed to be offset by better memories of this year if their marriage was to have a chance of becoming even halfway bearable.

"Higher with the topknot, please, Jessie," she said when she was getting ready for dinner. And then, when the task was done, she realized that she looked almost magnificent enough to be going to a ball. She was wearing the rose pink silk that she had had made for last Season and never worn before tonight. By the time the Season had begun last year, she had been married and with child and living—alone—at Reardon.

Staring at herself in the looking glass, she considered changing quickly into something a little plainer.

But there was no time. Besides, she needed the boost to her morale that her appearance would give her. She was terrified. She had already thought of and rejected a dozen excuses she might send down for not joining him at dinner. She would not show such cowardice. She was his wife, his countess. They had been married for almost a year. Was she to cower in her own room because he had requested the honor—his word—of her company at dinner? She would not cower.

His coat and knee breeches—knee breeches just as if he were going to court or to Almack's!—were black, his waistcoat silver, his linen a startling white. He looked magnificent. As she joined him in the drawing room, she felt the old catch in the throat and quickening of breath she had always felt at the sight of him. London's most wicked rake, the man most to be avoided, though he had never shown any particular interest in any of the young girls who had crowded the ballrooms and drawing rooms during the entertainments of the Season. She had fallen deeply—and secretly—in love with him from the moment she had first seen him. Just as almost every other girl had done, she supposed. The eternal attraction of the rake. Of forbidden fruit. She had woven dreams about him. She had hugged her pillow to her at night, pretending it was he. Poor silly girl that she had been.

He came toward her, holding out a glass. "Ratafia," he said when she hesitated. She felt herself flush as she took the glass and wondered if he remembered—or if he knew—that it had been gin at the opera house. She had never tasted gin until that evening. It had disgusted her and excited her. And four of them had made her light-headed, warm, and reckless. She had not been drunk in the way she thought of as drunkenness. She had not been insensible or fuddled in the mind. She had known clearly what was happening at every moment. It was just that she had been made into a different person, one who was willing to do everything that normally was confined to her dreams. Like leaving the masquerade with the Earl of Reardon—she had known who he was from the first moment even though he had been masked and wearing a black domino.

She should not have been at the masquerade at the opera house. No decent woman attended such scandalous affairs. But she had been feeling upset and mutinous at her parents' refusal to allow her to attend the Pearsons' Valentine's Ball even though, unlike the year before, she had made her come-out. They had been obliged to attend a concert, they had told her. There would be time enough for balls and parties when the Season began later in the spring. But Duncan had arrived during the evening. Duncan was her devil-may-care, irresponsible, lovable cousin, who had brought a message for her father from a mutual acquaintance and who was going to the opera house masquerade. She had always been able to wind Duncan about her little finger. She had done so that evening and much against his better judgment—and her own—he had been persuaded to take her with him. Just for a short while, he had said. Just for a short while, she had agreed.

But he had been a careless chaperon and appeared soon enough to have forgotten all about her. His companions had offered her drinks, and, nervous at the boisterousness of the masquerade, she had accepted. And got herself pleasantly drunk. And recognized with a leaping of the heart, the tall black-clad gentleman who had asked her to dance. She had danced with him for over an hour before agreeing that it would be more comfortable to be private together for a short while. She had made only a feeble protest when she had found herself outside the opera house, then inside a carriage, and then inside a comfortable house alone with him.

She had been drunk but not insensible. Not at all.

She could remember every moment. She could remember how his mouth had felt and how shocked and excited she had been when he had put his tongue in her mouth. She could remember where he had put his hands and what he had done with them. She could remember the weight of his body and its splendid masculinity. She could remember the moment he had entered her body. She could even remember her surprise at feeling no great pain and her realization that her inebriation was acting as a sort of painkiller. But not a pleasure killer. Fully aware of the horror she would feel when she was sober, she had enjoyed every moment of the intimate play of their bodies. This was what he felt like, she had thought. This was what happened. At least this was what happened with an experienced rake. It was wonderful.

She had underestimated the horror that soberness brought.

"I have not poisoned it," he said.

She looked up at him, startled. There must have been a long silence. She must have been staring into her glass.

"Or would you prefer something stronger?" he asked. The word *gin* seemed almost to hang in the air between them.

"No," she said. "I must keep my milk pure." It seemed an unbearably personal thing to say. But what did she say to him? And what would he say to her? She realized more fully than she had yet realized that they were almost total strangers. Before last Valentine's Day, they had never spoken. Since then they had married and had a child together, but they had rarely spoken more than a dozen words at a time to each other.

"Ah, yes," he said, and she was aware of his eyes straying to her breasts. She lifted her glass to her lips and realized that her hand was not quite steady. "Dinner is ready. I told Morse that we would come in as soon as you came downstairs." He took the glass from her hand and extended an arm for hers.

They had made love, she thought, remembering the feel of him inside her, what he had done there, and the sensations he had aroused there. And yet apart from that, they had scarcely touched each other. She set her arm along his. Her fingertips rested against the back of his hand. She felt an unbearable physical awareness.

What if he had come to exercise his conjugal rights? she thought suddenly and felt her fingers press down involuntarily on his hand. It was a thought that had not entered her mind until this moment. She had assumed that because he never had exercised his rights in almost a year of marriage, he never would. But perhaps her pregnancy had held him away at first. Certainly James's birth would have held him at bay in November. Perhaps now after three months he would consider her sexually ready again.

What if he had come for that? What if tonight . . . ?

"If I seat you at the foot of the table," he said, "we will have to shout to converse."

He seated her to his right, sitting at the head of the table, where she usually sat. He intended then that they converse? He seemed very close. The room seemed horribly empty. The presence of Morse and a footman only succeeded in making it seem emptier.

"Is my s— Is James a good baby?" he asked. "Does he give you any trouble?"

She resented the questions. They seemed an intrusion. James was her baby. She had resented his taking the baby into his own arms earlier and carrying him over to the window in order to shut her out. She had resented the way he had said, "Then he must be fed," as if she would not have thought of it for herself. How did he think she had managed without him?

"He is my joy," she said, not realizing until the words were spoken how theatrical they sounded. "Of course he is no trouble. He usually sleeps through the night now. That is good after only three months."

The conversation seemed to be at an end. What if he wanted another child? The possibility had not struck her before. There were plenty of women who had babies yearly. The thought of becoming pregnant again so soon, of going through the birthing process again, terrified her. And humiliated her. She would have no cause to complain if that was his reason for coming home. She was his wife. She had not fully realized the helplessness of her situation until this moment. The helplessness of all wives. Perhaps he intended to stay until the deed was done, and he could return to London and all his other women until the time came to come back to claim ownership of another son. He would doubtless want another son.

If that was why he had come. He had not said why. Perhaps only to spoil Valentine's Day for her when she might at this moment have been enjoying it with Hester and some of her other friends.

"Tell me about our son, my lady." His voice was soft, but the command was unmistakable.

He might have been there to know about James for himself. But he might miss too much pleasure in London if he did that. She looked at him. His dark eyes—she could remember how they had gazed down into hers while his body moved in hers—looked steadily at her.

She licked her lips. "He likes to sleep on his stomach," she said, "with his legs drawn up beneath him. He looks most peculiar. He was a very unhappy baby before I discovered that."

"I sleep on my stomach," he said.

She almost laughed and then did. Her laughter sounded nervous and quite out of place.

"It is strange what can be inherited," he said. "Perhaps I should tell you some of my other peculiarities so that you will know what to expect."

What to expect of James or what to expect of him? She looked up at him.

It seemed that he almost read her mind. "As he gets older," he said after a pause.

"Do," she said. "I know nothing about you." The admission brought a flush to her cheeks.

Quite unexpectedly he began to talk about his childhood and about his boyhood at school. It sounded as if he had had a rather lonely childhood and as if he had enjoyed his years at school.

"I always vowed," he said, "that if I ever had a child, he or she would have brothers and sisters."

So she had been right. Oh, dear God, she had been right. She had not thought of it. She had not prepared for it. It was so long. Although she could remember it very clearly, it was rather as if it must have happened to someone else. And with someone else.

He got abruptly to his feet. "You have finished eating?" he asked. "Let me escort you to the drawing room."

"I am sorry." She felt humiliation again. "I should have left you to your port some minutes ago."

"Not tonight," he said, taking her arm and leading her from the room. "Do you still play the pianoforte?"

Still? Had he heard her? She did not believe he had ever noticed her until her bold drunk person had taken his eye at the opera house.

"And sing?" he said. "You used to have a lovely contralto voice. I can think of no reason why you would not still do so."

"I play and sing for my own amusement," she said.

"And will do so this evening for mine," he said. "If you please."

If she pleased! As if she had a choice.

He stood behind her while she played and sang. She did not know how he reacted to her music, though each time she stopped he asked for more. After longer than an hour, she got to her feet.

"James will be ready to nurse," she said. And she was, too. Her breasts were full and heavy with milk.

"He must not be kept waiting then," he said, inclining his head to her.

She hesitated a moment before turning toward the door, expecting him to say more, expecting him to indicate that he would be visiting her room later. A part of her—a treacherous, unwelcome part—hoped that he would. She had been unbearably aware of his physical presence all evening.

"Give me your hand," he said suddenly, reaching out his own, palm up.

She placed her right hand on his, wondering if he intended to draw her toward him. She was having difficulty breathing.

"Your left," he said.

She looked at him in incomprehension as she obeyed.

He did not close his hand about hers. Instead, his free hand touched her wedding ring and then drew it off over her knuckle. He dropped the ring into his pocket. She had not removed the ring since he had put it there on their wedding day. Even when her fingers had swelled during her pregnancy, she had not taken the advice of the midwife to remove it. Her finger looked strangely bare.

"That, I believe," he said very softly, "was an encumbrance. Apart from the fact that we share a son, we have no ties that merit the ring, do we?"

She was paralyzed with shock. During the evening, she had come to expect to be bedded. Instead he intended to put her from him, to end their marriage. Could he do that? Could he refuse her support? Could he take their child from her?

"For tomorrow at least," he said, "we are unmarried, my lady. But I cannot call you that, can I? Amy. Tomorrow you will be my valentine, Amy." He smiled a rather twisted smile that did not reach his eyes, and raised her bare hand to his lips.

What? Her mind could not translate his words into any meaning. What did he mean?

"I am sure," he said, "that our son does not await a late meal with any patience. He is like his father in that, too. Good night, Amy."

She licked her lips and felt a flicker of—desire? as his eyes dropped to observe the nervous gesture. "Good night, my lord," she said, drawing her hand from his and turning to hurry from the room. Even so he was at the door before her, opening it for her and closing it quietly behind her.

Tomorrow you will be my valentine, Amy. That was what he had said. He had never spoken her name before. Except during their marriage service, she supposed. She had not heard a word of that service. *You will be my valentine.* Whatever did he mean? And what did he mean by taking her ring and telling her that it was an encumbrance. Her knees felt rather like jelly as she forced them to carry her up the stairs toward the nursery. And she was breathless enough to have climbed ten flights instead of two.

Whatever did he mean? Whatever had he planned? A repetition of last Valentine's Day? She had been his valentine then, too, she supposed.

The baby was doing nothing to hide his displeasure at having been kept waiting a full fifteen minutes after becoming aware of hunger pangs.

The idea had come to him quite on the spur of the moment. If it could be called an idea. He had decided to use the evening to try to establish some sort of ease between them, to try to get to know her a little better, to try to reveal something of himself to her. He had planned to do the same tomorrow in the hope that at the end of it there would be some sort of a relationship between them. Some small measure of friendship and respect, perhaps.

The evening had been more of a success than he might have expected. They had talked through dinner, somehow filling in the silence with stories of their lives. It had all been very strained, very self-conscious, but it was more than they had ever accomplished—or even tried—before. He had suggested music in the drawing room afterward because he did not think they could keep the conversation going much longer. And yet it was too early to go to bed. Besides, he had always admired her playing and had always been intrigued by the unexpectedly rich, low pitch of her singing voice.

He had stood behind her while she played and sang, so that he could watch her at his leisure. And he had wondered what she would do if he followed instinct and bent to kiss the back of her neck as it arched over the pianoforte. Or if he slid his hands beneath her arms to cup her full breasts—full with his son's milk. He was jealous of his son. He had wondered, looking at her wedding ring, if she always wore it, if she had put it back on, perhaps, when she knew he was coming. It was something of a mockery.

And that was when the idea came to him. The impulse to erase all that was between them—except their son—and all that was not. The need to cancel the past and start again. On Valentine's Day, the day for lovers, the day when everything had gone wrong for them. And so he took her ring, the symbol of a marriage that was really not a marriage at all, and put from his mind the thought that had been lingering all evening, the thought that perhaps he would go to her bed that night and try to win her with sexual expertise.

It seemed like a good plan to make her his valentine for the day. Except that Valentine's Day to him had always meant only a more than ordinary excuse for philandering. He knew nothing about wooing an innocent young girl. If he was to erase last year and all that had happened since—except his son—then she was an innocent young girl. She probably was anyway. He did not know quite how she had come to be at that masquerade ball, but he knew she was not supposed to be there. And he knew she would not have acted as she had if someone had not been busy plying her with gin.

He was up very early in the morning, after his usual almost sleepless night, down in the kitchen stealing a rasher of bacon off the grill and having his fingers slapped for it by the cook while a maid gaped. The cook had been in his employment and in his father's before him for as long as he could remember. He had been stealing food from under her eye and being slapped for it for as long as he could remember.

"How does one woo a young maiden on Valentine's Day?" he asked.

"Sit down at the table like a proper gentleman," she said, as she had been saying to him all his life, "and I'll make you up a plate of bacon and eggs. But don't pick with your fingers. You don't need to be wooing no young virgins. You have a wife."

"How does one woo a young wife on Valentine's Day then?" He grinned at her and sat. Why did food in the kitchen always taste more delicious than food in the dining room? "Three eggs? Are you trying to fatten me up?"

"You be nice to her, that's what," the cook said. "Just a pretty little thing she is that comes tripping down here every day to approve the menu, and never thinks to set her fingers on any of my food, and says thank you very much when I gives her a cake or a tart what I have just baked. And as fond as you please of Master James. He has the look of you. This time next year I'll have to have an eye to the currants and the apples when he is around, like as not. You be nice to her."

The gardener had come into the kitchen. A long-time employee, too, he looked not at all taken aback to see his master seated at the kitchen table digging into an early breakfast. He rubbed his hands and held them out to the fire. "There be roses coming into bud in the hothouse, m'lord," he said with a grin.

"Are there, by Jove?" the earl said. "They are good for Valentine's Day, Jenkins?"

"Magic," the gardener said. "Better than di'monds, m'lord."

Morse, standing in the doorway, dignified and immaculate despite the earliness of the hour, looked pained to see his master eating with such informality. But he said nothing. He would scold the cook later, though his words would do no more good than they had ever done, he supposed. Cook was a law unto herself.

"We are discussing Valentine's Day, Morse," the earl said, holding out his plate hopefully to the cook, who frowned and forked three more rashers of bacon and two slices of toast onto it. "And how one woos a young wife for the occasion."

"Music, my lord," Morse said, bowing and spreading a snowy, freshly starched napkin over his master's lap. He would remind Cook about that, too. "The Reverend Williams has his nephew staying at the rectory. He is an accomplished violinist. He has played for the Prince Regent."

"And Miss Williams is still at home?" the earl asked. "She is an accomplished pianist." Probably more accomplished than his wife, he thought disloyally.

The butler bowed.

"They play a treat, they do," the cook said. "They played at church last Sunday. Miss Williams on the organ, of course. He didn't sound a bit like a cat, he didn't, on his violin. I never heard a violin before without it didn't sound like a cat. Yours included."

"Yes," the earl agreed. "My violin lessons did not last long, did they? It seemed to be mutually agreed by all concerned that I had no talent whatsoever."

"Praise the Lord, we all said belowstairs," the cook said, while Morse frowned at her and the gardener chuckled and the maid gaped.

"Music," the earl said, mopping up the last of the grease from his bacon with his toast. "And roses. And candlelight and dancing. I like it. Arrange it, will you, Morse?"

"A party?" the cook said, looking alarmed. "I can't do it on such short notice. I won't. What do you want served?"

"A party for two," the earl said. "It will be far more romantic than a party for fifty. Would you not agree?" He fixed his eye on the gaping maid.

"Oh, yes, your lordship," she said, blushing hotly and bobbing three curtsies in succession. "The first man a girl sees on Valentine's Day will be her husband, your lordship," she added irrelevantly. She bobbed again.

"That was why you was in the stables gawking at Roger almost before the cock had time to crow this morning?" Jenkins said with a chuckle. "And he was gawking back, too, Sal."

Sal turned an even deeper shade of red.

"Take that greasy plate away," the cook instructed her, "and wipe up the crumbs. Some people could have a plate as big as a house and still have crumbs dotted about it. Her ladyship already has a husband. Though sometimes one wonders."

The earl got to his feet. "There can be no harm, anyway, in doing everything one is supposed to do," he said. "What time does my wife usually get up?"

"She gets up earlier than any of the rest of us," the cook said tartly, "to give Master James his feed. But then she goes back to bed. Jessie will be taking up her chocolate soon. It is shameful a man has to be told such things of his own wedded wife."

"If you will stop scolding and pour the chocolate for me," the earl said, "I shall play ladies' maid myself this morning."

Sal sighed, the gardener chuckled, Morse looked dignified, and Cook poured. The earl took the tray with his wife's cup of steaming chocolate on it and climbed the servants' stairs to her room. It had felt almost like old times being down in the kitchen. It seemed to him that he had spent most of his childhood down there. His parents were always too busy to be bothered with him, and his nurse was a careless creature who had liked to sit gossiping in the housekeeper's room or else nodding off to sleep in the nursery. He had loved his nurse.

But it did not feel like old times now. Today was Valentine's Day, and he was on his way to begin the wooing of the woman he had seduced and ruined exactly one year ago and married six weeks after that. He was on his way to try to erase a year of bad memories. It seemed a daunting task he had set himself.

It was her ring that woke her. Or rather the absence of her ring. She had not realized how much she had fingered the ring and turned it on her finger until it was no longer there. She had noticed that fact the night before while she had lain awake trying to sleep. Trying to make sense out of what he had said and done. Trying to ignore the fact that he was sleeping in the master bedchamber, separated from her room only by the dressing room between. Trying desperately not to admit to herself that she wanted him. Her woman's needs were beginning to reassert themselves now that her body had recovered from pregnancy and the experience of giving birth. She had been aware for some weeks that she was twenty years old, that spring was coming, that she was going to have to learn to live her life without a man in it.

How did one learn such a thing? The craving had been there, muted, not fully understood, denied, even before the night of the masquerade. But now that she had had a man, despite the ugliness of the circumstances, she knew what it was her body needed. She knew what it was she would never experience again. It had been hard to fall asleep knowing that he was there in the next room. Knowing that he was her husband and James's father. Knowing that he had taken her ring and called it an encumbrance. Knowing that he had said she was to be his valentine the next day.

And now, she thought, twisting the ring that was not there, the absent ring that had woken her, it was Valentine's Day. She had no ring, no marriage, no reason to get up to be mocked by the day. She wished she could get up to find him gone again, taking her ring with him, the one symbol of their marriage—apart from James. She wished she could be alone with her baby again as she had been for almost three months. She had made her baby her world. She had made motherhood her reason for living.

Jessie had been already and left her chocolate on the table beside the bed, she noticed, opening her eyes. That was unusual. Although Jessie never did anything as ill-bred as shaking her or shouting into her ear, she did make her presence felt, bustling about the room, opening the curtains rather noisily, rearranging the already carefully arranged pots and brushes on the dressing table, clearing her throat. Jessie knew that she valued her mornings, that she hated to oversleep, even after those nights when James was hungrier than usual or decided to take his meal at a more leisurely pace than usual.

She turned onto her back, stretched out her legs, lifted her arms up at full stretch, and yawned loudly.

And realized that there was someone standing at the window watching her. Obviously not Jessie.

"Oh," she said.

"Good morning," he said.

She was not wearing a nightcap, she thought, mortified. Her hair must be all wild tangles. It usually was when she got out of bed in the mornings. How long had he been standing there? What was he doing here? She felt a sudden treacherous stab of desire deep in her womb. But he was not in his nightshirt or his dressing gown. He was dressed in riding boots and breeches and a dark coat. He looked—gorgeous. One of her hands strayed to her hair, but it was hopeless.

"I brought your chocolate," he said. "It should be just the right temperature for drinking."

"Oh," she said again, looking at the cup. She was expected to sit up and drink it? She was wearing a nightgown. It was perfectly decent and no more revealing than any of her flimsier dresses. But still, it was a nightgown. It struck her as rather ludicrous that she was embarrassed for her husband of a year to see her in her nightgown. Especially when just a year before—exactly a year before—he had done that to her that had got her with child.

"Don't sit up yet," he said, walking toward her. "You are embarrassed to have me in your room. You are quite right. I ought not to be here. I just wanted to make sure that I was the first man you saw this morning, you see."

She stared up at him, unconsciously drawing the bedclothes closer to her chin.

"It is Valentine's Day," he explained. "There is a superstition about the first man a woman sees on that day. Sal told me."

"Sal?" Her brain felt sluggish, as if his words should make sense to her. "Sally? The kitchen maid?"

"She was in the stables early," he said, "to make sure that Roger was the first man she saw. Roger, I take it, is the good-looking young groom who is new to my stables?"

She nodded, feeling stupid. What was he talking about?

"The first unmarried man a maiden sees on Valentine's Day will be her husband," he said.

"But we are already m—"

"No." He set a finger firmly across her lips. A warm and masculine finger that smelled faintly of—bacon? "Not today. For today we are single. And thus my presence in your bedchamber is scandalous. Today you are my valentine. I claim you by virtue of the fact that I am the first man you have seen today, my son excepted."

She understood at last. Though only in part. She did not know what it meant to be his valentine. The same as it had meant last year? She did not want the same as last year. At the time it had seemed unutterably romantic to be danced with and held close by a black-masked, black-cloaked gentleman whose identity she knew. She had thought it romantic to be whisked off by him for a private tryst. She had thought it romantic to be made love to. But she had seen it all through the deceptively rosy haze of alcohol. It had not really been romantic at all. None of it. It had been sordid. It could have been called seduction if she had not been so very willing from the first moment.

She wanted romance. Pure, wonderful, chivalrous romance. But it was too late for romance with him. And too late for romance with anyone else. Her life was to be forever without romance. And yet he was pretending that they were unmarried. He was claiming her as his valentine on the strength of an old myth that she had used to believe in implicitly. And perhaps—oh, just perhaps—he did not mean this year to be a mere repeat of last year. Perhaps he meant something else. Some game a little more romantic. Her heart yearned, and she remembered how she had

loved him, how he had been woven into all her dreams
before she had come to hate him.

"Your valentine?" she said.

"My valentine, Amy," he said. "Will you join me
for breakfast in—half an hour?"

"Yes," she said. "Thank you." For offering her
breakfast in her own home? It felt strange to hear her
name on his lips.

"Dress for riding," he said. "You do ride?"

It was strange too that he did not know that about
her. She rode for an hour or more every morning and
always refused an escort, even though the elderly head
groom constantly fussed over her and asked her rhe-
torically what she would do if she took a tumble when
she was far from home.

"Yes," she said.

"Half an hour, my valentine," he said, and she was
very glad suddenly that she was lying down and had
nowhere to fall. He leaned over her and kissed her
full on the lips. His lips were firm and closed and
tasted of bacon. He had eaten already. He was going
to have a second breakfast with her. Or else he was
going to embarrass her by watching her eat. He pro-
longed the kiss for a few seconds and then lifted his
head and smiled at her. That was the moment when
she knew the truth of what she had suspected as soon
as his head had come down to hers. Her legs would
not have supported her if she had been standing on
them.

"Yes," she said.

He straightened up and looked down at her for several silent moments, his smile gone. Then he turned
and left the room. Amy closed her eyes and touched
her fingertips to her lips. And swallowed against what
felt like a lump in her throat. And fought tears.

He had made a ghastly mistake, he thought, waiting
for her to join him at the breakfast table. His hand

played absently with a fork. She was not ready for a day of valentine's romance with him of all people. He should have allowed her to go to Hester Dryden's and have some fun with her friends there. He should have stayed far away from her on this, the worst possible anniversary. He had made an idiot of himself and had doubtless ruined her day even before she had got out of bed.

God, she had looked inviting in bed—warm and flushed and rumpled. He put the thought ruthlessly from him.

There had been no response. None whatsoever. Merely the blank stare that had suggested she thought him out of his mind. And the monosyllabic answers. Even when he had kissed her, her lips had remained still and quite passive. All very different from the last time he had kissed her, when her lips had pressed eagerly back against his and her mouth had opened under the insistence of his own, and her body had leaned invitingly into his. And she had been hot with the desire to be possessed. She had been quite, quite drunk.

How had he thought it would be possible to woo her now?

He could remember the scorn with which she had greeted him when she had been sent to him the morning after, his remarkably uncomfortable interview with her father at an end. Scorn and defiance.

"You owe me nothing, my lord," she had said with more bravado than truth. He had owed her his name. No one in the kingdom would have disputed that except her. "Certainly not marriage. I will not marry you."

She had remained adamant even when her parents had joined them after ten minutes. She had been on her way into the country before the day was out.

He closed his eyes. And he remembered the icy hatred with which she had greeted him after he had been summoned back to her father's house, wondering what awaited him there. Both her father and her mother had been in the room, but she had been the one to speak to him. She had been standing before the fire, her back to it.

"If you can see fit to renew your offer of marriage, my lord," she had said with no preamble, "I will accept it. There is to be a child."

He had renewed his offer in front of their silent audience. He had never felt more uncomfortable in his life. She had accepted. She had added something before her father took up the conversation with a discussion of the practical aspects of the wedding, which must take place with all haste.

"I could bear the disgrace," she had said very quietly. "But I would not have my child live his life as a bastard."

And he hoped less than one year later to make her his valentine, to woo her?

He stood as she entered the room, looking pretty and elegant in a moss green velvet riding habit and black boots. The habit looked comfortable and well-worn, though by no means shabby. She must ride frequently, he thought, and realized again how little he knew of her. He seated her at the table and motioned to Morse to bring her coffee.

"Oh," she said, staring at the long-stemmed rosebud that lay across her plate. She darted him a glance. "They are in bud already?"

"Gold," he said, "for the start of the day. For sunshine and beauty." He nodded to the butler to leave the room. Morse's lips were pursed.

"For me?" she said. "Did you cut it yourself?"

"For you," he said, noting the flush along her cheekbones. "I did. What may I fetch you from the sideboard?"

She looked startled. "Toast," she said. "And a glass of milk, please."

"For my son?" he asked, walking across to the side-board, where sure enough a tall glass of milk had been prepared for her.

"For James," she said, and he winced at his faux pas.

"For our son." He set the glass down beside her coffee and set the toast rack on the table in front of her. She was holding the rose by the stem and had the bud against her mouth.

"Thank you," she said, but it was not clear whether she thanked him for the milk or the rose. "Are you not eating?"

"Coffee only," he said. "I ate earlier."

"Bacon," she said.

"And eggs, too," he said. "How did you know? Has someone been telling on me? Cook fed me in the kitchen. At least twelve rashers of bacon and three eggs and four slices of toast. It was indecent."

"Cook fed you in the kitchen?" Her eyes widened. "She is a dragon. A benevolent dragon perhaps, but a dragon nonetheless. I do not know where she found this very large glass, but she fills it to the brim with milk three times a day, and if I do not drain it quite dry, she wants to know the reason when I go down next morning. I quake in my slippers. Sometimes I almost expect her to swat me with her wooden spoon."

"She slapped me this morning," he said, "when I stole a rasher of bacon and ate it with my fingers. I would not be able to count all the slaps I have had from Cook in my twenty-eight years."

She looked at him, startled again, and then laughed. He laughed, too.

"Imagine the humiliation," he said, "of being the Earl of Reardon and being rapped over the knuckles by one's own cook for eating one's own food."

She laughed again. It sounded almost like a giggle. "Was that when you found out about Sally and Roger?" she asked.

"She did not admit to the charge," he said. "But if there is a brighter color than scarlet, her cheeks were it."

"I wonder," she said, "if it will prove true for her. The superstition, I mean."

"I wonder," he said, watching her face, afraid that he was making an idiot of himself again, "if it will prove true for us. No, don't say the obvious. Play the game with me for today. Will you, Amy?"

"What game?" Her voice was little more than a whisper.

"The game of innocence," he said. "The game of romance. Is it impossible? With me is it impossible?"

"With you?" she said. "Romance?"

"Can you pretend?" he asked. "Apart from the fact there there is my s—, that there is James, can you pretend that we are innocents and even strangers about to embark on a day of romance? We are nearly strangers, after all."

"Just for today?" She picked up her rose again and twirled it slowly by the stem. "And what about tomorrow?" But she answered her own question before he could. "Tomorrow does not matter. As a girl I always dreamed of having a beau for Valentine's Day. I never had one. And never a Valentine's party. The year before last, I was not allowed to go to the one in London that everyone else was attending because I had not yet been presented. Last year, Mama and Papa were obliged to go to a concert and did not think it important to find me some other chaperon so that I could go. So I persuaded Duncan to take me to the masquerade at the opera house. I thought the very fact that it was forbidden would make it wonderfully romantic." Her eyes remained on the rose.

He could just imagine the young, innocent, naive girl: she had been thinking to enjoy some forbidden but innocent pleasure to hug to herself in memory. The one valentine entertainment that she had at-

tended in her life. He might have given her that pleasure without ruining her. Had he not drunk so much
himself, perhaps he would have done so. He had been
in love with her for a long time before that evening,
after all. Perhaps he might have started a courtship
pleasing to both of them. Despite his reputation, perhaps she would have accepted him as a suitor if he
had treated her as a valentine last year instead of as
a whore.

"This year," he said, "you have a beau. Will you
accept me as such today and let tomorrow take care
of itself?"

She raised her eyes to his. "Why?" she asked. "Is
it because you feel guilty? Do you?"

He did not want these questions. He wanted his day
of fantasy. He was greedy for it. "Yes or no?" he said,
hearing with dismay that his tone was quite curt.

She considered him in silence for a while. "Yes,"
she said at last. "For today only. Tomorrow, life can
return to normal."

The words chilled him. "When is James going to need
you again?" he asked. "For how long can we ride?"

"For well over an hour," she said. "Two probably."

"Let's not delay then," he said, getting to his feet
and drawing back her chair. She had eaten only half
a slice of toast, he noticed, though she had averted
Cook's wrath by drinking the milk to the last drop.
He did what he had resisted doing the evening before.
He kissed the back of her neck before she turned. She
hunched her shoulders slightly, but made no comment.
She turned back to the table as she was about to move
away and picked up her rose.

"I'll fetch my hat," she said.

He watched her lift the bud to her nose as she left
the room.

She led the way from the stables and took her usual
route without really thinking about it. She rode along

the mile of back lawn to the trees, through the trees
to the meadow, and along the meadow. Then she followed the line of the trees to the lake, which could
not be seen through the denser trees that grew about
it, to circle back around the lake and the house at
some distance, until the latter came into sight again
when she had more than a mile of front lawn to canter
across to reach it. James prevented her from ever
going much farther from home, though he did not
nurse quite as often now as he had done at first. She
had always refused to have a wet nurse.

Her husband looked quite splendid on horseback.
But of course she had known that. She had used to
watch him with covert admiration in Hyde Park, when
he had not known of her existence. She wondered
suddenly how he had known who she was so that he
could call on Papa the next morning. Even though he
had removed her mask and seen her face, it must have
been a stranger's face to him. How had he known that
she was a lady and not a doxy—was that the right
word?—like the other women at the opera house?

"There is a meadow on the other side of the trees,"
she said as they slowed their horses and moved carefully to avoid branches and twigs. "I like to gallop
across it."

"The meadow has not been moved to another location then?" he said, making her feel thoroughly foolish. Sometimes it was hard to believe that this was his
home, that he had grown up here. "It was the one
place where galloping was strictly forbidden. It is a
favorite burrowing place for the local rabbits, apparently. The only time I disobeyed, I was given a hearty
walloping—by Davies, my father's head groom as he is
now mine. I have been much abused by my servants."

"The groom. The cook," she said. "Did your father
never object?"

"I never reported them, and they never reported
me," he said. "Shall we dismount and lead the horses

down to the lake? I believe we were all agreed that my parents would not have been much interested anyway. And so I pestered the servants, and they disciplined me and spoiled me and loved me, I do believe. Many of them are still with me. I think of them almost as family."

She had not known that about him. Until their conversation at dinner last night, she had not even thought of him as a child. A whole person. A man who had come to the present moment after twenty-eight years of living and experience. There must be so much to know. She felt a sudden pang of loneliness. He was her husband, and she knew almost nothing about him. He knew almost nothing about her. They were strangers.

But she was his valentine. During the day, perhaps, they could do something about the situation. Unless he meant the day to be romantic in a strictly physical way. Perhaps he planned to touch her and kiss her, and leave her lonelier than ever tomorrow. Physical intimacy without any sort of knowledge of the other person, without any sort of friendship could only make one achingly aware of one's essential aloneness. She knew that from bitter experience.

"I always vowed," he said, "that if and when I had children of my own, I would not neglect them. No, this will not do, will it? The trees have grown thicker, and the slope will get steeper soon. I'll tether the horses here, and we'll go down without them."

The lake was not ornamental or man-made. It was surrounded by trees and was at the foot of steeply sloping banks. It was a place where Amy had come frequently the summer before as she grew heavier with child and heavier too with despair. She had used to sit on the bank, staring into the deep water, trying to make sense out of the turn her life had taken.

"It is easy to slip here," he said, taking her hand in

a firm clasp. "I would hate to see you hurtling down the slope and plunging into the water."

She laughed. "I came here often last year," she said, "when I had an ungainly bulk to carry about with me."

"Did you?" His hand tightened on hers for a moment. "I spent many days here as a boy, swimming—another forbidden activity—or climbing trees or merely sitting, weaving dreams. Ah, look at that."

It was not just a stray clump of primroses but a whole bank of them, all in glorious bloom as they faced the unobstructed rays of the sun across the lake.

"Oh, springtime!" she said, and the unexpected ache of an unnameable longing brought tears to her eyes. "There is no time like it, is there? What would we do if spring did not come each year? I have longed and longed for it this year."

"Have you?" He spoke quietly, and lifted his free hand to blot one spilled tear with his thumb. "Was your heart really set on going to Hester Dryden's party?"

She closed her eyes. No, it was not that. It was just that spring always brought with it new hope, a promise of something new, some reason for living. Her son was her reason for living. But even so there was so much surrounding emptiness. So much loneliness. She remembered suddenly, and for no apparent reason, the day her husband had returned to London, two days after their child's christening. There had been no warning. Merely the formal visit to her sitting room late in the morning to take his leave. A stranger going away again, taking everything with him, though she had not known that there was anything else to be taken.

She remembered the unwilling, self-pitying tears. The knowledge that she was alone again—though he had spent no time with her even before he left. All hope went with him.

He felt the ground, found it to be dry, and drew her to sit beside him and beside the primrose bank. He still held her hand.

"You were there," she said. "So soon after. Before there was time to wash him properly and wrap him. Husbands are not usually summoned until everything has been made pretty, are they? Were you waiting outside the door?"

She had had the confused impression that he had been there very soon. Too soon.

"Inside the door," he said. "Did you not know that I was with you for the last two hours? Did you not know who it was who sponged your face with cool water?"

Perhaps she had known. But it had always been too dreadfully embarrassing a truth to admit. She hoped she had been wrong. And it was too puzzling a truth. Men did not witness such scenes. Why had he?

"It is not surprising you did not know," he said. "You had a far worse time of it than most women. The doctor thought you were going to die." His hand tightened painfully about hers.

"You came because you thought I was going to die?" she asked.

"I came," he said, and he inhaled slowly, "to see— to see what I had done to you. If you were going to die, I was going to witness the death I had given you. I could not share it. That was the damnable thing. But I could punish myself with it. It would have been something I could never have erased from my memory."

She stared at him, dumbfounded.

"Instead," he said, "I witnessed the terrifying miracle of birth. And I heard you laugh. You laughed at me when you were holding my son all blood-streaked on your stomach. You looked up at me and said, 'Look.' And then you cried. Do you remember?"

She remembered it clearly. It was the one clear

memory in a foggy recollection of pain and exhaustion. She had wanted him to bend over her, to touch the baby, to kiss her. She had not realized until that moment how much she had hoped that the birth of their child would bind them together as nothing else had. She had yearned for a sense of family. Instead, he had looked down at the baby, his face stony. She withdrew her hand from his in order to clasp her arms about her knees and rest her forehead on them.

"Yes," she said.

His fingers touched the back of her neck as his lips had done at the breakfast table. She no longer wanted the romance she had yearned for then. He was incapable of tenderness. She had learned that in the past year. She did not want the mockery of a valentine's romance with him. How would she bear his going away again?

"I did not intend talking about that," he said. "I did not intend talking about the past at all. I intended a day out of time."

"How can we pretend that we both came into existence only today?" she said. "And how can we pretend that we met only today? The past is there. The present cannot be divorced from it. The present is colored by it." She listened dismally to her own words. She wished they were not true. She wished she could accept the gift of the day that he had offered. It would be some small something to take into the future with her. But she had spoken the truth.

He sighed and ran his knuckles lightly back and forth across her neck. "I suppose you are right," he said. "The past cannot be changed either, can it?"

"No," she said against her knees.

There were several moments of silence. "How you must wish it could," he said.

"And you." And yet, she thought, and was surprised by the thought, she was not so sure she would change the past if she could. There would be no James if the past were changed. There would not have been that night, whose ugliness had been apparent only after it was over. There would not be this day and this moment. She shivered under the light stroking of his hand.

"Changed," he said. "Not erased."

"Changed how?" She closed her eyes tightly.

"Who was hosting a Valentine's Ball that evening?" he asked. "Someone must have been. I wish it had been that one we were both attending. I wish I had asked you to dance at that. I wish we had been surrounded by the eagle eyes of a hundred chaperons. I wish I had sent you flowers the next day and called to take you driving."

"No you don't," she said. "You never consorted with girls like me. You never even noticed us. You would have been bored. You would not have got from me what you want from women if I had not been unchaperoned and if I had not been drinking."

"Did you know what was happening?" he asked. "I have often wondered."

"Yes," she said. "I knew."

"Did you know who I was?" he asked. "Either before or after I removed my mask?"

"From the first moment," she said. "Your identity was unmistakable." She would not return the question. The answer was too humiliatingly obvious.

"You must have been very inebriated then," he said, "even to have agreed to dance with me. Were not all the little girls warned to have nothing to do with me?"

"Perhaps," she said bitterly, "you do not understand the attractions a rake has for girls who have been hedged about with dullness and propriety all their lives."

"Ah," he said. "And so you had your brief moment of adventure and defiance, Amy, and are now hedged about with dullness and propriety again."

That was it in a nutshell. Perhaps that was life. She knew so little about it. Perhaps life was a dull thing interspersed with brief moments of adventure, defiance, and joy. Had it been a moment of joy, their coupling exactly one year ago? Yes, it had. God help her, it had. On the spur of the moment, she could think of only two moments of pure joy in her life. That was one. The birth of their son was the other.

She was suddenly aware of a familiar tautness in her breasts. "James will be needing me," she said, lifting her head. "I must go back."

He got immediately to his feet and held out a hand to help her up. "I did not intend the day to develop this way," he said. "But perhaps it was inevitable. Perhaps now that we have begun talking to each other, we have to deal with the past before there can be any present. But it is Valentine's Day, and you are my valentine. Look at the primroses, Amy."

She turned her head obediently and looked. She had not been to the lake since last autumn. Perhaps she would not have come until summer if he had not suggested it today. She would have missed the primroses. How fleeting a thing joy was.

"Now look at me," he said.

She did so, raising her eyes slowly from his chin. It was not easy to look into his eyes.

"Smile for me," he said. "Because there is spring, beauty, and hope. And because it is February the fourteenth, and you are my valentine."

She knew that however foolish it was and however painful it would be, she would look back on this day with longing. She knew she was still a naive girl and not the mature woman she had thought she had become. She knew that she was still as much in love with him as she had ever been. She smiled, though her eyes dropped back to his chin as she did so. She watched him raise her hand to his lips and turn it over to kiss the palm.

If only, she thought. Ah, if only ... She drew her hand free and turned from him to scramble up the bank toward the tethered horses.

He set a pink rosebud across her plate on the luncheon table—pink to suggest the warmth of afternoon. But she was still busy in the nursery. He paced.

The day was not progressing at all as he had imagined it would. He was not at all sure that it was not quite disastrous, in fact. He had wanted to live through the day and to take her through it without either of them once thinking of the events that had brought them together and held them together. He had wanted to woo her as if they really had met for the first time today. It was an impossibility, of course, a romantic dream. It was surprising, he supposed, since he had never thought of himself as being even a remotely romantic person.

Perhaps, he thought, the only hope for them was to delve back into the past and to come to terms with it—together. But he did not want that to happen today. Tomorrow, perhaps, but not today. But perhaps there could be no today if one denied yesterday. He sighed and readjusted the flower so that the bud was on the plate instead of hanging over the edge.

He knew what he wanted to do at this very moment. He had resisted the urge to follow her to the nursery. She would not like it at all. But she was his wife, and her baby was his son. He felt excluded and lonely. Not self-pitying. He had deliberately excluded himself after being unable to do so while she was in the process of giving birth. He had no right intruding on their lives when his own part in them had been such an ugly and guilty one. She had been forced to marry him. He would not force her to live with him forever after. He had given her the only gift that seemed of value—the gift of freedom from his presence. But he felt excluded and lonely now—as he had every day of the two and a half months since he had dragged himself away back to London.

He paced a few more times, glanced at the pink rosebud, which needed no further readjustment, hesitated, hurried from the room, and dashed up the stairs two at a time to the nursery floor so that he would not have time to think and give in to a feeling of guilt.

She was sitting in a rocking chair by the window, her dress lowered to her waist and her elbow on one side, gazing down at their son, who was sucking contentedly. But she looked up, startled, flushed and glanced about her. There was no shawl or blanket to hand with which she could cover herself. She closed her eyes and leaned her head back against the frame of the chair while he shut the door quietly behind him.

He watched in silence for a while before strolling across the room toward them. She kept her eyes closed and rocked the chair slowly. There was something almost tangibly intimate about the scene, he thought. His wife and his son bonded together—the son he had put inside her with such careless pleasure, the son she had borne in such agony while he watched helplessly as he watched now. Excluded. By his own choice. By the nature of what he had done to her. Could he ever atone?

He reached out and touched the backs of his fingers lightly to the inner side of her breast, touching his son's hand as he did so. The child was sleeping, his mouth slack about her nipple. She opened her eyes and looked up into his. It was a moment of unbearable sweetness. It was a moment, the merest moment of time, when the three of them belonged together. A family.

"Amy." He heard the whisper of his own voice.

He watched her eyes grow luminous with tears before she lowered them to the baby, lifted him away from her breast, and covered herself with her dress. The tears alit hope in him—and doubt. Why did she cry? Because she had felt the moment, too? Or because he had spoiled a time of intimacy with their son? He was almost afraid to hope.

"Let me take him," he said, and he lifted the baby off her lap, cupping the warm little head in one palm and holding the feet against his stomach. The baby's mouth had fallen open. He felt that stabbing of love again. He had missed two and a half months. How could he miss any more? How could he let his son grow up at long distance? He lifted the child toward him and kissed his wet mouth. He tasted Amy's milk.

"You do love him, don't you?" she said, getting to her feet abruptly. But her voice was agitated and unexpectedly bitter. "Is that why you came? Did you suddenly realize that you have an heir to carry on your line and your title? Is that why you have decided to make up to me? Because while he is young and helpless, I am necessary to him and therefore to you?"

He looked helplessly about him. The child's crib was in an adjoining room. He went into it, set his son down carefully so as not to wake him, and covered him with a warm blanket. He remembered to set the child down on his stomach.

She was standing at the window of the nursery, looking out. "Yes, I love him," he said. "Because he is my son. I do not think of him as my heir. I think of him as my son. And no to all your other questions. I came to see you. Your letter requesting permission to go to Hester Dryden's reminded me of what anniversary today is." He had come up behind her and set his hands now on her shoulders. "The anniversary of the conception of our son." He heard her swallow. "I love him, and I cannot say truly that I wish he did not exist, but it is a ghastly anniversary for all that. And all that has followed it has been even more disastrous."

She laughed, though there was no amusement in the sound. "Ghastly. Disastrous," she said. "Is it any wonder I held out against your first offer even though Papa threatened dire consequences? I should have held out against his insistence that I call you back. But I could not, of course. My baby did not deserve to be punished for my sins. He had to have a name and respectability. You and I do not matter. I do not care that you think your entanglement with me ghastly and disastrous. Perhaps you deserve to suffer. And I do not care that my life is an endless misery. I certainly do deserve to suffer. James is all that matters. I do not know what your game is today exactly, my lord, but it might as well end here. I want no more of it."

She turned suddenly and hurried across the room toward the door.

"The baby?" he asked, going after her.

"His nurse will be back in five minutes," she said, opening the door and continuing on her way through it.

He stopped on the threshold. Their baby was more important than they were, she had said. He could not leave the child alone even for five minutes. He went quietly into the inner room and gazed down at his sleeping son, whose head was turned to one side and whose bottom was elevated beneath the blanket. He must have drawn his legs up beneath him.

Could he read hope into her bitterness? Into her misery? Into her accusation that he had come down only to see his heir? Did she want more from him? She had smiled at him at the lake, because he had ordered her to.

Or was there no hope at all? Was it he who perpetuated her misery because she had been forced into marriage with him and could never be free of him?

One thing was sure, he thought as he heard the nursery door open and strolled into the room to smile at the nurse's surprised face, he was going to have some answers before the day was over. Perhaps Valentine's

Day was not unfolding at all as he had hoped or expected, but it had begun something. And something was better than the nothing that had characterized the rest of their marriage. Whatever it was that had begun was going to be carried to its conclusion—today.

"He is fast asleep," he said. "I shall leave him to your care."

It was sweet-tasting, he thought irrelevantly as he walked downstairs to the dining room, wondering what awaited him there. He had not expected a mother's milk to taste sweet. He wanted to taste it again. He felt an unwelcome stabbing of physical desire.

The sight of the pink rosebud across her plate shook her. What was he trying to do? What was this day all about? She could not help but be reminded of his reputation as a very successful rake. Did it amuse him to come here and punish her for asking to go to Hester's party by making her ache for what could never be in her life? Or was she being unfair to him? She was afraid to hope that she was being unfair.

She picked up the rose and crossed the room to stare out of the window. Morse was fussing at the sideboard. She relived that brief scene in the nursery, that brief moment in time when dreams had become sweet reality. Unbearably sweet. It had started when she had had her eyes closed to hide her embarrassment and had felt his fingers against her breast. It had not been a sexual touch. James had been there, too, asleep.

She had opened her eyes to find herself looking directly into his. And something had happened—that momentary sweet something to which she could put no name. That sense of—oneness. Three in one, almost like the Trinity, she thought guiltily. That sense of family. But no. There was no real word to put to what had happened. It had been overwhelmingly powerful, though. Surely she could not have felt it alone. And he had whispered her name.

Would he have done that if he felt nothing? But was it not in just such situations that rakes excelled? She turned to face him as she heard him enter the room, but she did not look fully at him. She hurried to her place and set down her rose beside her plate. She wanted to thank him for the rose, but she could not bring herself to say the words.

They reached for conversation, but could find nothing but banal comments on the weather and on the earliness of spring and the possibility that winter would yet return before they could consider it quite over. It was a silly conversation, as most conversations were, in which they mouthed the obvious and said nothing at all.

"Thank you, Morse," the earl said at last. "You may come back later to clear away."

Morse bowed and left the room with the footman who had been assisting him.

Her hand was on the stem of the rose. His hand reached out so that he could touch his fingers to the back of hers.

"What shall we do this afternoon?" he asked. "Walk? Jenkins tells me the daffodils are beginning to push above the soil."

"I said the game was over," she said, watching his fingers. Long. Very masculine. She remembered exactly how and where they had touched her a year ago, while she was conceiving their son. Or just before she had conceived, to be more accurate. "I want no more of it."

But the lie struck sudden panic into her. She wanted the game to continue. Oh, she did. The rest of today might be all she would ever have. She did not care what his motives were. Sometimes pride did not seem to matter. She wanted the rest of the game, whatever it was to be. She lifted her eyes to his, and his face blurred before her suddenly. She bit her lip.

"Why?" she asked him, her voice high-pitched. "Why? Tell me why."

"You have been a millstone about my neck for a full year," he said. His fingers curled about hers and held on tightly when she would have scrambled to her feet. "When I saw you and recognized you at that masquerade, I could not believe the evidence of my own eyes for a moment. I could not resist dancing with you. I believe I had some idea of protecting you from all the unsavory characters that were surrounding you. Comical, no?"

It was a rhetorical question. She looked at their hands. She wondered if he knew he was hurting her.

"You were drunk," he said. "You did not slap my face when I whispered things into your ear that I had no business whispering. You did not shove me away when I danced indecorously close to you. And so I decided to attempt kisses. Yet when I drew you apart, you came so willingly that I decided to attempt more. I was not drunk. Irresponsibly inebriated, perhaps, but I plotted your ruin with cold intent. Knowing you both unchaperoned and incapable of protecting yourself, I ruined you. And impregnated you into the bargain. Wonderful gentlemanly behavior. Wonderfully protective."

She wanted to point out that she was at least as much to blame for what had happened as he. But she said nothing.

"I did the honorable thing too late," he said. "I married you in all haste as soon as you accepted me, and I brought you here where you would be safe from the gossip and the malice that would have followed upon the arrival of our son less than eight months after the wedding. And then I returned to my life in London. To find that it was impossible to return to. You were a millstone."

"You abandoned me," she said, abandoning in her turn the pride that should have kept her mouth shut. "Can you imagine what it is like to be a woman nineteen years old, with child, newly married, and abandoned on her wedding day in a strange place among strange people?"

He was a long time answering. "Better that than being stuck with my company," he said.

She did not ponder his reply. "It was suitable punishment," she said. "I deserved punishment for what I had done. And I will not blame the drink. As soon as I saw you, as soon as you asked me to dance, I wanted you. I was excited by your reputation and excited by the fact that you had taken notice of me. I was excited by your words and your touch. And by your suggestion that we be alone together. I was excited by what you did to me. All of it. I found it all utterly wonderful. As if I had never been taught about propriety or sin or the consequences of sin. I have deserved all the consequences—the terror of knowing myself with child, the humiliation of begging you to marry me, the misery of being abandoned on my wedding day and again only two weeks after the birth of our son. I have deserved it all."

"Amy—" he said. He seemed to realize finally how tightly he was holding her hand. He loosened his grasp.

"But I will no longer pretend that it was ugly," she said passionately. "I have been accustomed to call it so because it was sinful and ought never to have happened. But I lie to myself when I call it ugly. I will not have it said ever again that my son was conceived in ugliness. He was conceived in beauty. I don't care who you were or are or how carelessly you seduced me—though no seduction was necessary. I don't care. It was beautiful, what happened. I was not so drunk that I cannot remember. I can remember every moment. Even though it was sinful and even though I must be punished for it every day for the rest of my life, I will no longer deny it. It was the most wonderful experience of my life, and I am glad James came of it. I am glad."

She snatched her hand from his and overturned her chair in her haste to get to her feet.

"Amy—" he said.

"It is not very flattering to be told that one is a millstone about someone else's neck," she said. "But I don't care. If it is guilt that has brought you here, my lord, you can go back to London tomorrow with a clear conscience. I absolve you of any guilt in what happened. I wanted it to happen. And I am not sorry it happened. So you can go back to your life and all your other women, and forget about me."

"Amy." He tried to regain possession of her hand, but she snatched it away again.

"And no more games," she said. "Perhaps they are amusing for you. They are not for me. Go play them with some other woman. Go away. Leave me in peace again. I have lived without you for a year. I can live without you for the rest of a lifetime."

She turned to rush from the room, but she jerked back again, before she could stop herself from so spoiling the effect of her anger, to snatch up her rose. She hurried away, waiting for him to say her name again. But there was silence behind her. She had to climb the stairs and make her way to her room from memory. Her eyes were blinded by tears.

The day was over. The day that might have been hers.

It was wrong to be feeling so elated, he thought as he walked through the formal gardens to look at the bank that sloped sharply downward beyond them. Sure enough, the brown earth was being nudged aside by numerous green shoots from the daffodil bulbs. There would be blooms before the end of the month.

And he would see them too this year. By God, he would. The blooming of the daffodils had always been the highlight of spring. He could remember taking a bouquet of yellow trumpets to Cook one year. She had tapped Jenkins's predecessor none too gently on the wrist when he had called him a young jackanapes. She had ordered the man to leave the dear little lad alone. The aggrieved gardener had gone stamping off to cut away the abandoned stems.

Even now, long before the daffodils came into bloom, he felt that light soaring of the heart that spring always seemed to bring—except last year. Paradoxically, he had found her bitterness and her anger reassuring. Her words had given him hope.

I wanted it to happen, she had said. *And I am not sorry it happened.* She had been speaking of the experience he would have thought she had found the worst and the ugliest in her life.

He was conceived in beauty. It was the most wonderful experience of my life.

He went down on his haunches the better to see one shoot that was just peeking above the surface of the earth. He had been. Their son *had* been conceived in beauty. Strangely it had been beautiful. He had felt so much guilt over it since that he had ignored the memory of how it had been at the time. It had not been the quick, frenzied coupling that one might have expected of two people coming together under such circumstances. He had made love to her. He could not remember making love to any other woman, though he had bedded more than he could possibly count. He had suppressed the memory of the tenderness with which he had given her joy. And guilt had forbidden him to remember the answering joy he had found in her body.

"I love you," she had whispered to him over and over again when he was deep in her body. She had been gazing up into his eyes, and he had believed the words and not found them either amusing or alarming.

"I love you," he had whispered back. Three words that he had never strung together and spoken aloud before—or since. Words that he had forgotten saying.

What had made her doubt between that moment and the next morning when she had refused his marriage offer? He straightened up and turned his steps to the hothouses. Perhaps the same thing that had made him doubt—soberness and the memory of who she was, and who and what he was. In her inexperience, she had probably imagined that what he had done to her body and the words he had whispered to her were what normally happened between a rake and his doxy. And in his inexperience, perhaps he had imagined that a young and innocent girl with a few drinks inside her could not possibly know what she did or said—and could not possibly welcome the addresses of the man who had seduced and ruined her.

No more games, she had said. *Go away. Leave me in peace.*

Did she mean what she had said? And yet she had been distraught and crying. And then she had turned back to grab the rose that was part of the game. Perhaps he had spent too long believing what she said and what she seemed to say. People did not always speak the truth, he knew. People did not *often* speak the truth when they were trying to mask emotions and protect pride. Had he ever spoken the full truth? Perhaps telling only a part of the truth was as bad as telling none of it.

"Jenkins," he said, seeing that his head gardener was inside the hothouse where the roses grew, his pride and joy, the one part of the garden that no other gardener was allowed to trespass upon, "show me the loveliest red bud, will you?"

Jenkins looked glum. "Another one?" he said. "I'm only glad whoever thought of Valentine's Day did not have the bright idea of making it Valentine's Week. That one I would say, m'lord. Or would you prefer one that is partly opened?"

"No," the earl said. "The tighter the bud the better. That one? Yes, I think I would have to agree."

Jenkins sighed. "That one it will be then. Making up for lost time, are you, m'lord?"

The earl looked at him sidelong. "I will not dignify that impertinence with an answer," he said. "I shall come just before dinner to cut it."

"She has them side by side in a vase by her bed," Jenkins said. "So Jessie says. Cook thinks it must be working, m'lord. Which is more than you deserve, she says. And the rest of us agree with her."

"Well," the earl said, "I shall have to remember my servants' opinion of me the next time I hear a whisper about a raise in wages, won't I?"

Jenkins chuckled and moved off to another part of the hothouse.

She half expected that he would have left during the afternoon, gone back to London without a word of farewell. That was what she had told him to do, after all. But a casual question to Jessie, when the latter had come to dress her for dinner, revealed that he was still there.

"And such lovely rosebuds those two are, my lady," Jessie said smugly. "Cut them himself, he did. Mr. Jenkins don't allow no one else even to set foot inside that hothouse. Fat lot of good the roses do when there is no one but him to look at them, I always say. Except you, of course, my lady. You are allowed in. And now his lordship."

"Yes, they are lovely," Amy agreed. "I must press them and preserve them before they pass their best."

Jessie smiled with secret satisfaction.

She should send word down that she would eat dinner in her room, Amy thought, frowning at the first two evening gowns Jessie held up for her approval, finally settling for the white lace over white satin and the vivid red sash that matched the red rosebuds at the top of each scallop of the hem. And yet, instead, here she was picking out one of her favorite dresses and sending Jessie in search of her red slippers. She would not cower from him, she thought, as she had thought the evening before. She would return to her room after dinner, but she would eat in the dining room. And she was quite prepared to discuss the weather and the season with him again if he felt obliged to keep the silence at bay.

She did not feel as unhappy as perhaps she ought. She had spoken the truth to him and freed herself of some of the pain of the past year. She had freed herself from some of the oppressive sense of guilt and sin that had hung over her all that time. What she had done was wrong. There was no doubt in her mind about that. But it had not been ugly. She was glad that she had admitted that. She was glad that she had realized it. And glad that she had told him, though it must have been patently obvious how vulnerable she was to him. It did not matter. It had felt good to admit to both him and herself that what had happened had been beautiful. That it had been the most wonderful experience of her life. That their son was the product of beauty.

She did not care what it had been to him. To her it had been beautiful. It had been an experience of love. Oh, not a very profound love, perhaps, since she had not known him and did not even now know him well. But it had been a love that had induced her to give herself, and it was a love that had not died even though she had spent a year hating him—and for good reason. How could he so cruelly have abandoned her? She would not think of it. It did not matter.

Satisfied with her appearance some time later, she turned her steps to the drawing room, where he was awaiting her as he had been the evening before. Perhaps, she thought, before he left, if she was given the chance, she would throw the final defiance in his teeth and tell him the full truth. Perhaps she would tell him that the words she had spoken to him over and over again while he had made love to her had been true. And that they were still true. He thought she had been a millstone before? She would be a veritable mountain for the rest of his life. She smiled as he handed her a glass of ratafia.

She bit her lip hard and willed the tears to stay back out of sight a few minutes later when he led her into the dining room and she saw the deep red rosebud across her plate. He had paid no heed to her words then. He was still playing the game. Whatever it was, he was still playing it. She longed—and dreaded—to know what the end would be.

"Thank you," she said. "Oh, it is beautiful. And it matches my sash and slippers."

"A red rose tonight," he said. "Red for passion."

If her chair had not been pressing against the backs of her knees already, she knew she would have disgraced herself and fallen to the floor. She sat down hastily.

"I shall leave you to your port," she said, getting to her feet. She had scarcely touched any of the food that had been placed in front of her. "Thank you for the rose—for the roses." She picked up the long-stemmed red rosebud.

"Amy—" he said.

"I shall retire to my room if you will permit it," she said. "I have a headache."

He took her free hand in his. "I will not permit it," he said. "And I do not for one moment believe that you have a headache. Sit down."

She sat, her eyes downcast, her lips compressed.

"Our guests would not take kindly to your going off

to bed without even bidding them a good evening," he said.

"Our guests?" Her eyes flew to his face.

"Only two," he said. "I see from Morse's nod that they are in the drawing room already, awaiting us. Shall we join them?" He got to his feet, bowed to her, and extended an arm.

"You did not tell me you had invited guests." Her voice was accusing, aggrieved. "I do not want to entertain guests. If they are your friends, you may entertain them yourself. I want to go to my room. James—"

"—was given your full attention not very long ago," he said. "And will not need it again until much later. It is my turn, Amy. There are two men in your life, not just one. You promised me today. Give me what is left of it. If you still feel as mutinous at the end of it as your tone and your expression suggest at this moment, then you may consign me to hell before you retire for the night. I may even oblige you by going there."

He smiled and felt treacherously lighthearted. He watched her lips compress still further and resisted the temptation to soften them with his own. It was a little too soon for that yet. She might reward him with a resounding slap. Besides, Morse, busy at the sideboard with two footmen, was drinking in the whole scene. From childhood on, the earl had realized that his servants were neither deaf nor blind—nor particularly closemouthed. Doubtless, everyone belowstairs would be crowing with delight at the information that he had kissed his wife in the dining room. They could go to the devil with his blessing, the lot of them. He suppressed a grin.

"The evening cannot pass quickly enough for me," she said, sniffing her rose.

He wasted a smile on her bent head. And then sobered. He was sure of nothing. Perhaps he had totally misread the signs all day. Perhaps by tomorrow he really would be consigned to hell.

"Who are they?" she asked when he paused outside the drawing room.

Morse had excelled himself. The carpet had been rolled back, and the bare floor shone. The grand pianoforte, which usually stood in one window alcove, had been moved farther out into the room. Miss Sarah Williams, the vicar's daughter, sat at it with her cousin seated at her side, his violin resting on his lap. The only light came from the single branch of candles that stood on the pianoforte. A table covered with a stiffly starched white cloth stood at the other side of the room, a bowl of fruit punch on it—nonalcoholic out of deference to James—and also a cake. The cake was a surprise to the earl. It was decorated with pink icing and a sculpted red rose and was—yes, by God it was— in the shape of a heart.

Cook! Dear Cook. She was going to have to endure a hug and a kiss on the cheek tomorrow. He would probably get himself slapped for his pains.

Miss Williams and her cousin rose to their feet.

"Sarah!" Amy said, hurrying forward, both hands extended. "And Mr. Carstairs. What a lovely surprise. Have you come to play for us? We are privileged, indeed." She kissed Miss Williams's cheek and shook the cousin by the hand.

"We certainly are," the earl said, bowing to his guests and noting with some satisfaction that the mutinous expression on his wife's face had been replaced by a glowing smile. "Perhaps you would treat us to a private concert for half an hour or so?" He seated his wife at some distance from the pianoforte and drew a chair up beside hers. She looked at him curiously and silently as he sat down.

The earl felt privileged long before the half hour was over. Mr. Carstairs was indeed a talented violinist, and Miss Williams's accompaniment was in no way inferior. Although he was paying the two of them a sizable sum for the evening's work, he felt humbled by the beauty of the music they played.

Amy sat watching and listening with glowing eyes and parted lips. He smiled at her between pieces and, feeling his eyes on her, she looked up at him and half smiled back. He took her hand and set it on his sleeve, covering it with his own. With her other hand, she held the rosebud on her lap.

"And now," he said at the end of the concert, getting to his feet after applauding the players and praising them, "to begin the ball." He reached out a hand toward Amy.

"Ball?" she said.

"Ball." He drew her to her feet. "We will dance on an uncluttered floor with no danger of being mowed down by an enthusiastic dancer and without the necessity of changing partners between sets or of having a variety of different dances. Waltzes, if you please," he said, turning his head toward Miss Williams and her cousin.

"We are going to waltz?" Amy said. "Here? Now? Alone?"

"Last year," he said, taking her rose and setting it on the chair, "you asked no questions. Last year I felt alone with you once we began to dance. Did you not feel alone with me?"

She was gazing into his eyes as if mesmerized. Miss Williams's cousin was tuning his violin again. "Yes," she said almost in a whisper.

"It was this time last year," he said, "that things began to go wrong. That we began to make some unwise choices. Let us see if we can do better this year, shall we?"

Her eyes sparkled with unshed tears. Her hand reached up to his shoulder as his arm circled her waist and drew her closer. "Yes." He saw her mouth form the word, though he did not hear it.

"It was a pretty mask," he said as the music began, and he moved with her to its rhythm. "But you look far prettier without it."

"And you," she said.

He grinned at her. "Prettier?" he said. "Ouch!"

She smiled fleetingly. "More handsome," she said.

"I whispered improprieties in your ear last year," he said. "What shall I whisper this year? That your beauty has outshone each of the roses I have given you today or all three of them combined? That you were at your most beautiful early this afternoon when your dress was down to your waist on one side and my son was at your breast? That the envy I felt of him amounted almost to jealousy? That today I have not been able to regret the events of last year? What shall I whisper that will have you melting against me as you did then?"

She moaned.

Steady, he told himself. *Careful.* He had ruined things utterly last year. Let him not compound the errors this year.

"Or shall I just be quiet?" he said against her ear. "Shall we enjoy the music and the dance, Amy? My valentine?"

"Yes." Her face looked somewhat distressed. "Yes."

He stopped talking.

My valentine. It is my turn, Amy. There are two men in your life, not just one. His words rang in her ears, seducing her with every passing minute. And his whispered words, lavish and expert in their flattery. He would only have to whisper the suggestion in her ear, and she would go with him as she had gone last year. She would allow him his pleasure again and be his dupe again.

But the music and his closeness and the heady masculine musk of his cologne weaved their inexorable spell about her. The drink had been in no way to blame after all, she thought. This year she had not drunk one mouthful of alcohol. Yet this year she felt as light-headed as she had then, as unwilling to force her head to rule her heart.

The game was almost at an end, she thought. He would take her to bed—she had no doubt that he intended to do so, and now she knew that she would not refuse him—and tomorrow he would leave again. Perhaps he would return at the end of October again to await the birth of his second child. The game would be at an end, and she would be the bitter loser again. And she was as powerless this year as she had been last year.

She tipped her head back to look up into his face. He was looking back at her, his dark eyes steady and intent. She felt the seductive rhythm of the music and of their dancing bodies, far too close for propriety—as they had been last year.

"Hugh." She heard his name, spoken with her voice. She had never even thought of him by name. But she had spoken it now. "Please," she said, and did not know for what she pleaded. She did not know if he would know for what she asked. "Please."

His eyes smiled at her. Not just his lips, she thought, gazing up at him. His eyes smiled. He stopped dancing and signaled to the musicians. The music drew to a close. "Perhaps," he said, "Miss Williams and Mr. Carstairs will join us for cake and punch."

The spell was broken. Amy chatted gratefully with their guests for the following half hour or so. Perhaps by the time they left, she thought, she would have the strength to bid her husband good night and to put an end to a day that could only lead to another year of misery if she tried to prolong it or allowed him to do so.

Perhaps she would have the strength. He set an arm

loosely about her waist as he talked. It was a gesture of careless—or carefully calculated—possessiveness.

Miss Williams and Mr. Carstairs had left the drawing room together after effusive thanks on both sides. The earl looked down at the half-empty bowl of punch and at the cake with the base of the heart missing. Nothing ever tasted quite as sinfully delicious as Cook's icing. He must remember to tell her so in the morning—before he kissed her cheek.

"Thank you for the roses and for the surprise guests and the dancing," his wife said quietly. "Good night, my lord."

But he set his hands on either side of her waist before she could escape. "It was Hugh a short while ago," he said.

She appeared to be finding the folds of his neck cloth fascinating. And so she should. His valet had expended enough care and energy over them.

"Has it been better than last year?" he asked.

She raised her eyes to his. "I want to go to bed," she said. And blushed.

"So do I." He smiled at her discomfiture. "But not just yet. I want us to go there together if you will freely and gladly agree to do so. There is something I must tell you first."

"You wanted it to be better than last year," she said. "Let it be better then. Let it end here. It has been a—pleasant day. I will remember it with some pleasure when you have gone. Let it end here, my lord. Let me say good night and leave you."

"I love you," he said.

She looked up at him with helpless misery. "No, you don't," she said. "You don't have to say so. Perhaps you say it to all your other women. Perhaps it is what makes them compliant. You said it to me last year. But you need not say it this year. We both know that if you wish to come to my bed you may do so. I am not so lost to all good conduct that I would refuse you your conjugal rights. You do not need to seduce me with flattery and untruths."

"There was a sparkle of something in you," he said, "that set you apart from all the other girls who made their come-out two years ago. Something that made me notice you. Something that made me fall in love with you, though I was horrified by the feeling and very unwilling to act on it. Being in love with a virtuous young girl and courting her and marrying her were not in my plans for the foreseeable future. And so I loved you secretly and unwillingly until I saw you at the opera house a year ago tonight."

"You are lying." There were tears of anger—and perhaps something else—in her eyes. "Don't lie. You were unaware of my very existence until that evening."

"How did I know who you were then?" he asked. "How did I know whose father to call upon with my offer the next morning?"

She stared up at him. "I don't believe you," she said. "Why did you abandon me if you loved me?"

"Because I had ruined you," he said, "and destroyed that sparkle. Because I was forced to offer you a rake for a husband and could see in your eyes how much you hated me. I have hated myself for what I have done to your life."

"It was not hatred for you," she said. "I hated trapping you into marrying me when everyone knew that you had no intention of marrying anyone—especially someone like me. It was the situation I hated. My own helplessness. And then I hated you for abandoning me. You cannot imagine what my wedding night was like. You cannot possibly imagine."

"I can." He swallowed and touched the backs of his fingers to her cheek. "I lived through it, too, Amy. If that is what hell is like, I believe I am going to have

to reform my ways so that I can go to the other place
when I die."

"I always loved you," she whispered. "From the
first moment I saw you. I suppose it was not love. It
was hero worship or worship of the forbidden, more
like." She looked down suddenly. "I always loved
you."

"Well, my valentine," he said, lifting her chin with
one finger so that she had no choice but to look into
his eyes again. "Well."

"Please," she said, catching at his wrist. "Please,
Hugh. If this is seduction, have pity on me. Please."

He touched his lips to hers and found them cool
and trembling. He warmed them and stilled them with
his own, wrapping his arms about her and drawing her
against him. *Ah, Amy. Ah, my love.*

It was too late. A day too late. A year too late.
Perhaps two years too late. If she had never seen him,
perhaps she would have been safe. Having once seen
him, she was forever lost. She sagged against him,
pressed her lips back against his, opened her mouth
to the seeking of his tongue, twined her arms about
his neck.

It was too late. And she did not care any longer. If
there was to be only the night, then so be it.

He drew his head back a few inches after a while
and looked down at her.

"If I would freely and gladly agree," she said. "I
do. You may take me to bed."

He first smiled and then chuckled. "You look rather
as if you were inviting me to escort you to the scaf-
fold," he said. "It is not for tonight only, Amy. I am
hungry for a regular bed partner, you see, and I have
discovered over the past year that only my wife will
do. There has been no one else since our marriage,
you may be surprised to hear. That means there has
been no one at all since our marriage. I want you
tonight and every night. I want to live with you every

day and sleep with you every night. I want to be a father to my son—to *our* son—and to any future sons or daughters we may be blessed with. I want a marriage with you, Amy. I will settle for nothing less. If you can offer only tonight—with the martyred expression you just assumed—then no, thank you. I shall return to London tomorrow at first light."

The sense of peace was so overwhelming that she had to close her eyes and rest her face against his neck cloth. Sin was not irredeemable? Punishment was not eternal? There was to be a reprieve after only one year?

"You love me?" Her voice was muffled by the folds of his neck cloth.

"I love you."

"Not just because it is Valentine's Day and there have been the roses and the primroses and the music and candlelight and the heart-shaped cake?"

"Amy." She felt his cheek come to rest against the top of her head. There was soft reproach in his voice.

She sighed with contentment.

He rocked her against him, feeling her body relax against his. He kissed the top of her head after a while and chuckled. "Nothing has developed quite the way I imagined it today," he said. "I do believe you are on the verge of falling asleep, Amy, when I pictured this moment as one of blazing passion."

She raised her head and smiled at him slowly and sweetly, the smile extending all the way back into her eyes. "All in good time," she said. "James—"

"—is going to have to be taught that his father has needs at least as urgent as his own," he said. "I suppose I am going to have to let him be satisfied first, aren't I?"

"Yes," she said. She was still smiling. "Come with me? Don't leave me. Come, too."

He wrapped one arm about her waist and led her

toward the door. "And then afterward," he said, "my turn."

"Yes," she said with a sigh of utter contentment. "I am going to enjoy having two men in my life, not just one."

But he paused suddenly when he already had a hand on the doorknob. "Goodness," he said. "I almost forgot. The most important question is still to be asked. Will you marry me?"

She stared up at him blankly.

"You will observe that your finger is bare," he said. "Will you marry me, my love? Because you love me and for no other reason?"

"Oh," she said, looking down at her hand. "Oh, yes. Yes, Hugh. For that reason. And for no other."

"Well, then." He released his hold on her and reached into a pocket. "Let us cut this to the bare essentials, shall we?" He fitted her wedding ring over her finger and slid it on. "With this ring I thee wed, my dearest love. Because I love you. For all time."

He kissed her and smiled at her and drew her against his side with an arm about her waist again. She nestled her head against his shoulder as he opened the door. They climbed the stairs together slowly, murmuring nothing of any great importance to each other.

Morse, who had been waiting in the hall for a chance to get into the drawing room to clear up—that had been his excuse for loitering there, anyway—smiled with smug satisfaction and turned back toward the kitchen rather than proceeding with his intended task. He had something of importance to share with the other servants.

The Wooing
of Lord Walford

by Anne Barbour

"CONFOUND it, Sally, is this any way to treat a guest?"

Sarah Berners, the young woman thus addressed, gazed down at the gentleman who spoke so importunately. His dark eyes were intensely alive below a mop of dark hair, arranged in modish carelessness.

"Charlie." She lifted damp curls from her forehead as she spoke with some asperity from atop a rather wobbly ladder. She had been tending plants in her greenhouse, a sprawling collection of glassed-in buildings, and she had accomplished only half the tasks she had allotted to herself. For half an hour she had been laboring with several pots of maidenhair, set on a high shelf, and the heat and humidity and her uncomfortable position were beginning to take a toll on her temper. "You have been running tame in this house since you were in short coats, so even though you rarely grace the neighborhood with your presence these days, I hardly think I need consider you a guest."

"But I want to talk to you." Charles Darracot, the second son of the Earl of Frane possessed a great charm of manner, of which he was only too aware. He stretched a hand to Sally with a coaxing smile, and sighing, she accepted his assistance and slid down to ground level.

Really, it was too bad of Charlie, she thought, with an absence of rancor. She had much to do this morning, and had given strictest orders that she not be disturbed in her sunny haven. Orders, of course, meant nothing to Charlie. She could just picture the persuasive grin he must have projected at Carlisle, reducing the usually austere butler to stammering ineffectually.

"What is it, Charlie?" she asked, removing a clutter of clay pots and trowels from a nearby bench. "I have just started on the arrangements for Lady Winstaunton's Valentine's Ball, and there is much to be done."

"Valentine's Ball! Good God, we're hardly into December. Why are you beavering away at Valentine's Day already?"

"Because," she replied impatiently, "as you would know if you thought of anything but your own affairs, it always takes months to fill Lady W.'s order. She insists upon masses of dried flowers, as well as the forced fresh, and then there's the big jars of potpourri she likes to place in every room." Motioning Charlie to be seated, she settled herself, wiping grimy fingers on her already stained muslin skirt.

"Lord yes," he muttered. "I remember now. She gets the place smelling like a French—that is, it's always rather stultifying." The young man, after a dubious glance at the dirt-streaked surface of the bench, lifted the tails of his elegantly cut riding coat and perched instead on the relatively clean corner of a potting table.

Sally eyed him suspiciously. "What are you doing back in Somerset, Charlie? Come down from London on a repairing lease, have you?"

A shadow crossed his attractive features, but his grin crinkled as engagingly as ever. He sketched a bow from his seated position. "I came just to see you. Yes, truly," he added in response to her expression of unrelieved skepticism. "I have a proposition for you." Sally rose precipitously from her seat and began to reascend the ladder. "The answer is no. Or rather," she amended, "absolutely, irrevocably, and never in this world, *no*."

Charlie, too, shot upward and, plucking her from the ladder, replaced her on the bench. He remained standing above her to prevent any more such attempts at flight.

"You haven't even heard what I have to say," he said, a look of hurt dismay in his eyes that did little to diminish the mischief sparkling in their black depths.

"Stop bamming me, Charles George Darracot. If you think I am going to lend myself to another of your hair-brained schemes, you've gone barmy. Do you recall," she asked, her foot tapping ominously on the earthen surface of the greenhouse floor, "the last time you 'had a proposition' for me? You left me standing knee-deep in a duck pond at two o'clock in the morning while you hared off to Brighton with that brazen little lightskirt."

"Sally!" Charlie's voice was filled with shocked reproach. "She was *not* a lightskirt, that is, not precisely, and she ..."

"I rest my case," said Sally, attempting once more to rise. Charlie, however, possessed himself of her hands and drew her down again on the bench to sit beside him, the pristine folds of his riding coat forgotten. His expression turned serious.

"Sally, listen. Are you, or are you not, my best friend?"

"Of course, but ..."

"And have I, or have I not, always come to your assistance when you needed me?"

There was a moment's silence.

"Yes, I suppose," said Sally in a small voice, "but, Charlie ..."

"All right, then. Just listen. I think you'll find my, er, plan of great interest."

Sally felt her insides clench warily, but she returned his gaze without comment.

Charlie's eyes fell before hers, and he stared at his hands for a moment before speaking.

"Have you ever heard of a tontine?"

"A what?" Sally looked at him blankly.

"A tontine. It's a sort of wager, or rather ..."

He broke off and ran long fingers through his disordered locks.

"I'd better begin at the beginning. It all started a long time ago, when I was at Oxford."

"Oxford!" Sally's voice rose in startled query. "Charlie, is this going to take very long? I really do have a great many things ..."

"No, it won't take long," he replied testily, "if you'll just let me continue." He drew a deep breath. "As I was saying, one pretty latish evening during my last year there, a bunch of us were sitting about in Fremont Major's rooms. I won't say we hadn't been at the brandy barrel, but we weren't jug bitten, or anything of the sort. James Wentworth was complaining that his mother was already on the lookout for a suitable *parti* for him. And he only nineteen for God's sake. Then Freddie Bremerton chimed in to say that his bride had been chosen for him when he was still in his cradle. Pretty bitter about it he was, too.

"Before long, we were all in full cry against a system that forces a chap to marry just when he gets out in the world and has a chance at a little jollification."

"If you think it's bad for a man, what about a female?" interrupted Sally. "I mean, just look at you and me. If we hadn't dug in our heels three years ago, we would have found ourselves married to one another."

"Precisely my point. We were lucky. Our parents wished us to marry, but they had some regard for our feelings. Others, however, simply push their progeny into the pit with no regard to their preferences. Anyway," he continued, taking up the thread, "at the end of it, we all—there were twelve of us in the room—made a vow to resist all the parental machinations and society's expectations and all the rest."

Charlie rose and began to pace the floor.

"Then," he continued, "Horace Belwharton spoke up. He'd actually been studying his history, and he came up with this tontine idea. It seems," he went on hastily, observing further signs of impatience in his listener, "that a couple of hundred years or so ago, some of the more rapacious citizens of Italy, thought up a unique sweepstakes scheme. Simply put, a group of men would shove a fairish amount of money into a pot, and the last man alive would collect it all."

Once more, he was the recipient of a blank stare.

"I'm not saying it's a very sensible sort of undertaking—I rather think it must have led to some dirty work—stilettos in dark alleys and that sort of thing—but the whole idea seemed especially designed to fit our particular situation."

"Charlie," said Sally with great firmness. "You're babbling, and I really don't . . ."

"No, no." Charlie spoke impatiently. "Just listen, will you? I don't mean we wagered on who would live the longest. We amended the scheme. We each agreed to scrape together a hundred pounds and give it to Tom Falwell to invest for us. Tom is the best of good fellows, even though his father is a cit—owns a couple of banks or some such, and he's considered a financial genius. We solemnly vowed to fight our families' matrimonial plans tooth and nail, and the one who remained successful the longest—that is, the last of us left unmarried would claim the ducats."

Sally stared at him thoughtfully. "Well," she said at last. "The whole thing sounds idiotish in the extreme, but—let's see . . . You're, um, twenty-three, so that must have been six years ago. If your financial genius did well by you, I suppose there must be a fair amount of money accrued by now. You, of course, are obviously still in the running to capture the prize, but"—her eyes narrowed—"what has all this to do with me?"

Sally contemplated her friend uneasily. It was true, they had been in each others' pockets almost since they had been in leading strings. Their estates marched together, and they had been inseparable through all their growing-up time. A year Charlie's junior, Sally had acted first as worthy opponent in endless games of toy soldiers and mumblety-peg, and later as indefatigable carrier of his game bag and fishing pole, as well as target of daring ambuscades and brilliant military maneuvers. In turn, Charlie had put in duty as doll mender, defender against every other small boy in the neighborhood, and arranger of funerals for the assortments of birds, kittens, and rabbits discovered by Sally in various states of terminal distress on their tramps through meadow and forest land.

It was true, she reflected uneasily, that she and Charlie had delivered one another from more than one sticky situation. If she had aided him in some of his more totty-headed schemes, he had always been there to rescue her from the results of her own folly. That was all in the past, however, she reflected stiffly. The last time she had sought Charlie's aid—the episode of Lady Melksham's pet pug, if she were not mistaken—she had still been in her teens. She was now a dignified lady of twenty-two years and far beyond such escapades.

Charlie, on the other hand, had never outgrown his capacity to fall from one scrape into another. He was wild to a fault, and at a time when other young men of his class were embarking on careers in the military or the church, Charlie toiled not, neither did he spin, living precariously on the allowance he received from his father and monies inherited several years ago from an indulgent uncle. He seemed happy in his he-

donistic life-style, but lately—well, now that she came
to think of it—she had noticed a certain pensiveness
cross his features from time to time on the rare occasions when he had descended on the neighborhood from
London. He was still high-spirited, and yet, she could
have sworn he was not entirely happy these days.

She sighed. "What has all this to do with me?" she
repeated, in a gentler tone of voice.

Charlie instantly noted the change in her demeanor.
He grasped her hands again and spoke eagerly.

"Everything. You're right, of course, I'm still in the
running for the pot. Sally ..." He paused for a moment to let his words sink in. "... The tontine prize
is now twelve thousand pounds!"

"Twelve thousand ..." Sally's voice trailed off in
awe.

"Yes. And there is only one other man left of the
twelve of us who is still unmarried." He paused again,
and as Sally gazed questioningly at him, his eyes took
on a wicked glint. "The one remaining bachelor besides myself is—Lord Walford."

Sally's jaw dropped open. "Sedgewick Horne, Lord
Walford?"

"The very same. Earl of Walford, heir to the Marquess of Bridgeworth and cynosure of every swooning
maiden on the marriage mart."

"For heavens' sake, Charlie. Is that ...? No, certainly he has not remained unmarried in the hopes of
winning twelve thousand pounds."

Charlie snorted. "Of course not. Twelve thousand
pounds is—well, not precisely a drop in the bucket to
the Hornes, but it's certainly not an incentive to avoid
parson's mousetrap. The marquess is rich as what's-
his-name—Greek fellow."

"Croesus?"

"Yes, that's the chap. No, Sedge remains a bachelor
due to his own carelessness."

"What?"

"Well, he knows he must marry. His mother has been rattling on at him for years about it, but he's always got his head in a book, or he's busy blowing up some shed or other with his experiments, or he's off fishing, or . . ."

"Yes, I get the idea, Charlie, but I will ask you one more time. What has all this to do with me?"

"Why, I want you to marry him, of course."

For a full minute, Sally gaped at him. Several times she opened her mouth to speak, but whatever thoughts churned within her, they remained unuttered until, at last, she stood and faced him.

"Charlie, this time you've gone 'round the bend. Or perhaps I did not hear you aright?"

Charlie, too, rose to his feet.

"I'm sorry, my dear. I should not have sprung it on you so abruptly; but if you'll just think it over, I know you'll see what splendid sense it all makes."

"Sense!" Sally gulped indignantly. "You want me to set my cap for a man who has never indicated the slightest interest in me, or any other female! And how can you cold-bloodedly plan to marry off one of your best friends just to snatch a silly prize out from under his nose? Charlie, you've done some insane things before, but this—this is just wicked!"

Charlie did not reply for several moments. He paced the floor once more before stopping before her.

"Sally." His voice was quiet, and an expression Sally had never seen before rested on his features. His eyes grew serious, and his jaw was set in a manner that gave him a seldom-seen look of maturity. "Let me see if I can explain this to you. I know you think me—and with good reason—a reckless care-for-nobody, but things have been different with me lately. All the pastimes that seemed so important—the gambling, the larks—they seem trivial beyond bearing now."

He smiled faintly. "I never thought I'd be saying

this, but I want to do something with my life. And if I win the tontine, I can do so."

Sally sank back onto the bench. She had never thought to hear Charles Darracot say those words, and she listened unbelievingly as they echoed in the sunny peace of the greenhouse.

"Go on, Charlie," she said softly.

"Philip Grantham is selling his stud farm. Do you know the name?"

"I believe Father used to buy from him now and then."

"He was seriously injured recently, and he is no longer able to manage things. He told me that if he can't run the place himself, he would just as soon get rid of it altogether. He wants eight thousand for the farm and the stock. Sally, you know how I am with horses. I could do this!"

"Yes, Charlie," she breathed, recalling the hours he had spent in the stables as a boy. He had never been happier than in the company of the head groom at Westerly Court, the Darracot estate, and that venerable personage had eventually declared him as knowledgeable as any stablehand in the country—to Charlie's vast delight. "I believe you could. But why not borrow from your father? He was willing to buy you a pair of colors, or set you up as a barrister—or even to provide you with a living as a clergyman. Surely . . ."

"That's true, because those are all gentleman's professions. You know father; he's a right 'un, but he's got some old-fashioned notions, such as the idea that earning one's own living is somehow beneath the son of an earl."

"Mmm," replied Sally. "You are right. I imagine Lord Frane would cut up very stiff at the idea of one of his offspring raising horses. However, and be that as it may," she continued, sitting up very straight, "I fail to see why I should make a fool of myself over

Lord Walford just in order to fulfill your boyish dream."

"You can't tell me, Sally Berners, that you haven't got a few dreams of your own—and I'd wager some of them are woven about Sedge. When I think of the hours I've spent listening to you gush over him . . ."

"I never!" Sally's voice rose to a squeak. "Well, perhaps just a little, the year of my come-out. You must admit there's a great deal to gush over. It has been pointed out by more than one interested observer that he looks as though he just stepped off a Greek vase, with those masses of careless golden waves and the cheekbones of an Eastern prince. And his eyes! If ladies wrote odes to gentlemen, those smoky blue eyes would come in for their share of overblown verse. Then when one comes to his . . ."

"Yes, very well," interrupted Charlie with some asperity. "I'm willing to concede he's a pattern card of masculine beauty. And he's a nice fellow, too. So, how about it? Would you like to marry him?"

A feeling of unreality gripped Sally, and she clasped her hands in her lap. What was one to say when one's oldest and dearest friend suddenly started babbling wild impossibilities? She reached to lay her hand on his arm.

"Charlie," she began firmly. "Listen to me. I am not a—a toy soldier to march at your bidding. Neither is Lord Walford. He may be a prince among men, but I prefer to choose my own life mate. As does Lord Walford, I'm sure."

"That's just the point. You haven't chosen your own mate, and the way you're going on you never will."

"I see. Just what, precisely, do you mean, 'the way I'm going on'?" Sally's voice remained calm, but Charlie had no difficulty recognizing the ominous edge that had crept into it.

"Now, don't fly up into the boughs. I only mean—

well, you're not a beauty like Elizabeth, but you're a taking little thing."

"Why, thank you, Charlie," she interposed, the edge having taken on the property of a honed blade. "And I'm sure my sister would thank you as well if she were here."

"You're purposely being difficult," exclaimed Charlie in exasperation. "All right, you're more than taking. You're very attractive, or at least you would be if you took the slightest interest in your appearance." Ignoring Sally's menacing growl, he continued hastily. "Well, look at you. You have—nice hair. I know brown ain't a very fashionable color, but yours is more of a chestnut. You've got masses of it, and in the sunlight it has those reddish, glinty lights, but"—he reached to curl a tendril around his finger from where it had escaped its confinement—"you keep it stuffed up under a dreadful cap half the time, as though you were somebody's elderly aunt. And your eyes are big and brown, sort of like the heart of a pansy—except when you get angry and look at a fellow all squiggly-eyed. You ought not to squint, you know. It don't become you. No—wait," he added hastily, as Sally's hands clenched into balls. "I merely meant that when you are all togged out and your hair done up, you're a"—he drew a long breath—"a lovely young woman. And that being the case," he continued, beginning to perspire, "any gentleman would be proud to have you on his arm."

At this, Sally relaxed suddenly and began to laugh.

"Oh, Charlie, you are so absurd. "I am not on the catch for a husband, you know. I am much too busy keeping the Berners family afloat. You know how things have been for us since Papa died. He did not leave us very plump in the pocket, and Mama hasn't the knack of household management. Why do you think I toil away out here"—she flung out an arm, gesturing to the plants that surrounded her in damp profusion—

"raising the most luxuriant flowers, herbs, and medicinal plants in the county? Because people pay me for them! If we are to manage a respectable season for Elizabeth, and Chloe after that, and still have anything for William when he's old enough to . . ."

"That's what I mean," interrupted Charlie impatiently. "You go around carrying the weight of—who's that other Greek fellow?"

"Uh, I don't—Sisyphus, perhaps?"

"I don't know either, but the point is, you would be well-advised to quit worrying about your bird-witted sisters and think about yourself."

"Elizabeth and Chloe are *not* . . ."

"There's no arguing that Elizabeth is a diamond of the first water, I will admit."

"That's why it's so important that she have a really splendid debut. With Mama's connections, she would surely be granted vouchers for Almack's, and there's no reason why she shouldn't make a splendid *parti*."

"And that, I suppose, is how you plan to repair the family fortunes, by matching Elizabeth up with some doddering duke?"

"Of course not," replied Sally indignantly. "We would never force her to marry where her heart is not engaged. Only, as Mama always says, 'It's just as easy to fall in love with a rich man as a poor one.' "

"Precisely," declared Charlie, a note of triumph in his voice. "Which brings me back to my original point. Why not marry Lord Walford and solve your financial problems in one fell swoop?"

Again, Sally simply stared at him. She had never known him to be so tenacious—or so buffle-headed.

"Charlie, my dear idiot. Even if I were to acquiesce to this ludicrous scheme, just what makes you think that Lord Walford will suddenly glance down from his Olympian plateau and pluck squiggly-eyed little me from the crowd of female admirers at his feet?"

"Ah," said Charlie, a pleased expression crossing

his mobile features. "There is where you have the advantage, my dear, for you have me to advise you!"

Sally's derriere descended onto the bench with an audible thump. "Charlie," she began shakily, "what in God's green world are you talking about?"

Charlie sat beside her, once more clasping her hands in his. "Don't you see? Why do you think none of the females his mother's been hurling at him have never caught Sedge's attention?"

"I don't know," she replied slowly. "I always assumed he hadn't met the right lady. Or perhaps he isn't interested in—although, I understand he has been seen with the occasional ladybird."

"Never mind about that, my girl," Charlie said with asperity. "But, you're right. He hasn't been presented to the woman he'd like to spend the rest of his life with—simply because his, er, requirements are a little more unusual than most."

"I beg your pardon?"

"That is, Sedge doesn't care for ordinary pastimes—dancing and gambling and hunting and that sort of thing. He's of a serious turn of mind. His pursuits are—well, some might call them eccentric."

"Ye-es, I've heard that."

"And I," Charlie concluded triumphantly, "know just what they are. I'm one of his closest friends, and I know precisely what he wants in a woman. I know his favorite topics of conversation, I know what he likes to do on rainy days, I know just how he likes a woman to behave. Under my instruction, you'll have him falling for you like a felled tree in no time."

"Charlie!" Sally could hardly speak for the indignation that boiled within her. "That is the most callous—the coldest, most unfeeling—to say nothing of the deceit! How could you?"

"Well, perhaps it is a little callous, and yes, there's no question there's some deceit involved, but think of the outcome! Your mama is perfectly right about falling in love with a rich man. I think you're half in love with him already, and you'd make him a good wife, wouldn't you? Wouldn't you rather see him married to you than some other scheming harpy? That is," he amended hastily, "it isn't as though I'm asking you to learn Chinese. I just want to instruct you in Sedge's interests. That's all it would take. I know it."

"That's all it would take," she replied disdainfully. "Do you really expect me to turn myself into something I'm not in order to snare an unsuspecting gentleman? Lord Walford doesn't deserve such treatment, Charlie. Can't you see that? Besides, don't you think he would find it somewhat unsettling when, not long after the ceremony, he discovers that the dutiful bride he thought would enter into all his hobbies, actually has little or no interest in blowing up sheds?"

"I don't expect you to turn into something you're not," Charlie said with great dignity. "Nor do I expect you to take up the study of explosives. I merely believe that if you, er, looked into some of the things that interest Sedge, you'd find them of interest to you, as well. You've always been something of a bluestocking, after all."

"Am I?" she responded, her eyes glittering dangerously.

"Lord, Sally, don't take a fellow up so. I only mean that you and Sedge already share many of the same interests. Probably."

She frowned, then turned abruptly.

"How long do you think it would take to learn all my lord's likes and dislikes?" she asked.

"Sally! You'll do it?"

She put up a hand to stay Charlie from sweeping her into an exuberant embrace. "I have not said so, my lad. I would first know what his likes and dislikes *are.*"

"I shall tell you all, my little bird. The first thing we must do is lure him into the vicinity. Propinquity, you know, is a wonderful thing. Fortunately, it happens that he prefers dark women over fair, so we are well on the road already. We can get in some spadework right away, and I should think that within a month or two, you should have learned enough to capture his interest."

"A month or two? What will we be doing in all that time? You and I, that is?"

"Why, I must teach you how to tie flies for fishing, and bring you up-to-date on the latest archaeological finds. You'll have to learn a smattering of Greek—he likes to read Homer in the original—and, well, perhaps you should learn just a little something about explosives."

"Explosives?" she queried faintly.

"Yes. Sedge is always trying to find new methods to improve the efficiency of dynamite for use in mining and in military planning. I think a mere smattering would do in this area, however—no need to actually participate in the actual, er, process."

Sally groaned. "Why couldn't he be like every other man with a beautiful face. All glory and no brains?"

"I guess that's his problem. With his looks, everyone expects him to do nothing but spout bad poetry and fall into striking poses. He does enjoy poetry, by the way. He admires Coleridge but thinks Byron is humbug."

"A man of many parts, forsooth," said Sally, smiling.

"Yes," agreed Charlie eagerly. "Which makes it all just perfect since you enjoy poetry yourself. Now, here's the plan. Sedge has spent Christmas at our place for donkey's years. His parents always pick this time of year to go to Italy, and all his brothers and sisters are married with families of their own. We have about three weeks to teach you some of the basics. We can get started on the fly-tying and the Greek. I'll bring him over when he gets here, and you can start luring him into your net."

Sally shifted uncomfortably. "You're assuming a lot, old friend. You have not asked if I'll fall in with this dreadful scheme."

His expression grew serious, and he placed his hands on her shoulders. "Sally, I know the plan is what one might call underhanded, but the results will be of benefit to all. You and I and Sedge will all be happier in the end."

Sally gazed at Charlie for a long moment. She could never agree to such an underhanded, manipulative scheme. Could she? And yet, her heart leapt at the chance being held out to her. She had waited such a long time for this. She thought of Sedgewick and his heart-stopping, golden beauty. Charlie was right, after all. Everyone concerned would be happier if all worked out as he envisioned.

Sally stared unwaveringly into the dark intensity of Charlie's eyes. "Yes," she said at last. "I believe that's true. All right, Charlie, I'll do it."

Fanny, Lady Berners, relict of Sir George Berners, Bart., fairly squealed in her dismay. "Lord Walford is coming *here*? Why didn't you tell me? The whole house is at sixes and sevens, what with William down with the mumps and Elizabeth's patterns scattered all over the morning room. I don't know why she cannot confine her dressmaking to the sewing room."

She glanced reproachfully at her daughter Elizabeth, a dark, slender beauty seated across the table from her in the small breakfast parlor at The Ridings, the Berners' family home. It was a large, pleasant house, the original Tudor having been enlarged over the years to form a sprawling, comfortable dwelling place for many generations of Bernerses.

"Because there's not enough light there," said Elizabeth placidly in answer to her mother's plaint. She took a sip of coffee before passing the jam pot to her younger sister, Chloe, a lively young miss of fourteen summers, who had nearly upset the coffee urn in her efforts to reach across the table. "I shall remove my mess and have all tidy before our guests arrive." She turned to Sally, her deep blue eyes wide and questioning. "Why is Charlie bringing Lord Walford here? I believe he arrived only last night, and we're all going over there for dinner tomorrow."

"I would like the answer to that as well," interposed Lady Berners. "It seems to me," she continued, irritatedly waving aside the offer from a footman of more coffee. "That you and Charlie have become wondrous great of late. He appears at our front door as regularly as the postman. You two aren't planning some mischief, are you?" she concluded suspiciously.

"My goodness, Mama!" Sally's laughter sounded loud in her ears. "What makes you say such a thing? It's been ever so long since Charlie and I have got up to mischief together."

"Then why is Charlie here almost every day?" interposed Chloe, a saucy grin spreading across her freckled countenance. "And always with armfuls of the oddest things. Did I see turkey feathers the other evening?"

"Chloe," remonstrated Elizabeth softly. "Manners." She somewhat spoiled the effect by glancing questioningly at Sally.

"We're engaged in a—a project. I have always wished to learn how to tie flies for fishing. That is—do you remember? Old Mr. Wigmore used to do that, and they were so beautiful, that I—I would like to—that is, I thought I'd try ..." She trailed off, taking refuge in the bottom of her cup. "Of course, we're not up to anything, Mama," she said a few moments later in response to mother's continued expression of skepticism. "Goodness, you'd think we were still ten years old!"

"I don't think anything of the sort," replied her mother at length. She sighed. "Goodness knows, you rarely get up to anything at all these days. You spend most of your days buried in your garden plots and greenhouses. So unnecessary, my dear—I don't know what people must think!"

"Mama, I enjoy growing things, and as for what people think, you know the decoctions and infusions I make up are much in demand. Did you know that a London apothecary has sent to me for some of my preparations?"

Lady Berners squirmed in her seat. "But so beneath one, my dear." With one last sip of coffee, she rose hastily. "I must see to William. He has already driven three maids from his room in tears. I believe he is even more full of mumps than he was earlier in the week."

Elizabeth also rose, declaring her intention of repairing to "the mess in the drawing room," and after some coercion from her sisters, Chloe trudged up to the schoolroom.

Left to her own thoughts, Sally allowed herself to drift over the events of the last several weeks. True to his words, Charlie had become almost a permanent fixture at The Ridings. On the day after Sally's capitulation, he had ridden over with an armful of textbooks, culled from his father's library, on the study of ancient Greek. Unfortunately, after days in which Sally's ears rang with, "Alpha, Beta, Gamma, Delta . . ." her grasp of the tongue of Homer and Sappho remained tenuous at best.

The fly-tying effort had met with more success. To Charlie's vast delight, Sally picked up the intricate technique quickly, and after a few initial failures, she began producing acceptable specimens almost immediately. He was particularly pleased with her Dark Cahill, a wispy concoction of pheasant and turkey feathers.

"Of course," he stated quickly, cupping her fingers in his as he led them through a particularly convoluted knot in the silk thread used for binding the feathers together, "we don't want you to become too proficient." At her questioning glance, he continued. "Well, you certainly don't want to do a better job than Sedge. Puts a fellow off, you know. He will fill the role of instructor—with you fluttering your eyelashes in pretty admiration of his skill."

At this, Sally expelled an exasperated sigh. "Charlie, I don't know if I can go through with this. You're asking me to turn myself into a complete wigeon. When is the last time you saw me flutter my eyelashes?"

Charlie frowned. "Well, then you ought to do it more often. God knows, they're long and thick enough." He looked into her eyes for several moments, and when he continued, his voice had taken on an odd note. "Long and thick," he repeated. "Sort of like—like a fringe."

He swung away with a jerk, turning back to the array of flies lying before them in various states of construction. His tone became businesslike as he demonstrated yet another method of affixing feathers to the fly's hackles, and his confidence in her growing ability was apparently such that he no longer saw the need to guide her fingers. He left the house at an unusually early hour.

The next evening, Charlie chose to review Sally's knowledge of poetry. Here she felt herself on firmer ground, for she truly enjoyed poetry, and had discovered in past conversations with Lord Walford that they shared many favorites.

"Nonetheless," said Charlie, pulling a volume from the pile he had placed on the desk, "we shall take no chances. Here, how about this one?" he asked, having selected a poem at random. "It's by Coleridge, Sedge's favorite. "A LETTER TO MISS SARA HUTCHINS,' " he began.

"That doesn't sound very interesting, but let's go on. *'O, Sara! in the weather-fended wood thy lov'd haunt! Where the stock-doves coo at noon, I guess that thou hast . . .'* 'Stock-doves coo'?" he repeated in revulsion. "Good God, what drivel. And what's a weather-fended wood?"

"I expect it's a sheltered place in the forest," replied Sally with the merest tremor in her voice.

"Pho!" Charlie had declared. "The fellow's a fraud—can't put two words together that make any sense." He slammed the book down in disgust and had continued to animadvert against the fatheadedness of poets for the rest of the evening.

Sally smiled at the memory and reflected on her good fortune that at least the Earl of Frane's library contained no material on explosives. That subject, said Charlie ruefully, would have to be left for later instruction by Sedgewick himself.

"Very well, old friend," she had replied, "but I draw the line at mixing a batch of black powder. I fear I may find it difficult to flutter my eyelashes if they've been singed off to the roots."

Sally grinned again in remembrance, but a moment later, her expression grew serious. She had agreed to Charlie's plan much against her better judgment, admitting to herself only much later that her deception was as much likely to destroy her chances for happiness as it was to promote it.

She sighed and took herself off, her mind on the gown she would wear to welcome her future husband.

"What do you think, Charlie? Shall we be able to get a spot of fishing in this afternoon after our visit?"

"Sedge, it may have escaped your notice, but this is December," Charlie responded patiently. He cast a sidelong glance at the man who rode beside him, trying to view him with the eyes of a female—hopefully a susceptible female. Golden hair—intense blue eyes

... Broad shoulders admirably filled his elegantly tailored riding coat, and he rode his horse with a casual grace. Sedge was undoubtedly the handsomest fellow of his acquaintance, Charlie thought with satisfaction. "If you will look about," he continued patiently, "you will notice there is a light covering of snow on the ground. This is not a good day to expose oneself to the elements, not even for a sizzling plateful of trout— not even for a glutton for punishment like you."

Charlie allowed his horse to settle into a placid walk and glanced again at his friend's perfect profile. For the hundredth time, he considered Sally's unexpected capitulation to his plan.

To be sure, she'd almost always been willing to fall in with his schemes, but she had a deuced inconvenient conscience, and had dug her heels in on more than one occasion. There was no doubt, he reflected uncomfortably, that there was an element of dishonesty in his plan, yet she had surrendered after he had expended less than half the effort he had thought it would take to win her agreement.

Charles Darracot was not a man given to introspection, but he was struck with the unwelcome thought that in talking Sally into going against her conscience, he may have been doing her an irreparable wrong. Good God, he'd never want to hurt Sally. She was more dear to him than anyone else in the world.

He could not even remember the first time they had plunged into trouble together. Luckily, both sets of parents were of a forgiving nature, and each looked with fond eyes on the child of the other family. All their lives it had been expected they would wed. Indeed, they had both been almost conditioned to an eventual union. Sally would not have done for the heir, of course. No, his brother Tom had been leg-shackled long ago to the daughter of a marquess. He and his somewhat boring bride resided for most of the year in London.

The daughter of a neighboring baronet, however, was the perfect choice for younger son Charles. Such a little lady, said his mother. Good stock there, said his father. It had taken Charlie and Sally the better part of a year to convince their parents that, while the two young people would always be the best of friends, they were in complete agreement that marrying each other would be too much like being joined to one's sibling.

Sally was a pearl beyond price. Was it rationalizing, he wondered, to assure himself that in grooming her to win Sedge's affection, he would be creating for her the life of elegance and wealth she could never otherwise obtain?

For there was no getting away from it, if left to her own devices, Sally would end up a spinster aunt to her sisters' children, or she would find herself leg-shackled to someone entirely unsuitable, such as— what was the feller's name—Squire Jeffers, or Jeffreys or some such. Pompous blighter with a red face and a long nose. He'd been making sheep's eyes at Sally for a couple of years—ever since his second wife had died, leaving him with a brood of unruly children. Charlie was sure the man's attentions were unwelcome, but Sally was too tenderhearted to discourage him. And there was Horace Pilcher. He stood up with Sally at all the assemblies. Everyone knew he was well up in the world, but there was something about him Charlie could not like.

No, he thought, once more contemplating Sedge's magnificent physique, he had found the perfect man for Sally. In fact, they would probably want him to stand as godfather to their first child. He found this thought oddly unsettling. It was hard to picture Sally as a mother, after all.

"What?" he asked blankly, suddenly aware that Sedge was addressing him.

"I said, why were you so suddenly taken with the

urge to go visiting? I hardly had time to pay my re-
spects to your mother and father."

"Ah. Well, it's too fine a day to lurk about indoors."

"But you just said . . ."

To Charlie's vast relief, they had drawn up before
the large front doors of The Ridings. He dismounted
and sprang immediately to wield the door knocker
with imperious abandon. By the time Sedge had joined
him, Carlisle had opened the door to usher the gentlemen, with great gravity, into the entrance hall.

"Charlie!" He swung around at the sound of a feminine voice, but the young woman lightly descending
the stairs was not Sally, but her sister Elizabeth.

"Sally said you would be coming over this afternoon." Elizabeth floated gracefully over the ancient
stone floor of the hall and smiled captivatingly.

"Hullo, Liz," said Charlie, grasping her hand. "You
know Sedgewick, don't you? Lord Walford, that is?"

Elizabeth offered her sweet smile. "Of course. We
danced at last year's Christmas Ball."

Sedgewick swept her a graceful bow. "I remember
it well, Miss Elizabeth." He stood back. "But, you
seemed so much—younger last year."

"I was still in the schoolroom then." The smile
spread into an elfin grin. "This year, Mama let me put
up my hair."

"Yes," interposed Charlie, "but where's . . . ah,
there she is. Sally, come see who I've brought," he
finished.

"Good afternoon, gentlemen." Sally entered the
hall from one of the small salons that dotted its perim-
eter, and Charlie was gratified to note that she had
attired herself in a becoming gown of primrose muslin,
whose sunny hue seemed to bring out all the delicious
glints in her chestnut hair. Her hurried entrance had
lent a delicate flush to her cheeks. Altogether, Charlie
could not remember when he had seen her in such
looks.

Lady Berners bustled in from the direction of the still room, and the next few moments were filled with a flurry of greetings.

"Well!" exclaimed Lady Berners. "What are we all doing standing about here? Do let us repair to the drawing room. I have sent for tea."

Over the cups, talk was general, with the conversation being dominated by Lady Berners and the Earl of Walford. As he good-naturedly answered her questions about his activities in London and all the friends he had left there, Sally studied him covertly. Dear Lord, the man was beautiful! She shot a glance at Charlie, and was discomfited to note that he was watching her. She turned her gaze hastily back to the earl.

"No, I'm afraid I did not attend Lady Brisbane's ball," he was saying. "There was a meeting of the Surrey Institution, and I had been asked to read a lecture on the properties of sulfur."

"Indeed," said Lady Berners in a faint voice. "How very interesting, to be sure."

Aware that Charlie's gaze on her had turned into a minatory stare, Sally took a deep breath. "Yes," she said brightly. "I understand that sulfur, along with charcoal and saltpeter, is the primary ingredient for black powder."

Sedgewick set his cup down with such force that it clattered. "Miss Berners, are you familiar with the production of black powder?" His blue eyes were very intense.

Sally laughed deprecatingly. "Not really. That is, I have some slight knowledge of chemistry—I raise plants and herbs for their healing properties. I sometimes use charcoal and potassium in my potting soils—and in my reading, I came across mention of their use in making black powder. I found it interesting, and continued my reading on the subject. I—I really know very little," she added truthfully.

"But this is amazing. I have never met a female who has the slightest interest in explosives." Sally felt bathed in the warmth of Sedge's gaze.

"Oh, yes," interposed Charlie, his voice sounding loud in the sunlit room. "You'd be surprised at all the bits of useless information tucked inside that pretty little head." Aware of the fatuousness of his words, he turned to Elizabeth and Lady Berners for confirmation. The eyes of both ladies were still focused on Sally in blank astonishment.

"B-but, Sally," said her mother dazedly, "Sulfur?"

"Black powder?" echoed Elizabeth.

Sally felt as though the room was beginning to close in on her. Charlie's nearness provided an anchor of reality at the edge of her consciousness, and she wished she could reach out and touch him—to absorb some of the confidence that sat so reassuringly on his features.

"Whatever is that on your skirt, Sally?" It was Elizabeth who spoke. Darling Elizabeth, thought Sally with a sigh of gratitude, who possessed the tact of a diplomat and who must have sensed her discomfiture. Glancing down, she plucked a wispy smudge of pheasant feather from the bright-colored folds of her gown.

"Why, Sally," said Charlie, his dark eyes alight, "have you been tying flies?"

"Tying flies?" echoed Sedge. "Miss Berners, you are not going to tell me that in addition to an interest in one of my favorite hobbyhorses, you are a devotee of the piscatorial delights?"

Sally simply stared at him blankly.

"He means fishing," explained Charlie in an unsteady voice.

"Of course," said Sally calmly. From wishing to touch Charlie's hand, she had gone to wanting to strike him with a blunt instrument. Look at him. Settled into his chair with easy grace, he might have been watching an enthralling stage play. A play directed and produced by himself. Did he not realize that they teetered on a precipice? Why, she wondered wildly, had she agreed to this mad charade? Clenching her hands, she continued in a cool voice. "Yes, I have been trying my hand at it, but only of late. My father had some beautiful ones, and—and I thought I would . . ." Her voice trailed off, and she wished the sofa on which she sat could rise up and swallow her whole.

"But that is splendid, Miss Berners." The expression of interest and open admiration on Sedge's face nearly proved her undoing. Why did not Charlie stop that interminable grinning and come to her assistance?

In his straw satin chair opposite Sally, Charlie felt that if he had to keep smiling for one more instant, his face would crack. Lord, he had not thought his own part in the initial phases of the wooing of Sedgewick would be so tedious. Did Sally have to look up at him quite so adoringly? And look at Sedge. He appeared positively fatuous, gaping at Sally as though she'd just been served up to him on toast for breakfast. It was enough to give a fellow a megrim.

"Perhaps before Charlie and I leave this afternoon, you will show me some of your specimens, Miss Berners?"

Sally jumped. "Oh! I think not, my lord. My efforts are sure to provoke only laughter."

"Nonsense. Tell me, what are you creating at the moment?"

"A Royal Coachman," she replied with some trepidation.

"Ah, yes," said Sedge, nodding toward the pheasant feather Sally still held in her hand. "And you have chosen the proper material."

Blushing, Sally smiled faintly.

Later, after the gentlemen had departed, Sally fled to her greenhouses. There, she soothed the turmoil in her soul as she always did, by tending to the growing things that never failed to provide solace.

True to his word, Sedge had insisted on visiting the large, untidy chamber in a remote corner of the house that Sally had outfitted as a workroom. There, amid boxes of assorted feathers, silks of different colors and weights, and the various implements needed to turn these items into simulated insects, Sedge rooted knowledgeably. His praise of her efforts was genuine, she was sure, and before he left, he had promised to return the next day to further her instruction in this ancient art.

Charlie, drat him, had simply stood about, grinning like a Cheshire cat. Obviously, he was already counting the tontine money his, as well as visualizing himself as a prosperous breeder of horses, striding over his acres and lording it over his tenants. He had whispered on his way out the door that he had unearthed a volume of Gray, another of Sedge's favorite poets, and that he would return with it that evening for more tutelage.

Sally sank down on a nearby bench and stared unseeing through the steamy panes of the greenhouse. It had begun. Her campaign had swung into action. Would the outcome be all that she had hoped? She thought of the hours she would be spending with Charlie this evening. Charlie and the poet, Gray. With a grin, Sally turned to her work.

Christmas sped past in a blur. The scent of pine, the crackle of the hearth as loved ones gathered for dancing, feasting and gift-giving all passed into the memory of yet another year. Sally had been caught beneath the kissing bough by an oddly shy Sedgewick, who then stood by to watch Charlie kiss her first on the cheek, and then on the mouth for an unexpectedly long moment. Sedge had retaliated to this obvious attempt to make him jealous by pressing a kiss to Elizabeth's blushing cheek, but he danced with Sally twice that night.

Charlie reported with glee that Sedge, for the first time ever, had agreed to Charlie's proposal to stay on at Frane Park beyond the Christmas season. In fact, it appeared that his lordship would still be in residence for the Valentine Ball.

After that, talk was of nothing but Lord and Lady Winstaunton's annual affair, held at the couple's estate some thirty miles distant. This event was the highlight of the social year for those living in the area, and by early January, preparations were already in full swing at The Ridings.

"But, Mama ..." The family sat at luncheon, a rather spartan meal of cold meat, salad, and fruit, and the conversation had dealt with the upcoming fete. Chloe's voice was raised in a querulous whine. "*Why* can't I have a new gown? Elizabeth says it would be no trouble to make one for me?"

"For heavens' sake, my dear," her mother replied, in a tone that indicated she had heard this plaint more than once. "You will not be attending the ball, nor the dinner preceding it. You and the other children will be allowed to mingle with the guests earlier in the day, and you will be permitted to stand for a while in the gallery to watch the dancing. Your pink sarcenet will do very nicely for both occasions."

"But it makes me look such an infant," wailed Chloe.

"But you are an infant," interposed her brother William, now mercifully mumpless. He was a sturdy youth, just past his eleventh birthday, with merry brown eyes. His hair, also brown, sprouted from his head in a series of unruly cowlicks. He reached past Elizabeth for a comfit and had his fingers gently rapped for his pains.

"Mama ..." gasped Chloe, swinging on her brother, ready for battle.

"Now, children," said their mother agitatedly. The quarrel continued unabated until Sally, rousing herself from an abstraction, said quietly, "That will do, William. Chloe, stop railing at the boy. You know he only wishes to annoy you."

Chloe subsided into a series of resentful sniffs, while William, oblivious, made another attempt, this time successful, for the comfits.

"Elizabeth," said Lady Berners. "Have you decided on the trim for your gown? I think I rather prefer the blond lace."

"Oh, Mama," replied Elizabeth, "I don't think that would go with mulberry. I thought perhaps a border of deep pink silk rosebuds."

"Well," concluded her mother placidly, "I bow to your judgment. Your taste in dress is impeccable."

Elizabeth blushed at the compliment, then turned to Sally. "Will you come to my room this afternoon for a fitting on your gown? I have set in the sleeves, and I think you will be pleased."

"Yes, although I am meeting Charlie a little later."

"Charlie?" echoed Lady Berners. "Where on earth are you going to meet him?"

"Oh. Um, at the Shallows." Sally squirmed in her chair. "We are going fishing."

At this, her mother dropped her fork. "But—but it is February! Have you two children gone mad?"

Sally stiffened. "Mama, really. We do not plan to be gone long. We are merely going to test out the new flies I finished last night. They are meant to float, but Charlie insists they will sink like stones. I wish to prove him wrong."

"Can I come?" asked William eagerly.

" 'May I come?' " Sally's correction came automatically. "Yes, I suppose, if you think you can manage to keep from falling into the river as you did last winter."

"Pho! I was just a baby then."

Chloe, obviously unable to resist this opportunity, sang out, "You're still just a—" but closed her mouth immediately upon becoming the recipient of three severe stares. "May I come, too?" she concluded in a subdued voice.

Thus it was that an hour or so later, a large and merry party gathered on the bank of the River Croid, which flowed through the environs of The Ridings. Elizabeth, too, had joined the group, and when Charlie hove into view, fishing poles in hand, it could be seen that he had brought Sedgewick.

Sally presented her collection of lures, and they affixed them to the ends of their lines.

At the first cast, Sally squealed in triumph.

"Look! Look, Charlie, the Jock Scot is floating. See? You'd swear it was a live insect! I'll have my apology now, my good man."

"Never tell me you doubted Miss Berners?" Sedge laughed and handed his pole to Sally. "Would you like to try it?"

With an expert flick of her wrist, Sally cast the line into the stream and was delighted to observe that the second fly performed as well as the first.

"Ah, I see you have been fishing before," said Sedgewick.

"Oh, Sally and I have come to fish right here at this very spot hundreds of times," interposed Charlie, his eyes on the little fly still bobbing enthusiastically in the shallows.

"When I was much younger, of course," Sally hastened to add.

"If you would allow a suggestion," continued Sedge. "By holding the rod thus"—he placed an arm about her shoulder to adjust the rod to a different position—"and flicking the line just so . . . Yes, that's it. A much more accurate cast, don't you think?"

Sally's heart thudded wildly at the unaccustomed nearness of that splendid physique. How very broad his shoulders were, to be sure. And how strong, yet gentle, his hands. Feeling the heat rise to her cheeks, she stepped away.

"Like this?" she asked breathlessly, hurling the line into the river, where it splashed several feet away from its target, the base of a low-hanging branch.

"No, no." It was Charlie, springing forward impatiently. "Like this." Placing both arms around her, he grasped her hands in his and placed them around the rod. She turned to stare at him in surprise, and found that there was a vast difference from looking Charlie in the eye from across a drawing room and finding oneself just a heartbeat away from him. How odd, she reflected in that brief moment. Charlie's shoulders were not as broad as Sedge's, and he was not as tall, but she was intensely aware of the strength emanating from him like the energy waves from a magnet.

Charlie remained still for a moment, his hands on Sally's. She hoped he could not feel her still thundering pulse beneath his touch.

"There," he said at last, turning her wrists slightly. He withdrew from her hastily. "Now try it."

This time the tiny lure flew to its designated spot, and Sally turned to the group, flushed with triumph.

"Let me do it now!" cried William, his brown eyes sparkling in anticipation. He grasped the rod handed to him by Sally with enthusiastic, though inexpert hands. His first cast, as might be expected, was less than successful.

"Oh, you wretched boy!" exclaimed Elizabeth, disengaging the hook from her skirts.

"Here ..." said Charlie. "Let me ..."

He attempted to wrest the pole from William, but the boy, with an outraged "*No*! I can do it!", had already whipped the line rearward preparatory to a mighty cast.

Charlie watched in amusement as the line flew skyward and arced behind the group. His grin, however, turned to openmouthed dismay as he followed the line's path. The next moment, Sally uttered a soft sound of dismay and her hands flew to her face. To Charlie's horror, blood began immediately seeping from between her fingers.

Time seemed to slow, and to Charlie, an eternity passed before he was able to push past the others in order to reach her side. He was vaguely aware of Chloe's shrieks and of Elizabeth's quietly urgent request to Sedgewick for a handkerchief. Sally had fallen to her knees, and he sank down beside her.

"Sally! Oh, my dearest girl—let me see. What—where . . . ?" Gently, he pried her trembling fingers from her cheek, gasping at what he saw there. The tiny hook had imbedded itself in her temple, a mere fraction of an inch from her eye.

"Mmm," said a voice at his elbow. "It is bleeding somewhat profusely, but the barb does not appear to have gone very deep."

An unreasoning rage swept through Charlie at Sedge's tone of clinical detachment, and he gathered Sally in his arms.

"You seem upset, old chap," continued Sedgewick. "Would you like me to remove the hook?"

"No!" said Sally sharply, speaking for the first time. "Charlie, you do it, please." Her eyes lifted to Charlie's. "Please," she repeated.

Charlie said nothing, but his gaze remained locked with Sally's for a moment before he nodded briefly. Gently steadying her head, he grasped the lure, and with great care loosed it from the feathers, leaving the shank end of the hook free. He was thus able to ease it, by its barbless end, from her flesh. Grateful that his hands had not betrayed the sickening tremor he felt in the pit of his stomach, he dropped the wickedly sharp bit of metal into the snow and allowed Elizabeth to wipe the blood from Sally's face with the handkerchief Sedge had dampened in the river.

The group returned to the house in relative silence.

Charlie, suppressing an urge to shake young William till his teeth rattled, strode wordlessly beside Chloe. Ahead, Lord Walford walked with Sally, bending solicitously over her and turning to Elizabeth now and again to offer advice as to the treatment the wound would require when they reached the house. Sedgewick Horne was certainly an expert on everything, Charlie reflected sourly. The thought occurred to him that he should have allowed Sedge to come to Sally's immediate assistance. Surely, rendering aid to a damsel in distress would have drawn Sedge further into the net he and Sally had spread for him. Charlie shrugged. It had simply not occurred to him to let anyone but himself go to her. God, he shuddered inwardly, what if the thing had gone into her eye? Picturing those huge brown eyes, raised so trustfully to his, he bent a murderous glance on William, who had retired, pale, shaken, and remorseful, to the rear of the group.

Ahead, Sally reflected uneasily on her insistence that it be Charlie who removed the barb from her flesh. Her words had burst from her, uttered through pure instinct. It was Charlie she trusted—Charlie whose sure hands had mended broken dolls and sparrow's wings and who had never failed to come to her when she needed him. But what of their grand plan for Sedgewick? She watched Lord Walford covertly as he conversed earnestly with Elizabeth, and at that moment, he turned to bestow a look of concern upon her and to examine again the tear in her flesh that lay beneath the handkerchief she held to it. Sally smiled. All was well. All was proceeding as she had foreseen.

"Just listen to this one." Charlie spoke disapprovingly, his dark hair catching mahogany reflections from the candlelight. He and Sally had been poring over volumes of Wordsworth's works for some hours in the small study that Sally had claimed as her own. "Seems to me the feller's a dashed loose-screw. What the devil is he talking about here? '... *In thy voice I catch the language of the former heart, and read my former pleasure in the shooting lights of thy wild eye.*' Shooting lights of thy wild eye?" he repeated incredulously.

"I should think it means that his love's eyes are sparkling and tempestuous" replied Sally, smiling.

"Well, why didn't he just say so? Could have done the job in half the words."

"Yes, but it would not have been so well expressed."

"Sounds like a lot of hogwash to me. Why do these writing coves have to make everything so complicated?"

"It's not at all complicated, Charlie. Wordsworth is simply trying to express what is in his soul."

"If that's what is in his soul, the feller needs a good physicking, if you ask me." He turned again to the page he had been perusing. "Never heard such rot in my life."

"He's speaking of the woman he loves, Charlie. How would you describe a woman who was particularly dear to you? Let's say she's, oh, blond and blue-eyed and slender."

"Well, that's what I'd say." He struck a pose and, grasping Sally's hand, pressed it to his lips. "Wilt thou be mine, oh blond, blue-eyed, slender person?"

Sally giggled. "Charlie, you are so absurd. Just how far do you think that would get you? We females, you know, like to have our hair compared to a cascade of sunshine. Or, in my case, a—oh, let's see—a cloud of—" After a few moments in thought, she fluttered her fingers in a gesture of defeat. "Well, I guess there's not much you can do with plain brown hair."

Charlie gazed at her with narrowed eyes. "I told you before, idiot, your hair is not plain. No—if I were one of those poet blokes, I'd call it—um . . ." His hand reached to touch a curl that fell in charming disarray over her forehead. "I'd call it a deep, spicy brown with russet highlights that puts one in mind of late afternoon sunlight falling on brown silk, or perhaps the river, where it runs clear and sparkling through a spring meadow."

"Why, Charlie!" Sally blushed with startled pleasure.

Charlie, too, flushed a deep scarlet, and he hastily withdrew his hand from the curl he had been stroking and closed the book with a snap.

"That should do it for tonight," he said briskly. "Now tell me, how are you coming on your gown for the Valentine Ball?"

Sally blinked. "Why—why, all right, I suppose. Elizabeth is making it for me, you know."

"Mmm. I know she's handy with a needle, but do you think you can trust her to turn out something really stylish?"

"Elizabeth always dresses in the first stare, and most of what she wears is her own handiwork."

"That's true, but . . . Tell me what it looks like."

"My ball gown? Well, the underdress is amber satin, and—"

"That's good. Amber is vastly becoming to you."

"Thank you," she replied with some asperity. "It has a gold tunic that will be sewn with brilliants. The sleeves are puffed and caught up with gold ribbon. Does that, too, meet with your approval?"

Charlie rubbed his hands in satisfaction.

"You'll look smashing, particularly if you get your maid to do something with your hair. Pile it on top of your head in one of those loose knots. What are you doing?" he interrupted himself, staring at Sally in bewilderment as she gathered paper and pen to her and began writing.

"I want to get this all down," she replied, her color high. "Since I cannot be trusted to rig myself out in proper style, I do not wish to miss any of your extremely instructive comments."

He lifted his hand in a placating gesture. "Sally, that's not what I meant. I just want you to look your best, that's all."

"Of course! I want to be in prime condition when you lead me into the ring to auction me off to Sedgewick Horne?"

He looked at her, puzzled. "But wasn't that the idea? And I'm not auctioning you off. We entered this bargain together, after all."

"And do you," she continued, her eyes fairly spitting sparks by now, "believe that I cannot attract a man without you to see to the placement of every hairpin in my head?"

"Good God, Sally, what's come over you? I believe nothing of the kind! I only meant ..."

Sally silenced him with an angry gesture. "Oh, never mind, Charlie. you said you were leaving, did you not? Do me the courtesy of seeing yourself out. If you will excuse me, I shall retire now."

Charlie stared after her receding back, and remained so for several minutes after the door closed behind her.

It was three days before Sally again saw Charlie. In the meantime, Sedgewick visited the ladies at The Ridings with an assiduousness that astonished and delighted Lady Berners.

"I believe he is becoming quite smitten with you, my dear." She beamed on her oldest daughter, who sat opposite her at the breakfast table. "And you say he is planning a visit this morning?"

"Yes, Mama. He has been attempting of late to compose some verse of his own that he wishes to read to me."

"How very delightful," replied Lady Berners with a broad smile.

However, when Lord Walford put in an appearance some hours later, he found Sally in a small room adjacent to the greenhouse, wherein hung row upon fragrant row of dried herbs and other plants.

"I am so sorry, my lord, but Mr. Fletcher's gout is acting up again and Mrs. Fletcher has sent for some of my mixture. I blend goutweed with a sprinkle of Good King Henry, and of course, a little madder. Then I must see to to my fairy roses. They are Lady Winstaunton's favorite bloom, and I have promised her several tubs full for the ball. They are at a rather critical point, I'm afraid."

"Ah, yes, the famous Valentine Ball. I must confess I am looking forward to it. Lady Frane speaks of it with great anticipation. I understand there is to be some unusual entertainment."

"Oh, yes—the Token Auction." Sally dimpled in laughter. "Lady W. has proposed it as an innovation this year. Each unmarried lady present is to bring with her a token. It must be a personal item, but not one that would be well-known to her friends. She must keep it in hiding until the night of the ball, when it will be placed with the others in full sight of everyone. The unmarried gentlemen will bid on the tokens, and the lady who furnished the token of his choice will be his dinner partner, as well as his partner for not two, but *three* dances. Most improper, but it is for a good cause. The funds raised will be donated to charity."

"I see." Sedgewick grinned broadly. "I suppose it would do no good for me to ask what you plan to bring? Or Miss Elizabeth, either," he added hastily.

"Not a particle," replied Sally, her eyes sparkling with mischief. "And speaking of Elizabeth. She and Mama and Chloe are in the morning room. If you would join them for a few moments, I shall be through here shortly and will come then."

"Of course." Sedge's bow was a miracle of manly perfection. "By the way," he added as he stepped through the door to the outside, "I have been allotted a shed—a thoroughly isolated structure you may be sure—for my explosive experiments. Would you and Miss Elizabeth care to examine my efforts?" He smiled his devastating smile. "I promise not to blow up anything while you are there."

"Oh. Ah, yes, that would be delightful." Sally hastily shepherded him through the door, and when it closed behind him, she leaned against it limply. In a moment, she shook her head resignedly and returned to her work.

As it turned out, a great deal more than a few minutes had elapsed before Sally was able to put in her appearance in the morning room. Lord Walford, however, appeared perfectly at his ease. A packet of verse lay on the table, and he was reading aloud to the ladies.

"But, my lord," Lady Berners was saying, "you have a rare talent. Have you thought of taking your poems to a publisher?"

Elizabeth and Chloe said nothing, but gazed on Lord Walford with rapt attention. Really, thought Sally, advancing into the room, the three of them might have been in the presence of the Bard, himself. Seeing Sally, Sedgewick sprang to his feet, scattering papers in all directions.

"Ah, my dear," said Lady Berners, "Lord Walford has been entertaining us with his excellent verse." She turned to Sedgewick. "Do please read again the one about the sunrise."

Sedgewick assisted Sally into a nearby armchair before settling himself again. Retrieving the pages, he cleared his throat modestly and began:

ON BEHOLDING A SUNRISE
The morn calls and I rise to greet the day.
From my window I behold the palette of the sky,
Where streaked colors play.
Pale azure blooms to rose, then to flaming red . . .

I wished to put in crimson there," he broke off, "but I couldn't think of a rhyme."

Until at last, sleepy Apollo
Rises from his cloudy bed.

He lay the paper on the small table before him, a dreamy expression in his eyes. "I haven't finished it yet, but I rather fancy I have a good start." He looked expectantly at the faces before him.

"Oh, yes," breathed Elizabeth. Chloe echoed this sentiment, though she had begun to squirm visibly during the recital, while Lady Berners merely nodded, spellbound.

"Yes, it's very nice," agreed Sally in a kind voice. "It's a little derivative, don't you think? But that is surely understandable in a beginner. Are you working on anything else?"

"Not at the moment," he replied a little stiffly.

Sally smiled inwardly. No matter what Charlie said, she simply could not transform herself into a spiritless wigeon just to win a man's approval. Besides, it was time her unsuspecting swain was granted an inkling of her true character.

The next moment, with another of his charming smiles, Sedge had swept his papers into a packet. Shortly after that, he was gone.

Sally stood in front of the mirror in Elizabeth's room and gazed at the vision before her. Elizabeth had finished her tucking and pinning, and now stood back to admire her handiwork.

"Oh, Sally," she sighed happily. "I knew this was the perfect gown for you. You look like a fairy princess."

Indeed, thought Sally dazedly, Elizabeth was not far wrong. The amber silk fell from her breasts in alluring folds, dropping softly against the outline of her body.

Over the tunic floated a cloud of cream-colored net, sparkling with hundreds of tiny spangles. Gold ribbons caught up the fabric at her hemline and her puffed sleeves, and more ribbons of the same color were woven through the mahogany wavelets of her hair.

Sally took a long breath. She had not known she could show to such advantage. During her Season, she had dressed with propriety and elegance, but always in frilly muslins of white or a pale pastel that did nothing for either her shape or her complexion. She had always reminded herself, when garbed for a ball or soiree, of an underdeveloped child dressed for a party in finery stolen from her big sister.

But this ... She swung about and watched the amber silk move about her in a sensuous flow. Hugging herself, she turned to Elizabeth.

"You are a genius, Liz. I wish you had had the dressing of me when I was in London." She transferred the hug to her sister, who blushed in pleased modesty.

With some regret, Sally removed the gown and dressed herself in the serviceable muslin she had worn when she came into the room. Casting one more glance at the amber silk, now resting in the arms of Elizabeth's maid, she left, feeling a little like Cinderella relegated once more to the cinder heap.

Reaching her own room, she flung herself into a small emerald-striped armchair and gave herself up to reflection. The ball was only three days away. Sedgewick had garnered a promise from her of two dances, though that thought did not elevate her self-esteem as much as it might have, since he had asked the same favor of Elizabeth and had even asked Lady Berners to save a country-dance for him. Nonetheless, Charlie had seemed pleased when she had related this news to him.

Charlie. She allowed her thoughts to drift back over the last few weeks. As her relationship with Sedge grew apace, Charlie had grown oddly pensive. Now that Sedge had taken up her instruction in fly-tying and ancient Greek, and now that she and Sedge spent long hours discussing poetry of which he had no knowledge, he appeared to feel somewhat at a loss. He seldom appeared at The Ridings by himself any-more—Sedgewick was nearly always at his side. On these occasions, he had begun to keep well into the background, satisfied, Sally supposed, that Sedgewick was well and truly under her spell.

Except for last Tuesday. The strangest thing had happened last Tuesday. Charlie had appeared at The Ridings. It had been quite late, and he came not to the great front door, but to the French doors that opened out from Sally's workroom.

"Charlie!" Sally had started, nearly oversetting the candle that stood near the book she was reading. She observed that he was carrying a slim volume, and she gestured him to a seat across the table from her. "What in the world are you doing here at this hour? Mama would have a fit if she knew you had come."

"Yes, I know," replied Charlie, placing the book on the table with a thump, causing the nearby piles of feathers to sir fretfully. "Young ladies do not receive gentlemen unattended in the dead of night."

He moved about the room in a restless fashion, absently sifting though the feathers and riffling the pages of the several volumes of poetry that lay nearby. Sally watched him silently as his shadow danced and grew and shrank against the wall in the flickering candlelight. At last, he threw himself into a chair next to her.

"Sally . . ." he began, and then fell silent once more. He met her eyes and grinned ruefully. "I am having an attack of cold feet, I fear." At the questioning lift of her eyebrows, he continued hesitantly. "I have been wondering if we are doing the right thing—in hood-winking Sedge."

"Charlie Darracot!" Sally bestowed upon him a look of astonished indignation. "You have done nothing for the past month and a half but throw me at his head, and now you wonder if . . ."

"I know, I know," responded Charlie hastily. "And the whole plan is working splendidly. I just wondered if—you know . . ."

"No, I don't know—and I wish you would explain this sudden about-face."

"I'm not doing an about-face. I just thought—well, I just thought that if you were having second thoughts, it's not too late to abandon the whole thing."

"I see." Sally studied him, noting that it looked as though he had not been sleeping well lately. She rose, and with an angry swish of her skirts, began pacing the path just abandoned by Charlie.

"Of course I had second thoughts," she said slowly. "And third and fourth thoughts as well. But I have concluded that we are doing the right thing. Particularly since, as you say, the whole thing seems to be working out so splendidly. Sedge spends nearly every waking hour here, you know."

"Yes, I know," said Charlie, with a marked lack of enthusiasm. "He rode out this morning and did not return until almost dinnertime. What were you doing all that time, anyway?" he asked idly.

"Oh." Sally mentally reviewed her day with Sedge. Or rather, the small portion of the day she had actually spent with him. "We read some poetry and went for a walk."

"Oh? Where?"

"Down to the river and back. We discussed some of Sedge's ideas on Homer. He's doing a translation of the Prologue to the *Odyssey,* you know."

"No, I didn't know that."

"Yes, he found himself in such disagreement with the Wolf translation that he decided to attempt one of his own."

"Ah."

"Then he read the latest stanzas of a pastoral ode that he's composing."

Sally saw no reason to mention to Charlie that she had managed to escape the reading by foisting Sedge off on Elizabeth and her mother while she fled to her greenhouse. Sedge's poetry was not truly dreadful, but she had discovered in herself an extremely small tolerance for the massive doses he dispensed on a daily basis. She was grateful that her mother and Elizabeth, particularly Elizabeth, seemed content to listen for hours to the stuff.

In an effort to turn the conversation, Sally picked up the little volume Charlie had placed on the table. She opened it to discover that it was a book of verse by one Ambrose Philips.

She looked up at Charlie, and was surprised to discover that a flush had crept over his handsome features.

"Oh, that," he said awkwardly. "I was browsing through some more of father's stuff, and I found . . . That is, some days ago I tried to describe you in poetic terms and failed rather miserably. I found something that I thought—more appropriate. May I—may I read it to you?"

Sally's mouth formed a small *O* of surprise, but she said nothing, merely nodding in acquiescence.

Charlie opened the book to the place he had marked, and with one more quick glance at Sally, began to read:

For the dark-brown dusk of hair,
Shadowing thick thy forehead fair . . .
O'er the sloping shoulders flowing,
And the smoothly pencil'd brow . . .
And the fringed lid below,
Thin as thinnest blossoms blow,
And the hazely-lucid eye,
Whence heart-winning glances fly . . .

Charlie closed the book and replaced it gently on the table, and turned to face her. To her horror, she felt her eyes brim with tears, which in a moment began to spill over her cheeks.

"Sally!" exclaimed Charlie. "What is it? Good God, I never meant to . . ."

"Oh, no," she sniffed, hastily wiping away the tears. "It's—it's just that no one has ever said anything half so beautiful to me in all my life."

"You like it then? You don't think it's—rubbish?"

"Of course not!" She blew her nose purposefully on the small handkerchief she kept in her pocket. "I do thank you, Charlie, for thinking of me when you read it, and for bringing it tonight."

"You're welcome," he said gruffly. He appeared to fall into a reverie then, from which he jerked himself a few moments later.

"Valentine's Day is next week," he observed.

"Oh. Yes."

"I suppose you and your sister have made all your preparations."

"Yes."

"I should imagine Sedge will want to bid on your token. What is it to be?" he asked casually.

"Charlie! You know I can't tell you that!"

"Oh, for the Lord's sake, Sally, don't come all over missish on me." She turned an innocent stare on him, and he continued irritatedly. "This is me, after all. How is Sedge going to know what token to bid on if I can't tell him which is yours?"

Sally glanced down to her lap where her fingers were pleating her skirt with great precision. "I suppose he will just have to guess, like everyone else."

"You know good and well that everyone else is going to know the identity of the owners of every token on display. That's the point of the whole thing, goose. Otherwise, how would all the eager swains end up with the ladies of their choice?"

Observing the stubborn tilt of Sally's chin, he sighed. "All right, but assuming he guesses right, he will probably dance the waltz with you. Do you remember your steps?"

She stared at him. "Charlie, I do not know how to waltz at all."

"Of course you do," he said patiently. "Your mama had a caper merchant out here for both you and Elizabeth just before you went to London."

Sally's gaze dropped again to her now severely wrinkled skirt. "Yes, but I never quite got the hang of it. Elizabeth learned to perform it in no time, and Signor Canelli was so impressed with her grace that he spent all his time in pirouettes with her."

"Yes, but when you were in London . . ."

"Oh, Charlie, you know how it was with me in London. I never even received permission from the patronesses to waltz—not that anyone would have asked me anyway."

"Nonsense," he said briskly. "I would have."

"But you never appeared at Almack's," she observed pointedly. "And besides, you don't count."

"I beg your pardon?" His voice carried an unmistakable edge.

"I only meant," she returned soothingly, "you've always told me that dancing with me is like taking a turn around the floor with your sister."

"Did I say that?" He stared at her in some confusion for a moment before continuing. "Well, there's no help for it. You'll have to practice on me."

He rose and extended his hand

"You mean right now?" she exclaimed, startled.

Charlie did not reply, but bowed low from his waist. "It is I, Sedgwick, Earl of Walford. Would you do me the inestimable honor, Miss Berners, of joining me for the waltz?"

Sweeping her skirts into a curtsy, she glanced up at him and laughed.

"It would be my great pleasure, my lord."

Leading her to the center of the room, he placed his arm around her waist. "One, two, three, one, two, three. Remember how it goes?"

It appeared that she did. As Charlie hummed a light tune, she settled herself against him, feeling as though she had stepped into a dear, familiar haven. Around the cleared space in the center of the chamber they whirled, and he bent to whisper, "But you dance divinely, Miss Berners."

"Why, thank you, my lord."

They danced for a few more moments before Charlie stopped suddenly. He gazed down at her, an arrested expression on his features.

"You are utterly captivating, Miss Berners," he continued in an unsteady voice. "And you have won my heart."

"Have I, my lord?" she whispered. She gazed up at him, mesmerized, feeling as though she were being drawn into those dark eyes. Sally prayed he could not feel the thunderous beat of her heart beneath the plain fawn muslin she wore. She was totally unnerved by Charlie's closeness. The feel of his body against hers was having an astonishing effect, and it seemed as though everything in her was suddenly focused on the unfamiliar sensations that coursed through her. "Will he really say that, Charlie?" she whispered.

"Oh, yes," he replied in a strangled voice. "He will tell you your eyes are like deep, mysterious pools, and he will kiss your hand." He brought Sally's fingers to his lips. "And then ..." His face was very close to hers, and she could feel the feather touch of his breath on her cheek. She was filled with the familiar soap and leather scent of him, and she thought she might simply die right there in his arms.

"And then ..." Charlie repeated in a barely audible voice. He clasped her to him, and one hand cupped the back of her head. Slowly, he bent his head and brushed her lips tentatively with his. She stood unmoving, lost in the unexpected wonder of the gentle contact. Then, with a sigh that was more of a groan, his mouth came down on hers once more, and this time the kiss was deep and urgent and achingly tender, seeming to reach into her very soul for a response that was only too freely given.

Sally had no idea how long they remained thus, but suddenly Charlie released her and stood back. A growing expression of horror crossed his face.

"Sally, I ..." He spoke in a barely recognizable rasp.

"And will Sedgewick do that, too?" Sally interrupted, her own voice emerging in reedy thread.

It was some moments before Charlie answered, and when he did so, his tone was light. "He may, but not, let us hope, until after he has proposed marriage."

"But you did," she said softly.

"And I apologize, Miss Berners," finished Charlie, still in that light, faintly bored tone. "I was overcome by the, er, wine and the music."

Sally smiled demurely. "You have a vivid imagination, Charlie."

Charlie had said nothing in reply, and after a few more moments in idle conversation, he left the house, slipping through the French doors into the darkness.

Returning to the present, Sally shifted in her emerald-striped armchair and smiled again in memory. The smile spread into a grin as she rose and began to dress for dinner.

"You can't mean to tell me," moaned Lady Berners, "that you plan to arrive at Winstaunton Hall in a farm wagon!"

"Of course not, Mama," replied Sally soothingly. "I have only to see that the dried arrangements and the potpourri are packed properly in the wagons. Then I must assure that the flowers in tubs are put into the heated wagons. Masters will see to it that they are delivered at the servants' entrance, while I shall arrive in proper style at the front door with you and the others in the landau."

"The landau." Lady Berners' mouth turned down in a moue of disparagement. "Really, Sally. It's so dreadfully out of date, I cannot see why we don't sell it and purchase a nice barouche. They are ever so much more fashionable."

"And ever so much more expensive, Mama."

Lady Berners sighed. "Yes, I suppose you're right, my dear." The two had just emerged from the linen room where, with the assistance of Mrs. Lamb, the housekeeper, they had been taking inventory. "By the way," she continued. "Did Lord Walford leave already? I thought he just arrived a few minutes ago."

"Um, yes he did," said Sally, "but I really couldn't spare the time to visit with him. I have a great deal to do if I am to leave tomorrow for Winstaunton Hall. He is in the morning room with Elizabeth. And Chloe."

"Oh?" responded her mother thoughtfully. "Did Elizabeth not drive into the village with him yesterday because you were terribly busy?"

"Why, yes. Come to think of it, she did." Sally pulled a thread from her skirt with great care.

"And the day before that Elizabeth and Lord Walford went skating with Chloe and William, did they not? While you were immersed in your greenhouse?"

This time Sally merely nodded.

A long moment passed, during which Lady Berners stared penetratingly at her daughter.

"Are you sure you know what you are about, my dear?" she asked at length.

"Yes, Mama, I am sure."

This time it was Lady Berners who nodded. They had by now reached the Great Hall, and she began to ascend the staircase, but turned to ask, "Charlie has been a frequent visitor of late, too, has he not? At some rather odd times of day, I believe."

"Yes, Mama," repeated Sally, allowing a small smile to creep into her eyes.

"I see" was her mother's only response. She acknowledged the smile with one of her own, and looked as if she might say more. Instead, she shook her head and resumed her journey up the staircase.

The remaining days before the ball passed without incident, unless one counted the explosion—really a very small one—caused by Lord Walford's experiments. Lady Frane maintained with steadfast courtesy that since the shed had not been used for years, its destruction was of little account. Upon hearing the news, the ladies of The Ridings were quite pale with apprehension until the earl himself arrived, none the worse for wear, to proclaim his well being.

Thus, two days before the Valentine's Ball, the ladies mounted the despised landau with hearts full of lighthearted anticipation. And if the delight on the part of one of them was tinged with apprehension, she joined the others with a determined smile pinned to her lips.

In the elegantly furnished room at Winstaunton Hall where he had been billeted, Charlie stared blankly at his mirror while March, his valet, hovered in an agony of apprehension over his master's demeanor.

"I see no fault in the cravat, sir," the man said diffidently. "The Osbaldston, after all, is quite suitable for ball wear."

"What?" With an effort, Charlie tried to focus on March's words. "Oh, the cravat. Yes, perfectly adequate. You may consider me togged and ready, March. Be a good fellow and leave me now—and don't wait up. I'll see myself to bed."

March, stiff with injured dignity, merely nodded and let himself silently from the room.

Charlie slumped in an armchair near the fire and gave himself up to gloomy reflection. What the devil was the matter with him? he wondered. Everything was going as planned. Sedge had obviously fallen victim to Sally's charms and if he weren't planning to propose to her tonight, Charlie was prepared to eat his quizzing glass. Sally had promised to insist on an early wedding, so that within the year the tontine money would be his. He could buy the stud farm, and he would be free to live the life he had envisioned for himself, self-sufficient and beholden to no one. Self-sufficient—and all by himself.

He sat up suddenly, arrested by this thought. Was that what was blue-deviling him? The idea that Sally would soon retire to a life of wedded bliss, leaving him to reign alone in his little empire? But what was there in that to put him in a megrim? True, Sally and he had been close as pennies in a pocket for donkeys years, but of late they had led their own lives; he as one of the *ton's* most dashing bachelors, if he did say so himself, and she as titular head of her little family in the country.

Yet, he mused, even though they did not move in the same circles now, the knowledge that she was always there for him, snug in the rural fastness of The Ridings, had been a sort of talisman for him over the years. It created a small haven of brightness in the back of his mind, a place he could warm himself when he was troubled and needed solace.

Now, his haven would be gone. She would belong to Sedge, and he would have no place in her life. The feeling was growing in him that he didn't want Sally to belong to Sedge. The thought of Sedge folding her in his arms and kissing her, as he, himself, had done those few nights before made him physically ill.

His thoughts fled back to that moment when they

had shared that impromptu waltz. She had looked up into his eyes, and it was as though he had never seen her before—never noticed the mysterious, womanly beauty that had settled on her while he wasn't looking. And now she was on the verge of becoming betrothed to Sedge.

Sally had not discussed her feelings for Sedge with him, but it was all too obvious that she thought him the pinnacle of a maiden's desire. Charlie felt like the merest nonentity, standing in the shadow of handsome, wealthy, intelligent Sedge, who was a perfectly decent sort, to boot. No, though Sally was no doubt fond of the Honorable Mr. Charles Darracot, she still looked on him merely as her old comrade in arms, so to speak.

And yet . . .

There was that kiss. When he had pressed his lips against hers, her response had not been that of a female bussing an old chum. Her soft curves had molded to his body in an embrace that had set his pulses pounding and his blood racing. Her mouth had opened beneath him, leaving him to probe the wonder within. It had taken everything in him to withdraw from her before he dishonored the fabric of their friendship.

In the days that followed his late-night visit to The Ridings, neither mentioned the incident, and Sally had maintained her usual, friendly behavior toward him. He was forced to the conclusion that she had been, as he claimed to be, a victim of the lateness of the hour, the candlelight, and the pretense.

Charlie rose abruptly and, giving a final flick to the perfection of his cravat, left the room and proceeded downstairs.

Most of the ball guests had already assembled on the ground floor of the huge manor house, drifting through drawing rooms and overflowing into the Great Hall from whence branched the wide main staircase to the gallery above. Lord and Lady Winstaun-

ton, a handsome couple in their late fifties, stood near
the door, greeting guests who had arrived the day before and were descending from their rooms, or who
were neighbors and newly come in carriages. Tubs of
Sally's roses, and her other hothouse flowers stood in
every corner, and masses of dried flowers filled vases
set on tables and stands. Jars filled with potpourri
were scattered throughout the rooms, saturating the
air with their heavy fragrance. Excited young misses,
looking very much like floating blossoms themselves
in their gaily colored muslins and silks, drifted from
chamber to chamber trying to look bored and unaware
of the masculine attention that followed their progress.

Charlie looked for Sally, but could not find her.
Sedge was standing with a group of acquaintances
near the fireplace in the Hall, and Charlie strolled
over to join them.

"I think the silk rose is Vivian Carew's, but I'm not
sure," one of the young men was saying. "Though, I
rather thought she'd set out the gold locket she wears
to the assemblies."

Sedge welcomed Charlie, explaining that the gentlemen had been guessing the identities of the owners of
the tokens laid out on a table in the ballroom. "Have
you seen them?" he asked. "You must take a look—
there's quite an assortment," he said, laughing, as
Charlie shook his head in a negative gesture.

They strolled into the ballroom where, on a large
pier table, lay an assortment of feminine belongings.
Hair ornaments jostled with scarves and ribbons, and
flowers of silk and velvet twined about necklaces and
even a shoe or two.

"And how about you?" asked Charlie. "Have you
guessed which token belongs to your chosen lady?"

"Ah," Sedge responded, his blue eyes sparkling
with mischief. "I do not need to guess. I know!"

"Indeed? You never told me you were blessed with
second sight, old man."

"I don't need it, my boy, when I have the cooperation of the lady's sister. Young Chloe, you see, is not
as closemouthed as the rest of the family, and is, I
discovered, susceptible to bribery."

"But, you are a scoundrel"—Charlie smiled lazily—
"to win a lady by such contemptible means. Fie on
you, sirrah!"

"Ah, well." Sedge shrugged, his face still alight. "When
needs must, you know. And once having gained
knowledge of Chloe's passion for comfits, I could not
pass up the temptation. There." He pointed to a small,
plain silver bracelet lying among the glittering cluster
on the table. "That is the token upon which I shall
bid."

Following Sedge's gaze, Charlie stiffened, the
amusement draining from his gaze. For a long moment
he studied the little bracelet, and when he turned back
to Sedge, his jaw was clenched with the effort it took
to speak calmly.

"And if you gain the token," he asked, and held
his breath to hear the answer, "will you also win the
lady?"

"That is for her to say," answered Sedge, his face
breaking into a wide grin.

A vision rose up before Charlie's eyes, hot and brilliant, of his fist plunging into Sedge's mouth, smashing
that stupid smirk and scattering those perfect white
teeth in a bloody explosion. Swallowing, he swung on
his heel and walked away.

The bracelet! My God, why had Sally pledged the
bracelet he had given her on her sixteenth birthday?
He could still remember the expression on her face
as he slipped it on her wrist that day so long ago.
Lord, he'd thought she was going to burst into tears.
She had looked up at him with shining eyes and told
him that it was the first piece of real jewelry she had
ever owned. Her words had made him feel wretched
because it had been the cheapest of all the bracelets

lying in the tray at the jeweler's. After that, Sally was rarely seen without the trinket, until ... He narrowed his eyes. That's odd, he thought. She had worn the thing constantly until the day the two of them had held a long conversation about their parents' marriage plans.

Charlie had railed against the fates that would shackle him before he had scarcely had time to taste the delights of the world. He didn't want to marry Sally—he didn't want to marry anybody. And Sally certainly did not want to marry him. Did she? He had asked her the question, looking straight into her eyes, and she had responded lightly that, of course, marrying Charlie was the last thing in the world she desired. She had yet to find her heart mate—yes, that was the word she had used. She and Charlie would, she said, simply have to explain all this to the senior Darracots and the Berners. Present a united front.

And it had worked. Oh, not right away, but eventually the old folks had given up, and Lady Frane had cast her eyes over the wider world for a wife for her second son. All to no avail, of course. He had been too busy enjoying his bachelorhood, savoring the pleasures of town life to consider taking a wife. If a serious thought flew by mistake into his head, it was waved away immediately, like a bothersome insect.

Now Sally had found her heart mate, and he had at last grown into a measure of adulthood. He was through with mindless pleasuring. He wanted more in his life now, something deep and satisfying. My God ... He almost stumbled as the thought struck him like a physical blow. He wanted Sally! He had always wanted Sally, he realized with a sudden, painful clarity, only he had been too stupid to see it. And now it was too late.

Slowly, he made his way back to the main hall, where more of the guests were descending the great staircase from the floors above. He lifted his eyes and experienced a moment of deep shock. Sally, with Elizabeth behind her, floated down the staircase, the amber silk of her gown caressing her lissome body. The brilliants sewn on to the gauze tunic reflected the candlelight like sparkling points of flame, enveloping her in a blaze of brilliance matched by her sparkling eyes. Her hair, piled high on her head in a luxuriant curve also caught the candlelight in russet highlights, and her cheeks were lightly flushed.

"God, she's beautiful!" he murmured involuntarily.

He had not realized that Sedge had followed him from the ballroom, but behind him, he heard a strangled gasp.

"Beautiful," whispered Sedge in echo.

Shaken, Charlie retired to a far corner of the Hall and watched Sally's progress through the crowd. Her eyes searched the room, sweeping past Sedge at first, then returning to him. She greeted him with an engaging smile and allowed him to lift her fingers to his lips. A surge of bitterness curled in Charlie's belly, and he would have fled the chamber but for Lady Winstaunton's voice cutting through the buzz of chatter that surrounded him.

"Ladies and gentlemen, we are going to start off the festivities tonight with the Token Auction." To much laughing banter, she explained the rules of the auction, concluding with the reminder, "Remember, the lady who owns the token you purchase will be yours for the evening. At least until the last dance is played," she added with a smile, as more laughter and several ribald shouts greeted her statement.

Charlie crossed his arms and settled against the wall, and watched the proceedings sourly. Silk flowers, scarves, hair bows, and shoes—all went beneath the gavel of Lord Winstaunton, who acted as jovial auctioneer, until finally his lordship's fingers touched on the little silver bracelet.

"And what am I offered for this charming bauble?"

he called. Against his will, Charlie drew closer to the group surrounding the table.

Sedge started the bidding with five guineas, and when the others saw who was bidding, a few other voices called out in competition. Squire Jeffers, or Jeffreys, or whatever his name was, chimed in until the bidding reached ten guineas. He fell silent then. The bidding rose to twelve guineas before the other voices ceased.

"Twelve guineas, five shillings," called Lord Winstaunton, and the crowd murmured, for this was the highest bid reached all evening. To Charlie's utter astonishment he heard himself call out, "Aye!"

Out of the corner of his eye, he was aware of Sally's astonished gaze on him. He was also made aware of a small disturbance arising from the gallery overlooking the ballroom, where several of the children of guests attending the ball stood watching the scene below. Among the young observers was Chloe, who had just wriggled her way to the front of the group. She was now waving wildly to Sedge, who, oblivious, signaled his intention to raise the bid to thirteen guineas.

"Thirteen guineas, five shillings," croaked Charlie, and his body was suddenly covered in perspiration. What in God's name was he doing? Sally would be furious with him! Sedge would probably try to destroy him bone by bone. Coming to himself, he heard his voice raise once more.

"Fourteen guineas."

He was dimly cognizant of Chloe's antics in the gallery, and apparently so was Sedge, for he turned and, lifting his head, favored his co-conspirator with a puzzled stare. Charlie looked at Sally, who had turned her gaze to him. He tried to read her expression, but her cinnamon eyes were opaque and her face was closed to him.

"Fourteen guineas," Charlie cried again, and was surprised that his words were greeted only by silence.

Lord Winstaunton glanced questioningly at Sedge, but Sedge shook his head.

"Sold!" Lord Winstaunton held the silver bracelet out to Charlie, who stepped forward dazedly. He turned and moved almost without volition until he reached Sally's side. He held the bracelet up, and slipped it on her wrist. She touched it gently with one finger before slipping her arm into his. As they turned away from the crowd grouped around Lord Winstaunton, Charlie caught a glimpse of Sedge, bidding on another token.

"I'm sorry," Charlie whispered hoarsely.

"Sorry?" Sally replied with a smile. Her eyes were wide and held a disturbing expression in their depths. He could have sworn he saw a hint of laughter there. "Do you mean you do not wish to sit next to me at dinner?"

"No, of course that's not what I mean." The guests were beginning to move toward the dining room, and he placed his hand beneath her elbow to guide her through the crush. "I know you wished Sedge to buy your—token." He could not utter the question that hammered in his brain. *Why did you put up the bracelet I gave you for another man to possess?*

She smiled again, but said nothing. Their dinner conversation was mundane, but all through the six lavish courses set before him, Charlie was aware of a simmering excitement beneath their commonplace chatter. At one point during the meal his hand inadvertently brushed hers, and it was as though he had been touched by a charge of electricity. Did she feel it, too? he wondered. Was Sally aware of the tension that seemed to simmer about them? Charlie felt as though by stretching out his hands in the space between them, he would create rivulets of lightening. He studied her covertly and noticed with some small pleasure that she was merely toying with her food.

After dinner, Sally slipped away to visit with friends

on the other side of the room, and Charlie did not see her again until it was time for the ball to start. Contrary to custom, the first dance played was a waltz, and it was the first of the three dances granted to the young men who had purchased tokens. Laughing couples took the floor. Charlie found Sally deep in conversation with Sedge and Elizabeth. Joining them, he nodded awkwardly to Sedge. In his preoccupation, Charlie had not considered the puzzling fact of Sedge's dropping out from the bidding on Sally's bracelet, and now the gaze he turned on his friend was questioning.

"I see you decided against the bracelet, after all," he said at last.

"I made a mistake," Sedge answered calmly. Which really, thought Charlie, didn't tell him anything at all. The music began then, and Sedge turned to Elizabeth.

"My dance, I believe, Miss Elizabeth," he said, whereupon he led a shyly smiling Elizabeth out on the dance floor.

"My dance, I believe, Miss Berners." Charlie made her a low bow and stretched out his hand to her.

Sally, raising her head to gaze into Charlie's eyes, felt the lilt of the music pulse through her veins. She lifted her arms and as his hand settled at her waist, gave herself up to the feelings that surged within her.

Charlie was dancing with her! And if she were not very much mistaken, there was little danger that he mistook her for his sister. There was an intensity in his gaze that had never been there before. And a measure of confusion, she thought, and smiled to herself.

"I see you have not forgotten your lesson," Charlie said after a moment.

"The lesson? Oh—the other night." Sally could feel heat rise to stain her cheeks at the memory of Charlie's lips pressed against hers in the candle-lit workroom. "No, I have not forgotten our—our dancing lesson."

"You waltz beautifully—we must do this more often." Charlie's arm tightened around her and an odd breathlessness crept into his voice. "Sally, why did Sedge give up on the bidding?"

"Why? Do you object to sharing the evening with me?" She fluttered her eyelashes in what she conceded to herself was probably a futile effort to appear ravishingly coy.

Charlie did not take the bait. Instead, he stared at her through narrowed eyes.

"What game are you playing at, Sally?" he demanded suddenly.

To Sally's vast relief, the music ended, and she prepared to disengage herself from Charlie's embrace. Charlie, however, had other ideas. They were on the periphery of the dance floor, and, keeping her hand in his grasp, he pulled her from the group of dancers into a corridor leading away from the great room.

"Charlie, what . . . ?"

"I thought you might like to take a turn in the conservatory," he said grimly, opening a door leading from the corridor.

Once inside the warmth of the moist, vaulted chamber, he swung on her.

"What's going on, Sally? You and Sedge have hardly spoken to each other all evening. Have you quarreled? Or have you already come to an—an arrangement and simply do not wish to broadcast the fact until his lordship has a chance to notify his parents!"

"Charlie!" Good God, she thought wildly. Charlie was glaring at her as though she were his worst enemy. Had she been mistaken in him? Was he angry that she had not wrung a public declaration from Sedge? "Charlie," she repeated, failing miserably to suppress the quiver that arose in her voice.

"Sally." He gripped her shoulders. "Why did you put up your bracelet for the auction?"

She dropped her eyes. "I wondered if you would recognize it," she said softly.

"Of course, I recognized it," he growled. "How could you just—toss it down for Sedge to claim?"

Sally lifted her eyes once more. "But, he didn't claim it, Charlie." She drew a deep breath. "Would you have cared if he did?"

For a long moment, Charlie simply stared down at her. Then almost without volition, his hands left her shoulders to encircle her, and the next moment his mouth had come down on hers. Sally's lips parted beneath his and her pulse throbbed to the beat of a joyous song that flooded every cell of her being. She had dreamed of this moment, and now that it was here, she pressed against him, memorizing with her heart every line of his body.

"Oh, God, Sally," gasped Charlie, when at last he drew back. "I've thought about it and thought about it, but I just cannot face the rest of my life without you. Would you—that is . . . Oh my God, Sally, I don't want you to marry Sedge, I want you to marry me!"

Sally's eyes were clear and bright as sunlit pools. "But we decided years ago that we would not suit. Didn't we?"

"But that was before I—Lord, Sally, I've loved you for years, but I was too stupid to understand that until it was finally brought home that I was really about to lose you."

"Do you, Charlie? Really love me?" Her gaze was piercing in its intensity, but he did not falter before it.

"Yes." He had not released her from his embrace, and now he tightened his arms around her. "I know I've acted the colossal fool for a number of years, living like a care-for-nobody. But all that time, I did care for you. I thought it was just friendship that bound us together—and I guess that's what it was during our growing-up years. But you grew into a magnificent woman, while I—I grew up to be an idiot."

"Oh, Charlie, no." Sally raised a hand in gentle protest.

"Well," he grinned uncertainly. "Anybody who falls

in love with a girl and doesn't even know it can't be very bright."

"That's true," she said gravely, only the lurking brightness in her eyes belying her words. Charlie traced the curve of her cheek with one finger and bent his head to hers once more. Some moments later, when she emerged breathless and shaken from this embrace, Sally felt as though her blood had been replaced by the finest, bubbliest champagne. She laughed up into Charlie's eyes, only to discover that his own were penetrating and somewhat somber.

"Sally, I practically forced you into a betrothal with Sedge. I must know—how do you feel about him? How do you feel about me?"

Her own expression grew serious, or at least as serious as she could manage with the joy that surged within her. "Oh, Charlie, I have loved you since before I could walk or talk, I think. It's always been you and only you, my dearest."

"But—when our parents wished for us to marry, you said . . ."

"I know what I said, but I lied. Well, not lied exactly. I said I did not wish to marry you, and that was true—at least at that time, for I realized you did not want it. I could only hope that one day you would come to know your heart and that there would be a place in it for me."

Once more, Charlie drew her into a crushing embrace, drawing back moments later to utter a stifled exclamation.

"Sedge! Oh, God, Sally, what are we to do about Sedge?"

"Oh, that."

"Yes, oh, that. My dear and only love, I want to marry you with all possible speed, even if it means losing out on the tontine. I shall find some other way to support a wife. Do you fancy the diplomatic life, my dear?"

"Well, as to that . . ." began Sally, dropping her eyes once more, but Charlie interrupted.

"I do feel badly about Sedge. After all we went through to make him fall in love with you, to suddenly turn him off like a tap . . ." He sighed. "You were right, my dearest love, we have served Sedge very ill."

"As to that," Sally said again, "there is something I must tell you, love."

At this, Charlie felt compelled to kiss her once more. "I do like the sound of that on your lips. Will you always call me 'love,' even when we are old and toothless?"

"Even when you grow bald," replied Sally, her eyes alight with tender laughter. "But let me continue—love."

Obediently, Charlie stepped back without releasing her hands.

"About Sedge," she continued. "It may be that . . ."

"There you are," called a voice from the conservatory entrance. In a moment, Sedge hove into view from behind the shrubbery bordering the path on which they stood. With him was Elizabeth and, Charlie noted with astonishment, they were holding hands.

"Elizabeth!" cried Sally, running to her sister. Elizabeth turned a glowing gaze toward her. "Are you . . . ?"

"Yes, Miss Berners," answered Lord Walford, bending a tender glance upon the girl beside him. "Elizabeth has promised to become my bride."

"I'm so happy for both of you," breathed Sally, hugging first Elizabeth and then Sedge.

"But—" said Charlie.

"I spoke to your mother late this afternoon," continued Sedge, oblivious, "and received her permission to ask for the hand of the dearest, most beautiful, most precious young woman in the kingdom."

"Goodness," interposed Elizabeth softly, the light in her face almost blinding in its expression of love, "Chloe almost ruined everything. When Sedge began bidding on Sally's bracelet, I thought my heart would break."

"But—" said Charlie again.

"I couldn't imagine," Sedge spoke in a burst of laughter, "what Chloe was about, waving from the gallery to me, after I had already inveigled the information I needed from her. The silly chit," he concluded, "made a mistake. She told me that Elizabeth would put up a silver bracelet and that the velvet rose lying near it was Sally's, but it was, of course, the other way around."

Charlie stepped forward and grasped Sally's elbow. "Is anyone," he asked in an ominous tone of voice, "going to tell me what is going on?"

Sally and Sedge exchanged glances, and Sedge turned to Elizabeth.

"I think these two would like to be alone, my love. Let us seek out your mother to tell her our news. And we must discuss with her the date we have set."

After one quick look at Sally, Elizabeth lifted her face to Sedge, and the light that filled her eyes seemed to flood the room.

After the two had left, Sally turned again to Charlie.

"Charlie," she began tentatively. "I have some rather lengthy explaining to do."

Charlie said nothing, but drew her down on a stone bench set next to a small fountain in the center of the conservatory.

"As you can see, we need not feel badly about Sedgewick." Sally's voice held a degree of laughter, and Charlie eyed her suspiciously. "I have to confess to you, my darling, that I never intended to make him fall in love with me."

Charlie's brows shot skyward. "What? But you said . . ."

"I never said I would try to attract him. If you'll recall, I said only that I would do the things you asked—learning Greek, and fly-tying and all the rest. And I said I would practice the conversational arts you taught me."

"Well, isn't that—?"

Sally lifted her hand. "Yes, I did mislead you—but, if I'd told you what I had in mind, you would have fled The Ridings and never returned."

"You see," she continued, when Charlie again made no response, "when you first proposed this incredible tontine scheme of yours, my first response was to refuse outright. Then I began to think over the possibilities. Your plan involved your spending a great deal of time with me, and I hoped . . ." Sally flushed to her roots. "That is—you see, I had observed a change in you. You had become more mature in your outlook, and serious about making a life for yourself on your own. In short, my dearest, you had at last grown from a boy to a man, and I hoped the time had come for you to know your own heart as well." She took a deep breath. "Oh, please, Charlie, don't be angry. I know I must seem like a scheming, manipulating harpy, but . . ."

Charlie reached to touch her hand. "Scheming, yes, and manipulating, too, but you are constitutionally unfit to be a harpy." He smiled. "How can I be angry at having been the target of such a—a loving plot. It is surprising to me, however, that after so much time in your company, Sedge did not fall head over tail in love with you."

"Oh." Sally's eyes fell once more to her hands, which were engaged in twisting the little silver bracelet. "Actually, I did not spend all that much time with him. Most of the hours he spent here were in Elizabeth's company."

There was another long silence before Charlie responded with a grin. "And I suppose that was your doing?"

"Um." By now the silver bracelet was twinkling in the candlelight as it fairly spun about on Sally's wrist. "I noticed that when they first met, an expression came into Sedge's eyes that—well, I thought it couldn't hurt for them to, er, get to know each other better. After all, Sedge is, as you pointed out so assiduously, an excellent catch, and I thought it a perfect opportunity for Elizabeth. And she was in such raptures over him, I knew I would not be forcing anything to let—to let nature take its course."

Charlie burst into laughter. "I think it is you who should take up a career in diplomacy. You will make a much better negotiator than I. With your talents, you would have every head of state in Europe eating out of your hand within moments of meeting you."

"As to that, Charlie, I think you need not worry about a career with the Foreign Office. You see, Sedge wishes to marry Elizabeth within the next three months. He says he has no qualms about marrying without his parents' approval, but he would just as soon present to them a fait accompli when they come home at that time. I think we can wait until after that, don't you—for twelve thousand pounds?" She dimpled engagingly at him, and Charlie took her in his arms once more.

"If you persist in looking at me in that fashion, I fear the ceremony will come too late if it is not held within the next five minutes."

"Charlie, you shock me," she said, nestling further into his arms. "Actually, I was thinking we should wait until next Valentine's Day to be married. Don't you think that would be apropos?"

"No, I do not. I think three months and one day would be more like. And I shall make every day Valentine's Day for you, my little love."

"Why Charlie"—Sally giggled—"I think that is quite the most poetic thing you have ever said to me."

"Yes," replied Charlie consideringly. "It probably is, and I hope you won't get used to it. That sort of thing is terribly wearing on a fellow, you know."

With that, in order to silence the protest he saw rising to her lips, he pressed his mouth on hers once more, and silence reigned in the conservatory.

Cupid's Dart

by Melinda McRae

1

SEBASTIAN Cole seethed with frustration. He'd spent the better part of the afternoon standing sentinel in the library, staring glumly out the window at the empty drive, waiting for a carriage that hadn't yet arrived.

She wouldn't abandon him like this; Willi couldn't be so cruel. But as each minute dragged past, he grew more and more doubtful. Despite all his hopes, his trust, she was going to condemn him to a miserable fate. And she claimed to be his friend!

The moment he heard the familiar crunch of carriage wheels on gravel, he jumped to his feet and ran to the window. An elegant traveling carriage, its glossy black finish only faintly obscured by dust, rolled up the drive.

Thank God.

Seb dashed through the hall and raced down the front steps, halting at the edge of the drive just as the carriage stopped. Waving the footman aside, he sprang forward and flung open the door.

"I didn't think you were coming," he said accusingly.

Light, fluid laughter greeted his ears. "Really, Seb, you know me better than that. How could I fail to come to the aid of a friend in need?"

Taking his hand, Wilhelmina, the widowed Lady

Taunton, stepped daintily from the carriage. Seb grinned in delight at the sight of her tall, shapely form.

"Forgive me for having even a moment of doubt," Seb said, kissing her cheek.

She frowned ever so slightly. "Tell me Seb, what is so dreadfully wrong that you needed to bring me all the way from London? You know the Season is starting."

Seb took her slim, gloved hand and raised it to his lips. "I would not have brought you here unless it was a matter of dire importance." He gave her a warning glance and nodded toward the attending footman. "Come, let me take you inside." He tucked her arm in his and led her up the steps.

He escorted her through the high-ceilinged, marble-tiled entry hall, and into the library, where he shut the door firmly behind them. "Brandy?"

Willi nodded. While she removed her cloak and bonnet, Seb poured them each a brandy from the decanter on the side table. He turned to hand her a glass, and halted in mid-step, staring at her in bold amazement. "What have you done with your hair?"

Willi patted her short curls. "*Tres chic,* is it not?"

Seb circled around her. The long chestnut hair he'd so admired was gone, but he was forced to admit she looked utterly charming—and years younger. He laughed to himself. No doubt Willi had deliberately intended that result. But as a man who'd ruefully noted the increasing gray in his own blond hair only this morning, he could not fault her for her vanity.

"I like it," he said at last. "It suits you."

Willi eyed him doubtfully. "What, exactly, is that supposed to mean?"

Seb sat down, crossing one leg comfortably over his knee. "It is stylish, unusual, daring, and attention-provoking. Like yourself."

She looked nonplussed. "I do not know if you are complimenting me or insulting me."

Seb laughed and reached over to squeeze her hand. "Dear Willi. You are the most extraordinary woman I know. Sometimes I regret we decided to be friends rather than lovers."

She waved a dismissive hand. "Lovers can grow tiresome over the years. Friendship is a sturdier relationship. Now stop being so mysterious and tell me why you brought me here."

Seb frowned. "It's Lavinia."

"Your sister-in-law?"

He nodded. "She's really done it this time. I warned her not to try something again, but she wouldn't listen. Finally, she's gone too far."

"What has she done now? Starched your nightshirts? Banned your valet from the house?"

"Don't be silly. It's worse. Much worse." Seb shook his head. "She's holding a Saint Valentine's Day party."

Willi smothered a laugh. "What is so terrible about that? I think the idea rather charming."

"You wouldn't if Lavinia was trying to match you up with one of her fubsy-faced nieces."

"I am beginning to see the problem—and my role. I'm here to protect you, aren't I?" Her hazel eyes lit impishly. "And suppose I'm not interested in saving your rakish neck?"

Seb stared at her in dismay. "But you will—you must!" His voice took on a pleading tone. "I thought we were friends, Willi. And friends always help each other out."

She carefully examined her evenly trimmed nails. "You wish me to attend a dull country party when I could be dancing until dawn in London?"

"I'll make it worth your while," he said cajolingly.

She arched a questioning brow. "Oh? What did you have in mind?"

"A new bonnet?"

She laughed. "I have more bonnets than I need."

"How about a kitten?" he offered anxiously. "There are new ones in the barn. Think how much you'd like to have a pet."

"I don't think I'd like a cat. No doubt the creature would sharpen its claws on my furniture."

"A new piece of porcelain for your collection?"

"I'm tired of porcelain."

Seb threw up his hands in exasperation. "What do you want, Willi? If it's in my power to grant it, I will."

She smiled triumphantly. "Nothing, actually. I believe I have everything I need."

Seb's face fell. "You mean you won't stay?"

Willi laughed and patted his arm. "Of course, I'll stay, Seb, and protect you from Lady Wexford's machinations. I cannot allow one of my dearest friends to be put in such peril."

He grabbed her hand and brought it to his lips. "I thank you."

"Of course," she continued, looking at him mischievously, "I may decide later that I am entitled to some reward."

Seb tossed back his head and laughed. "Anything you want, Willi, anything at all." He took a relieved swallow of brandy. "I am totally in your debt."

"Tell me more about Lady Wexford's plans. I do hope there will be a few amusing guests."

"Don't count on it," Seb said grimly. "Lavinia has, as usual, managed to collect the most boring collection of friends and relatives imaginable."

"Wonderful." Willi darted a look at the ceiling. "Perhaps I spoke too hastily when I said I wouldn't demand anything from you."

Seb leered at her. "Ah, but you already have the opportunity of spending five days in my company. I can think of several women who would give anything to be in your shoes."

"Then why didn't you ask one of them?"

Seb laughed. "Precisely because they'd expect more than that from me."

"And I won't."

Seb nodded. "That's what makes you so special—I can count on you in a pinch. I only hope you won't be too bored during your stay."

Willi reached out her hand and ran her long fingers down his smoothly shaven cheek. "Boring is never an adjective I'd use to describe you, Sebby dear."

Seb grabbed her hand and planted a kiss on her palm. "And I can think of more than one way to while away the hours."

Her eyes lit with amusement. "If I didn't know you better, I'd almost think you lured me here for immoral purposes, Seb Cole."

He laughed softly and leaned over to brush her lips with his. "I've always found them to be much more delightful than moral ones." He tilted her chin with his finger. "As you well know."

Willi gave him a speculative look from under her long lashes. "Are you trying to seduce me, Seb Cole?"

"I wish I could," he said.

They both looked up when a short, plump lady dressed in lavender bustled into the room.

"Ah, Lady Taunton." Lavinia, Lady Wexford, hastened forward. "There you are. So glad you arrived safe and sound. The roads can be so dreadful this time of year." She cast a baleful look at her brother-in-law. "You should have brought her directly to the drawing room, Sebastian."

Willi smiled. "Hello, Lavinia." She exchanged cheek kisses with the older woman. "I was just telling Seb how much I'm looking forward to my visit. I hear you have special plans for us."

"Well, yes, I have arranged a few modest entertainments." She frowned at Seb. "Sebastian dear, Richard wanted you to meet him at the stables. Something about one of the horses, no doubt."

"Do not tire Willi with your talking," Seb warned Lavinia. "She has just arrived and probably wishes to rest."

"Oh, bosh." Lavinia laughed. "She'd probably feel much better with a nice cup of tea and some good gossip." She took Willi's arm and dragged her toward the door. "Harriet—Lady Stone—is here already. And, of course, you know my sister-in-law, Lady Kirby. Her two daughters are with her. Such delightful girls."

Willi cast an imploring look over her shoulder at Seb as Lavinia dragged her toward the stairs. He had the nerve to laugh at her plight, and went the opposite way. Resigned to her fate, Willi followed Lavinia up the stairs to the drawing room.

Not that Willi minded Lavinia. She knew Seb heartily disliked his brother's wife, but Willi didn't find her so terrible. She was a dull, settled matron, whose conversation was filled mostly with talk of her children, her friends, her friend's children, and amusing, but not scandalous, gossip. She and Willi had little in common, but Willi regarded her with amused tolerance, rather than Seb's antipathy.

She could sympathize with him, however. She did not have to spend any length of time with Lady Wexford. And Lavinia, after all, was not trying to find Willi a husband. Despite Seb successfully reaching the age of forty without so much as getting close to the altar, Lavinia was bound and determined to drive him there.

And that was precisely why Willi was here. To protect Seb from any and all attempts on his bachelorhood. She was quite content to help him in the matter. After all, Seb was one of the few male friends she had left. Others had married over the years, and despite her protestations of disinterest, she knew that their wives viewed her with discomfort. Seb, she knew, would remain a bachelor forever—and therefore would always be her friend.

She herself had no desire to remarry. Men could be amusing playmates, but she enjoyed her independence far too much to give it up. Even for someone she liked as much as Seb. Oh, they had enjoyed a passionate liaison for a time, but they'd limited themselves to friendship for many years. Because neither wanted entanglements, they were free to enjoy each other's company without worry.

Willi smiled to herself. Despite Seb's apprehensions, it would be a pleasant visit. An amusing diversion before the full force of the London Season was upon her.

And it would be pleasant to spend so many days in his company. They had not seen much of each other as of late, and she was forced to admit she missed him. She had no shortage of escorts, whether she was in London or the country, but Seb was her one, true friend. And sometimes one needed a friend more than a lover.

Seb's predictions about the guests were borne out, Willi discovered, when she was introduced to the others before dinner. In addition to the Stones and Kirbys, there were two other middle-aged couples, three giggly young ladies, Seb's newly married niece and her husband, and three young gentlemen. A totally unexceptional gathering, she declared to herself, a pronouncement that was borne out during dinner.

When the ladies retired to the drawing room, Willi observed the young girls Lavinia invited. Surely Lavinia did not think any of them could capture Seb's attention? It was like setting an untrained puppy after the wiliest fox in the neighborhood. It was clear that Seb really hadn't needed her help in this matter, but Willi was glad he'd invited her anyway. It would be amusing to watch him elude their clutches.

When the men rejoined them, Lavinia clapped her hands to gather everyone's attention. "Now that we are all here, it's time to begin our party."

Willi smiled at Seb, who grinned in a manner bespeaking supreme confidence. She was immediately suspicious. What mischief was he planning? Something to thwart Lavinia, no doubt.

"As you all know, Thursday is Saint Valentine's Day." Lavinia blinked brightly. "To make your stay more memorable, each of the gentlemen will draw the name of the lady who is to be his valentine for the next few days. I've planned all sorts of delightful activities, culminating in a ball on the fourteenth." She shot a pointed look at Seb. "Saint Valentine is the patron saint of lovers, and perhaps he will work his magic on our party this week."

Seb's niece, Sophie, sitting next to her husband of a month, giggled.

Willi looked at Seb. He looked unconcerned and composed for someone who was about to be paired up with a lady for the duration of the party. If the men drew for names, however was he to be certain he could avoid those giggling girls? She darted a glance at Maria, Lady Kirby's eldest daughter, whom Seb had assured her was Lavinia's choice. The girl might not be exactly "fubsy-faced," as Seb called her, but she was certainly not the type of girl to attract his attention. How could Lavinia plan for Seb to draw that particular name?

It was all too confusing.

The married men went first. Sir Stanley Wright, a portly neighbor, drew the first name. "Lavinia!" he cried in delight as he read the name.

The Earl of Wexford drew Lady Kirby, his sister-in-law.

Willi felt the tension rise within her as each name was drawn, even though she wasn't included in this round. She would be in the other basket, with the unmarried "ladies."

It was mildly amusing to wonder how Seb was going to wiggle his way out of this one. There were five names in that basket; he couldn't possibly know which one he would draw. However did Seb intend for her to protect him if she was paired with another man?

Willi smiled at the thought. Perhaps her swain would be the young curate, Samuel Ford. He was an earnest and sincere-looking man—a rather odd type to be included in a Valentine's party. Of course, Lavinia may have been desperate to balance out the numbers. Seb's invitation to Willi had probably sent her into fits of desperation.

Willi's attention returned to Lavinia when the first round concluded. Out of the corner of her eye, she saw Seb sitting back, relaxed in his chair, a sly smirk on his face. He didn't look at all worried. Well then, neither was she.

The curate went first, and Willi found herself holding her breath as he unwrapped the paper. She released it in relief when he called out "Lizzie" and Lady Kirby's youngest daughter blushed prettily.

She heard Lavinia choke back a gasp when Seb's nephew Christopher drew his cousin Maria's name. Willi glanced at Seb, who smiled back at her with an expression of innocence that marked a guilty conscience. The scamp! He *had* figured out a way to thwart Lavinia's plans. She smothered a laugh.

"Seb, you're next."

Under Lavinia's baleful gaze, he rose from his chair with smooth unconcern and sauntered across the room. He winked broadly at Sophie and reached his hand into the basket. With great deliberation, he carefully unwrapped the rolled scroll, then squinted at it as if unable to discern the name.

"Why, I do believe it is Lady Taunton." He tossed a grin of triumph at Lavinia, who glared back. Strolling over to Willi, he sketched her an elegant bow. "My lady."

"Sit down before I start laughing," she whispered to him, and he plopped down beside her. "However did you manage to accomplish that trick?"

Seb looked indignant. "Are you accusing me of having manipulated the drawing?"

"Yes," said Willi, bluntly.

He placed a hand over his heart. "My lady, you wound me. It was luck, sheer romantic luck, that you are to be my valentine lady for the next few days."

Willi rolled her eyes.

If she was disappointed in the outcome of the drawing, Lavinia did not show it. "Now, gentlemen, over the next few days, you will have to prove yourselves worthy of your ladies. After each task, they will consult and decide which man has most exemplified the spirit of Saint Valentine. The man who wins the highest marks will be king of our Valentine's Ball—and his lady the queen. Your first task—to compose a poem of love and adoration for your valentine. We will read them tomorrow at luncheon."

A chorus of good-natured groans issued from the men.

Lavinia held up her hands. "Now, no complaints. The library is well stocked with paper, pens, and ink— and several books of poetry. There is to be no plagiarizing, but you can certainly use the masters of love poetry as your guide."

Seb leaned toward Willi. "I wonder if she includes Rochester in that group," he whispered in her ear.

"She said 'love,'" Willi hissed back. "Not indecency."

"Why are my favorite writers always branded indecent?" he complained.

"I wonder."

"I can't write poetry. This is ridiculous." Then his

expression brightened. "But no matter. I don't want to be king of her blasted ball anyway."

"You think to cheat me of my tribute?" Willi stared at him icily. "Remember just why I am here—and at whose invitation. I expect an admirable poetic effort from you, Seb Cole."

"I thought you were on my side," he grumbled.

"Shall I tell your nephew that you wish to switch partners?" she asked, glancing at Christopher.

Seb frowned. "You are going to wring your pound of flesh off me, aren't you?" He shook his head. "At least writing a salute to you will be easier than trying to say anything nice about Maria." He grimaced in distaste at the thought of his brother's niece.

Willi patted his hand. "That's the spirit. I might even deign to help you."

"Will you?"

He looked so eager that Willi laughed. "Perhaps. *If* you treat me properly."

"I will lay myself at your feet," he promised.

Seb's brother, the Earl of Wexford, drew near. "Don't know how you managed that so neatly," he said to his brother with a smile. "Lavinia's fit to be tied."

Seb laughed. "She should know better than to try to manipulate me." They shared a conspiratorial grin.

"She'll never learn, will she?" the earl asked. He turned to Willi. "And so generous of you, my dear, to lend yourself to Seb's masterful counterattack."

Seb held up his hands. "I swear, it was pure coincidence."

Richard and Willi laughed derisively. The earl clapped his younger brother on the shoulder. "You be careful now. Cupid's on the rampage and no telling who might get shot. Keep your armor up."

This time, Seb joined Willi in a jeering laugh. Then, placing his hand casually on the small of her back, he guided her toward the pianoforte.

"Play something romantic," he suggested as he pulled out the bench. "To put yourself back into Lavinia's good graces."

Willi gave him an arch look. "*I've* done nothing to irritate her," she said. But she followed Seb's command and began the notes of Burns's, "My Love Is Like a Red, Red Rose."

When she finished, the other guests offered suggestions, and she played several tunes before she gave up her seat. "Let Maria play," she offered, relinquishing the instrument. She looked around for Seb, finally spotting him on the far side of the room in an animated talk with his new nephew-in-law. Was the worldly bachelor passing marital advice to the new husband? Willi smiled at the thought. She'd better rescue George before Seb destroyed all his illusions.

As she made her way across the room, Willi realized she had spent quite enough time with the guests for one night. She must ration her exposure. Giggling young misses, and aging matrons were best enjoyed in small doses.

She lay a hand on Seb's arm. "I'm tired," she said bluntly. "Give my excuses to Lavinia."

"I'll escort you upstairs." Seb appeared as eager as she to escape the company.

"There is no need," she replied cheerfully, wiggling her fingers in farewell. She was not going to let him flee so easily.

Despite her tiredness, Willi did not fall asleep immediately. She was still curious what Seb had done to the valentine drawing to ensure they were together. The man had a crafty mind when it came to managing his sister-in-law. It would be amusing watching Seb and Lavinia trying to outwit each other over the next few days.

As it would be amusing to spend time with Seb again. The last time she'd seen him at a country house, they had both been in the company of others. It would be nice to have him to herself again—even only as a friend.

Willi sighed. Giving up Seb as a lover had been one of the hardest things she'd ever done, but she was still convinced it had been the right decision for them both. They'd only be distant acquaintances now, rather than firm friends, if she hadn't insisted.

Still, there were times . . . such as tonight. It was an unfair comparison, of course, for Seb was really the only eligible man here, her tastes not running to university students or curates. But even so, he far outshone the others. He looked as handsome and elegant as ever, whether dressed in trousers and frock coat or formal evening wear. Just one glimpse of his lazy smile could still make her knees feel like Mrs. Potter's Lamb Jelly. Perhaps because she knew exactly what she was missing.

For a moment, Willi was tempted to take advantage of their intimate situation—just while they were here, of course. Would any harm come from a few days of pleasure? But she knew, instinctively, that it would never work. Sadly, she recognized that one could never go back. She and Seb had decided on friendship, and friendship they would have.

Even if he sometimes made her want more.

Seb watched Willi leave with a mixture of amusement and regret. He adopted an air of cool detachment and deliberately set out to charm Lady Kirby. As long as he could avoid her daughters, Seb didn't mind Lavinia's sister.

The ladies gradually drifted off to bed, and finally only Seb, his brother, and Squire Ford were left in the drawing room. The brandy decanter was brought out, and it was quite late when Seb finally made his way to his room.

As he pulled off his evening slippers, he glanced guiltily at his watch. He'd meant to talk to Willi

again—perhaps even get some ideas from her about
that blasted poem. But it was far too late now; she'd
be asleep. Sighing, he stripped off his coat and cravat.

All in all, the evening had gone well. His devious
machinations had achieved the desired result—Willi
was now his designated valentine. No matter what idi-
ocies Lavinia had devised for the next few days, he
was safe. Thank God Willi had answered his
summons.

Of course, that was what friends were for—helping
out when the need arose. This situation might not
have appeared life-threatening to some, but it was to
Seb. He wouldn't put it past Lavinia to stage some
ridiculous incident in an attempt to trap him into marriage with one of her insipid candidates. Seb was an
honorable man, but he wouldn't allow honor to destroy him either. With Willi here to protect him, he
would avoid any awkward situations.

As well as enjoy her company. Willi was attractive,
witty, entertaining, and undemanding. If he ever sat
down and made a list of the characteristics he desired
in a woman, he imagined Willi had most of them.

Sometimes, in her presence, he could almost forget
his vows of bachelorhood. It was probably good Willi
was as content with the single life as he, or they might
have made a dreadful mistake years ago. Marriage
would have quickly destroyed their friendship.

It was much better this way, he reassured himself.
They were free to enjoy each other's company when
they wished, without any obligation. She knew she
could call on him to escort her to the theater, and he
needn't feel guilty about dragging her to the country
to save him from Lavinia's plots. All in all, it was a
convenient arrangement.

She'd looked most fetching this evening, in her stylish blue gown with that nipped-in waist, those impu-
dent curls giving her a teasing look. For a moment,
he'd almost been tempted ... He could never ignore

the fact that she was a very desirable woman. But he didn't want to ruin the relationship they'd perfected over the years. He could satisfy his physical needs with any number of women. Willi was the only one who could provide him friendship, and that was far more valuable. He'd never do anything to destroy that relationship.

2

With a frown, Seb crumpled the sheet of paper and tossed it onto the growing pile littering the floor of the library. "This is a damnable idea."

Willi laughed at his irritation. "It is scarcely flattering to think you are having such a difficult time of it."

"I'm no poet," Seb grumbled. "Wherever does Lavinia get her stupid ideas?"

"You should be thankful she didn't plan a more difficult task. This is at least something you can master."

He darted her a pleading look. "Won't you help?"

"What, write my own love poem?" She looked at him scornfully. "Hardly a romantic notion."

"You don't want me to look a total fool at lunch, do you?"

Willi remained silent.

Seb tossed down his pen. "That does it. I've no desire to participate in any of Lavinia's claptrap anyway." He glared at Willi. "I thought you came here to help me."

"I saved you from being paired with one of those silly girls, didn't I? How ever *did* you manage that, by the way? You couldn't have known you were going to draw my name."

Seb grinned. "Merely my good fortune."

"That I find difficult to believe."

"Are you accusing me of cheating?"

"I can't believe you would have left anything so important to chance," Willi said with a laugh.

"Perhaps I shall tell you someday—if you're very good. Now, how about a few games of billiards before lunch?"

"Do you intend me to be the only lady without a poem? You are a cruel man, Seb Cole."

"Help me then."

"This sounds suspiciously like blackmail," Willi replied, laughing. "All right, Seb, pick up your pen." She rested her chin on her hand, thinking for a moment. "You need a theme."

"I thought love was the theme."

Willi shook her head. "It's fortunate you never tried to seriously woo a woman, Seb. You would have been a miserable failure."

He adopted a hurt expression. "Keep speaking to me like that, and I won't write a word."

"Don't be silly. Your vaunted male pride is at stake here. Now, let's see. Something with flowers? That's a common image."

"My love is like a flower?"

Willi sighed. "You are hopeless, Seb. How about: My love is a garden of earthly delights; she lightens my days and brightens my nights."

Seb chortled. "Brilliant. I knew you could do it." He frantically scribbled her words. "More, more."

Willi paced across the room, deep in thought. "In the morning she is fresh and new, like the flowers bedecked with dew."

Seb hooted. "This is brilliant!"

"It is not. It's drivel, and you know it. But at least I came up with something. You are too cowardly to even try."

Seb bristled at the insult. He wrinkled his brow in concentration, then began: "By midday she is flushed and gay, after a tumble in the hay."

"Seb!"

He grinned wickedly. "Later on, she goes to hide, after she's taken her afternoon ride."

Willi turned her back on him.

"At night, she's quiet as a mouse as she sneaks out to the garden hothouse."

A loud shout of laughter greeted his ears, and he leered at her with a self-satisfied smirk.

"You are simply, utterly impossible, Seb Cole. You'll have every lady in the house kneeling over with fits of vapors if you dare to write such things."

Seb took up his pen and looked at her expectantly. "The next line . . . ?"

Willi threw up her hands in surrender. In the next half hour, they jointly composed what she finally pronounced as an acceptable effort.

To Seb's chagrin, their collaborative effort was not pronounced the best. That award went to Sophie's husband, who by the luck of the draw, or perhaps deliberate design, had drawn his wife's name.

"We should have won," Seb grumbled to Willi, as they bundled up in their cloaks for the next contest. "What were you thinking of, voting for George instead of me?"

"His poem was so much better," Willi said with a sly smile. "I thought it wonderfully romantic."

"Nearly turned my stomach—it was like an overdose of sweets." He grabbed Willi's gloved hand. "But this next contest should be a snap."

They followed the others out onto the back lawn, where bales of hay had been set up for the archery competition. Bright red hearts were affixed to the hay, each bearing the name of their particular lady.

Lavinia herded them together. "Just as Cupid shoots his arrows of love, you gentlemen will do the same. Each swain is to shoot five arrows at the target bearing your designated lady's name. Every arrow that strikes the heart will earn you a point."

"What if I hit another lady's heart?" Seb asked with a wicked grin.

Lavinia turned a dampening look on him. "Then you will be disqualified. Now, ladies, do you each have a token to bestow upon your fair knight?"

Willi tied a silk scarf of brilliant red around Seb's sleeve. "Do not disgrace me," she said warningly, although her eyes danced with laughter.

"I will do my best, my lady." Seb saluted her with his bow.

The women stepped back as the archers stepped forward. Successes were met with enthusiastic "ahs" while failures elicited loud groans. When everyone had shot their five arrows, Lavinia stepped forward, tallied up the points, and announced the scores.

"Mr. Ford, one; Freddy, one; Richard, two; Squire Ford, two; Lord Stone, two; Sir Stanley, three; Lord Kirby, three; Christopher, four; George, four; Sebastian, four."

Willi jumped up and down, clapping her hands with glee. "Good job!"

Seb grinned. "I told you I'd redeem myself."

The five men with the best scores retrieved their arrows and prepared to shoot again. Seb watched with open amusement as Sophie planted an enthusiastic kiss on her husband's cheek. He turned to Willi with a pleading look. "Don't I deserve any encouragement?"

She chucked him under the chin "You will get your reward later—if you win."

Seb put a hand to his brow. "Ah, the pressure. Will I be able to bear up under the strain?"

Willi laughed. "You had better. You already lost the first contest."

Seb stepped forward to his mark and carefully sighted the target. This competition was more his style; at least he knew what to do with a bow and arrow. Strangely, he had an unexpected urge to show off before Willi. He might not be able to write poetry, but he could do something to win the admiration of his lady fair.

With that thought firmly in mind, he sighted on the target and let loose his first arrow.

After the second round was completed, only Seb and his nephew Christopher were left.

"Want to defer now to age and experience?" Seb teased.

"Youth and daring won many a battle, Uncle Seb," Christopher shot back. "I'll not concede anything."

Seb saluted him. "To the death then." He turned to Willi. "Do I get a kiss for good luck?"

"Of course." Willi pressed her lips to his cheek. "Do well."

Willi stamped her feet to ward off the chill, but never took her eyes off Seb. Despite the cold, he'd shed his coat and stood in shirtsleeves. He'd retied her red scarf around his arm, and the ends fluttered gaily in the breeze. That same wind ruffled his blond hair, giving him a thoroughly rakish look.

For a man who'd seen his fortieth birthday, he still looked incredible attractive. Standing next to his nephew, Seb was far the more imposing of the two, even if he was twenty years older. The slight touch of gray around his temples only added a touch of distinction to his already handsome face. There was no other concession to age in his trim figure; he had the body to rival men many years younger.

Willi did what she could to hide the traces of aging in herself, but she wasn't so vain to think that they weren't noticeable. It was most unfair that men aged more slowly than women. She'd mentioned it to Seb a few times, but he'd only laughed and insisted he preferred experience over youth any day.

It was one more sign of how comfortable they were with each other. Like an old pair of slippers—they might be a bit frayed around the edges, but they didn't pinch the toes either.

She narrowed her gaze as Seb stepped up to the line again. Holding her breath as he loosed each arrow, Willi clapped her hands in delight when they reached their target. He and Christopher both shot a perfect round.

"Ready to concede?" Seb teased his nephew.

"Not a chance."

Willi danced over to Seb. "I think you might win that reward, after all," she said, trailing her fingers enticingly down his cheek.

"Watch me," he said with a grin, and gave her a quick kiss.

They shot again, arrow for arrow. Through four shots they were evenly matched. Seb loosed his last arrow, which hit the target dead center. He stepped back, and Willi ran to his side, grabbing his hand as Christopher shot again.

His arrow hit the hay, but not the heart.

Willi stared at the target in surprise. "You did it!"

"Told you I would," he said without a trace of modesty.

Christopher ran up and presented Willi with her much-tattered heart. "Looks as though Cupid's thoroughly stung you," he said with a grin. He winked at Seb. "I'd be careful if I were you, Uncle. The lady might get ideas."

Seb chortled. "Oh, the lady has ideas, all right." He put his arm around Willi's waist and squeezed. "But only the most improper ones, I assure you."

"Seb!" Willi slapped playfully at his hand.

Christopher clapped his uncle on the back. A few more guests crowded around, offering their congratulations, then they all scurried back to the warmth of the house.

"Lavinia did not seem pleased with your win," Willi said, as she and Seb walked arm in arm up the path.

"Not only did I thwart her matchmaking plans, but

I won her ridiculous Cupid contest. Now she's afraid I might end up king of her dratted ball."

"That is a sight I'd like to see," said Willi. "King Seb, and his court."

He waved a warning finger. "Remember, if I'm king, you'll be queen."

She looked at him in feigned horror before they both burst out laughing.

"Of course, after that triumphant win, my spirit of competition has been aroused," Seb said, as he helped her off with her cloak once they were inside. "After all, I am tied for the lead."

"What has Lavinia devised for the next challenge?"

Seb shook his head. "Lord only knows." He shivered and rubbed his numb fingers together. "Quick, let's retreat to the library. Nothing like a nice brandy before a warm fire to take the chill out of February."

"You never told me you were such a skilled archer," Willi said, as she curled up in the overstuffed chair before the fire.

"One of my many hidden talents."

"Oh? What are the others?"

Seb handed her a glass and took the other chair. "A man must have some secrets."

"I thought that was a woman's prerogative."

"You tell me yours, and I'll tell you mine."

Willi shook her head. "Never mind. It will only imbue you with a certain aura of mystery."

Seb tried to look mysterious, but Willi only laughed. "You look as if you've eaten a rather bad oyster."

He poured himself another brandy instead.

Willi sipped hers silently, watching the dancing flames in the fire.

She'd seen a new side of Seb this afternoon—cool, concentrating, controlled. He'd joined in that archery competition with a determination that belied his usual casual attitude toward life. Seb could be ruthless when he wished.

Thinking back over the years she'd known him, she realized he'd always been that way. He'd shown that same determination when he'd involved himself in that messy situation with Lady Monkton and her brother. That ridiculous duel with Lord Plover didn't appear so ridiculous now. And he had expended a great deal of time and energy in helping Penhurst regain his position in the Foreign Office. Yes, there was much more depth to Seb than he let on.

"You look to be thinking far too hard, Willi."

Seb's drawling tones drew her back to the present. "I was merely fantasizing about being the Valentine's queen on Thursday." She batted her eyelashes at him. "Will I make an acceptable consort?"

Seb grinned. "Wouldn't Lavinia have a fit if we won the rest of her stupid games?"

"She'd probably never invite you back here again."

Seb laughed. "That, my dear, would make success all the more worthwhile." He raised his glass in salute. "Shall we fully enter into the spirit of competition and set Lavinia on her ear?"

"You are a wicked, wicked man," said Willi.

"I try." He grinned. "I try. Which reminds me—when do I get my reward? I did win the Cupid contest, after all."

"Very spectacularly, too, I may add. Which means I must come up with an appropriate prize. I shall need to think on it."

"Don't think *too* long," Seb said. "I might grow impatient."

"Ah, but is it not said that sweets postponed are all the sweeter?"

Seb glanced at the clock. "We've plenty of time before dinner . . ."

Willi clapped a hand to her mouth and jumped to her feet. "I almost forgot—I promised to help Sophie with her hair." She brushed her lips against Seb's cheek and fled through the door.

*   *   *

Following dinner, Lavinia did not allow the men to linger over their port, but hustled them into the drawing room for the next challenge.

"Isn't this exciting?" she twittered. "Two of you have already won an event in our little Valentine's festival. Tonight, you all have another chance to show your skill. And this time, gentlemen, the ladies may help you with your task."

"See that you live up to my example," Seb whispered into Willi's ear. She batted him away like a pesky fly.

Lavinia quickly distributed paper and pencils to each of the couples. "We will all take the word 'valentine,' " she explained. "Starting with the letter *v*, make as many words as you can using only the letters in that word. You have two minutes to think of as many words as you can. Then we shall read them aloud. If you have a word that no one else has, you will get a point. After that, we will go to the *a* and so on to the end. The team with the most points wins."

"You have an advantage, Lavinia," Sir Stanley protested. "Probably spent the last week studying the dictionary."

"No need to worry," the Earl of Wexford said. "She can't spell." Everyone laughed.

"Does 'valentine' have two e's or two i's?" Lizzie asked with a puzzled frown.

"Two minutes, everyone," Lavinia said, then took her place beside her partner.

"Piece of cake," Seb whispered in Willi's ear.

"The curate could be tough competition," she whispered back. "He's bound to know a lot of strange words."

"We'll write down our words separately," Seb said. "It'll be faster that way."

"But we could duplicate efforts."

"There isn't time to cross-check two lists. Just write down as many words as you can think of."

Willi nodded her head and began staring at the word. Vale—that was easy. And valet. Vat. Vane. She scribbled each word on her paper.

"Time!" Lavinia called in what seemed far too short an interval.

"It can't be two minutes yet," Lord Kirby grumbled.

"Now, remember," Lavinia reminded them, "you get a point only if no one else has the same word. Christopher, read the list you and Maria wrote."

"Vat. Vale."

"There goes two of yours," Seb said, crossing out the duplicates on Willi's list.

"Valet."

"And one of yours," she retorted, drawing a line through his.

"I've got a good one," Maria called. "Valient."

"Wrong!" Sophie giggled. "Valient has two *a*'s."

"Told you Maria was a dolt," Seb whispered to Willi. "Thank God, Christopher is stuck with her as a partner."

Lavinia looked eagerly around the room. "Does anyone have a word not yet mentioned?"

"Venial," cried the curate.

"See?" Willi flashed Seb a superior grin.

"Ventail," Seb announced.

Willi turned to look at him. "What's a ventail?"

"Yes, what is it, Uncle?" Christopher eyed him skeptically. "Sounds pretty suspicious to me."

"It's part of a medieval helmet," Seb explained with such assurance that no one dared challenge him.

"Now I discover you're an expert on medieval armor," Willi said in a low aside. "You never cease to amaze me, Seb Cole."

He grinned.

By the time they came to the *n*, only three couples were still in the running—the curate and Lizzie, Viscount Stone and Lady Wright, and Seb and Willi. Seb and the curate each gained a point on that letter and the score was tied.

"Tiebreaker," someone called. "Think up a new word. Cupid. Love."

"There's one more letter left," Seb protested.

"But it's another *e*," Lizzie argued back.

"Lavinia said every letter in the word, and we are going to do every letter," Seb insisted. "Two minutes."

"I don't know any more *e* words," Willi said in a low undertone.

"Neither does our curate," Seb said.

"And you do?"

He smiled smugly and scribbled something on his paper, not letting her see.

"Time," Lavinia called.

The curate shook his head. She turned to her brother-in-law. "Seb?"

"The fair Elaine," he said.

"Not fair," shouted Lizzie. "That's a name."

"You let Eve pass in the other round," Seb argued.

Lavinia turned to Mr. Ford. "Since you will be the loser, you may decide."

"Elaine is acceptable to me." He stood up and shook Seb's hand.

"Hooray!" Willi flung her arms around Seb in an exuberant hug. "Two wins now. You're well on your way to being king."

Seb smiled smugly.

"Lavinia looked like she wanted your head on a platter after tonight," Willi told him later.

"I know," he said grinning widely. "I'm thwarting all her romantic plans."

"Maybe we shouldn't try to win whatever she thinks up for tomorrow," Willi said. "I would hate to see her truly angry at you."

"Lavinia and I have been at daggers drawn ever

since she married Richard," Seb said. "She'll hold me in aversion no matter what I do."

"Strange that you two don't get along," Willi mused. "You seem to deal so well with most women."

"Lavinia made up her mind about me from the first moment we met," Seb explained. "She decided I was Richard's scapegrace brother, in need of reform, and she's been trying to do just that ever since."

"As I understand it, you *were* rather wild in those days."

"Well, I admit I had more than my share of adventures." He grinned. "But you can testify as to how well I've reformed."

"I don't think you've reformed at all," Willi said. "You're just as wicked as you always were."

"Are you so certain? It has been a long time since you've experienced the full force of my wickedness."

Willi actually felt herself blushing, but she nodded. "Very, very wicked."

Seb laughed. "Good. I'd hate to think I've grown soft in my middle years."

No, Willi thought to herself, Seb had not grown soft in either mind or body. She knew that he had some far-ranging intellectual interests—like his unexpected knowledge of medieval armor—that were beyond her scope. Yet he was an active sportsman, a devotee of the theater, and a talented dancer.

She'd never given much thought to how accomplished Seb was, taking his skills for granted. But when she deliberately compared him to the other gentlemen she knew, no one came up to his level.

It was strange, when she considered how long she'd known him, that she'd never appreciated his talents until now. She'd always accepted Seb as Seb, without realizing how very special he was.

She stole a glance at his handsome face. His brilliant blue eyes were alight with amusement while he regaled Christopher with some silly tale. At times like these, he almost took her breath away.

Quickly, Willi turned away. Across the room, Sophie and her new husband sat together on the settee, their heads so close together they were nearly touching. In London, their interest in each other would have been considered unfashionable, but here in the country, no one seemed to mind that they spent every moment in each other's company. Willi found the glowing adoration in their faces appealing. What would it be like to be in love like that?

In an instant, she dismissed the thought. She would not want to be that young and green for anything. She doubted that their idolatrous love would last for long. It rarely did. It would dwindle into comfortable companionship, if they were lucky, or outright hatred if they were not.

Willi realized how cynical she sounded, but she could not help herself. She'd seen too much over the years to regard the world through a rosy glow. Men and women were very different creatures, and it took an exceptional pair to make a marriage endure.

She didn't have the strength. With someone like Seb, maybe . . . but that was not possible. She'd deliberately stepped away from an intense relationship for fear of spoiling it. It was only when she looked at Sophie and George, that she wondered whether it really was possible to sustain a love like that for a lifetime. Could passion grow rather than decline over the years? Had she tossed away a real chance at happiness when she'd pushed Seb away?

3

After breakfast, Lavinia gathered the guests in the morning room.

"Today, we are going to split up our lovebirds. The

ladies will be coming with me to town, while you men are free to amuse yourselves about the house."

"Thank God," Seb whispered in Willi's ear.

"Then this afternoon, it will be the gentlemen's turn to go to town. While there, we are each to buy a little token for our valentine. The gentleman and lady who each buy what is judged to be the best gift will be declared the victor."

"Unfair," cried Christopher. "Unless you're going to increase my allowance."

"Not necessary, dear. There will be a strict spending limit of one pound," Lavinia said.

"That isn't going to buy much of a present," Maria grumbled.

"It is not the cost of the item, but the sentiment that counts," Lavinia explained. "Search for something that particularly suits your special valentine. Gentlemen, help your ladies with their wraps and then depart!"

"Whatever can I get for George?" Sophie wailed to Willi.

"I'm certain you'll find something suitable."

"Will you help me? You have such excellent taste."

"Then you'll have to tell me more about George," Willi said, as they hastened down the steps toward the carriage. "He did such a lovely job with your poem—is he fond of poetry?"

"I . . . I think so."

Willi smiled to herself. She could not imagine not knowing such an important detail about her husband. Sophie had a lot to learn. Surprises were all well and good, but not in a marriage.

Willi insisted upon learning all she could about any man who interested her. Of course, little things like Seb's skill with a bow and arrow, and his fascination with medieval armor didn't really count. But Willi knew that Seb detested poetry, loved hunting and cards, preferred claret to port, liked to sleep on his

left side, and had never kept the same mistress for
longer than a year. He liked his cravats starched just
so, hated having his hair cut, and would do anything
in his power to help his friends.

Those were the things a wife should know about
her husband. Perhaps she would need to explain matters to Sophie.

When they reached town, Willi accompanied Sophie
to several shops, pointing out things that might be
suitable for her new husband. They finally settled on
a book of poems by Wordsworth.

That task taken care of, Willi turned her mind to
Seb. Whatever would she get the man? Innumerable
things crossed her mind, but they were all too expensive. She saw a nice pair of calfskin gloves, but she
knew Seb liked to have his made especially for him.
The watch fob that caught her eye in the jeweler's
shop was nice, but cost more than one pound.

The decision was complicated by the fact that the
man didn't need a thing. Seb had always been one to
watch over his creature comforts and lacked nothing
in a fine gentleman's accoutrements. She'd have to
find something that he wouldn't ever think to buy
himself.

Biting her lip, she glanced down the street at the
other storefronts. She could purchase something amusing, like a withered apple from the grocers, or lady's
garters. Seb would laugh at that. There was always
tea, or a jar of chutney, but that was too dull and
mundane. Willi wanted to find something particular,
something special for him. Only she didn't know what.

She'd almost given up hope when she spotted the
window of a toy shop. With a laugh, she pushed open
the door. If she couldn't find anything sensible, she
would buy him something whimsical. Seb would appreciate the jest.

Willi inspected the array of toy drums, trumpets,

and flutes. There were tops, rolling hoops, and cricket bats. Seb was not much of a cricketer, she knew. And she couldn't see him playing battledore and shuttlecock in his rooms at Albany.

Then she saw exactly what she wanted and clapped her hand over her mouth to stifle her laugh. It was perfect. The very thing. Without hesitating, she paid the shopkeeper and waited impatiently while he wrapped up her purchase. Tucking her package under her arm, she stepped out of the store with a smug grin.

She did not stop smiling all the way back to the house. Willi couldn't wait to see the look on Seb's face when he opened his present. It was perfect, utterly perfect for this silly Valentine's party.

"What did you find?" Sophie asked her.

"It's a secret," Willi said with a mysterious smile.

"Oh, do tell."

Willi shook her head. "Not until Seb opens it tonight."

Seb was nearly as persistent in his importuning when Willi returned to the house.

"What do you mean, you aren't going to tell me what you bought?" He put on his best hurt-little-boy expression. "However am I going to know what to get you?"

"You will have to think of something on your own, Sebby dear." Willi tapped him lightly on the nose. "Surprise me."

"I hate surprises."

"I don't. I love to be surprised."

"What did the other ladies buy?"

"Seb Cole, I am not going to tell you a thing. You've a head on your shoulders—use it. Good Lord, you've bought women enough gifts over the years. Certainly, you ought to be able to think of another one."

"But not with only a pound to spend," he moaned. "That won't buy anything."

"It is not the price, but the thought, remember."

"I've never yet met a woman who didn't judge the value of a gift by the price."

Willi reveled in his distress. "Are you accusing me of being mercenary?"

"No, no," Seb replied hastily. "Not you. But I don't know how to buy anything but expensive gifts."

"Then it will be good for you to have the experience at least once in your life." Willi pointed him toward the door. "Take your place in Richard's carriage and do your duty."

Scowling, Seb complied.

He didn't have a clue what to buy. Willi certainly didn't need anything—she had more than enough money to buy herself whatever she wanted. Hadn't she already refused to accept a gift from him for coming to his rescue?

Earlier, he'd thought Lavinia's silly little party wasn't turning out half-bad, but now he wondered. What could he possibly buy a lady like Willi for less than a pound?

Richard dug an elbow in his side. "Why looking so glum, brother?"

Seb smirked. "This is all your fault, you know. If you kept a tighter rein on Lavinia, she wouldn't make my days such a misery with these silly games of hers."

"Can't think of what to buy, eh?" Richard laughed. "You can afford to be complacent, after winning two events."

"I don't give a rap about Lavinia's stupid contest." Seb glowered at his brother. "I just don't want to offend Willi."

Richard's eyes narrowed. "I still haven't figured out how you accomplished that, little brother."

Seb smiled guilelessly. "Accomplished what?"

"You know what I mean. Arranging it so Lady Taunton was your assigned valentine."

"Chance, pure chance."

Richard laughed. "That I don't believe. I know perfectly well you invited her here to protect yourself from Lavinia's young ladies."

"Would I do a thing like that?"

Richard clapped his brother on the shoulder. "Most certainly. And Lavinia was sorely vexed, I assure you."

"Serves her right. She should leave me alone instead of trying to match me with those ridiculous girls she comes up with."

"Lavinia's not happy unless she's managing some-one's life," Richard said. "Now that she's found a husband for Sophie, she's bound to redouble her efforts with you."

Seb shuddered. "Remind me to remain in town this summer."

"There's an easy solution to that—get married."

Seb stared at his brother. "You have been married too long; you're even beginning to think like her."

"Just think how furious she'd be if she didn't have a hand in it."

Seb laughed. "Rather a high price to pay for trumping Lavinia. Besides, I can't abide all those giggly young girls. Were they really that feather-headed back in our youth?"

"Probably." Richard laughed. "We didn't mind it then."

"We're growing old," said Seb with a mocking shake of his head. "Ear trumpets and Bath chairs come next."

The carriage halted before the town's main inn. Richard jumped out. "Good luck with your search, Seb."

Seb scrambled out behind him. "Wait. Where are you going? What are you getting?"

Richard turned and waved him away. "Time to do your own thinking, lad. Meet me back here in an hour."

Seb wandered up the street. There were enough

shops here; he was bound to find something. He tried
to tell himself it really didn't matter what he bought;
Willi would know that with only a pound to spend,
she couldn't expect anything spectacular.

He recalled all the emerald jewelry he'd bought her
when they'd been lovers. He still thought they suited
her more than any other stone, bringing out the rich
color of her hair and the flecked hazel of her eyes.
Willi in green was irresistible.

But he couldn't buy her emeralds today. Still,
maybe he could find something in that hue. She'd remember his other gifts, and know what he intended.

Cheered, he pushed his way into the first shop.

Seb paused in front of the inn, consulting his watch
with a dismal frown. The hour was nearly up, and he
hadn't found a thing. Not that Richard would leave
without him, but Seb didn't want to endure any rib-
bing on the way home either. Somehow, he had to
find something—fast.

There were those silk flowers in the milliner's shop.
He supposed that was as good an idea as any. Hastily
he turned to retrace his steps. Out of the corner of
his eye, he noticed a small shop tucked down the side
street. The three golden balls caught his attention, and
he stopped. Maybe he could find something there.

The pawnbroker's store was dim and crammed with
a hodgepodge of items. But he didn't think Willi
wanted a gilt armchair, and he rather thought the ivory-
handled parasol was years out of style. He turned to
inspect the glass cabinet where the smaller items were
displayed.

There was the usual assortment of men's jewelry—
fobs, watches, stickpins, card cases, snuffboxes, and
the like. One could put something besides snuff in a
box, he supposed, but it didn't seem quite right. He
glanced in the next cabinet.

Lady's things. This was more like it. Most of it was

probably cheap trumpery, but perhaps he could find something that Willi would like.

There was a nice pin of jet set with pearls, but he didn't think mourning jewelry would suit a Saint Valentine's Day party. Fortunately, there were a few other pieces that looked more appropriate.

"Hey there," he called, looking about for the shop owner. "Is anyone here?"

A wizened old lady materialized from the rear of the shop. "You wish to buy?" she asked.

"Maybe. I'd like to look at these pins here."

Drawing out a long key from her pocket, she unlocked the cabinet. Seb pointed to the items he wanted to see, and she drew them out, almost reluctantly, and laid them on the counter.

On examination, the first pin was cheap and shoddy. Seb thought a dark opal looked nice, but there was no question that the pin with garnets and pearls was the best the store had to offer.

"How much?"

"Two pounds, six."

"What?"

"It's easily worth ten times that."

"And you probably paid the owner a third of what you're asking me."

The old lady shrugged.

Seb debated. No one would really know if he cheated. But it galled him to think that he couldn't complete his task.

"What have you that's cheaper?" he asked finally. "Something under a pound."

She gave him a dubious glance, then turned back to the cabinet. She rummaged inside it for several seconds before pulling out something and setting it on the counter.

The piece was black with tarnish, and Seb could barely discern the faint design on the surface. "This is all?"

" 'Tis silver," the old lady said. "It'll polish up nicely."

Seb picked up the heart-shaped ornament and examined it closely. Discovering it was a locket, he flipped the catch open, but there was nothing inside.

Frowning, he examined it with a critical eye. It had to be real silver, as badly tarnished as it was, so it was not a bad bargain.

"It needs a chain," he said. "Have you any?"

The woman shook her head.

Never mind, Seb thought, he could pick up a length of green ribbon. He reached in his pocket and counted out his change for the old shopkeeper, who watched him carefully.

By the time he left the shop, Seb was whistling a jaunty tune.

Upon discovering that Willi was resting in her room before dinner, Seb headed up the stairs and rapped softly. "Willi?" he hissed.

She pulled open the door and motioned for him to enter. "Did you have any success in town?" she asked, her eyes twinkling.

Seb looked at her coldly. "Are you angling for a clue to your gift, Lady Taunton?"

She tossed her head indignantly. "Of course not. I only hope that you finally were able to compromise your principles and spend a mere pound."

"It was a difficult challenge, I admit." He shuddered in mock horror. "And never again, I promise you."

"You are the one who is making it so difficult, now that you've determined to win this competition," she reminded him.

Seb smirked confidently. "We will, too, after everyone sees what I bought for you."

"Your successes have positively gone to your head." Willi shooed him out of the room. "I need to dress for dinner."

Seb headed for the door, then turned and winked at her. "I am certain my gift will be declared the winner."

"Wait until you see mine," she said with a grin.

Seb headed for his room with a confident air. Finding that locket had been a marvelous stroke of luck. What could be more appropriate for a Valentine's party than a heart-shaped necklace? A pity he did not have a miniature of himself to place inside. Although the locket was so small, he doubted even a miniaturist could paint anything to fit.

What other sentimental things did women keep in lockets besides pictures of their loved ones? Scraps of treasured fabric? A dried flower petal from a favorite beau's bouquet?

Seb realized he was lacking education in some of the necessary matters. Never having been involved in a sentimental relationship, he'd never had to worry about the silly little things women treasured. He himself had kept boxes and boxes of rocks in his youth, but he didn't think Willi would like a stone rattling around in her necklace. No, he had to think of something.

He could put in a snip of the green ribbon he'd bought. That might work. He fully intended to buy Willi something nice in return for helping him out—a scrap of green would hint at what was to come. He'd find her some emerald bauble when he went up to town.

Then he had an idea. It was perfect! Grinning at his inspiration, he went in search of Lavinia's sewing scissors and the silver polish.

Even the men didn't argue about skipping their after-dinner port this night. They were all as eager to receive their gifts as the ladies. The guests barely touched their desserts before they eagerly filed into the drawing room, where the presents were heaped in two piles on the Queen Anne table.

"This is nearly as exciting as Christmas—or my birthday," Seb said.

"Only one of them is for you," Willi reminded him.

"I know." He looked at her hopefully. "Which one is it?"

"I won't tell you. You'll be over there shaking and rattling the package, trying to guess. You have to wait until it's your turn."

"You really don't want a man to have any fun, do you?"

Willi laughed. "Men are the most impatient creatures on earth."

Seb guffawed.

"It's true." Willi looked at him smugly. "Can you envision a man standing still for the hours and hours it takes for dress fittings? Or enduring nine months of childbearing? Goodness, we'd never have another baby on this island if we had to depend upon the men. They'd tire of the event after a month."

"But what of the endless hours we spend cooling our heels in drawing rooms and halls, waiting for the ladies? 'I must get my bonnet' or 'Let me find my gloves.' " He shuddered. "Men spend half their lives waiting."

"Which proves my point," Willi countered. "Men are short on patience."

Seb opened his mouth to reply, but clamped it shut when Lavinia clapped her hands. "Is everyone ready?" Conversation ceased and everyone looked to her with rapt attention. "Ladies first. Sophie, dear, you begin."

Giggling, Sophie walked over to the table. She looked carefully through the packages until she found the one with her name, then brought it back to her seat.

"What will the newlyweds do?" Seb whispered to Willi. "Something sticky and sentimental again, no doubt."

Willi jabbed him with her elbow. "Speak more kindly. This is your niece, after all. And they are rather sweet to each other."

"They're disgusting," he mumbled under his breath.

Sophie unwrapped her gift and blushed prettily.

"It must be good." Seb looked crestfallen.

"A baby rattle!" Christopher was the first to recognize the article she held aloft. "Sophie, is there something you haven't told us?"

Blushing furiously, his sister modestly ducked her head.

"Sophie!" Lavinia screeched and ran to her daughter's side. "Are you . . ?"

Sophie nodded.

"Oh, God." Seb groaned. "Just what we needed to complete the romantic atmosphere. Babies."

The present opening halted for several minutes while the young couple was congratulated. Richard led them in a toast, while Lavinia alternated between wiping her eyes and beaming like a proud grandmother-to-be.

"Just think, you'll soon have the majestic sounding title of 'great-uncle,' " Willi reminded him.

"I don't see anything great about being related to any of Sophie's offspring." Then his eyes twinkled wickedly. "Although, I rather like the idea of being able to call Lavinia, 'Granny.' "

Willi smothered a giggle. "Do you think she'll allow it?" she whispered.

"Not from me." He glanced at the rest of the presents. "I think the only thing that could top this would be a real, live baby."

"Well, I hate to disoblige you, but I didn't get you one."

"Thank goodness. The only thing worse than being called 'Uncle Seb' would be 'Papa.' "

"Oh, you're such a fake curmudgeon," Willi chided him. "I've seen how you play with your godchildren."

"They're not my relations," he explained.

Order was finally restored, and the other ladies rapidly opened their presents. There were fans, silk flowers, ribbons, books, and all sorts of knickknacks.

Willi was the last to open her present. She took the oblong box back to her seat and carefully unwrapped the paper around it.

"Faster," Seb urged with a grin.

She gave him an exasperated glance. Lifting the lid, she looked inside, only to find another, smaller box. She caught Seb's wide grin. She lifted the lid of the second box and peered inside apprehensively, expecting to find a further puzzle. She was relieved to find a paper-wrapped packet, tied with a green ribbon.

"Did you spend all afternoon putting this together?" she asked, as she struggled with the knot.

"Hours," Seb insisted with a grin. "I knew how *patient* you are."

Inside the paper was a small, velvet pouch. "Am I getting closer?" Willi asked. Seb nodded. She untied the strings and emptied the pouch into her hand.

Her eyes widened with surprise at the sight of the locket. "Oh, Seb, how lovely!"

He beamed proudly at her delight. "Isn't it, though? Cleaned up nicely, if I do say so myself."

Willi held up the silver heart for everyone to admire.

"Look inside," Seb urged.

She unfastened the catch and flipped the locket open. A lock of blond hair was curled inside. She looked quickly at Seb. "Yours?"

"Of course," he said with mock indignation. "As your valentine, you shouldn't be wearing anyone else's."

Willi's fingers curled about it. "I'll treasure it always, Seb. Thank you."

Seb darted her a curious glance, surprised by the huskiness he heard in her voice. Willi, who probably

owned a fortune in jewels, was thrilled about a little
trinket he'd picked up in a pawnbroker's shop for less
than a pound?

Seb cleared his throat. "You can hang it on the
ribbon," Seb said, taking the locket from her and
stringing it.

He leaned over to fasten the locket around her
neck, but when his fingers brushed against the soft
skin of her neck, he nearly jerked his hand back. It
was like touching fire, and a sharp stab of desire shot
through him. In his confusion, he made a hopeless
tangle of the knot.

"There," Seb said with relief, when he'd finished.
"A valentine for my valentine."

"I've never been given a lock of hair before," Willi
said, blinking her eyes in a suspicious manner.

"See that you guard it well," said Seb gruffly,
shaken by her reaction.

"Oh, I shall." Willi smiled warmly. "I will forever
keep it close to my heart."

Seb's eyes strayed to the creamy white skin that lay
above the low-cut neck of her gown. He couldn't see
the actual beating of her heart, but did notice the rise
and fall of her chest with each breath. He felt a sudden
twinge of envy for the locket, nestled there in the
valley between her breasts.

Willi, with her combination of earthy frankness and
feminine charms, had to be the most alluring woman
he knew. And he was falling under her spell all over
again. He was acting like an overeager schoolboy, but
he couldn't help it. He had a damnable urge to sweep
her up in his arms and carry her off—somewhere, anywhere—where they could be alone.

He lifted his gaze, and their eyes met. Willi's were
filled with bemusement, and Seb wondered if she'd
discerned his thoughts, sensed his discomfort. He
wanted to laugh off the sudden awkwardness with
some outrageous remark, but he stopped himself.

Willi had long ago convinced him that they couldn't be both friends and lovers. Now, he began to wonder if it really was an impossibility. Mightn't it be worth trying? If she'd been wrong ... they'd wasted so much time.

He stared at her, confused and disturbed by these new, troubling feelings. Did he dare speak to her about it? The matter was delicate, and one false move could ruin everything. He'd grown cautious over the years.

But caution was not what he wanted or needed now. He wanted to know the answers to all his questions: why he felt this sharp rekindling of desire for her, whether she felt the same, whether they could become lovers again. He knew he couldn't let her leave without finding out.

Willi fingered the silver heart. It was lovely. Seb was really making romantic gestures tonight; he must truly wish to win Lavinia's silly contest. Willi felt a twinge of guilt over the silly present she'd bought Seb. At the time, it had seemed like the perfect thing, but now ... A child's toy was highly unromantic. She wished she'd bought him something more elegant, even if she'd had to spend more than her allotted pound. But how was she to know that Seb was going to surprise her with such a gift?

She hoped Seb would understand.

The men eagerly started to open their presents. There were handkerchiefs, snuff, and Sophie's book of poetry. Seb, like Willi, was last.

"It must be good," he said with a grin, hefting the misshapen package in his hand. "It certainly weighs enough." He sat down and gleefully tore at the paper, then halted and stared in surprise at what lay in his lap. Seb burst out laughing.

"What is it?" Christopher demanded.

Seb held up a tiny, metal archer. "Soldiers. Bowmen."

"Archers for the archer!" Christopher cried.

Seb darted a delighted glance at Willi.

She shrugged dismissively. "I thought your stirring achievement should be commemorated forever."

"It's perfect," he declared, leaning over to give her a hug. She could barely hide her pleasure at his own.

"Now we must vote," Lavinia announced. "The best present for the ladies and the best for the gentlemen."

Sophie's silver baby rattle was easily declared the winner for the ladies. The voting was close for the men, but Seb's archers won the battle. Lavinia shot him a fierce glare when the votes were tallied. Seb had now won three points.

Seb sat back in his chair, a triumphant smile on his face. "That's three points now. With this lead, no one will be able to beat us," he said confidently to Willi.

She waved a warning finger at him. "Pride goeth before a fall."

Seb smiled weakly, but inwardly he cringed. He didn't give a damn about Lavinia's silly contests. What he did care about was Willi. Could he convince her that they could be more than friends? He was afraid to even broach the subject, for fear it would ruin their friendship if she did not feel the same.

He'd never thought of himself as a coward before, but Seb realized that in this matter, he certainly was.

4

If Seb hoped a night's restless sleep and the cool light of morning would clear his mind, he was mistaken. When he found Willi alone at the breakfast table, his first instinct was to beat a hasty retreat.

Instead, he pulled out a chair and greeted Willi with a cheerful face. "Today's the last day of the competition," he announced. "Tomorrow night, I'll be king of the Saint Valentine's Day ball."

"An honor that will follow you throughout the Season," said Willi dryly. "And to think you were looking upon this party with utter dread at one time."

"Ah, but now I have a chance to hoist Lavinia by her own petard. She won't forget this defeat for an age."

"There are still two more competitions," Willi reminded him.

"Two? I thought there was only one."

"She said something about two last night. You were probably too busy crowing about your latest triumph to listen."

"I still think your locket was a better prize than a baby rattle. No imagination, there."

"As you observed, only a live baby could have topped that. Even your brother looked pleased at the news."

"I can't believe Richard is going to be a grandfather," said Seb, with an incredulous shake of his head. "He can't be that old."

"I'm afraid he is," Willi said, taking a sip of her tea. "As you are yourself."

"Too late for grandchildren now," he said with a self-satisfied grin. "Instead, I'll have to settle for being king of the Valentine's Ball. Won't Lavinia be livid when she has to crown me King Seb?"

Willi pressed the back of her hand to her head. "I'm not certain I shall be able to serve as your consort. I feel a megrim coming on . . ."

"It's no use, Willi." Seb licked a sticky dab of marmalade off his fingers. "If I'm to be king of the ball, you'll be my queen."

"I wonder which gown I should wear?"

He leered at her in his most obvious manner. "I'd be more than happy to help you decide."

"And ruin the element of surprise? Never."

Seb laughed, then sobered with remembrance. He'd accompanied her to the dressmakers many times to help her make her selections. Later, he'd had the pleasure of taking them off her. That was the best part. Willi, naked beneath him in bed.

He shook himself. He was lusting after her as he had when they'd first been lovers. Not that he'd ever ceased to desire her, but he'd felt quite comfortable with their current arrangement—until last night. Now, he couldn't help but remember just how pleasurable their relationship in bed had been.

It must be that damned hair. She was the same old Willi, but then again, she wasn't, and the difference piqued his interest. Would it feel different to have those short curls beneath his hands, instead of her long hair spread over the pillow?

And would it feel different with her in bed after the passing of time? It had been three—no, four—years since they'd last shared a bed. For an aching moment, he wondered how many lovers she'd had in that time.

It was Lavinia and her insipid Valentine's Day plans. The forced atmosphere would make even the heartiest misogynist romantic. He was starting to think of Willi as his real valentine, rather than the partner he'd commandeered through trickery.

But he was afraid to say anything to her. She was the one who insisted they remain friends. Was it because she knew he could never be more to her? Or did she only think it was what he wanted as well? He wished there was some way he could find out without having to ask her. It would make things so much easier.

Lavinia called to them from the hall. "Hurry you two. We're all waiting."

Seb grimaced. "The general commands our presence."

"Your next challenge," Willi whispered to Seb. "Are you ready?"

Seb frowned. He wanted to talk with Willi, not participate in Lavinia's silly little plans. But he knew he had no choice in the matter.

"Let's hope this goes quickly," he whispered to Willi.

Lavinia waited impatiently at the door of the drawing room until they were seated, then raised her hand for attention.

"We are nearing the end of our little adventure, and the competition has been keen. Several of you are in a position to win." Studiously avoiding Seb, she beamed at her new son-in-law, who was only a point behind.

"This afternoon, we will begin the treasure hunt. But first, gentlemen, you are to make valentines for your partners."

"How thrilling," Seb whispered.

"Hush." Willi jabbed him with her elbow.

"In the morning room, I've gathered paper, ink, paste, lace, and other items you can use to make a creation worthy of your valentine." Lavinia took a breath. "However, these valentines are not to display the name of the intended lady—or their maker. Tonight, the ladies will vote on which valentine they deem the best, and I want the contest to be fair." She glared at Seb. "Is that understood?"

"Tell us more about the treasure hunt," Christopher called out.

Lavinia smiled. "Not for a while. Gentlemen, if you will retire to the morning room, your labors await you."

Seb grimaced at Willi. "I can't put together a frilly valentine. This is worse than writing that damn poetry."

She patted his hand. "Do your best. I'm sure most of your competitors will be equally inept."

"Comforting words," said Seb dryly.

In two hours, Lavinia ordered the men to stop their work and luncheon was served.

"How did your artistic endeavors go?" Willi asked Seb.

"Dismally," he said mournfully. "I think my godson could have done a better job." He bent down and flecked a bit of dried paste off his trousers. "The only vote I'll get is yours."

"What makes you so certain I will vote for yours? Lavinia said we are to vote for the one that pleases us the most."

"Mine better please you—it's yours. And I suffered mightily for it."

"I will take that into account," said Willi, teasingly.

"Did Lavinia say more about this treasure hunt?"

"Not a word."

Seb shook his head. "She'll probably have us scampering about the house like a bunch of idiots. Her treasure is likely to be a volume of some insipid romantic verse."

"Careful," Willi warned him. "If you take such a dim view of things, you may lose your chance to be king."

"I'm losing my desire to spite Lavinia," he said, then grinned. "Good Lord, did I really say that? I must be getting soft in the head."

After luncheon, Lavinia herded them into the drawing room again. "The treasure hunt is the last part of our little valentine festivities," she said. "You will work in pairs—except for Sir Stanley, who I'm afraid must go alone—and decipher the clues. One will lead you to another, and the first pair to solve the final clue will find the prize."

"Do we all have the same clues?" George asked.

Lavinia shook her head. "Each team has a separate puzzle to solve. Only the final location is shared."

"What's to stop us from putting our heads together and solving the riddles together?" Christopher asked.

"The spirit of competition," Seb yelled out. "If you think I'm going to help you, you've got bats in your belfry."

"Are all the clues hidden in the house?" Richard asked.

"Perhaps," Lavinia said. "And perhaps not."

"Wonderful," said Seb in a loud undertone. "We'll be out digging in the frozen ground by the end of this, mark my words."

Lavinia shot him a dampening look. "Any more questions?"

"What's the prize?" Lizzie asked eagerly.

"Something nice for both the lady and the gentleman," Lavinia assured her.

"Hopefully a good bottle of brandy," Seb said. "I've a feeling I'll need it after this is over."

"What if no one finds the prize?"

Lavinia looked puzzled. "I had not thought of that."

"Can't happen," said Seb with overweening confidence. "In fact, I'm willing to allow you to concede to my superior reason right now."

Expressions of derision greeted his ears.

Lavinia picked up a basket and walked toward her husband. "To make this fair, no one look at their clue until everyone has theirs." She drew out a folded piece of paper and handed it to Richard.

Seb drummed his fingers impatiently on his knee. "This shouldn't take long," he said confidently to Willi.

"Lavinia specially designed these clues," she said. "We will probably have the hardest ones."

Seb hadn't thought of that. "Do you really think she'd do that to me?"

Willi laughed. "Why on earth would she not? You've made a shambles of her carefully orchestrated plans already by winning too many events. She'll do anything to see you lose."

"Then we won't," Seb said with fierce determination.

Willi took the paper Lavinia handed her.

"Let me see that," Seb said, grabbing for it.

Willi held it away. "You heard what she said. Not until everyone else has one."

"Spoil sport."

"All right," said Lavinia. "You may open your clues. Good luck."

For a moment, the only sound was of paper rustling. That was followed by a few groans and exclamations of "what?"

"This is ridiculous," Seb said, as he read the note Willi held. "It makes no sense."

"Look under the cross, and you will find something to help you with your find."

"There's no cross that I know of in the house," he grumbled.

"Anything that looks like a cross?" Willi asked. "Remember, she said some clues might lead outside."

Seb shook his head slowly. "It doesn't mean a thing."

"Great," said Willi. "Finished on the first clue." Already two pairs had left the drawing room in search of their next clue.

"She might not mean a religious cross," Willi mused. "It could be anything with a x shape."

Seb's eyes lit with excitement. "Come on," he said, grabbing her by the hand and dragging her out of the drawing room. He raced down the stairs and across the hall. Without stopping to grab a coat, he pulled Willi out the door.

"Let me get my cloak," she said.

"No time." He ran around the side of the house toward the stables.

"What are we looking for?" Willi asked.

"The hay forks," he gasped. "They're always hung crossways."

They reached the stables. Seb raised a quick hand to the startled groom and pulled Willi into the dark interior. "There," he said, pointing to the far wall. He dropped her hand and darted toward the forks.

Willi stepped up behind him. "Do you see another clue?"

"No." Seb's voice dripped discouragement. "I thought surely this was the place . . ."

"Look around," Willi suggested. "She might have put it nearby."

Squinting in the darkness, Seb examined every surface at that end of the stable, but found nothing. He turned to confess his failure to Willi, then halted.

A shaft of light from the high windows bathed her face in a radiant glow, and he sucked in his breath at the sight. Almost without thinking, he moved toward her.

Willi rubbed her arms. "It's freezing! Let's go back to the house," she suggested. "I can think better where it's warm."

"I've just the thing to warm you," said Seb, too entranced to stop himself. He drew Willi toward him and wrapped his arms about her. "Better?"

He felt her shiver—from the cold, or was it some other reason? Seb bent his head and nuzzled at her ear. Those dainty pink shells had been calling to him from the moment he'd seen Willi's new, short hair. "Mmmm. Your ear's warm, at least."

He moved his hands up and down her back, hoping to ease the chill. He didn't know about her, but his temperature had risen several degrees already.

"Oh, Seb," Willi whispered, as he pulled her closer.

Seb trailed his lips along her jawline, halting for a moment before he pressed them to her mouth. Instantly, her lips parted beneath his and he deepened the kiss, teasing her lips with his tongue, tasting the warmth of her mouth. His arm tightened about her waist, and he brought up a hand to run through her curls. They were soft and springy beneath his fingers.

"God, I've been wanting to do that since you first arrived," he said, tearing his mouth away momentarily before kissing her again.

She felt so good, so right, that he didn't want to stop. He wanted to make up for all the lost time, the years when he hadn't dared to hold her and touch her like this. He shuddered with desire—and at the same moment, felt her stiffen in his arms.

Seb sensed her confusion and pressed a gentle kiss to the top of her head. He held her close, feeling the rapid beating of her heart against his chest.

"I fear I'm getting a bit old for a tumble in the hay," he said with a wry laugh. "Shall we go back to the house?"

Willi nodded. "It's best, I think."

Seb lifted her chin with a finger. "Sometimes it's so hard to remember to behave myself when I'm near you," he said with a wide grin. "Am I quite forgiven?"

Willi nodded. Seb released her and, taking her arm, led her quickly back to the house.

"Brandy?" he asked, when they'd entered the library.

Willi nodded and took a chair near the fire. She rubbed her arms again, as if to warm them, but it was more to calm herself.

Those kisses in the stable had shaken her more than she cared to admit. There could be no denying Seb's desire after what had happened. He still wanted her—as badly as she wanted him. But desire was a very dangerous thing.

Seb was her nearest and dearest friend. She could laugh and cry with him; share most of her thoughts and know that he cared for her. She must preserve their friendship, no matter what.

Yet how was she to explain what she felt for him? Those kisses in the stable had only confirmed her feelings. Feelings she had before she even arrived here. She remembered the deep thrill of excitement she'd felt when she'd received Seb's invitation. She'd canceled all her engagements without a second thought and rushed to his side.

So what did she want from Seb?

She'd thought she was content with her life. But she

now was plagued by a vague discontent—a feeling that there was something more that she wanted—but what?

Willi realized, with a dawning sense of wonder, that she wanted Seb. She wanted to sit beside him night after night before a fire, fetch him his slippers, massage the aches from his shoulders. She wanted to sleep with him—and wake up beside him in the morning. She wanted to grow old with him.

Willi smiled sadly to herself. She was in love with him, she acknowledged. And probably had been for a long time. She'd known it instinctively when she'd changed the tenor of their relationship, knowing that she couldn't expect the same from him. By insisting on friendship, she wouldn't have to face his rejection.

He still wanted her—she was certain of that. But did his wanting translate into deeper feelings than mere physical desire? Willi wasn't certain. Seb could be very closemouthed about his feelings; like most men, he wasn't comfortable revealing them.

If she allowed him, he would take her into his bed. For the night, and for the night after that. But how long would it last? If it wasn't forever, it would not be long enough. And if it couldn't be forever, she didn't want it at all.

She'd go back to London immediately after Lavinia's party. Willi thought it might be a good idea for her to keep away from Seb for a while, until she got her feelings back under control again. She would never let him know how she felt—she would not want to see the sadness in his eyes when he knew he couldn't reciprocate her feelings. That, more than anything she could say, would kill their friendship forever.

Seb poured them each a brandy. Handing her the glass, he stood beside her, staring glumly into the fire. He had almost forgotten himself in the stables. She'd barely said a word since they came back inside—was she angry that he'd kissed her like that? Should he apologize—or kiss her again?

"You still have the power to surprise me, Seb," Willi said at last, breaking the silence.

Seb glanced at her. "I must admit, I surprised myself."

She smiled. "I do not mean in the stables. I've seen you in an entirely different light this week. I honestly think I'll have to change my opinion of you."

"Favorably, I hope."

Willi looked at her glass for some length of time before she spoke. "I do not think I could ever look unfavorably upon you, Seb. No"—she darted a side-long glance at him—"I only sense that you are looking upon things differently these days. I suspect you are beginning to realize you are growing older, and wondering if there is more that you wish to do."

"I am?"

She laughed lightly. "Of course you are. It is a common trait among men of your age. Youth is gone, you are well into your middle years, and wonder what the future will bring."

"Do women feel the same way?"

"Some," she replied.

"Do you?"

"Occasionally. I wonder what my life would be like if Taunton had not died, or if we'd had children." She looked down again. "Or if I had remarried."

Once again, Seb felt that cold chill creeping over him. Willi had always scoffed at the idea of remarrying, saying she enjoyed her freedom too much. Now here she was, saying she sometimes thought about it after all.

Willi looked at him sharply. "Are you going to London after Lavinia's little party?"

"I'll be there eventually. Thought I might hike over to Devon and visit Alford."

"At this time of year?"

He shrugged. "I'd only admit this to you, but the Season's beginning to become a deuced bore."

She nodded. "I know how you feel. I'm rather glad I'll miss most of it myself."

He looked at her in surprise. "Where are you going?"

"To Italy. Didn't I tell you?"

"No," he said with a hurt expression. "Who with?"

"Felsham."

"Felsham?" Seb turned his head and glared at her. "That old bore?"

"I don't find him boring," Willi said. "And I do so want to see Italy. I've always wanted to travel there."

"Why didn't you say something? I would have taken you. And no doubt shown you a better time than Felsham."

"You didn't ask me," she said pointedly. "He did."

Seb shook his head. "I didn't know you wanted to go."

Willi hugged herself. "What Englishman would not want to visit sunny Italy? I want to find an elegant hillside villa, and I shall sit on the sunny terrace and eat apricots and nectarines and grapes and do absolutely nothing for days on end."

"You'd be bored within hours," Seb said.

Willi shivered. "After this weather? I'm tempted to depart early."

"You might be able to tolerate the sun. It's Felsham who'd drive you to tears."

Willi cast him a dampening look. "I'll have you know he can be utterly charming."

Seb snorted derisively. Felsham. Willi had professed to be as opposed to marriage as he, but the rumors about her and Felsham had flown fast and thick last season. Now he was taking her to Italy? Seb didn't like it. He didn't like it one bit. It was too ... cozy. Almost as if they were an old married couple.

A pain so sharp that he almost dropped the glass

ripped through his chest. Was that what Felsham planned—a honeymoon in Italy?

He couldn't believe Willi wouldn't have told him if she was planning to wed. She could be decidedly closemouthed about her personal affairs when she wanted to, but would a friend keep such an important piece of news from him?

Of course not. It was as she said—they were only traveling together. For all he knew, their relationship was as platonic as his and Willi's.

But somehow, he doubted it. Felsham might be a bore, but he was known to be a man with sensual appetites. The type who would appreciate—and appeal to—Willi.

Were they lovers? It was something they'd long ago agreed never to discuss among themselves. It was part of their friendship pact. But Seb had a burning desire to know—and a sinking dread that he didn't want to, if it was true.

It was a dangerous combination. Italy. Felsham. Thoughts of remarriage. He had to nip it in the bud, or he'd lose her. That was one thing he could not bear.

"Willi, are you really certain that—"

"Sebastian Cole!" Lavinia stood in the library door, a frown upon her face. "Whatever are you doing here? I happen to know that none of your clues will be found here."

Seb waved a dismissive hand at her. "I've conceded, Lavinia. The puzzle is too hard. Leave us to our brandy."

"Nonsense. You have to participate."

He set his mouth in a stubborn line. "I don't want to."

"Really, Sebastian, you surprise me." She turned an imploring glance at Willi. "Surely you can persuade him."

"Seb's a determined man when he's made up his

mind," Willi said, inwardly glad that Lavinia had interrupted their conversation. How could she tell Seb that she was glad to be going to Italy—for it would take her away from the temptation he posed.

"How many clues did you find?" Lavinia demanded.

"None," Seb admitted reluctantly.

"What? You silly fool. It's in the drawing room." Lavinia flung up her hands. "I never would have thought you so obtuse."

She stood there, one hand on her hip, with an expectant look on her face.

Seb accepted defeat. He held out his hand to Willi. "Should we try again?"

She stood. "We really ought."

Seb set down his glass, scowling at Lavinia as he did so. "To the drawing room, then. But I won't waste more than five minutes on the next clue."

Actually, he was almost glad Lavinia had interrupted them. He needed more time to think about Willi—and Felsham—and himself. Lavinia's silly little treasure hunt would be a welcome diversion while he decided how best to confront Willi.

With a look of triumph, Lavinia showed him that the cross proved to be in a watercolor of the village church hanging on the wall. The next clue was stuck in the frame.

Seb chortled. "This one is easy. 'Look for the lamp that's always lit.' That was to be the one at the end of the upstairs hall." He dashed out of the room.

They found the next three clues in quick succession. They were puzzling over the fourth one when a loud shout captured their attention.

"It sounds like Christopher," he said, turning back to Willi. "I think he found the treasure."

They hastened upstairs to the drawing room where Christopher and Maria had indeed found the treasure—a silver card case and a lacy fan.

"Paltry rewards," Seb whispered to Willi.

"You can say that only because you are still in the lead."

"Wait until you see my valentine," he groaned.

Lavinia waited until after dinner before the ladies were allowed to judge that contest. She warned the men to stay in the dining room, while their efforts were spread out on the card table.

Willi recognized Seb's effort immediately—or at least thought she did. It was creased and smudged, with errant spatters of paste along its lace border and lopsided red hearts. It was, as he'd warned her, a sorry specimen.

Not that the others were much better. Only one showed an artist's hand. The lace about the edge was even, the sentiment written in an elegant copperplate script, and the drawn hearts were evenly matched. Indeed, every lady pronounced it the winner.

"Oh dear," said Lavinia, when she was told the results. "We have a problem. Our score is tied."

Willi smothered a laugh. Seb's kingship might be salvaged after all.

"Who?" Sophie asked eagerly.

"George and Sebastian."

"Think of another contest," Lady Kirby suggested.

"But what?" Lavinia moaned. "I'm completely out of ideas."

"Trial by combat," said Willi mischievously.

"Swords!" Lizzie clapped her hands eagerly.

Sophie gasped. "Heaven's no!"

"Let us vote," Lady Wright suggested. "We shall decide which one is the worthiest."

"Tomorrow night!" Maria added. "Keep the men in suspense until then."

Willi grinned. She could only imagine how Seb would take *that* news.

"Well ..." Lavinia said reluctantly. "You are certain you wouldn't like another little contest?"

"No, no," they all chorused. "We'll crown the king tomorrow night."

Lavinia was gracious in defeat. "All right. Tomorrow night, you are to choose between George and Sebastian."

"And may the best man win!" Sophie cried.

Seb accepted the news with an equanimity that surprised Willi. No doubt he was plotting his campaign. He'd probably devise some outrageous scheme to induce all the ladies into voting for him. Bribery, blackmail, even outright trickery were not beyond him.

Willi prepared for bed that night with a mixture of relief and confusion. Relief, that she had managed to avoid being alone with Seb again. Confusion over what she must do.

She walked to the dresser and picked up the silver heart. Back in London, her jewel boxes were crammed full with elegant and expensive pieces, yet she would never treasure any of them more than this. It had cost less than a pound, and yet its value could never be calculated. Because Seb had bought it specially for her.

She flipped the locket open and ran her finger over the soft curl of blond hair. Memories of those moments in the stable rushed over her. She suddenly wished they hadn't come to their senses, that they'd thrown caution to the winds and had their "tumble in the hay," as Seb had so aptly put it.

Maybe, then maybe she would have been able to tell him how she felt. But now, she was too afraid of his reaction, too afraid to find out what he really thought. It was cowardly on her part, but if she did not know for certain, she could always hope. Maybe later in London the opportunity would present itself, or during the summer ...

The summer she planned to spend in Italy.

Seb had almost sounded jealous when she'd told

him of her plan to go to Italy with Felsham. Could it be true? If he *was* jealous, it could only mean ...

Willi smiled smugly to herself. She was not above using a bit of feminine guile. If she could arouse Seb's jealousy by flaunting her plans for Italy, she would do it. For then she would know—one way or the other.

And she could plan her future accordingly. Italy with Felsham or—she could only hope—some kind of future with Seb.

5

Seb sat in front of the library fire, nursing his brandy.

He'd never had the chance to talk to Willi about Felsham, and their trip to Italy. But what was he to say? That he didn't want her to go? She'd just laugh and go anyway. He had no right to order her around.

He could offer to take her instead. She might agree to that. Yet if she accompanied him, she'd still be subject to gossip and speculation. Even a widow as popular as Willi had to observe the conventions. Traveling to a foreign country with a gentleman not her husband was a bit too outrageous for most circles.

So what was he going to do—marry her so he could take her to Italy without destroying her reputation?

Seb nearly choked on his brandy. Marry Willi? Where had that idea come from? She'd be horrified at the very thought.

Although she shouldn't be, Seb thought defensively. He wouldn't make *that* bad a husband. He didn't have too many annoying habits—Willi was already acquainted with the worst of them and hadn't seemed to mind overmuch. As her husband, he'd be expected to escort her to balls and the theater—but didn't he do that already? It would not be a drastic change.

Except that they would be lovers again. Lord knows they were comfortable in bed together. Sometimes Seb thought they had been too comfortable—and that's

why they'd allowed their affair to cool. It would have
been too easy to allow it to become permanent. That
thought had frightened both of them.

Yet now he was thinking of that very thing and
wondering if it would be so very frightening after all.

But would Willi want to marry just to placate society? It was a high price to pay just to see Italy.

Would she really prefer him over Felsham?

Seb shook his head. He couldn't put it to her in
that way or she would object right away. He'd have
to couch his offer in gentler terms. Women—even
ones as practical as Willi—liked that sort of thing. This
was Saint Valentine's Day eve, after all, the time for
love and romance. He ought to be able to come up
with some sort of story that would satisfy her. Something about how Lavinia's Valentine's party had released his own ardor, and he realized he couldn't live
without her.

Would Willi believe such a thing?

Only if it were true.

The thought chilled him. Was it true? Was he ready
to throw off forty years of bachelorhood to save Willi's reputation?

No. Not to save her reputation. But because he
wanted to. Because he wanted to have Willi for himself, for as many years as they had left. He didn't want
her going to Italy, didn't want her going to the theater
or the country or anywhere else without him. He
wanted to lay beside her at night, see her face when
he awoke in the morning. He wanted to make love to
her in their own house, in their own bed.

However was he going to convince Willi of that
when the very thought frightened him nearly witless?

Seb poured himself another brandy and thought.
Pretty words weren't going to convince her. It would
take more than that. He'd have to convince her he'd
undergone a complete change of heart over the last
few days. To convince her that besides friendship,

there was more he could—wanted—to share with her. Not just sex, but everything that marriage entailed. Companionship, sharing—even arguing. No marriage was perfect. But he and Willi, knowing each other so well, knew exactly what to expect. They wouldn't be starry-eyed lovers like Sophie and George, but friends who'd chosen to spend their lives together.

And if that didn't frighten her away, he was halfway there.

An idea formed in his mind. Tomorrow was Valentine's Day—wasn't it the old superstition that the first man you saw on that day would be your valentine—and husband? Maybe he could put the old saying to the test.

He remembered that miserable paper creation he'd slapped together in the morning room earlier. What if he made Willi another? One that was especially for her, that told her how he felt, how he wanted her.

Would she listen? Would she believe?

He had to try. For suddenly, the years in front of him stretched on and on, and he knew he did not want to spend them alone. Her words earlier had struck a chord. His life was at least half over and what did he have to show for it? He didn't regret not having a family—he had enough nieces, nephews, and god-children to entertain him when the urge struck. It was the thought of growing old alone that sounded so frightening. He wanted someone to share those years—the good and the bad—and to know that when he was gone there would be someone who would re-member him as more than a friend. With Willi by his side, the coming years would not be frightening, but filled with laughter and good times.

He'd enjoyed his single life up until now, but he was eager to try life with another. With Willi.

Willi was asleep when he stole into her room shortly after dawn. He'd been up the entire night, working on endless versions of his valentine until he had finally achieved something worthy of her. Afraid she would awaken early and ruin his plan, he'd hastened to her room without shaving or even changing his clothes. He wanted to be the first thing she saw when she opened her eyes.

Seb sat down in the upholstered chair and set his valentine on the dressing table. Yawning, he stretched out his legs before him. He could wake her, but wasn't sure the superstition would work if he did. He would wait patiently until she awoke.

He watched her sleep, idly wondering what she was wearing to bed these days. When they'd been lovers, she'd been partial to diaphanous creations that he'd almost regretted removing. Had she switched to long sleeved flannel in the intervening years? He stifled a laugh. Willi would probably be wearing frothy lace negligees when she was sixty.

And he knew he'd still want her as badly then as he did now.

As Willi drifted toward wakefulness, a strange noise reached her ears, and she dreamily tried to recognize its source. A drafty fire? Buzzing bees? Snoring?

Snoring? She sat bolt upright and looked across the room. Seb was sprawled in the chair, asleep.

Willi shook her head, smiling fondly. What on earth was the man doing here? He looked as if he hadn't even gone to bed; his clothes were wrinkled and he certainly hadn't shaved. Had he been here all night?

Carefully, she slipped from bed and wrapped her dressing gown around her. She crossed the floor to where Seb sat and gently shook his shoulder.

"Seb," she called. "Wake up."

"What!' He looked at her with sleepy eyes that suddenly grew wide with alarm. "Damnation! I fell asleep, didn't I?"

"It appears so," Willi said with a laugh. "Would you care to tell me why you're here, or dare I ask?"

Seb stretched uncomfortably. "It's Valentine's Day," he mumbled. "I was supposed to be the first person you saw when you awoke. Except that I fell asleep."

"I assure you, I haven't seen another soul this morning."

"Really?" Seb brightened momentarily, then he remembered why he was here. He pressed his hand to his head. "Oh, Lord."

Willi nodded sympathetically. "A bit too much brandy, perhaps?"

Seb groaned. He pointed to the valentine on the table. "I made that for you."

Willi picked up the carefully decorated sheet of vellum. Dainty lace encrusted red hearts surrounding a written verse. "You made this?" she asked suspiciously.

Seb nodded. "Rather better than my first attempt, isn't it? Read it."

"Roses are Red, Violets are Blue, Sugar is Sweet and so are you. I'll take you to Italy, to a villa in the sun, Marry me and we'll have some fun." Willi laughed shakily. "I see your poetic ability hasn't improved."

"Maybe not, but you've always said it's the sentiment that counts." Seb smiled weakly. "I mean it."

Willi's gaze turned incredulous. "You wish to marry me?"

Seb smiled. "I know, it's rather a shocker, isn't it? Thought so myself when I thought of it last night." He took the valentine from her and set it on the table, then took both of her hands in his. "But the thing is, I want to. I'm glad we're friends, but I want us to be more than that." He grinned wryly. "We're not getting any younger, you know. And I can't think of another lady with whom I'd rather spend my declining years."

Willi stared at him. "I honestly do not know what to say—or even what to think." She placed a hand on his brow. "Do you have a fever? Did you receive a blow to your head?"

"You aren't making this easy," he growled. "Look, you can't go traipsing about the Continent with any man who asks you. It just isn't done."

"Why, Seb Cole! Are you suffering from an attack of respectability in your old age?"

"Perhaps. But if I am to turn respectable, I want to do it with you."

Her eyes twinkled merrily. "But what if I don't wish to become respectable?"

He put his arm about her waist and drew her closer. "You can be as disreputable as you wish when you're with me," Seb said with a leer that made her laugh.

Willi sobered. "Seb, you are talking nonsense, and you know it. How many years have you insisted you never wished to marry? And now, suddenly, you've had a complete change of heart?"

"Blame it on Saint Valentine," Seb said. "I've been struck with a blinding passion that only you can satisfy."

Willi desperately wanted to believe his words. But how could she? Seb couldn't possibly want to marry her. Because it was exactly what she wanted, it couldn't be true.

Seb abruptly pulled her down on his lap. "I see I am going to have to use my powers of persuasion on you," he said, and lowered his lips to hers.

"Are you persuaded yet?" he asked a few minutes later.

"I'm not sure," Willi gasped. "Perhaps you should—"

Seb's mouth came down on hers in a ruthless kiss that took away her breath and thought. She melted against him, responding to the expert touches of his lips and hands.

"Willi?"

"Yes?"

"Shall we get married?"

"Ummm," she replied, as he ran his fingers lightly across her neck.

"Is that a yes?" he asked hopefully.

Willi put her hand to his cheek. "Are you so very certain, Seb?" she asked, her eyes wide and curious. "I don't want you to come to your senses next week and think it's all a dreadful mistake."

"The only mistake I ever made was not doing this sooner," he said with such firmness that Willi believed him.

"I will marry you then," she said, emphatically. Then she laughed. "Lavinia will be stunned."

Seb laughed with her. "Knowing her, she will take all the credit. When she had nothing whatsoever to do with it."

"Oh? I thought you said it was Saint Valentine who persuaded you."

Seb eased Willi off his lap and stood. "Saint Valentine had nothing to do with it," he said, as he fumbled with the sash of her robe. "Blame it on Felsham, if you must blame someone."

"Felsham?"

"I was crazy with jealousy at the thought of you going to Italy with him," Seb said, as he drew her down onto the bed. He parted her robe, then grinned. "Thank God."

Willi looked at him quizzically.

He fingered her filmy night rail. "I was worried you might have taken to wearing flannel," he said, planting a kiss at the hollow of her throat. "I warn you, Willi, as my wife you will not be allowed to wear flannel to bed." His eyes gleamed wickedly. "If I allow you to wear anything at all."

"I promise to be a dutiful wife," Willi said, her eyes brimming with laughter as she pulled Seb to her.

*   *   *

It was long past noon before Willi finally ventured into company. Thank goodness the ball was tonight. No one would think it unusual that she had slept late.

Except, of course, it had not been sleep that had delayed her.

She looked for Seb the moment she entered the drawing room. He looked handsomer than ever. A wide grin split his face when he spotted her, and she blushed under his approving gaze. She wore the silver locket around her neck.

Seb hastened to her side, taking her hand and pressing a soft kiss to her fingers. "You look exquisite," he said, never taking his eyes off her face. He clasped her hand tightly in his and cocked a questioning brow. "Are you ready to shatter their peace?"

Willi smiled teasingly. "You wish to commit yourself publicly so soon?"

"I dare not give you the opportunity to change your mind," he replied with a grin. Still holding her hand, he turned to the group. "If I may have your attention!" He waited while they quieted, then casually slipped his arm about Willi's waist. "I am delighted to inform you all that Lady Taunton had agreed to exchange that title for the simpler, but even more enviable one of the Honorable Mrs. Sebastian Cole."

A moment of stunned silence greeted his words.

Richard was the first to come forward, and he clapped Seb heartily on the back. "About time," he said, and leaned over to kiss Willi's cheek. "Welcome to the family."

Lavinia fanned herself frantically. "I cannot believe it," she observed loudly to her sister. "Seb! And Lady Taunton!"

"Looks like you should have been watching your backside, Uncle," said Christopher with a smile, as he offered his congratulations. "Cupid's dart found it's mark."

"I think it's so exciting," Lizzie gushed breathlessly. "An engagement at a Valentine's party. How romantic!"

"The vote!" Maria cried. "We must take the vote for our Valentine's king."

"I'll concede defeat," George said graciously. "Any man who proposes to his lady on Saint Valentine's Day eve deserves to be king at the ball."

Christopher's loud laugh rang out. "I know you wanted to be king, Uncle, but isn't this a rather drastic measure?"

Seb grinned. "It was a near-run thing, wasn't it?" He squeezed Willi's waist. "I can only thank the lady for helping me cement my victory."

Lavinia lay a hand on Seb's arm. "Sebastian Cole! You are a rascally devil." She hugged Willi. "I hope you keep him under a firm rein."

"Oh, I will," Willi assured her.

Seb's eyes twinkled with mischief. "Just think, Lavinia, I'm to be married at last, and you didn't have a thing to do with it!"

"Oh!" She looked at him archly. "Who arranged this little party? You thought to foil my designs by inviting Willi, but it looks as if I have the last laugh!"

Seb turned red as everyone chuckled. He bowed to his sister-in-law. "You are a matchmaker beyond compare, Lavinia," he acknowledged. "For which I will be eternally grateful."

He drew Willi into his arms and kissed her soundly before the entire company.

Devil's Luck

by Anita Mills

The Red Ram Inn, February 1795

THE taproom was nearly silent, deserted save for a single table. A smoking cruzie lamp cast the eerie shadows of four men onto the ancient, soot-streaked wall. An assortment of bank notes, silver, and scraps of papers before a very bored Lord Trevaney gave testimony to his incredible luck, while the other three men sat glumly playing, attempting to recoup losses.

Finally, one threw down his cards in disgust." 'Tis the devil's luck you've had this night." Reaching for a nearly empty bottle of burgundy, he drained it, then leaned back wearily. "I'm done up, Gary."

Beside him, Peverel Pennyfoote, an overdressed young dandy, stared at his cards, trying not to betray his distress. As the gentleman pushed a pile of the crumpled bank notes into the pot, he felt the bottom of his stomach drop. Already he'd wagered far beyond his means, and now he held a losing hand.

Reluctantly, he folded his cards and mumbled, "I'm out also. I will, of course, settle on quarter day."

"As you wish." The viscount's dark eyes met the last player's. "And you, Merriweather—what of you?"

The older man considered his cards, then nodded. "I am in for—" He hesitated, knowing he had already lost everything, that if he did not win he might as well put a bullet into his brain. "One hundred pounds," he said. Leaning over to dip his quill into the ink pot on the floor, he tore off a corner of paper and began to write his vowel.

"I don't think so," Trevaney decided lazily. "You are already into me for nearly two thousand."

The enormity of the sum sent a visible shudder through Charles Merriweather, and tightened the knot in his stomach. He could not lose again. He closed his eyes, seeing Fanny and his daughters, and the desperation of his situation nearly overwhelmed him.

" 'Tis you and I, Merriweather," the viscount prompted.

"Wait—" The older man began loosing his watch fob from his waistcoat. " 'Tis all I have, my lord."

"Paltry." Trevaney stretched, then stood, towering over the table. "I cannot say it has not been a pleasure, sirs," he murmured, scooping his winnings into his black felt ramillie.

"Wait! You cannot!" As the young lord turned back to him, Merriweather ran his tongue over parched lips. His heart pounded so loudly he could scarce hear himself beg, "You got to let me recoup, my lord."

Trevaney's cold eyes considered him, then he shook his head. "You have nothing to wager."

"One hand—one hand for double or nothing, sir— 'tis all I ask."

"And you are offering—?"

"For God's sake, Gary, don't do it—'Tis a fortune you've won," Edward Hawkewood spoke up. "You've already put me and poor Pennyfoote into dun territory. That ought to be enough for you."

"You are out, Ned." His gaze still on the squirming man, Trevaney raised one black brow. "Well—what do you propose to wager?" he asked softly. "Other than paper, that is."

Taking a deep breath, Merriweather let it out heavily, then took the gamble of his life. "I have daughters, my lord, and—" As the viscount's brow lifted higher, he hastened to assure him, "Ain't a one of 'em as ain't prettier than any London miss, I promise."

"No!" Pennyfoote screeched.

"You got to have an heir, don't you?" the older man argued. "And m'girls' breeding's good—better than you'd think looking at me—wife's a relation to the Devonshire Tracys, and—"

" 'Tis a monstrous thought! To offer an innocent female to—to a—a hardened lecher is an outrage, sir!"

"It ain't your affair, Peverel!" Merriweather snapped. "I ain't asking him to give her a slip of the shoulder, after all's said."

Ned Hawkewood knew Trevaney was far more drunk than he appeared. "Don't do it, Gary—you cannot wish a wife you've not seen," he argued reasonably.

But the viscount still watched Merriweather. "What a fond parent you are," he murmured sardonically. "You remind me of my father."

Encouraged that Trevaney had not rejected the wager out of hand, Merriweather coaxed, "Taking creatures, every one of 'em—got pleasing manners to match the looks, too."

"Veritable paragons, no doubt," the viscount acknowledged.

"Got everything any man could want in a wife," Merriweather insisted. "Now if you was to take Charlotte—she's m'beauty."

Red-faced, Pennyfoote shouted, " 'Tis a horrid, evil notion! You might as well toss her into the Hellfire Club, sir!"

"Or Melisande—or even Arianne, but Annie's only seventeen. "Course you could make her into what you wanted," the older man allowed, ignoring the dandy.

" 'Tis my experience that one female is very like another, and every last one a wigeon," the viscount declared dryly. For a long moment, he continued regarding Merriweather, then a faint smile lifted one corner of a decidedly sensuous mouth. "But there is the matter of the heir, as you said."

"You'll take the wager?" Merriweather asked eagerly.

"Done. I shall give you one hand and one hand only," he decided, taking his seat again. Pushing his hat to the center of the table, Trevaney nodded curtly. "You may pass the pasteboards."

Silently praying, the older man took the deck and shuffled it in his hands, then slowly, deliberately counted out the cards. As beads of cold perspiration damped his brow, he picked his up and his heart sank. It was as though he saw the pits of hell beckoning to him. Looking across to Trevaney, he saw nothing to encourage him, for the man's expression was detached, as though the money on the table were nothing to him.

"Your wager, my lord," he managed to croak out.

Once again, one of Trevaney's black eyebrows rose. "But I have already bet the whole, as you will recall."

"Aye, of course. D'you want to play or show?"

"I shall display, I think."

His throat nearly too tight for speech, Merriweather waited as the viscount slowly turned over his cards, one at a time. His lordship had the winning hand. Meriweather stared, too sick to speak.

"Well?"

When the older man did not move, Trevaney reached across the table to take the cards from seemingly nerveless hands. Turning them over and spreading them out, he betrayed no emotion.

"No!" Peverel Pennyfoote stood up. "This is outrageous, I tell you!"

Charles Merriweather's head sank to his hands as tears of self-pity rolled down his cheeks. "Done for," he mumbled.

Trevaney rose again and leaned to retrieve his hat. Straightening, he looked to his thunderstruck friend.

"Well, Ned, aren't you going to wish me happy?"

"Is everyone here insane save me?" Pennyfoote demanded hotly. "Mr. Merriweather—sir, you cannot! Every decent feeling must revolt!"

" 'Tis over, Peverel," Merriweather mumbled. Rising with an effort, he addressed Trevaney, his voice hollow, "I shall go home and apprise my family. No doubt you will wish to call upon the morrow to look m'girls over."

"I shall be there later today—shall we say 'round eleven?"

"And I'll see you in hell first!" Pennyfoote threatened the viscount. "You'll not debauch an innocent!"

Hawkewood caught the dandy by the collar of his coat, holding him back. "Don't be a fool," he growled low. "If you call him out, he's like to oblige you."

But the object of his anger appeared more interested in pulling his lace-edged cuff down over his wrists, then straightening his coat sleeve, before he glanced the younger man's way. "*Are* you calling me out?" Trevaney asked silkily.

Shaking himself free and backing to a safe distance, Pennyfoote boasted, "I ain't afraid of you, my lord."

"You'll be crow's bait," Hawkewood warned him. "Don't be more of a fool than you already are." Grasping the dandy's arm, he pushed the fellow toward the door. "The cemeteries is full of fools. Here—" Reaching for the young man's hat, he jammed it over his head. "Good night, Pennyfoote," he said flatly. "Go home and sleep your wine off."

Peverel cast one last comically malevolent look at Trevaney, then fled the taproom.

Trying to maintain the tattered shreds of his dignity, Merriweather collected his hat and cloak from a chair, put them on, and turned back briefly. "Got to be going also," he mumbled.

As the door closed, Hawkewood muttered, "Idiots both."

"Aye."

"What are you going to do with the chit? Surely you do not mean to wed her?"

"No," Trevaney admitted. "What would I do with a green country miss? The accomplished ones are tedious enough."

Relieved, his friend declared, "Well, I did not think so, of course, but—"

"I should be bored within the hour, Ned. Not to mention that I have no intention of leg-shackling myself to a chit won over a card game."

"Aye, you owe more than that to your consequence, don't you?" Hawkewood rubbed his head. "I still don't see why you allowed the wager."

The viscount shrugged. "I have never suffered fools lightly, my dear Ned. 'Tis time Mr. Merriweather learns a lesson, don't you think?"

"Aye, but—"

"By the time I have slept and bathed, I expect he will have stewed sufficiently to be let off the meat hook, don't you think?" The corners of Trevaney's mouth lifted into a faint smile. "I don't need to fleece lambs, old fellow—not whilst I have you."

The chill rain pelted thick-paned windows, and in the front saloon below, the clock struck the hour of three. Still awake, Melisande Merriweather lay in the darkness, wondering how her sister Charlotte could be such an utter pea-brain.

Charlotte Maria Louisa Corisande Merriweather Pennyfoote. The mere sound of such a name, if not "dearest Peverel's" effete dandyism, ought to have scotched the romance, but it hadn't. Far from it, in fact. And now, while thoughtless Charlotte slept no doubt blissfully down the hall, it was Melisande who remained awake to wrestle with her own conscience.

Her wretched sister had extracted a promise of silence, then had stunned Mel and Annie with the news that "Given Papa's almost certain opposition, Mr. Pennyfoote and I see no other course but to elope." And the argument that they wouldn't have a feather to fly with had not dissuaded Charley in the least.

"Oh, if it means I shall have dearest Peverel's arms about me, I shall count it a blessing to practice even the most shocking economies," the silly idiot had responded airily. It had taken a great deal of self-restraint to keep Melisande's supper down after that.

It was all Mama's fault, and the chickens ought to roost on her head for it, Mel reflected grimly. If she had not intentionally let it slip out at Lady Washburton's country Christmas party that "Our Charlotte can expect a goodly portion from Charles's Uncle Thorndike one day soon," Mr. Pennyfoote would never have so much as cast a glance at Charley. And it was the baldest of lies, designed only for repeating later in London, but "dearest Peverel," being Lady Washburton's nephew, had immediately laid siege to Charlotte.

As if Uncle Thorndike would give any female so much as a farthing. Having suffered a bitter romantic disappointment in his youth, he'd denounced "that perfidious sex," and settled into the miserable, solitary life of a miser. But Mama defended her ploy as harmless, saying it was needed merely to gain the lovely Charlotte a boost into the matrimonial saddle. After all, at twenty-one she was a bit long in the tooth for a London Season.

Well, there was no help for it, Mel reflected. Come morning, she was going to have to break her oath to Charley by telling Papa. After all, he'd squeezed every last shilling from his impoverished estate to lease a small, not very fashionable London address for the spring. And the whole winter, they'd nearly starved while Mama employed a village seamstress to copy from fashion dolls, using cloth and ribbons she'd carefully bought at market stalls. Indeed, if Mel never saw another potato or turnip, she'd not miss them. The more she thought of the sacrifices all of them had endured, the more she wished to throttle her ungrateful sister.

Each girl knew what was expected from the trip to London—"Marry a fortune at best, an independence at least, and do so quickly," Papa had said. But foolish Charley had set her cap for Mr. Pennyfoote, while shy, seventeen-year-old Arianne professed more interest in Papa's horses than in finding a suitable husband. Which left only Mel herself, an inauspicious circumstance, given that she was cursed with bright red hair and a body that her mother decried as being "of Amazonian proportion." No, if everything depended on her, she sighed, Papa might as well resign himself to debtor's prison.

So she would have to tell on Charlotte, she reasoned for at least the fiftieth time of the night. But no matter how much she herself was irritated with her flighty sister, she still felt a pang of guilt at the thought of betraying her.

"Open up! Open up!"

Jarred from her thoughts, Mel realized that her father had returned from his Thursday night of drinking at the Red Ram, and once again he'd misplaced his key. As their lone footman hastily trod the back stairs, Papa continued pounding the heavy wooden door.

She could hear poor Sack try to apologize for being asleep, but her father's voice filled the house with earthy epithets, demanding that everyone be rousted out, that there'd been a disaster. Alarmed, Mel sat on the side of her bed and felt with her feet for her slippers. At the other end of the hall, her mother's door opened, and soft, quick footsteps passed Mel's room.

"Charles! Whatever—?"

"Wake 'em up, I said! Don't just stand there, Fan! Get the daughters down here!"

"Unless they are all dead, I expect they have heard

you," her mother answered dampeningly. "What has happened?"

"Everything's wrong, Fan—everything! Damn, where are they?"

"Charles, you are foxed—utterly foxed," she decided with disgust.

"I ain't begun to drink! You hear that, Fan? I ain't begun!" Rounding on poor Sack, he ordered loudly, "A bottle of port!" Turning back to his wife, he lowered his voice, but there was still a truculence to it. "I ain't going to tell it but once, Fan," he muttered. "Go on into the book room, so as you can sit down."

"Tell what?" *Will* you make sense?"

"Mama, what is going on?" Charlotte asked sleepily.

"I am sure I have not the least notion. One of your father's queer starts, I expect."

"Come on down, puss—this concerns you! In the book room, Fan!" He caught his wife's arm and pushed her ahead of him through the doorway.

Mel opened her door and slipped into the dark hall, where she nearly collided with her younger sister. "Watch out, will you?" Arianne whispered. "Are you going?"

"Yes," Mel answered tersely.

"What do you think has happened to set him off so?"

"I don't know." Noting that the younger girl had a candle, she added, "You go first, for you have the light."

"Do you think he found out about Charley and Mr. Pennyfoote?" Arianne asked nervously.

"No—how could he?"

"I don't know. But he sounds—"

"Drunk," Mel finished for her flatly.

"You have no sensibility, Mel," the girl complained.

"Stuff."

"Sometimes I think you are a changeling," Arianne muttered. "You do not even look like me or Charley."

"I am supposed to favor Uncle Thorndike, lest you forget it."

"Only because he has money."

"One of us *has* to be said to resemble him, after all. And I am told he had red hair in his youth," Mel reminded her.

"Well, I am sure I don't remember it, for he hasn't had so much as a sprig of it since I've been alive."

At the foot of the staircase, Charlotte waited anxiously for them. Leaning closer, she murmured for their ears alone, "If he says anything about Peverel, I shall simply die."

"Charley, you are a pea-goose."

"But I love Peverel! You aren't going to tell Papa, are you?"

"I don't know," Mel answered truthfully.

The book room was dark, save for a large brace of candles hastily lit by Sack, and the air within was musty and chill. Mr. Merriweather sat sprawled in his large leather-covered wing chair, a bottle in one hand. Behind him, Frances Merriweather waited grimly, her mouth drawn into a tight line of disapproval.

"Uh-Papa, are we going to have a fire lit?" Arianne asked timidly. " 'Tis cold."

"Can't afford it," he mumbled thickly. "Can't afford anything. Money's gone." A tear of self-pity trickled down his cheek as he paused to peer at each girl.

"Charles, if you have wakened us in the middle of the night to watch you drink—well, I shall not abide it," Mrs. Merriweather told him.

It was as though he did not hear her. Taking a deep pull directly from the bottle, he swallowed greedily, then wiped his wet mouth with the back of his free hand. Once again he surveyed his daughters with bleary eyes.

"Devil of it—sorry—"

"Sorry for what?" his wife demanded grimly. "Charles, you are making no sense."

"Lost. Lost bad, Fan."

"I don't wish to hear this—I am going back to bed," she snapped.

"No, you ain't. Got to help decide who to give him."

"Give who to whom?" Charlotte asked.

Ignoring the first part, he answered the second. "Trevaney." As he said it, he looked down at his feet. "Ain't got a farthing as I don't owe," he mumbled.

"Trevaney?" Melisande repeated blankly. "Lord Trevaney?"

"Ain't but one of 'em," he acknowledged. "Last of his line."

"Lord Trevaney!" Arianne echoed, her eyes round with shock. "But he's—he's that odious—that awful—"

"Arianne!" her mother said sharply.

Her father nodded. "They was at the Ram, puss, and I should've known they was playing too deep for me, but—"

Reaching around him, Mrs. Merriweather pried the bottle from his hand. Very deliberately, she flung it into the empty fireplace grate, where it shattered, spilling the wine onto the blackened stone hearth. "Go back to bed, girls," she ordered quickly. "If this concerns Lord Trevaney, 'tis not for your ears."

"Is," he maintained stoutly. "Just don't know how to say it, that's all." Looking up, he sighed heavily. "I'm telling you I lost."

"There is nothing to lose!' You have nothing that is not encumbered save Wynwood Manor!" As she said it, the color drained from her face. "Charles—"

"Trevaney don't know it—gave m' vouchers until he wouldn't take any more of 'em." As her face mirrored her disbelief, he nodded. "Was winning at first—I swear it." He lifted his hands palm up, then let them fall to his lap. "By the time I knew how far I was down, I was desperate, Fan."

"How much?"

Once again, he looked as though he could cry. "Fifteen hundred—no more'n two thousand."

"Fif—two—two *thousand*?" she echoed him. "Oh, Charles, we are ruined!"

"I was trying to recoup m' losses," he mumbled defensively. "When he gave me a chance to win it back, Fan, I had to take it. Don't you see? I had to try, and he wouldn't take m'vowels," he added, his voice nearly too low to hear.

"And?" Mel leaned over him. "what did you wager, Papa?"

He swallowed visibly. "No help for it—" His voice dropped even lower. "Had to wager one of you."

"What?" As the import of his words sank in, Mrs. Merriweather clutched her breast. "To Trevaney? I shall not bear it!"

"Papa, you didn't!" Charlotte cried.

"Did you win?" Arianne asked hopefully. "Surely you won that hand at least."

"No, my dear, I did not."

There was a moment of total silence as those around him could only stare. Then, as it sank in and her mother collapsed dramatically to the floor, Charlotte hurried to retrieve her aromatic salts. But Arianne and Melisande were waiting for him to say something more. Finally, Mel found her voice.

"Which—which one of us?" she asked faintly.

He opened his eyes. "I don't know—going to let him choose, I guess."

"Well, he cannot choose me," Charlotte announced, coming back into the room. "Papa, how *could* you wager your own flesh and blood?" she demanded, as she waved the salts under her mother's nose.

"Man's last of his line—got to wed, and—"

"Trevaney!" Arianne fairly spat out the name again. "The man's a—a—"

"You will not say such words, Annie," her mother declared awfully. "You have been reared as a lady."

"Well, he is! Did not Lord Larchmont call him out when Lady Larchmont's last infant looked like Trevaney?" Arianne demanded hotly. "And there was that business about Mrs. Compton, wasn't there? Not to mention the duel he fought over Lady Standish—nor that little matter of Miss Featherstone's awful suicide. They said she left a love note for him."

"Don't know what they teach in schoolrooms these days," Mr. Merriweather muttered. "Gossip—must be all gossip."

"Papa, Trevaney must be old!" Charlotte all but shouted. "And the man's naught but a shameless debaucher of females! There—I have said it, Mama!"

"Charlotte, you will lower your voice to your father." Rounding on her husband, Frances Merriweather gave vent to her own anger. "Charles, this is outside of enough, do you hear me? When the hour is civil, you will send 'round to Lord Trevaney, declaring that you will make arrangements to pay the money somehow, do you hear me?"

"The whole world hears you, Fan," he grumbled. "And how the devil am I to pay, I ask you?"

"Well, I expect we shall have to apply to your uncle, and—"

"He wouldn't give a starving man a hen!" he snorted.

"Then there is only Wynwood."

"Sell the manor!" Charlotte and Arianne cried together. "No! Then we shall truly have nothing!"

But their father seized on the notion. "Aye, we could sell and begin anew in America." Then he recalled himself and shook his head. "If I was to satisfy all I owe to the tradesman and to Trevaney, there'd not be naught so much as a penny left for passage."

Melisande sucked in her breath, then let it out slowly. "No," she said calmly, "this manor has been in this family since before the Restoration, Papa. And a gentleman must settle his gaming debts properly, mustn't he?"

"Aye, but—"

They were all looking at her incredulously. Taking a deep breath, she nodded. "There is no help for it— one of us must take Lord Trevaney. Papa, are you quite certain you did not name one of us?"

"Don't remember—don't think so," he muttered.

"Have you lost your mind, Mel?" Charlotte demanded furiously. "You know very well that my heart is already attached, and—"

"What's this, puss?" her father asked, rousing.

"Nothing, Papa," she said quickly.

"And do not be looking at me," Arianne added. "I should rather wed Satan than Lord Trevaney."

"Perhaps if his lordship had as much to drink as Charles, he will not remember this sordid matter," Mrs. Merriweather offered hopefully. "In that case, we shall merely have to pay him."

"We can't, Mama," Melisande reminded her. Looking to her siblings, she forced a crooked smile. "This is more than a matter of debt, you know. It is a matter of family honor. If Papa reneges, none of us shall be able to hold a head up before the world, and we might as well not attempt London."

"Sorry, puss—truly sorry."

"I should rather die of mortification rather than wed him," Charlotte insisted.

"Well, you will die a viscountess, in any event," Melisande said practically. "A viscountess able to help the rest of us."

"Mel!" the girl wailed.

"Fudge. Stuff. Besides, given his reputation for dallying with all sorts of females, I cannot think a bride won at the tables can be expected to engage his heart." Melisande went on, "I should think that once the heir is assured, he would be more than happy to leave you to your own amusements."

"Me! It should be you or Annie! At least you have no hopes to dash!"

"Charley, I will not!" the youngest girl shouted at her. "I should abhor being married to the lecher!"

"Girls, what have we come to?" Mrs. Merriweather asked feebly. "If Melisande has any notion, I am sure *I* am prepared to listen."

"I do, Mama. I propose we settle the matter by chance, with the loser taking Lord Trevaney. Suppose we find the broom, pluck straws, then compare them. We draw from the middle carefully, without bending or breaking the one we choose."

"And?"

"The shortest straw loses."

"Mel, have you lost your mind?" Charlotte demanded hotly. "I don't want Trevaney, I tell you! I shall take Mr. Pennyfoote only!"

"You will do no such thing, missy!" her father shouted at her. "The man's naught but a fortune hunter!"

"Well, if he is, he's brought his horse to the wrong pond, hasn't he?" Melisande pointed out dryly. "You know, Charley, he could be a dashed difficult husband when he discovers you have no money."

"Peverel loves me for myself!"

"Then why don't you tell him you have no hopes of Uncle Thorndike's money?" Arianne chimed in.

By now, her mother had digested the whole of her proposal and was beginning to accept the totality of her husband's loss. "Yes, well, it would solve a great deal, wouldn't it? Although I own I cannot like—" She caught herself and settled her shoulders. "Well, if he is any gentleman at all, which I am by no means disposed to believe, surely Lord Trevaney will wish to offer settlements to the family." She looked around her, then added hopefully, "Don't you think so?"

"Mama!" Charlotte appeared ready to weep. "I won't draw a straw—I cannot!"

"Well, I own I cannot like the connection at all myself, but I am told he is very rich," Mrs. Merriweather said. "And certainly if he is willing to take a penniless bride—"

"Mama, you cannot approve this!" Arianne protested.

"In the ordinary way of things, no, but it could be a practical solution to more than one coil, dearest. Besides, females of our class do not throw themselves away on nobodies. Your father may be a plain mister, but we at least may claim noble descent. And Mr. Pennyfoote is naught but nephew to Lady Washburton, who was a miller's daughter ere Sir Ralph elevated her."

Stung, Charlotte retorted, "Peverel is not a nobody!"

Ignoring her eldest, Mrs. Merriweather addressed Arianne again. "You will find the broom, Annie, if you please. And you, Charlotte, will draw first."

"Papa, *please*!"

"You got to do as your mama wants," he answered, brightening. "Good notion, if you was to ask me."

In no mood to be teased, Melisande took her morning chocolate in her bedchamber before coming down to a decidedly late breakfast. She'd scarce slept all night, a circumstance which did nothing to improve her disposition. Charley and Annie pulled out full broom straws, but hers had accidentally snapped, making it the shortest. She had gone to bed feeling truly cursed, and her headache this morning had done nothing to dispel the notion.

While she'd not been to London since her childhood and had never actually encountered Viscount Treva-

ney, her mind had formed a distinct impression of a
man raddled by dissipation, a stout fellow constrained
by corsets, no doubt, with a florid complexion from a
lifetime of drinking and carousing. But it did not matter if he were pockmarked and utterly disgusting, she
reminded herself resolutely. She had, to put it mildly,
been hoisted on her own petard. As she went downstairs, she considered trying to give him a disgust of
her, then discarded the notion as unworthy. No, she
could only hope he did not live forever.

"You look like death," Arianne told her as she took
her place at the table. "You'd best hope he does not
come today."

Charlotte looked up. "You do appear hagged, Mel."

"I've had no sleep."

"La, but I shall like having a viscountess for a sister," the older girl decided. "Perhaps Trevaney can
be persuaded to help Peverel obtain a commission."

"In what?" Mel asked sourly.

"Well, since we are no longer at war, Pev rather
fancies himself a dragoon. And I do like the uniform,"
the older girl conceded. Turning to Arianne, she murmured, "He would look dashing, don't you think?"

"I think Papa will never let you wed him."

"Well, if you make the brilliant marriage, I cannot
see why Papa would care."

"I don't think I could call it brilliant," Arianne said.
"I mean, it is one thing to be a viscountess, quite
another to have oneself tied to Lord Trevaney."

"Hopefully his lordship will have forgotten the
whole matter, and we have worried ourselves over
nothing," Melisande muttered. "Is there any jam
left?"

"There is no need to be hateful," Charlotte said
smugly. "After all, drawing straws was *your* idea."

"I expect we will discover Trevaney to be rather
old, and given the life he has led, mayhap he will die
while you are yet young enough to find another."

"I've no wish to discuss this," Mel muttered.

Realizing that they'd goaded her enough, they turned the subject. "Papa is still abed," Charlotte observed suddenly.

"Weasel-bit, no doubt."

"And Mama has gone to lie down again, saying she has the headache from last night."

"So do I." As soon as a manservant placed a plate of sausages on the table, Melisande reached to take one. Cutting it carefully, she carried a bite to her mouth.

At the front of the house, the iron knocker struck the heavy oak door. There was a muffled sound of voices, then Sack presented himself apologetically.

"Fellow's askin' ter see the master," he announced. "Said I was ter rouse him." Holding out the card, he squinted at it, then read aloud, "Gareth Ro-Rowland, I think."

"But we don't—oh, lud! Mel, could that be Trevaney?" Charlotte gasped.

At that, Melisande choked on the sausage, coughing until tears came to her eyes. "It—it cannot be," she managed when she caught her breath. "Surely not already."

But the footman studied the pasteboard rectangle at arm's length and added, "Tre—aye, 'tis Trevaney, it says." Seeing that they all stared, he hesitated. "D'ye think I oughter get the master?"

Melisande found her voice. "No. I expect Papa is either ill or still disguised." Sucking in her breath, she let it out slowly. "I shall see him."

"Mel, you cannot face him wearing that," Charlotte declared practically. "He'll bolt."

"Charley—"

"Well, you cannot. I mean, you are supposed to induce him to settle something on you, after all."

Arianne regarded Melisande critically for a moment, then agreed. "No, it will not do at all, Mel—not

at all. He will think you no more than a housemaid
in that. And you simply must do something with your
hair—I mean, you look like a wild schoolgirl."

"With my height?" Mel retorted. Nonetheless, she
felt an inner panic at the thought of facing Lord Trevaney. Time, she needed time to compose herself and
her thoughts, and yet she had almost none. Looking
down at her plain cotton sacque, she had to own that
it bespoke a poverty that would not serve the family
interest. She turned to the waiting footman. "Pray tell
his lordship that he shall be attended directly."

"I'll help with your hair," Arianne offered. "A
crown knot ought to improve it greatly."

"There's not enough time." Rising, Mel added, "I
cannot think it would serve anything to make Trevaney wait any longer than necessary."

"Well, at least wear the green satin stripe—it be-
comes you best!" Charlotte called after her.

"At least cover your hair!" Arianne insisted. "And
go up the back way that he will not see you ere you
are ready!"

In the small front saloon, the object of their distaste
sat surveying his surroundings with contempt. It was
as he'd suspected—everything from the worn carpet
to the faded paper fairly cried genteel poverty. If there
was anything worth more than a passing glance, it was
only the clock.

There was nothing worse in his books than a fellow
who gamed where he could not pay, and yet he'd sat
there and let Merriweather give him worthless paper
promises. Even then the fool had not known when to
stop, offering up his own flesh and blood for one last
chance to come up even.

He ought to have dangled the fellow for a day or
so to teach him a lesson, but there was always the
possibility that Merriweather would have put a ball in
his brain, laying yet another scandal at Gareth's door.

There was, after all, no way of telling what fools would do—the Featherstone chit was proof of that.

Miss Featherstone. Even though he could not remember her given name, he still felt a twinge of conscience whenever he thought of her. Hawkewood had called it his fatal charm, but it was nothing of the sort. How could he have possibly known that standing up for a minuet or two with the goose would have had such an effect on her? Perhaps he ought to have been kinder when she began writing romantic drivel to him, but he had little patience for silly females, and particularly not one scarce out of the schoolroom. If he had sinned at all, it was that he'd merely told her to leave him alone. The next morning she'd been discovered in her bedchamber hanging from a silk cord, a farewell note to him pinned on her nightgown.

He glanced irritably around the room once more. A few moments, the footman had promised. A few moments and he would be attended. Trevaney passed a weary hand over his eyes as though he could somehow wipe the cobwebs of excess from his mind. God, but he was tired, and his head ached like the devil from far too much wine. Drawing out his watch, he flicked the cover off and checked the time. Eleven o'clock, it said.

Where the deuce was Merriweather? He had not all day to wait on the man. Heaving himself up from the chair, he walked to stare out the window into the gray day. Absently, he loosened his neck cloth, letting the frilled shirt beneath hang open at his neck. No need to stand on ceremony, he decided. The man would no doubt be far too grateful to care about a piece of linen.

"Would yer lordship care fer—" The footman hesitated as Trevaney swung around impatiently, a frown marring his handsome face. "Fer coffee?" he finished lamely. As the viscount's scowl deepened, he added quickly, "Or there's port and a mite of hock ter be had, sir."

"Nothing, thank you. Just tell Merriweather I have not all the day, if you please."

There was no mistaking the clipped tone of Trevaney's voice. "Aye, sir," Sack responded promptly, "I'll tell 'im."

"In another ten minutes, I shall leave."

"Tell 'im that also, sir, I will."

Backing from the saloon, the footman turned and fairly ran up the stairs. For a moment he wondered if he ought not to attempt rousing the master. But as he paused at Mr. Merriweather's chamber, he could hear the sonorous rumbling of heavy snoring, and he knew he would not be thanked. Instead, he went to rap at Miss Melisande's door.

"Ten minutes he's giving her," he said as Bess, the maid the mistress and girls shared, peeped out.

"Well, she ain't done, Will, and that's all there is to it."

"In the devil's own taking, he is, and he ain't a cove ter wait, or my name's not Will Sack."

The door opened wider, providing the veriest glimpse of white-stockinged legs about to be swallowed in voluminous petticoats. As the starched garments settled over the whalebone hoops, Miss Melisande's fiery head appeared, then her white shoulders. Will couldn't help himself—gulping, he gawked at the swell of her holland-covered bosom. Gor, but them as favored the delicate ones was fools, he decided. Bess caught his rapt expression and slammed the door in his face.

Having heard him, Mel searched frantically for her stomacher, then held it to her chest while Bess quickly threw the green gown over her head and threaded the rolled satin cords over the starched stomacher. Her heart pounding in her ears, she sought her kid slippers with her toes, wriggled into them, then headed for the door.

"Wait—yer hair!" the maid wailed. "We got ter put it up fer ye!"

"There is no time—he'll be leaving," Mel said over her shoulder.

It wasn't until she had nearly reached the bottom of the stairs that she looked down and discovered she'd forgotten to tuck a lace fichu into the crevice between her breasts for modesty. Torn between fleeing and brazening it out, she half turned to retreat quickly when she heard the saloon door open. She spun around as the tall gentleman looked up at her, and her breath caught painfully in her chest. She gaped at him.

"You—you cannot be Lord Trevaney!" she choked out, her hand covering her breasts.

Two things crossed his mind at once. She had hair like spun copper, and she was almost as tall as he was. Inclining his head slightly, he murmured apologetically, "Unfortunately so, I'm afraid."

"Oh, but—"

He thought the blush became her. "Alas, but my sad rep precedes me, I see," he lamented.

"Yes."

"And if half of it were true, I must surely be nigh to dead?"

"I shouldn't say that, precisely," she managed.

"But you have thought it."

"Yes." She knew he was amusing himself at her expense, but being missish now would not serve. She sucked in her breath, then let it out slowly. "My lord, I am Melisande Merriweather, and, uh, if you do not mind it, I should like to be private with you for a moment." As one black eyebrow lifted quizzically, she could feel her face grow hotter. "Please—in the saloon, I think."

An unholy light warmed his dark eyes. "Private? You find me intrigued, Miss Merriweather."

"Well, I can scarce be expected to conduct any business in the hall, sir," she retorted stiffly.

He stood aside to let her pass, then followed her back into the small room. "Would you prefer to sit?" he inquired politely.

"No." She wiped damp hands on her wide silk shirt and eyed him cautiously. He was not what she'd expected, not at all, and she needed time to collect her thoughts, to think what she should say to him. "Er— would you care for some tea, perhaps?"

"No. Actually, I have come to speak with your father."

"Yes, I know, but Papa is rather unwell today, you see, and—"

She moved away, then turned back to look at him. He was perhaps the handsomest man she'd yet seen, possessed of dark brown eyes, an utterly arresting countenance, and a tall, well-proportioned frame. And with his ruffled shirt open and his black hair tied at the nape of his neck, there was an air of recklessness about him that drew her.

Aware that he waited, she took yet another deep breath, let it out, then declared baldly, "I'm afraid, Lord Trevaney, that I am your prize." When it looked as though he might speak, she went on hastily, "Please, let me finish, I beg of you. I know I am two years past a London Season, for I was twenty last June, but Papa has had little money to send me or my sisters. And I am well aware that I am overtall, but there is no help for that. As for my hair, I have tried lemon water to lighten and boiled walnut bark to darken it, but 'tis determined to be naught but red. I do however have a modicum of accomplishments." Taking a quick breath, she plunged on, adding, "I watercolor miserably, sing indifferently, and play the harpsicord without a great deal of enthusiasm."

Her chin came up and her blue eyes dared to meet his. "On the other side of the coin, I read Latin and French tolerably, am versed in the classics, and I have a mathematical inclination. And as I have lost the draw, I am obliged to offer my hand and person to you as a matter of honor. Moreover, as long as you expect nothing more than your heir from me, I shall not object to your—your fancy pieces— providing you behave with discretion," she declared, blushing furiously. "There—I have touched upon everything, I think."

There was a pregnant silence, punctuated only by the loud ticking of the clock. "Well," she demanded finally, "aren't you going to say something?"

For answer, he regarded her lazily, letting his eyes sweep from her thick red mane to her kid-clad feet, lingering ever so briefly on the low-cut bosom of her dress, then returning to her face. One corner of his mouth twitched as he fought down a smile.

"Despite your rather—er—compelling presentation, Miss Merriweather, I am afraid I must decline."

"Decline?" she said, obviously relieved. "Well, then I suppose I ought also to tell you that neither of my sisters is wishful of wedding you. Charley would rather die of mortification, and Annie says she would prefer the devil."

"Wise of them," he murmured, his mouth twisting wryly. "I expect I should make a miserable husband."

"And I suspect you are funning with me, sir," she retorted. "You cannot like my height or my hair, which is quite all right with me."

"Not at all. In fact, I think it would be unfortunate if your hair were to change color; I have not the least objection to tall females; I abhor watercolors, dislike sitting through poor musical presentations, and enjoy the classics also. But I have absolutely no interest in a wife who intends to give me carte blanche to pursue other females, nor am I wishful of one whose mathematical calculations are directed at my purse."

"Your purse?" For a moment, she was taken aback, then she found her voice. "Oh, of all the—" Her blue eyes flashed briefly, displaying her temper. "Lord Trevaney, you surely do not believe I would wish to wed with you?" she asked sarcastically. "Had papa not lost our money—and had I not gotten the wrong straw—you are without doubt the last man I should want! I abhor shameless libertines, if you would have the truth, sir—and you had no right to stand there, letting me throw myself at you!"

"Throwing yourself at me?" he repeated incredulously. "You call that pitiful speech throwing yourself at me?"

"Yes—or at least I tried! But you stood there amusing yourself whilst I attempted the matter."

"Miss Merriweather, I have had my share of importuning females, I assure you, but yours was the most over-the-left-shoulder proposition I have gotten in my life. Never have I experienced such an unenthusiastic and wholly unconvincing effort."

"Because I lost the draw! What would you expect?"

"Passion."

"Passion?" she echoed blankly. "Oh, 'tis coming it too strong, it is! With your rep, 'twas all I could do to choke out my words, sir!"

"Well, if you must speak of mathematics and watercolors, you are sadly lacking." Reaching beneath his coat, he drew out wadded, wrinkled bits of paper. "No, if I were inclined to wed, I should choose fire over mathematics any day, my dear." Opening her hand, he thrust them into it, then closed her fingers. "Fire," he repeated softly, looking into her bright blue eyes.

Before she had the least notion what he meant to do, his hands slid up her arms, drawing her nearer. Her eyes widened with shock, then closed quickly as she felt his warm breath on her cheek, but nothing in her life had prepared her for the intensity of his kiss. His lips were hot, demanding, stifling her feeble protest, taking her very breath away. A shiver coursed down her spine, chased by the heat that rose within her. For a moment, she held her fists clenched tightly at her sides, but as his mouth possessed hers, her father's gambling vowels scattered at her feet. She caught his waist to steady herself, then struggled to push him away.

As suddenly as he'd kissed her, he released her and stepped back. "That, Miss Merriweather, was but a taste of fire," he whispered, "and you cannot deny you liked it."

"You, sir, are no gentleman!" she spat at him.

"La, Mel, but whatever—?"

Whatever Charlotte had intended to say died on her lips as she stared at Trevaney. Her face flaming, Melisande brushed past her, not daring to turn back before she reached the safety of the door. Holding the door frame, she declared, her voice strangling, "Pigs will fly, sir, ere I should ever again consider allying myself with you!" Then she fled up the stairs.

"Well, I cannot think what—that is, she is never given to freaks of temper . . ." Charlotte's voice trailed off uncertainly as she looked at him.

But he was staring oddly after Melisande. Then he sighed and reached to pick up his hat. A faint smile played on his lips as he turned to her. "Which one are you, I wonder? The one who'd prefer death—or the one who'd choose Satan?" he murmured. Setting the hat at a raffish angle over his black hair, he let his smile broaden. "Make my apologies to Miss Merriweather, will you? Tell her I was mistaken about the fire."

With that, he left her standing there. Looking down, Charlotte saw the scattered bits of paper, then bent to gather them in her full skirt. Turning one over, she could see that they were her father's gambling vowels. Still holding them in her skirt, she ran upstairs.

"Mel! Annie! Mama!" At Melisande's door, she rapped loudly, then slipped inside. "Lud, Mel, but what happened? Look, he left Papa's vouchers!"

But Melisande was watching at the window as the viscount emerged into the gray day, then mounted a sleek black horse.

"You aren't attending me, Mel," Charlotte chided.

"Be still, my treacherous heart," Arianne said, coming into the room behind her. "That cannot have been Trevaney—it cannot have been."

Melisande turned around. "It was."

"But he is—is"—Annie groped for a word, then settled on—"beautiful!" Recovering, she went to the heart of the matter. "Well? Is he going to wed you?"

"No, Annie, I have managed to escape."

"Escape?" As the import of Mel's words sank in, the younger girl's face fell. "Then we are not going to London? We are still ruined?"

"Trevaney left Papa's vowels," Charlotte spoke up. "Though why, I am sure I do not know."

"He gave them to me," Mel said tiredly. "He let me make a complete fool of myself, then he gave them to me."

"Charlotte, whatever is this nonsense? You have nearly brought down the house with your unseemly—" Mrs. Merriweather stopped. "Gave what to you, Melisande?"

"Papa's vowels. Please, I have the headache from no sleep, and I should like to lie down."

But her mother was not easily deterred. "He gave them to you? Oh, you dearest, dearest child! I vow I am cast into transports! But why did you not summon your papa? There are settlements to be discussed, arrangements to be made, and—"

"He didn't take her, Mama," Charlotte said.

"He didn't take her! Well, I am sure I do not know whether to be in alt or the pits of hell! This certainly is not what I would have wished for her, of course, but—" She caught herself, then looked to Melisande. "Why ever not?"

"I botched it," Mel answered dryly. "I spoke of Latin when he wished for passion."

"Passion! Well, of all the indecent—"

"Please, Mama—I am very tired."

"But he did give you your papa's notes, didn't he? Well, at least that means we shall be able to go to London," Mrs. Merriweather recalled, brightening. Peering more closely at her middle daughter, she nodded. "Yes, you do look a trifle hagged, dearest. Perhaps I ought to send Bess up with a tisane for you."

"I just need to sleep."

"She wants rid of us, Mama," Charlotte murmured, going to hold the door. As the other two passed into the hall, she turned back to Melisande. "He said the oddest thing, you know—he said to tell you he was mistaken about the fire, whatever that means."

"I have not the least notion," Mel lied.

As soon as the door closed, she lay down on her bed and stared at the ceiling. She ought to be gratified that Trevaney did not want her, she told herself. But as she recalled the scene, she could not help remembering the feel of his arms around her. Her hands crept to her lips, and her eyes closed as she relived the heat of his kiss.

"Psssst—Mel!"

She rolled over in the dark and covered her head with her arm.

"Are you awake? Mel, Charley's gone!"

"Huh?"

"I said Charley's gone—she's bolted!"

Melisande sat up at that, then rubbed at her eyes. "Oh, 'tis you, Annie."

"Did you not hear me? I said Charley's bolted!"

"What time is it?" Mel asked sleepily.

"Past midnight. You slept through supper, you know."

"My head hurts worse than ever."

"Did you not hear me? I said Charley's bolted."

"What? Don't be a goose, Annie!"

"Shhh—not so loud." Pulling a chair closer, the younger girl held out a piece of paper. "Here—you'll see. Wait, and I'll get you some light so you can read it."

When Arianne returned with a nearly guttered candle, Melisande held up the note and tired to decipher it. "Not Charley's hand, Annie," she muttered. But as she read, her stomach knotted.

"Dearest darling Miss Merriweather," it began, followed by, "Every day I am desolate without your joyous presence to lighten my life. You must say you will make me the happiest of men and come away with me. I shall await you tonight at the RR." It was signed, "Yours evermore, P."

"Where did you find this?"

"It was on her writing desk. But wait, there's another." Very carefully, she smoothed out a half sheet for Melisande. "Look at this."

"Dearest Papa, when you read this, Mr. Pennyfoote and myself will be on our way to being wed. I know you will be vexed, but I am convinced that Peverel and I were destined for each other. I pray you will forgive and wish us happy." The wretch had ended with "Yr Obedient Daughter, Charlotte."

"Mel, there are clothes strewn everywhere, and her cloak and walking boots are missing! I would have wakened Papa, but I knew he would be in such a taking. Do you think perhaps Mama ought to tell him?"

"The goose—the silly goose!" Mel muttered. "No, if 'tis only midnight, I daresay they may still be there. I cannot think they will travel before dawn."

"But how could she have gotten there?"

"She probably walked—'tis not too far, after all."

Throwing back her covers, Melisande rose quickly and tore across the room to her wardrobe, where she yanked her heavy wool habit from the hook. Pulling a plain waist over her head, she drew on the habit skirt, then the jacket. Her nimble fingers flew, fastening the braided frogs over the cotton waist. Without bothering to tie her stock, she rummaged in the bottom of the cabinet for her riding boots.

"Mel, you cannot go after her!" Alarmed, Arianne threatened, "I'll have to tell Papa!"

"If Papa goes, she'll not be able to sit for a fortnight, and well you know it. Besides, I dare not think what he'd do to Pennyfoote," Mel added under her breath. "And I'd not see him hang for putting a ball into the coxcomb."

"But 'tis dark! And what if you are accosted?"

"At this hour? In the country? Besides, I'm going to ride, so I will merely leave the road and take the fields."

"I'm going to waken Mama."

"No, you are not. If I am successful, I mean to bring Charley home and put her to bed. Then there's none but us to be any the wiser, do you understand?"

"But—"

Her boots on, Melisande stood. "Promise you'll not say anything ere morning, Annie."

"Mel—"

"Word of a Merriweather."

"But—"

"Word of a Merriweather," Melisande repeated sternly. "Otherwise, Papa is going to make hell on earth for Charley."

"I know, but what if something happens to you? I should never forgive myself."

"It won't." Catching her sister by both shoulders, Melisande stared the younger girl down. "Look at me—ten to one, I shall be mistaken for a man in the dark."

"In a sidesaddle?" the other girl countered timidly.

"Astride. A sedate pace serves nothing." Leaning forward, Melisande brushed her lips against Annie's cheek. "If you want to do something, pray that I find her before 'tis too late. Now, go back to bed as though nothing has happened." As she spoke, she picked up her winter cloak and threw it over her shoulder.

"Papa was right," Annie observed as Mel opened the door. "He said you ought to have been a boy."

"Nonsense."

Once out in the dark hall, Melisande felt her way along the wall to the back stairs, then crept down them, and let herself outside. Cold air hit her, clearing any lingering sleep from her head. Pulling her cloak about her, she walked quickly to the small stable, her boots crunching on frosted grass. Above her, clouds hung on the cusp of a crescent moon.

The stable door creaked on rusty hinges, opening to a dark, musty interior. Cursing the lack of a lantern, Melisande whistled softly. And one of the horses moved within a stall.

" 'Tis only I, Algy," she whispered, feeling gingerly along the rough wood until she touched the horse's hard, bony nose. "Good boy." Her hand found the latch, then slid upward seeking the bridle on the peg. Letting herself in, she spoke softly as she slipped the bit into his mouth and fastened the bridle over his head.

"Come on, fellow, 'tis time we rode," she told him, drawing him outside. Bracing herself on a gate rung, she swung a leg awkwardly over the animal's back, struggled to straighten her skirt as best she could, pulled her cloak more tightly about her shoulders, and nudged the animal forward into the lane.

When they reached the main road, she lay low against the wind and gave the horse his head. It responded eagerly, taking the muddy, rutted road with a steady, pounding gallop that sent Melisande's cloak flying out behind her.

The colder she got, the angrier Mel got at Charlotte

for being so utterly, totally stupid. When she found her, she intended to ring a peal the idiot would not soon forget. And on the way back, no matter how much she protested, Charley was going to sit behind.

The raw wind bit into her skin and whipped the hood back from her face, tangling her hair wildly. Her eyes watered and her nose ran as she hunched lower, hoping that Charlotte had nearly frozen herself to pay for her perfidy.

The inn appeared ahead, its painted ram's head swinging in the wind, its upper windows shuttered against the cold. Above it, the weathercock twisted nervously, as though it did not know which way to go. In the stable behind, a horse neighed, and an ostler sleepily called out to silence it.

Above the door, a lantern, its horned chimney panes nearly black from smoke, flickered a valiant yellow to show any laggard travelers the way. As Melisande's eyes took in the lower windows apprehensively, she could see the faint glow of light inside. At least there was still someone to be found in the taproom, someone who might know if Charlotte was there.

She swung down from Algy and tied the big horse to the iron ring on one of the posts. Straightening her habit over her cold legs, she pushed her hair back from her face and strode to the door. Pushing on the latch, she opened it and stepped inside, where the smoky warmth enveloped her.

If Charlotte and Pennyfoote were indeed there, then what? She could scarce burst into a bedchamber, and if she asked for her sister, she might well cause that which she wished to prevent. Too much of a scandal and they'd be obliged to wed, anyway. She hesitated as she heard the voices in the taproom.

"Alas, but what a fickle dame is Fortune," Trevaney murmured, tossing down his hand. As Hawkewood raked in his winnings, Gareth rose and stretched.

"And I have never been fool enough to court any reluctant female, Ned, so I shall merely go to bed."

"But you've scarce lost a hundred, Gary—'tis a pittance to you," his friend protested.

"Ah, but now you know how 'tis done." Trevaney leaned over and lowered his voice as though he would share something of import. "Never let yourself get so far down that you must play to survive, old fellow. Always wait until the old girl comes back on her own." Straightening, he yawned.

"You going to bed already? Surely not!"

"There's naught much else to do in a damned country inn, is there? If the roads are not sufficiently dried by morning, I damn well may try them anyway."

"Poor Gary—in the middle of nowhere without so much as a wench to warm you," Ned murmured sympathetically.

Picking up a nearly full bottle of burgundy, Trevaney turned to go upstairs. Then he saw Melisande Merriweather standing in the foyer. Her face was ruddy from the cold, her hair windblown and tangled. As he watched, he saw her pull her cloak hood up to cover it, shadowing her face. Moving quickly to intercept her before Hawkewood noticed her, he caught her arm and pushed her into a private parlor, where the dying embers of an earlier fire glowed eerily in the darkness.

"Lord Trevaney! What—?"

Before she could finish, he clamped a hand over her mouth and whispered, "For God's sake, keep your silence."

"Mmmmumph!"

"Shhhhh."

"Gary? Gary?" Hawkewood called querulously. "Where the devil did you go? Gary—" He stood in front of the half-opened parlor door and listened. "Must've gone on up," he decided finally. "Odd though—thought I heard voices." Shaking his head, he muttered, "Damned wind, I guess."

Trevaney waited until he could hear the other man's footsteps overhead, then he released her. "What an unexpected surprise," he murmured.

"What do you think you are doing?" she demanded, pushing back her hood.

"I could easily ask the same of you," he countered. "I suppose I ought to be flattered, but I am still not in the market for a wife."

"Oh, of all the—" she choked out. "Listen, you arrogant lecher, if you think I have come to see you, you are way wide of the mark," she told him haughtily. "If you must know, I am looking for someone else." But as she said it, she had to sniff back her running nose, ruining the effect of her words.

"At this hour?" he gibed. "Coming it too strong, my dear.

"Have you seen Mr. Pennyfoote?"

"Ah, I see. Though quite frankly, you disappoint me—I should never have guessed you held a tendre for such a little man."

"A tendre?" Her voice rose incredulously. "Do not be absurd—I should rather die than look twice at him," she snapped.

"Do all the Merriweather females express themselves so dramatically," he asked curiously.

"No, but I count Mr. Pennyfoote no more than a fortune hunter." Taking a step back from him, she asked more civilly, "Well, *have* you seen him?"

"I thought he left to go upstairs about an hour or so ago."

Not wanting to tell Trevaney everything, she sucked in her breath for courage, then let it out quickly. "I do not suppose you would mind discovering if he is alone, would you?"

He was about to say something cutting, but then he saw the anxiety in her face. Having opened his mouth, he shut it for a moment. "No, Miss Merriweather, I will not," he said finally.

"Then I suppose I must waken the innkeeper."

She made no sense, none at all. "You'll be ruined," he declared brutally. "Absolutely ruined just by being here. I suggest you return home before you are discovered."

"But I must find my sister—I must find Charlotte!" Knowing he had to think everyone in her family insane, she dared to meet his gaze. "She believes she loves Mr. Pennyfoote, you see, and they are eloping. I must get her home ere she ruins her future, my lord—I must!"

"And what of your own rep? Surely—"

"As I am not like to get a suitable offer, anyway, I cannot see that it matters. But Charlotte—Charlotte is the beauty, and all of Papa's hopes are in her." When he said nothing, she lifted her chin almost defiantly. "It is none of your affair, anyway, so I am sorry to have asked you." Moving toward the door, she pushed it further open. "Perhaps if you directed me to his chamber—"

Impressed by her determination, he sighed. All right," he conceded grudgingly. "Though being the irate rescuer is a rather unusual role for me, I'll attempt it."

"Tell her that I will do all in my power to see Papa knows nothing of this."

"Wait in your coach, and if I discover her, I'll bring her down to you." When she did not move, he snapped irritably, "Go on."

"I don't have a coach."

"Then how the devil did you get here?"

"I rode a horse." Seeing that he clearly disbelieved her, she retorted, "Well, I thought it rather cold to walk. At least on that head I am not quite so stupid as Charley."

"You'll die of a lung inflammation," he predicted direly. "How will I know I have found the right wigeon?"

"I told you—she is the family beauty, possessed of golden hair, and—"

"There are beauties everywhere," he said impatiently. "While I am gone, don't leave this room."

As he went up the steps, she moved to the fireplace, where she stared into the glowing embers. Beneath the heavy cloak, she rubbed her cold arms, trying to warm them. Overhead, she could hear Trevaney pound on one of the doors, then the disgruntled shouts of those he'd awakened. She listened intently for Charlotte's indignant screeching, but heard none. At least she wasn't making a greater fool of herself.

Then there were quick steps coming down, and he was back. "They are not here," he said tersely. " 'Twould seem Pennyfoote fled as soon as he departed the taproom. And apparently his groom could have been your sister, for he arrived with one and left with two."

"I see," she said heavily. "Did—did any see their direction?"

"Unless I mistake me, they are most likely headed for Scotland." Her expression was so utterly cast down that he actually felt sorry for her. "Come on—I'll see you home."

She shook her head. "I have to find her. And they cannot have gotten very far, can they? 'Tis dark and cold and the roads are poor."

He nodded. "I expect the fools will be mired ere they are ten miles."

"Yes, of course." Pulling up her hood again, she started to leave him. "Well, in any event, I must thank you for inquiring for me."

"Are all the Merriweathers idiots?" he demanded harshly.

"You have no right—"

"Oh? Your father bets his flesh and blood where he cannot win, your sister runs off with an improvident

pink, and you—you, Miss Merriweather, have ventured out alone on a winter's night without so much
as a by-your-leave to anyone!''

"Good night, sir," she responded stiffly.

He caught her arm again, pulling her back into the small
parlor. "I said I would see you home, and I shall. You will
sit down at this table, and you will wait whilst I fetch my
cloak and send out to roust my driver."

"It is unnecessary, my lord."

"No, as much as I regret to admit it, Miss Merriweather, common decency requires it. Sit down."

"You must be foxed," she muttered under her breath.

"Not nearly enough."

She waited only until he'd left, then she bolted for the
door and let herself out. As the roads were worse for a
carriage than for a single horse, she felt she had a fair
chance of catching Charley and Mr. Pennyfoote ere they
spent the whole night together. Grasping Algy's
reins, she stepped onto the mounting stone, pulled up
her wide riding skirt, and flung herself onto the beast's
back. Flicking the leather ribbons lightly against the
horse's neck, she nudged it away from the post.

Letting it canter easily through the narrow village
street, she waited until she got to the north road before
she dug her booted heel into its flank. She had to spare
him, she knew, but she also knew she had to hurry.

The bitter, biting wind caught her skirt, lifting it,
freezing her legs above her boots. If she were a man,
she'd roundly curse Charley for this escapade, she told
herself. Drawing her knees up, she tried to push the
heavy wool down and pin it with her limbs to no avail.
Her teeth chattered from the cold that seemed to possess her very bones.

The road was dark and eerily deserted, as though
everyone in the world avoided it but her. They could
not get far, Trevaney had said, but there was no sound
of them, none at all. Somewhere in the distance, a
hound bayed, sending a shiver down her spine.

Then she heard a carriage, not in front, but behind her. She kicked harder, but Algy was tiring, dropping into a bone-jarring trot. The coach passed, splattering mud on her cloak and boots, then rolled to a halt a few yards beyond her, forcing her to rein in.

The door opened, and Viscount Trevaney jumped down. Scowling angrily, he caught Algy's bridle, yanking the reins from Melisande's hands. His eyes flashed eerily, reflecting the faint moonlight, as he reached for her waist and dragged her down.

"Get in," he said curtly. "You are nigh frozen."

"Y-you have no-no right t-to—"

Her words died as he grasped her elbow, thrusting her toward his carriage. Without ceremony, he threw her through the door, then went back for the horse. She had landed half off the padded leather seat, half on the muddy floor, her boots tangled in the wide wool skirt of her habit. With an effort, she managed to struggle to sit.

"B-but I h-have to find Char-Charlotte!" she called after him. "And y-you have no right to st-stop me!"

He didn't answer as he led Algy behind the coach. When he returned, he swung his tall body up and into the seat across from her. Leaning to shut the door, he ordered his driver to turn back.

"N-no!"

He regarded her balefully, saying nothing, as the carriage teetered precariously while the driver made a narrow turn.

"Wh-where's my h-horse?"

"Tied behind," he responded tersely.

The carriage lamp beside him smoked, and the sway of the carriage made the flame flicker, chasing shadows above its yellow glow. He pulled his hat forward, then sat back, his face barely discernible in the faint light.

"You s-said they c-cannot have g-gone ten miles!" she stammered out.

He did not answer.

"S-she'll b-be ruined!"

Nothing.

"P-please!"

Clearly he did not mean to listen. Defeated, she pulled her cloak closer about her, trying to wrap everything from her shivering shoulders to her boots within its folds. Turning her head against the seat, she drew up her knees, seeking an elusive warmth.

"I don't know which of us is the greater fool," he muttered finally. "By the right of it, I ought to have let you freeze yourself to death."

"Why d-didn't y-you?"

"Why didn't you wait?"

"B-because I knew y-you wouldn't g-go after Ch-Charlotte!" As she spoke, she had to sniff. "If 'twas y-your sister's r-rep—"

"Don't chatter!" he snapped. He reached into his pocket and drew out a lawn handkerchief. "Here—blow your nose."

"I c-cannot h-help it!" Taking the cloth, she blew loudly, then wadded it in her hand. "M-my t-thanks."

"Come here."

"H-huh?"

"I said to come here."

"I w-will not! I—I—d-don't—"

Exhaling his disgust, he grasped the pull and lurched across to her seat, where he tugged at the tassels on her cloak. Shocked, she stiffened and tried to move away.

"Don't be a complete ninny." Loosening the outer garment, he pulled it away, then he lifted his own. Reaching out, he grasped her shoulder, dragging her back against him. As she struggled, he folded both garments around them. "Sit still, will you?"

"No!"

"Now's a damnable time to get missish," he said, settling his arm around her shivering shoulders. "Believe me, Miss Merriweather, just now I do not feel the least inclined to seduction. But I will not have your death laid at my door, thank you," he added sarcastically.

" 'Tis n-not meet," she protested.

"You are like ice. Here—lean against me." When she did not move, he wrapped his arms tightly about her, effectively forcing her against his chest. "We've got to get you warm before you are made sick from your own folly."

Admitting to herself that she was overmatched, she ceased struggling and sat as still as her shaking body would let her. Gradually her nervousness receded, replaced by a curious sense of forbidden closeness. Never in her life had she been held like that by any man, not even her father, and she was acutely aware of the soft wool of his coat, the tickle of his lace-ruffled shirt against her cheek, the slight roughness of his cheek, the warmth of his breath as it intermingled with hers, the steady beat of his heart. But most of all she was surprised by the hardness of his shoulder and chest. And by the warmth of his body.

Embarrassed by her own thoughts, she lapsed into silence as the cold ebbed slowly from her. Finally, he shifted her weight slightly but did not release her. "Feeling more the thing, Miss Merriweather?"

"Actually, I was thinking how my cat must feel," she murmured.

"Your cat?" he asked, taken aback.

"Have you never held a cat against its will, sir? It will tolerate the treatment, but run as soon as it perceives it can escape."

"I much prefer dogs myself, Miss Merriweather," he countered. "They will lie still until pushed away."

"Alas, but I suspect females are more like cats."

"Claws and spit? Or devious?"

"I should rather think them clever."

"Like your sister?" he gibed. As soon as he said it,

he wished he hadn't. "Your pardon, Miss Merri-weather. Not knowing her, I should not have presumed."

She was silent for a moment, then conceded, "Actually, Charley *is* a bit of a wigeon."

"Charley?"

"Charlotte. Charlotte Maria Louisa Corisande Merriweather, to be precise. God aid that she should not add Pennyfoote to it."

"Egad."

She couldn't resist smiling. "Well, Mama used to be of a romantical nature, so we are named for her fancies. My sister Annie was christened Arianne Philomena Diana Catherine Merriweather, if you can believe it."

"And Melisande?"

"Actually, I have probably got the worst of it. Papa's fortunes were declining when I came into the world, so I am Melisande Thomasina Thorndike Merriweather. My sisters do call me Mel, however."

"Thorndike is rather unfeminine, I should think," he murmured, trying to keep a straight face.

"Ah, but my father's maternal uncle is Thomas Thorndike, you see, and since every farthing that crosses his fingertips tends to stay with him, he is quite rich. Not that we shall ever see any of his money, no matter what Mama chooses to believe."

"Why not?"

"Having suffered disappointment of one in his youth, he hates females."

The corners of his mouth twitched. "I cannot say I altogether blame him."

"Well, we are not all cut of the same cloth, my lord. Not that he knows it, for despite my being named for him, he merely sent two pounds to my christening." She sighed expressively. "And I should have preferred to be an Elizabeth or Anne or even Catherine. But I suppose it was my hair that gave Mama her hopes."

"Oh?"

"Uncle Thorndike had red hair also, but the resemblance ends there, I'm afraid. He is rather short and squat." She paused a moment, then added, "I am warm now, Lord Trevaney."

"And I am quite comfortable."

"Well, no doubt Lady—" She bit back her words. "That is—"

"If you meant Lady Larchmont, I can tell you that bit of gossip was just that—malicious speculation and no more. And I met Lady Standish's husband over an insult, not her."

"Well, I had heard—"

"But you ought not repeat it. However, now that you have brought it out, all I can say is that Larchmont was the fool. Had he waited until the infant ceased looking like a raisin, he would have discovered a distinct resemblance to himself."

"Oh."

"While I've not lived a monkish life, Miss Merriweather, even I must find it difficult to live up to the rep I am given."

"I suppose foolish females pursue you."

"Without mercy," he answered dryly. "It is, alas, the price of a title and a handsome purse."

"Not to mention a handsome face, I expect," she murmured. She longed to ask of Miss Featherstone, but knew that would be beyond the bounds of civility. It had been quite bad enough to nearly mention Lady Larchmont.

This time, when she sat up, he let her go and returned to his own seat, making her think she'd angered him. She turned her body and laid her head against the padded leather seat, drawing her cloak up over her shoulder. Once again, silence filled the small space between them.

She must've finally dozed, for when she awakened, he'd stretched his long legs out, resting his booted feet on the seat beside her. When she looked up, he was regarding her lazily.

"You know, most females of my acquaintance would have it by now that I am obliged to wed them."

She sat up at that. "Well, I should think an unwilling husband would be the next thing to a curse. And the same could be said for an unwilling wife, don't you expect?"

"Perceptive of you," he acknowledged. "Unfortunately, my experience leads me to believe that women will do anything to share my title."

"I should rather have my husband's regard." She hesitated, then blurted out, " 'Tis why I must find Charlotte, my lord—Mr. Pennyfoote believes her to be an heiress when she is not. And she believes he loves her. Can you not think what that marriage would be when both are found out?"

"Rather bitter, I should think."

"Yes."

His eyes were intent on hers, his expression quite odd for a moment, then he looked away. "You were willing to wed me yesterday."

"That was a matter of family honor, my lord. And there would have been no pretense between us, for you would have been collecting a just debt."

"And you, Miss Merriweather? Would you have truly gone through with the marriage?"

"I told you—we drew straws to determine which one of us should accept you. And I lost," she answered simply.

He stared out his window into the darkness. "My father hated my mother," he said slowly. " 'Twas because her father lied to him."

"That must have been a burden to you," she said softly.

"Yes." Abruptly, he sat up and pounded the ceiling of his coach to get his driver's attention. The carriage slowed, then his coachman leaned over the side.

Opening his door, Trevaney shouted, "Turn 'round! We are bound for Scotland!" Relatching it, he leaned back. His mouth twisting wryly, he looked at Melisande. "I hope we can still catch them."

"The roads—"

"Are wretched," he finished for her. "But you are within the best that Weddington Carriage Works has to offer, and we are pulled by a team of four, whilst Pennyfoote has but a post chaise and pair. If we can make it to the toll road, we ought to be able to go all the way to Scotland, if we have to."

"Surely we can overtake them before then," she said faintly. "I mean, I don't want her to have spent a whole night with him."

"Ten to one, they'll be mired in mud before they reach the tollbooth," he reassured her. "But they have a start on us, so in worst case, we ought to at least be able to stop the marriage."

"I hope so."

"If she is underage, they cannot wed before the border," he said bracingly.

"She is one and twenty."

"Oh." He exhaled heavily. "Yes, well, that does put a different complexion on the matter, doesn't it?"

"Yes. Do you still think they are for Scotland?"

"I don't know."

For a moment, she was afraid he meant to turn back again, but instead, he looked out the window. "I'll give it to the next posting house," he decided. "If they have passed there, we'll go on. If not, we are out."

"Thank you, my lord."

At first it seemed that he hadn't heard her, but then he spoke. "I would not wish my mother's fate on anyone, Miss Merriweather."

She longed to ask him what happened to her, but could not. As if he heard her thoughts, he spoke, his voice low. "For years I thought she was naught but a silly, foolish creature like the rest of her sex," he said finally. "Her life was but one of endless diversions—her dogs, her needlework, her cards, her gossipy friends—everything but her family, it seemed to me. It was not until she died, and my father could not tear himself away from London long enough to bury her, that I read her diaries and realized how empty it all was to her."

"Did she love him?"

He snorted derisively. "If she did, there was no solace in it. For whatever love she bore him, she had but me and her empty title to show for it. My father, on the other hand, kept more mistresses than I could count."

"And because of what was between them, they could not love the child they brought into this world," she said quietly.

"I have no need for pity, Miss Merriweather," he responded coldly. "The fault was his, not mine."

" 'Twas not pity I offered, Lord Trevaney. 'Twas commiseration." Reaching out, she dared to touch his hand. "Though not nearly so marked by it, I have oft felt—wrongly so, I think—that my parents have been inclined to regard me less, for I was born in the middle. Charlotte was their miracle, and Arianne their babe, you see."

" 'Tis scarce the same."

"And so I said. In my case, it was but the feeling. Unlike the others, I have never been petted or cosseted, and I have always been the one expected to have common sense."

His strong, warm fingers closed over hers. "I'd say you have it."

"No, not really. If I did, I should not be here. If I did not believe there to be more than Pennyfootes in this world, I'd have stayed home in bed. I fear I have a rather romantical disposition, you see."

"So you have risked contracting an inflammation of

the lungs, for which you will not be thanked," he observed, smiling again.

"You make me sound noble, when I am not," she murmured, retrieving her hand. "There is the matter of Papa also. He quite depends on Charlotte making the grand match in London."

"And now we are returned to the sensible Miss Merriweather," he chided.

"Well, if Charley does not truly love Mr. Pennyfoote, then she should see if there is someone who will value her for herself, don't you think?"

"Indubitably."

"Now you are funning with me, but I do not mind it," she admitted, smiling also.

"I suppose the local squire's son has a corner of your heart, Melisande?" He asked casually.

"Hardly." Her smile twisted ruefully. "I am a good three inches taller than both of his sons—in fact, they think me naught but an Amazon."

"I don't think you are an Amazon at all."

At that moment, they hit a deep rut, then bounced into the mud. The coach teetered precariously before coming to a sudden halt. Above, the driver could be heard cursing and shouting at the team of horses, and the whip cracked, all to no avail. Finally, the coachman got down from his perch on the box and wrenched open the door. "Stuck in the mud, milord," he acknowledged apologetically. " 'Er won't budge a-tall."

"Damn!" Trevaney muttered, his good humor vanishing. Turning to Melisande, he was clearly disgusted. "We were fools to try this."

Guilt washed over her. "I'm sorry. Perhaps we can be dug out," she offered hopefully.

"Mud's up to the hub," the coachman said.

Trevaney's jaw worked visibly as he struggled with futile anger. "Well, unless you wish to wait here for help, Miss Merriweather, I hope you can walk," he managed evenly. "How far, Tom?"

"Dunno. Mebbe a mile—mebbe two" was the discouraging answer. "Post house at th' gate."

"I can walk, for I have my boots," Melisande said, "but I think I should rather take Algy, if you do not mind it."

"Algy, Miss Merriweather?"

"Algernon, then—the horse you tied behind. And before you say anything, I can ride astride and without a saddle—indeed, I have already done so."

"No, I'll ride Alger—Algy, was it? And you'll sit sidewise with whatever decorum you can manage." He jumped down, then reached for her, lifting her as she leaned out the carriage doorway. "You are not precisely light, are you?"

"No, but 'tis unkind of you to note it," she muttered. "I weighed nine stone on Papa's scales when we sheared the sheep last year."

"Not a dieaway miss, I'd say." As he spoke, he walked behind the carriage and untied her horse. "Come on, Algy. God aid you, you poor creature, for between us, you'll be carrying past twenty-two stone."

"He has a rather temperamental disposition," Melisande warned him. "You'd best let me take the reins."

"Miss Merriweather, I am accounted a fair hand with horses," he retorted. "Although," he added, "it has been a very long time since I have ridden without a saddle." He lead Algernon to where she stood and handed the reins to his driver. "Come on, Mel—I'll boost you up," he said bracingly.

"Lord Trevaney, you are becoming rather familiar," she protested.

"Friends merely," he assured her, cupping his hands for her foot. "I am usually called Gareth—or Gary."

Putting one hand on his shoulder and stepping into his hands, she caught the horse's mane and swung up, throwing her leg over the big horse's back. Before Trevaney could say anything, she reassured him, "I am accounted to have a good bottom, my lord." With an effort, she pulled her voluminous riding skirt down as far as she could over her legs, then loosened her cloak enough to slide back and make room for him.

He grinned up at her. "Oh?" As she flushed, he braced himself with the carriage step, then heaved himself up before her. Leaning down, he took the reins. "Cut loose two of the team and follow," he told the driver and coachman. Settling back, he clicked Algy's reins, and the horse moved forward. "Bottom or not, I'd advise you to hang on, my dear—I am accounted a bruising rider," he said over his shoulder.

"Really, but—"

Her words were lost as he goaded the animal with his heel, and Algy broke first into a hard trot, then stretched into a gallop. Throwing whatever reservation she had to the wind, she flung herself against the viscount's back and held on for her life. Within a hundred yards, he reined back to the trot.

"You just did that!" she choked out.

"I was merely checking your bottom, Mel. There's naught wrong with your arms either," he added, teasing her.

"A gentleman would never—"

"A lady would never ride astride," he countered, cutting her off. "So I would guess we are an even match, aren't we?"

"No," she retorted, "we aren't a match at all."

At least it was not raining, she consoled herself. But it was cold, and as the wind whipped at her cloak, she found herself leaning into Trevaney's back, seeking warmth and shelter from it. She had to give him one thing—he mastered Algy expertly without the saddle, guiding him between the deep ruts in the muddy road with speed.

Had the night not been so bitter, it would have been truly beautiful, almost like a fairy world, where clouded light from the crescent moon touched the sparkling rime on fields and hedges. And there was no sound beyond that of Algy's hooves clopping in the frosted mud.

Off to one side of the narrow road, a lonely post chaise leaned, a tilted sentinel bearing silent witness that someone else had been caught in the mire. Melisande shouted at Trevaney, "Could that be Mr. Pennyfoote's?"

"I don't know!"

They came over a hill, and in the distance, a small pinpoint of yellow light could be seen. Abruptly, the viscount reined in, and dismounted.

"We cannot stop now!"

But he was blowing into his hands, cupping them over his face to warm it with his breath. When he lowered his hands, the steam from his nose and mouth crystalized before his eyes. He took off his gloves and chafed his hands for a moment, then put them back on. Turning back to her, he ordered curtly, "Swing your leg over."

"Here? But we are nearly there!" she cried.

"Mel, you cannot ride pillion into a post house," he said reasonably. "You'll have to sit sidewise, and I'll have to hold you on." As he spoke, he reached up to steady her against a fall. "And we'd best think what we mean to say when we get there."

"If I find Charlotte, I'm going to say a great deal," she declared with feeling.

"In any event, we'll have to stay the rest of the night. If you discover your sister, you can share a chamber—if not, I doubt if there will be much room."

"I am not the least tired," she lied feebly.

"I am, and I've got a devil of a head. Unlike you, I've imbibed a fair amount of wine." His face was deceptively sober as he looked up at her. "What I am saying is that you may have to be my sister or my wife."

"*What*?"

"I pray you will not screech," he muttered.

"But—'tis preposterous!"

"Look, if there's enough room, I pay the shot for two—otherwise, we'll have to share."

"No!" Recovering, she decided, "Well, Charlotte will be there—I know it."

"Lud, but I hope so." The faint moonlight reflected in his eyes. "Otherwise, I suppose you must be my sister."

"Do you have one?" she asked curiously.

"No—my parents did not like each other enough to try again, I'm afraid. Go on—turn around. I'll catch you if you fall," he promised.

Favoring him with a disgusted look, she slid forward, then leaned to grasp the horse's mane. Hanging on tightly, she drew up her cold-stiffened left leg, then struggled to bring it over. For a moment, she slipped precariously, but he caught her and boosted her back.

"I shall feel the veriest fool," she grumbled. "And I do not see what it matters, for I shall have no rep left, anyway."

"If it comes to that, I won't let a scandal touch you," he said, drawing the horse off the road to a tree. Bracing his boot against the trunk, he swung his tall body up behind her, and put his arms around her to take the reins. "Now," he murmured above her ear, "you are going to need every bit of bottom you have—and a great deal of aplomb to carry this off."

As the horse broke into a bone-jarring, teeth-chattering trot again, he went on conversationally, "I think I shall call you Elizabeth, and you may call me John—John Tremont—that ought to do. Elizabeth and John Tremont."

"You sound as though you have done this before," she commented acidly.

He didn't answer. Instead, he shifted the reins to his left hand and encircled her waist with his right arm, pulling her close and covering the both of them with his cloak. When he finally spoke again, it was to say, "We'll tell them we've had a carriage accident to explain why we are arrived so late."

"What were we doing on the road at night?"

"We took a wrong turn—at Pembly, I think."

Though it was still dark, ostlers were already in the post house yard when they arrived, and the smell of food steamed from the inn's chimney. Several coaches were drawn up, their doors open whilst hot bricks and carriage rugs were laid within. Seeing Trevaney and Melisande, one driver called out, "Coach for Birmingham leaves at four sharp! Room for two on top!"

Melisande shuddered visibly. "It sounds like an invitation to freeze."

"It is, but the price is cheap enough," Trevaney murmured. "God willing, there will be a bed when they leave."

"But Charlotte—what if they have gone on?"

"Right now, I am too tired to chase the fools."

Whistling for an ostler, Trevaney threw the reins down. As a boy hurried to take them, he leaned over and slid easily from the horse. Turning, he caught Melisande's waist and set her down. Then he squared his shoulders.

"Come on. No matter what I say, you will not dispute it."

At the door, he cleaned the mud from his boots on the bar, then waited for her to precede him inside. Several men milled outside the taproom, waiting either to depart or to eat. The innkeeper, his apron stained with food, saw them, took in the viscount's expensive boots, the fineness of his cloak, and rubbed his hands together as he hurried forward.

But Trevaney's attention was on two gentlemen emerging from a small private parlor. "Damn," he muttered succinctly.

"How to serve ye, sor?" the innkeeper asked obsequiously. "Food fer ye and the lady?"

"A bedchamber—for myself and my wife."

As she gasped, one of the men hailed the viscount. "Gary! Damn if it ain't Trevaney!"

"Trevaney!" The innkeeper's mien was gleeful. " 'Tis welcome ye are to the White Horse, milord. 'Tis Trevaney, Peg!" he bawled out to a rotund female with a cleaner apron. "His lordship'll be a-wantin' clean linen!"

"What the devil are you doing here, Gary?" the gentleman demanded.

"I could ask the same of you, Pemberton."

The man's eyes raked over Melisande, making her acutely aware that her face was red and raw, her hair sadly tangled, and her habit and boots muddy. Trevaney's hand reached back to grasp hers, squeezing her fingers in warning.

"Well, now—what's this?" Pemberton asked slyly. "Don't believe I know this one. Harry, come have a look," he called out to his friend.

" 'Tis the devil all right," the other man acknowledged, coming up to them. "Hallo, Trevaney. Fancy encountering you here—ain't taking the stage, are you?"

"Merely had an accident, Wilbanks," the viscount responded tersely.

"You, Gary?"

"Yes."

But Pemberton's gaze was still on Melisande. "Ain't you going to make me known to your"—he hesitated knowingly, before finishing his sentence with—"fancy bit?"

Trevaney's grip was now like iron. His jaw tightened visibly, and his dark eyes went cold. "You will, of course, wish to apologize to my wife," he said with deceptive softness.

Thunderstruck, they looked at each other, then at Melisande again. Her face hot, she wished she could disappear through the floor.

"Well, Jack?"

The man swallowed. "Your—your *wife*, Gary?"

"Didn't know you was even betrothed," Wilbanks managed weakly. "Wish you happy, of course—just never—"

But Trevaney's eyes were still on Pemberton. "My wife," he said evenly.

"Heh—heh." The other lord's face was pasty white. "Didn't mean a thing, of course—just a bit of a jest— sorry for it," he offered. "You wasn't insulted was you, my lady?"

"Uh—"

Trevaney appeared distracted by a crease in his cloak. Smoothing it out, he shook his head. "Utterly insufficient, I'm afraid."

"Shocked—too shocked for anything." Looking at Melisande again, he managed to stammer out, "Terribly sorry, my lady." Casting a quick, nervous glance at Trevaney, he tried again. "That is, you have my most sincerest, most total apology, Lady Trevaney."

Still shocked herself, Melisande finally found her voice. "I did not think anything of it," she murmured faintly.

"Well, ain't you going to present us?" Wilbanks asked querulously. "I mean, she's going to be the gossip of the Season!"

Once again, the viscount seemed absorbed in his cloak, picking at a bit of lint, then dusting it off with his gloved hand. "Lady Trevaney has no wish to have her name bandied about," he said coldly. Turning to her, he actually smiled. "My dear, the boor on your left is Baron Pemberton, while the other is Sir Henry Wilbanks."

"How-de-do?" Wilbanks said quickly.

"My lady," Pemberton acknowledged.

"Gentlemen, Melisande, my viscountess." Openly possessing her hand, Trevaney murmured, "Good day."

As he drew her away from them, she could hear

one of them say, "Must be a love match, for she's too tall by half."

"But she's pretty enough, and with his name and that hair, she'll be all the crack," the other predicted.

She waited until they were out of hearing before rounding on him. "Why on earth—?" she demanded awfully.

"They both know I have no sister."

"That still does not give you leave to—to lie, my lord!"

"Mel! What are you doing here!" a voice gasped from the stairs.

" 'Twould seem we are about to have a fond reunion," Trevaney murmured.

"You know very well why I am here, Charley," Melisande retorted crossly. "I am taking you home ere Papa finds out." But even as she said it, she knew she was already too late. "Well, in any event, I'm taking you home."

"Miss Melisande!" Pennyfoote choked out. "Whatever—?"

"You haven't wed him yet, have you?" Mel demanded.

But Charlotte had spied Trevaney. "More to the point, why is he here?" she asked haughtily. " 'Twould seem you have the explaining to do."

"Trevaney! Egad!" Pennyfoote shrank behind Charlotte.

Her eyes still on her sister, Mel reminded her, "I am still waiting for an answer—are you wed or not?"

"Yes," Charlotte said at the same time Pennyfoote answered, "No!—that is, not yet."

"Does he know you have no portion?"

"I am sure he does not care."

"But her uncle—" Pennyfoote began weakly.

" 'Twas Mama's lie to make certain that she would attract a London beau, nothing more," Melisande said.

"Mel!"

"Well, you said he does not care, didn't you?"

But the dandy was looking at Charlotte. "Your Uncle Thorndike—you are his heiress, ain't you?"

"He is as like to give her a farthing as hell is like to freeze," Melisande declared brutally.

"Mel!" Charlotte wailed.

"Is this true, Miss Merriweather?"

"Mel, you have ruined me!"

"Would you rather have him find it out after you are married, Charley?" Mel countered reasonably. "Would you truly wish to be tied to a man who loved you for money you do not have?"

Drawing his slender body up to his full height, Peverel Pennyfoote faced Trevaney. " 'Twould seem I have been utterly deceived, my lord," he said stiffly. "I am afraid I will have to wait beyond quarter day to settle the matter between us."

"Peverel!"

"As for you, Miss Merriweather," he told Charlotte, "I am only thankful that mine eyes have been opened in time to prevent what I can only consider would have been a mésalliance—and so I shall tell my Aunt Washburton."

"Oooh—Mel, look what you have done!"

"At least I love you, Charley."

"I cannot go home unwed—Peverel," Charlotte tried desperately, "You cannot abandon me! Not after we have eloped! Not after I have been hours in your company!"

"Er—I'm afraid he has to do so, Miss Merriweather," Trevaney murmured apologetically. "Pennyfoote, you will explain to her, of course."

Looking away, the dandy fidgeted with his neck cloth, then mumbled, "Ain't got so much as a feather to fly with—got to find an heiress, you know."

"Peverel!"

"Well, it ain't like you didn't lie to me also."

"Oh, I say, Lady Trevaney!" Coming back into the foyer, Sir Henry approached them. "Just wanted you to know that when Gary brings you to London, Lady Wilbanks and I will be most happy to have a reception for you."

"Thank you, Henry," Trevaney murmured sardonically. "We appreciate that, don't we, my dear?"

"Yes, of course," Melisande answered, her face flaming, her voice nearly too low to be heard.

"Well, well—just never thought you'd step into parson's mousetrap, that's all," Wilbanks said, clapping the viscount on his shoulder. "But damn if I don't wish you happy—truly I do. Got to run—see you in London, no doubt."

Charlotte stared after him, then turned to her younger sister. "Lady Trevaney?" she asked archly. "Well, Mel, 'twould seem you have some explaining to do also, haven't you?"

"No." Once again, the viscount's hand sought Melisande's. "Unlike Pennyfoote, I have no intention of bolting."

"Well, I think—"

"But they got to be here! Ain't nowhere's else for 'em to go! First post house on the toll road past Pembly, ain't it?"

All the color drained from Charlotte's face as she recognized her father's voice. "Mel, I am going to swoon, I swear it! 'Tis Papa!"

Pulling away from Trevaney, Melisande went to her sister's side. "No, you are not, Charley—not now. You are going to face him."

"I cannot! Oh, I feel so much the fool!" She tried to turn and run up the stairs, but Melisande caught her. "Please—Mel, I cannot!"

"Cannot what, puss?" Mr. Merriweather demanded sharply.

"Papa, you were not supposed to know until 'twas done!" Charlotte cried.

Her father regarded both of his daughters balefully. "At least one of m'girls has some sense, you know.

'Twas Annie as wakened me, and I'm damned grateful for it. As for you, Mel, I don't know what you was thinking, going off in the middle of the night. You ought to have let your papa attend to the matter."

"Er—I believe we ought to step into one of the private parlors first," the viscount murmured.

"Trevaney! What is the meaning of this, sir?" Then his eyes caught the movement of Peverel Pennyfoote trying to slip undetected out the back way. "No, you don't, Pennyfoote! I'll have your hide on m' stable door, sir!"

The young man froze guiltily. Turning back, his expression was glum. "It ain't what you was to think," he protested.

Aware that a small, curious crowd had gathered, Melisande spoke up. "His lordship is quite right—unless we wish to air our linen before the world, we'd best remove ourselves to a more private place."

"Precisely," Trevaney said.

Charlotte looked around her. "Please, Papa—I should prefer to be private also."

"Aye. You ain't done yet, Pennyfoote," Merriweather growled. "You go before me, you hear?" Looking to Trevaney, he muttered, "And I mean to hear from you, my lord—I ain't got this sorted out yet."

"I shall be most happy to oblige," the viscount murmured, holding the door. As everyone passed by, he drew Melisande aside. "Chin high, my dear—I've no intention of abandoning you."

"No," she whispered.

"Eh, what's this, puss?" her father demanded, turning around.

"Yes, why don't you ask dear Mel what she is doing here?" Charlotte suggested maliciously.

"Mean to—in time."

Trevaney stepped inside the small parlor and shut the door behind him. Merriweather looked from Charlotte to Pennyfoote to Melisande, then his gaze rested on the viscount.

"I don't know what you got to do with this, but I mean to find out, sir."

"Papa, I went to the Red Ram to look for Charlotte," Mel spoke up quickly. "And as she and Mr. Pennyfoote had already left there, I came after them."

"Foolish thing to do, puss."

"I know. And when Lord Trevaney realized I was alone, he was most insistent upon seeing me safely back to the manor."

"Then why are they here?" Charlotte demanded. "Make her tell you how it is that—"

"I'm telling this, Charley!" Mel snapped. Drawing a deep breath, she hastened on. "On the way back to Wynwood, I was able to convince Lord Trevaney that marriage to Mr. Pennyfoote would be Charlotte's ruination, and we turned around to follow them."

"Ruination of her!" Pennyfoote snorted. "What of me? I was sadly deceived, I tell you!"

"You let me think you had money also!" Charlotte shouted at him. "You said you would carry me off to a life of luxury, as I recall it! You promised me heaven on earth, you clunch!"

"I expected to live on your expectations, Miss Merriweather—until I came about, anyways," he amended hastily beneath her father's glower. "Then I was going to set us up in the first style."

"You said you loved me!"

"Is this true, sir?" Mr. Merriweather asked awfully.

"When she was an heiress, but now—"

"You'll do right by the gel, do you hear me?"

"I should rather die than wed him!"

"You ain't got nothing to say in the matter now," her father retorted. "Rep's in shreds, ain't it?"

"No more than Mel's!" Charlotte wailed. "Why don't you ask her how it is that she is pretending to be Lady Trevaney!"

"It is no such thing, Charley, and well you know it!"

"Oh? Then how is it that that man out there offers to have a London reception for you and Trevaney?"

"Puss?" Mr. Merriweather turned his attention to Melisande.

"Er—if I may be allowed—" Trevaney murmured apologetically. "There is no need for rancor among us."

"No need!" Merriweather sputtered. "No need, sirrah! Aye, there is!"

But everyone else was watching the viscount. His dark eyes met Melisande's. "I'm sorry, my dear—I'd hoped to do this properly, you know."

"No," she whispered, her throat constricting, "I won't let you."

He looked past her to her father. "There is no need for rancor," he repeated. "We shall merely give out that Miss Merriweather and I decided upon a romantical elopement to Scotland, and"—for a moment, his gaze returned to Melisande—"I assure you, I do not mind it." Seeing that tears brightened her blue eyes, he nodded. " 'Tis the only answer, my dear."

"That don't save Charlotte's rep, sir."

"Papa, I should not wed Peverel if he were the last man on earth!"

"Peverel Pennyfoote accompanied us to support me," Trevaney went on smoothly, "and as for Miss Charlotte, she came to provide propriety for Melisande."

"To Scotland, sirrah?" Merriweather asked. "But if you was wishful of wedding her, why—"

His eyes still on Melisande, Trevaney responded, "Given my utterly reprehensible reputation, you have opposed us, forcing the elopement. We shall give it out as a love match."

"Sounds deuced odd to me," her father muttered. "But I ain't saying as it might not work," he conceded, rubbing his chin. "But, damn, if you was wanting the chit, why didn't you take her in the first place?"

"No one need know of that."

"I say, 'tis a capital notion, sir!" Peverel Pennyfoote declared enthusiastically, reaching to pump the viscount's hand.

"Don't," Trevaney said curtly. "If I could avoid the certain scandal, I should call you out on the instant."

"No." Swallowing hard, Melisande repeated it more loudly. "No."

Everyone turned to her. "No?" her father fairly yelped. "No? Why the devil not?" he wanted to know furiously. " 'Tis the answer to everything! With the settlements, I could come about!"

"Mel, you have to take him!" Charlotte protested loudly. "You have been seen in his company at this inn!"

"Aye, and you've told 'em you was married," Pennyfoote added nastily. "Besides, I ain't sticking my foot in parson's mousetrap now, I can tell you. Well, I ain't! And you heard Miss Charlotte—she don't want me."

"I'm sorry, Mel," Trevaney said again. "I wish I could wrap everything up in clean linen for you, but I cannot. 'Tis me or ruination."

"You got to wed him, puss—you got to," her father insisted. "Ain't no other way about it."

"My lord, I am exceedingly honored by your generosity," she began, her voice low, "but I—well, I cannot allow you to do this."

"His generosity!" Pennyfoote snorted. "If you was to ask me, he ain't got any!"

"Shutter your mouth, sir!" Merriweather snapped. "Melisande, sweet—you cannot mean it," he coaxed his middle daughter. "Take him now, puss, and reform him later."

"Mel, he is obliged to wed you!" Charlotte screeched at her.

"I have no wish to reform him, Papa." Hot tears stung her eyes, nearly blinding her, as she held out her hand to Trevaney. "I am sorry for all the inconvenience, my lord, and I wish you well."

"Mel—"

"No. You are not obliged, for the fault was mine." She forced a smile. "And should I hear your name slandered again, I shall not hesitate to defend you." Turning to her incredulous father and sister, she managed to tell them, "As I do not go about in society, I cannot think any will truly care about my poor reputation."

"Puss—"

"And there is no need to take me to London with Charley, Papa—I should not take, anyway."

The viscount squeezed her fingers briefly. "Believe me, Mel, you have my greatest admiration. I know not how I shall explain your disappearance to Wilbanks, but I expect I shall contrive something."

Disconcerted by the warmth in his eyes, she wanted to cry outright, but dared not. "I am sure you will, sir."

"You—you ain't going to listen to her?" Merriweather asked weakly.

"Yes." Lifting her hand to his lips, he kissed her fingers lightly, then he released them. As they all stared in silence, Trevaney readjusted his black felt hat, then opened the door. Turning back briefly, he murmured softly, "Good-bye, Melisande."

As the door closed behind him, Peverel Pennyfoote allowed plaintively, "Well, I wasn't afraid of him, but I say 'tis good enough riddance."

"One more word out of you, sirrah, and *I* shall put out your lights for you," Merriweather told him sharply. "Suffice it to say that I am only thankful the knot between you and Charlotte was never tied. I would not for the world wish her burdened with an effete pink."

"Well!"

Wiping her wet cheeks, Melisande told him, "You'd best go, Mr. Pennyfoote."

Not needing any further urging, the young man gathered his shredded dignity and made good his escape. For a long moment, the Merriweathers stared at each other, until Mr. Merriweather sighed heavily.

"Now what's to do?" he asked helplessly.

"As there is but Mr. Pennyfoote and Lord Trevaney who know—and Lord Pemberton and Sir Henry Wilbanks, but they have not seen Charlotte, of course—well, I think we should merely go home," Melisande answered.

"So do I," her sister concurred.

"Ain't nothing else to do, I suppose," he decided finally.

It was a rainy Valentine's Day, less than a fortnight since the debacle at the posting house, and everyone except Melisande seemed to have forgotten Charlotte's unfortunate attempt at elopement. But Mel herself was afflicted with a lingering melancholy, a sense of loss she could scarce explain.

Far too often, her thoughts turned to the viscount, wondering if he'd left the neighborhood, if he counted himself well rid of the Merriweathers, if he thought of her at all. It was beginning to seem as though she thought of little else. Over and over, she relived nearly every word spoken between them, recalling the incredible intimacy of being held by him, of being warmed by his body. And far too often, her treacherous mind shamelessly wandered back to his kiss.

Passion and fire, he'd said he wanted. And yet out of a mistaken sense of honor, he'd actually forced himself to offer for her, trying to save her from her father's ire. Idly, she allowed herself the luxury of imagining what it would be like to be wedded to him. Then she brought herself up short, scolding herself severely for such a foolish notion. The viscounts of this world did not wed plain country misses with no fortune and no connections.

For nearly the five-hundredth time, she drew her knees up beneath her wide skirt and resolutely directed her attention back to Fielding's *Joseph Andrews*. Under any other circumstances, she would have enjoyed it, but just now it seemed that she did not enjoy much of anything.

"La, Mel, but there you are!" Charlotte declared, bursting into their father's book room. "Only fancy—Lady Washburton has loaned Mama the latest fashion dolls from Paris!"

"We have no money, Charley," Melisande responded shortly.

"Fiddle—a bit of ribbon here, a snippet of gauze there, and Mama shall contrive to make me look fashionable. But I will need some net gloves, you know. Mrs. Washburton's maid told Bess that they can be bought cheaply in London."

"I hope you do not mean to spend Papa's last farthing."

"I don't know what ails you, Mel. You were not used to be such a—a dullard," Charlotte complained.

"I'm sorry—I'm just a bit blue-deviled today, I suppose."

"Today? You've acted as though you were at last prayers since—" The older girl stopped, flushing. "That is—"

"Since you ran off with Mr. Pennyfoote?" Melisande inquired mildly.

"I pray you will not remind me. 'Twas foolish—utterly foolish of me to believe him."

"Well, as you have recovered rather quickly yourself, I collect your heart was not bruised very much either."

"Mine eyes were opened, and I can only be thankful that—" Charlotte stopped in mid-sentence to gape at the small window. "That I came to my senses," she finished lamely.

"What's the matter?"

"Nothing—nothing at all. Yes, well, I expect I ought to see if Mama wishes me to help her sort buttons."

"You know, you are behaving quite oddly yourself, Charley."

"Am I? I expect it is but that I am rather excited." With that, the older girl quickly disappeared.

Melisande sighed. The sooner her papa found a husband to rein in Charley's volatility, the better. Once again, she turned the page and resumed reading with a grim determination, thinking that poor Joseph was a bit of a bumbler, that he ought to be making a clearer effort to scotch his employer's advances. If she were writing the tale, she'd have done it a bit differently. But, she conceded, at least the tale was not nearly so unrelentingly moral as Richardson's *Pamela*.

She paused, thinking she heard Charlotte go outside, then discounted the notion. It was, after all, raining.

"Ah-hem."

She looked up, and her heart nearly stopped as Lord Trevaney came through the door. Smiling, he removed his wet hat and crossed the room to her.

"Hello, Mel."

"Trevaney, what a surprise," she managed faintly. "I thought perhaps you had returned to London."

"I had," he admitted. "In fact, I was gaming just the other night in one of the hells."

"Oh?" He was far too near, far too handsome for her to think rationally.

"Hawkewood said I had the devil's own luck, in fact." Moving so close that his soaked cloak dripped spots of water onto her skirt, he towered over her. "Hoping 'tis the truth, and considering that 'tis Saint Valentine's Day," he said softly, "I've come back to put my luck to the touch."

"I—" Her heart pounded loudly in her ears, and her throat constricted too tightly for speech.

Without warning, he dropped to his knees before her, murmuring, "I've no experience in begging, Mel." As her eyes widened, he caught her hands. "I know 'tis soon, but I wanted to say it at the posting house even." He looked up, his dark eyes warm, his smile decidedly crooked. "I admire you for everything, you know—your sense of right and honor, your devotion to your family, your—Lud, I'm botching this, aren't I? I ought to just get it out, so you may decline again, I suppose." His warm fingers tightened on hers. "Mel, if you can bring yourself to wed me, I am prepared to love you for the rest of my life."

For a moment, it seemed as though the room spun whilst his words hung in the air. "Wed you?" she echoed. Then as they sank in, she smiled through tears. "Oh, Trevaney!"

"Is that aye or nay?" he asked, his smile broadening into a grin.

"Aye," she answered happily. "But are you quite certain?"

He stood up, pulling her with him, drawing her slender body against his. His arms closed about her, and as she leaned into him, he kissed her thoroughly, taking her breath away. She clung to him eagerly, savoring the heat between them.

When at last he left her mouth, he looked into her eyes. "Hawkewood was right," he whispered huskily, "I do have the devil's own luck." With one hand, he brushed back the mass of red hair from her temple. "You give me fire, Mel."

"Here now, puss—what is the meaning of this?" Mr. Merriweather asked gruffly from the doorway.

Still within the circle of his lordship's other arm, she turned to face her father.

"It means, Papa—it means you may wish us happy."

"*What?* Well, damn if I don't—aye," he declared,

beaming, "damn if I don't. Fan! You got to come down!" he shouted loudly. "Our Melisande's going to be a viscountess!"

"Oh, I almost forgot," Trevaney murmured, reaching beneath his cloak to his coat. "Here," he said, handing a folded paper to Melisande.

She looked down, seeing that it had been addressed to "Viscount and Lady Trevaney."

"What is it?"

"Your first social engagement—a reception given by the Wilbanks. But you may decline, if you wish."

Lady Trevaney. Even the sound of it sent a shiver of delight down her spine.

"No, I shall like it excessively," she decided.

The Imposter

by Sandra Heath

PLEASE do it for me, Felix," Francis begged desperately. "It's only a little out of your way."

"No."

"I don't think it's very much to ask."

"Indeed? Well, I do."

"Won't you even put yourself out for the sake of our old friendship?" Francis entreated.

"*No!* You can do your own damned courting," Felix replied rather testily as he stood in front of the fireplace in his Park Lane house. The flames behind him made his shadow sway over the rich Axminster carpet, and the curtains were drawn because the January evening had closed in and it was wet and blustery outside.

He wore formal evening black in readiness for the ball he was to attend at Spencer House, and at the age of twenty-eight was ruggedly good-looking and tall, with the broad shoulders and slender hips that were ideally suited to the tight-fitting fashions considered obligatory for gentlemen of *ton*. His aristocratic Anglo-Saxon ancestry was evident in his thick fair hair, keen blue eyes, fine-boned face, and natural elegance. What was also evident at the moment was his obstinate determination not to accommodate Francis.

Felix sighed inwardly. This last day of January was proving all that was wretched. He'd woken up suffering from the aftereffects of last night's excesses, and had then had to endure a long lecturing visit from his fearsome great aunt, Lady Fullingworth, who thought him quite mad to call off his forthcoming St. Valentine's Day betrothal to Miss Amelia Whitworth. Maybe his aunt was right and the full moon had had something to do with it, but there was no disputing the way his doubts had been gathering momentum over the thirty-one days of this most odious of months.

As friends he and Amelia had always hit it off splendidly, but they would have done very badly together as husband and wife, of that he was now quite certain. Nevertheless, the ending of a match was seldom a light undertaking, hence the overindulgence at his club, where he'd seen the bottom of several wine bottles too many, and now he felt far too disenchanted with himself and with the world in general to agree to Francis's outrageous request.

Francis was lounging back in a nearby armchair, with his long legs stretched out untidily toward the fire. He was very handsome, indeed almost too handsome, and if Felix epitomized an Anglo-Saxon lineage, so Francis epitomized his French ancestry. The dark-haired, dark-eyed Vinings had come over with the Normans in 1066, and the two friends had often pondered the possibility that their forebears had faced each other at the Battle of Hastings.

Francis possessed the sort of romantic looks that were sighed over by the fair sex, with whom he was extraordinarily successful, although to his discredit he was inclined to boast about this. His brown eyes were long-lashed and melting, but their softness concealed a vain character. The Honorable Francis Vining was fully aware of his masculine beauty, and as a result was exceedingly conceited, but he did have some redeeming features. He was amusing company and could be kind, but his outstanding quality was his apparently endless capacity to enjoy himself. There were few gentlemen in London more prepared to revel in every diversion the capital offered, and it was one of these diversions that was now causing the strain between the two old friends.

Francis was annoyed by Felix's intractability. "For Heaven's sake, a few hours of your time really aren't all that much to ask. I *know* you always go home to Northwood by way of Faringdon, which means that Priors Court isn't far off your route. You are still going home in a few days' time, aren't you?" he asked as an afterthought.

"I fear the answer to that is yes, I'm still going, although my family doesn't yet know it. I have a great deal of explaining to do," Felix replied heavily.

Francis sat forward to help himself to another measure of his friend's best cognac. "I must say, I'm rather surprised you've cried off where Amelia is concerned. I would have thought you and she were an excellent couple."

"I don't intend to discuss it."

"As you wish." Francis sat back again, swirling the cognac a little pensively. "Look, you may have decided to end your contract with Amelia, but I daren't act so high-handedly. If I showed a clean pair of heels to *my* match, I'd have my allowance severed at the very neck." Francis drew his finger expressively across his throat.

"If the match is all that important, I suggest you—"

"It isn't personally important to me—indeed, I'd prefer to be without it—but it is to my old man. He's the one who's set up on it. The lady is an heiress, and that's what the Vining coffers require. I don't expect that to mean very much to the future Lord Northwood, who has the indecently bulging Vestey family fortune to look forward to."

Felix was a little tired of the endless Vining wringing of hands over the supposed parlous state of their finances. Francis's father, Sir Horace Vining of Long-acre Court in Wiltshire, was proud of the care he took with his fortune, but what he regarded as care, others saw as miserliness. The baronet of Longacre Court was a skinflint whose exceedingly full treasure chests were so seldom dipped into that their hinges were rusty, which made Francis's present moans a little difficult to endure, and Felix's temper was already short. "If you insist that the Vining coffers are what matters, I fail to understand why you're cutting up rough about visiting your suitably wealthy bride-to-be," he observed a little scathingly.

"I wouldn't cut up rough about it if it were not for—"

"If it were not for a certain actress," Felix finished for him.

His tone pricked Francis a little. "This isn't a run-of-the-mill seduction, you know. I want Dolly to be more than a mere conquest, I want to establish her as my mistress."

Felix blinked in astonishment. "My dear fellow, Dolly Ainsworth is the darling of London's theaters, and will never condescend to be anyone's mistress, with the possible exception of the Prince of Wales. She prefers to bestow her favors as the mood takes her, but that is as far as it goes. You delude yourself if you think otherwise."

"You're wrong."

"No, Francis, you are."

"I don't want to argue the point, Felix, I just want to secure the lady while she's wavering toward me. She's about to leave for Bath, something about a contract with the Theatre Royal, and she will be there when I'm supposed to be kicking my heels at Priors Court. If I don't go to Bath as well, I'll probably lose her to Creighton."

"Creighton?"

"The fellow has wagered he'll succeed before me."

Felix's eyes cleared. "Ah, so now we have the nub of it!"

"Not entirely. I *do* hold the lady in high esteem."

"Yes, and a pig just flew over St. Paul's," Felix remarked dryly.

"I want her, and I mean to have her," Francis replied shortly.

"Dolly's favors may be enticing, but they are resistible. Your match with Miss Martin is of far greater importance, and I advise you to turn your mind to paying her some long overdue attention. After all, she is your bride-to-be!"

"A bride-to-be I haven't even met yet," Francis observed sulkily. "The only member of Plain Jane's family I've met is her father, and that was on the day he and my old man deigned to inform me they'd settled my future."

Felix was a little taken aback. "Not even met? Then how can you possibly call her Plain Jane?"

Francis searched in his pocket and drew out a little portrait in an oval silver frame. "Here she is, Miss Plain Jane Martin of Priors Court in the county of Oxfordshire."

Felix took the miniature and studied the painted face. The young lady smiled sweetly at him, her gray eyes unexpectedly large and expressive. She had a cloud of magnificent flame-colored hair, and her face was striking, if not exactly pretty. In his opinion Miss Martin was many things, but certainly not plain, although she lacked the glory that made the incomparable Dolly Ainsworth the toast of Drury Lane. "You do her an injustice," he said, handing the miniature back again.

"Oh, come now, with hair like that she no doubt possesses a vile temper and a positive rash of freckles," Francis grumbled unreasonably, stuffing the miniature unceremoniously back into his pocket. "Be honest, Felix, would *you* want to spend several days dilly-dallying in pointless politenesses with such a creature, when you could be lying in Dolly Ainsworth's arms?"

"I really couldn't say," Felix replied a little evasively, for if the truth were known he'd already spent a night in Dolly's arms and found the experience somewhat disappointing. For all her beauty, the actress was not passionate; going through the motions was more her style. The brief liaison was something he'd tactfully refrained from mentioning to Francis, who'd been completely preoccupied since seeing her in *The Taming of the Shrew*. Nothing would do but that he lured La Ainsworth to his bed.

Francis got up and went to the window, holding the curtain back to watch the rain dashing against the glass. Park Lane was lamplit, and Hyde Park opposite was in darkness. "Dear God, what a dismal night," he murmured.

"It suits my mood," Felix replied.

"That much is obvious." Francis looked at him, and then doggedly returned the conversation to the prickly matter of Miss Jane Martin and the visit to Priors Court. "Felix, if you would but oblige me in this request, I'd be eternally grateful."

"Francis—"

"Just call in on your way to Northwood, and tell the lady how much I regret not being able to arrive as promised on Saint Valentine's eve, but I'm unwell at the moment and will not have recovered sufficiently by then to travel. You're leaving for Northwood at least a week before then, which will hardly be leaving it to the last moment as far as they're concerned. Pour on your inestimable charm and convince Plain Jane, that's all I ask."

"I don't feel inclined to lie to her on your behalf," Felix answered irritably. Why wouldn't the fellow let the matter drop?

"There's not a great deal of fibbing involved, and it would help me no end if you'd do it," Francis wheedled. "It isn't even as if this meeting is all that vital at the moment. The official betrothal isn't for another six months, so there'll be plenty of time for me to woo her properly before then."

"How modest you are, to be sure," Felix murmured dryly.

Francis raised a knowing eyebrow. "My dear Felix, in that particular respect I have no need for false modesty. I'm peerless when it comes to laying siege to the fair sex."

Felix let the remark pass. His own reputation was a match for Francis's, he simply didn't crow about it.

Francis drew a long breath. "Will you do it for me, Felix?" he asked again.

"No."

"Why not?"

"Because I don't see why I should attempt to pull the wool over poor Miss Martin's eyes simply and solely to enable you to get Dolly Ainsworth between the sheets!"

"Oh, how I loathe the green-eyed glint of envy," Francis retorted. "Be honest and admit that you won't help me because you want Dolly yourself."

"I won't dignify that remark with a response," Felix murmured.

"What sort of friend are you?" Francis muttered pettishly, moving toward the cognac again, but Felix placed the decanter out of reach.

"You've consumed five since you arrived, and if you have any more you'll drive your damned phaeton into the nearest lamp post."

"Are you accusing me of being in my cups?"

"No, I merely see that you are drifting in that direction."

"That's rich, coming from someone who became totally inebriated last night because he'd arbitrarily decided to cancel his match!"

Felix raised an eyebrow. "There was nothing arbitrary about my decision, and as to the rest of your remark, I may have been inebriated, but I wasn't in charge of a team of four."

Francis sighed. "You're right, of course, damn your eyes." He studied Felix again for a moment. "Look, would it avail me more to come tomorrow, when you're in a better temper?"

"Not if you still mean to ask me to call at Priors Court."

Francis scowled and was silent for a long moment. Then he fixed Felix with a serious look. "Very well, you leave me no option but to point out that you are obligated to me," he said bluntly.

Felix was incredulous. "That obligation was the result of a serious matter of life and death, which I hardly think describes your animal urges toward Dolly Ainsworth!"

"Nevertheless, I'm calling upon your indebtedness now," Francis insisted. "I got you safely to a diplomatic doctor after you were wounded in that duel, and no one was ever the wiser. Now I expect you to repay me."

"You're a fool, Francis."

"Possibly, but it's what I want. I mean to succeed with Dolly in Bath. Indeed, if I don't, I believe madness will ensue."

"It already has," Felix replied flatly.

"Think that if you wish. *Now,* will you do as I ask?"

"You leave me no option."

Francis exhaled with relief. "Thank God for that."

"But after this I will no longer consider myself beholden to you," Felix reminded him.

"Naturally."

"Very well, I'll do your dirty work for you, but under protest."

"To the devil with your protests. I'm only interested in your cooperation, willing or not." Francis searched in his other pocket and drew out another miniature, this time of himself, and placed it on the table next to his chair. "Just present the lady with this, and it will suffice until she can have Adonis himself."

"Does your vanity know any bounds?"

"It has no need," Francis replied unblushingly.

Felix looked at him. "I still think you're quite mad. What if I don't succeed in placating the lady and her family?"

"You will."

"Don't bank on it, for there's nothing certain in this life."

Francis sighed and picked up his tall hat and gloves. "I can't stand you when you're in this frame of mind."

"Well, while I'm in it, let me also remind you that Bath is almost as public a place as London, and your presence there and not in your Mayfair 'sickbed' might reach Priors Court."

"That's an outside chance I'm prepared to take. Anyway, why on earth should the Martins find out? They'll all be safely at home."

"So you fondly hope," Felix murmured.

Francis tugged his hat on irritably. "You really are in a mood, aren't you? Are you quite sure you've done the right thing regarding Amelia? Maybe—"

"I'm absolutely sure."

Francis shrugged. "Well, *I* think you're already having second thoughts, hence your excessive bile."

"Just go, Francis," Felix replied, nodding toward the door.

"Aren't you going to wish me luck with La Ainsworth?"

"Go!"

Felix remained by the fireplace as the door closed behind Francis, and a moment later he heard the phaeton and four turning slowly out of the gates in front of the house. As it drove away toward Piccadilly, he sat down in the chair by the fire. The firelight shone in his blue eyes as he pondered the exceedingly disagreeable beginning of the new century. The year 1799 had been odious enough, but 1800 was beyond the pale. So far, anyway.

And yet he had celebrated New Year's Day with such high expectations. It had been a delusion, however, based on the deliberate wearing of blinkers where his relationship with Amelia was concerned. It was as well he'd decided against the match, for the parting of the ways had revealed her in her disagreeable true light. He'd done his best to be diplomatic when he'd explained his reasons for withdrawing, assuring her that she wasn't at fault in any way, but she'd taken very public umbrage, using her waspish tongue to excellent effect, hence his great aunt's visit. As far as his family and friends were concerned he'd behaved monstrously, and was to be condemned for treating "poor Amelia" in such a way.

Toying with his gold signet ring, he leaned his head back, weary in the knowledge that he had to brace himself for what was bound to be a difficult visit to Northwood Castle, his family's ancestral home. There had been an uninterrupted line of Vesteys there since the thirteenth century, and they had borne the title of Viscount Northwood since their judicious support for the winning side in the Wars of the Roses. Felix knew that his father set immense store by the marriage with Amelia, and would therefore be furious as well as incredulous. A great deal of tact and convincing argument would be required to smooth over this awkward storm in the otherwise tranquil Vestey pool.

Felix sighed heavily. He'd taken the precaution of not advising his parents of his impending arrival, for that way at least they wouldn't have time to prepare their full case against him. A flying visit was what he intended, to allow them the courtesy of haranguing him in the dock, without permitting them too long in which to do it! One thing was certain, come St. Valentine's Day he'd be back in London, for the thought of facing them all on the day he should have been betrothed to Amelia was too awful for words.

He glanced down at the signet ring with its entwined initials. *F* and *V*. Felix Vestey. Fair and Valorous? Or Foul and Villainous? He'd like to believe the former, but Amelia had set out to have him thought of as the latter. So far she was succeeding.

Priors Court was an Elizabethan mansion situated near the Thames and the numerous small backwaters that marked the otherwise busy river in this part of the country. It was set in a park into which some of the shining fingers of quiet water wound between banks of willows and alders, and was visible from the Faringdon–Oxford turnpike as a magnificent cluster of balustraded towers decked with armorial emblems. The park was thick with trees, both deciduous and evergreen, and Priors Court was therefore a very secluded and private place.

As Felix was in London mulling over his unsatisfactory January, Miss Jane Martin was wondering what the rest of 1800 had in store for her. She sat clasping her knees on one of the window seats in the candlelit top-floor gallery at Priors Court, watching the rain sluicing down the glass. It was dark outside, and she could see only her indistinct reflection.

She wore a long-sleeved dark green velvet gown, with a froth of cream lace at the neck and cuffs, and there was a warm cream cashmere shawl around her shoulders. Francis hadn't gauged her at all well from her portrait, for her skin was devoid of freckles, and her flame-colored hair was not an indication of a fiery temper; indeed, she was very sweet-natured. Her figure was slender and graceful, and her gray eyes were as expressive in life as they were in the silver-framed likeness. Light could pass through them in a moment, but so too could shadow, and her lips were as quick to smile as they were to tremble a little with sadness.

She was a creature of tender emotions, endlessly patient and understanding, but capable of being very deeply hurt, which was why, if she had but known it, a callous and selfish man like the Honorable Francis Vining wasn't at all right for her.

The gallery's paneled walls were hung with Flemish tapestries and portraits, and at regular intervals were crimson silk chairs with heavily carved backs and legs. The same silk had been used for the curtains that stretched from floor to ceiling at the many windows. In daylight the view from those windows was quite breathtaking, but for days now it had been raining. The January chill was hard to keep at bay in spite of the two immense stone fireplaces that added their dancing light to that of the candles, but in spite of the cold it was one of Jane's favorite parts of the house during the winter months. She came here when she wanted to read, and that had been her purpose tonight, but now she was lost in thought. Her face was pale in the flickering light as she hugged her knees, and a book of poems lay open by her feet on the window seat. Some of the lines had quite unsettled her.

Those awful words 'Till death do part'
May well alarm the youthful heart:
No after-thought when once a wife;
The die is cast, and cast for life;

Cast for life. Three words with an ominous ring. She liked poems, especially those by Mr. Nathaniel Cotton, but on this occasion he'd given her too much cause for thought. What would life be like with the man her father had chosen for her?

Suddenly she felt restless, and got up from the window seat to pace along the gallery. As she reached the end she was halted by the renewed vigor of the rain dashing against the window panes. Please don't let the weather be like this when Francis is here. It wasn't long now. Soon they would meet at last. She lowered her gaze, for she knew so little about him, except that he was said to be one of the most handsome gentlemen in London, and that one day he would be Sir Francis Vining. And that he was probably left-handed, if his backward-sloping writing was anything by which to judge. She wished she could picture him, but although she'd sent a miniature, he hadn't yet sent one in return, even though she'd asked. All she'd had was a letter.

She took out the sheet of folded vellum she carried in her pocket. It was only a brief communication, penned from his London address and bearing his family coat-of-arms. She wished it said more, but it was formal and very correct.

> *Hanover Square,*
> *January 16th, 1800*
>
> *Dear Miss Martin,*
>
> *I am writing to express my happiness upon being granted your hand in marriage. Such an honor is not lost upon me, and I trust we will soon be able to meet. Until then,*
>
> *I am,*
>
> *Yours very sincerely,*
> *F. Vining*

With a sigh she refolded the vellum and pushed it back in her pocket. There were so many unanswered questions, so much she yearned to know. . . .

The wind blustered again, and she returned to the window seat, where she leaned her head back to resume her study of the water patterns on the glass. Her thoughts moved to St. Valentine's Eve, when Francis would be here. She'd embroidered two handkerchiefs with his initials, but now she didn't know whether or not it would be proper to give them to him on St. Valentine's Day itself. One moment it seemed right because she was to be his wife, the next it was wrong because they didn't know each other. Her mother thought it was quite acceptable to give him a Valentine gift, but her father did not, and her friends were equally divided, which meant that the weight of opinion was evenly balanced. The fate of the handkerchiefs was unresolved, and would probably remain so. Maybe they would have to keep until next year, when Francis would be her husband and there would be no problem at all about what to do on St. Valentine's Day.

Suddenly there was a rough pattering of large paws, and she got up with a laugh as two large Irish wolfhounds bounded along the gallery toward her. They were called Romulus and Remus, and were by no means as wild and dangerous as they looked; in fact, they were just playful overgrown puppies. The only trouble was that their notion of play was somewhat boisterous, for they didn't know their own strength and were certainly no respecters of fashionable clothes. Their claws slithered as they reached her and stood up on their hind legs to lick her face.

She laughed again as she hugged them both, and all her pessimistic thoughts were suddenly dispelled. The future would be happy, and she and Francis would fall in love. She just knew it!

"Miss Jane?" A footman's voice echoed along the gallery from the staircase.

She turned swiftly. "Yes, James, what is it?"

"Mr. Martin wishes you come to the great parlor."

She got up and hurried toward the staircase, with Romulus and Remus trotting at her heels.

The great parlor was on the floor below, and as its name denoted, it was a very large and lavish room indeed. In the past it had served as a bedchamber for Good Queen Bess herself, but now it was the drawing room. Leaving the wolfhounds outside, Jane entered.

Her parents were alone. Her father was standing with his back to the fire and looked a little strained, she thought with growing unease, while her mother, who wore a mauve dimity gown and was twisting a handkerchief in her hands, looked very upset indeed.

Jane hesitated uncertainly by the door. "What is it? What's happened?" she asked. Her mother sniffed and dabbed her eyes, and Jane hurried to crouch beside her chair. "Mother?"

Jane's father cleared his throat uncomfortably. He had become stout in recent years, but was still a handsome man. He wore a maroon coat and beige breeches, and his balding head shone because he'd removed his wig and tossed it onto a table. "Jane, my dear," he said, "I fear there is unwelcome news from Bath which means that I must go there first thing in the morning. It concerns my interest in the canal venture, and the distinct possibility that I have been swindled by my, er, partner." He glanced unhappily at his wife. "I'm sorry, my dear, but I cannot leave the matter as it stands. I know that Henry is your cousin, and that by challenging him I will be casting a shadow over your family's name, but I'm damned if I'll stand by and allow him to fleece me in order to settle his gambling debts."

Jane was shocked. "Cousin *Henry* has done such a thing?" she gasped.

"So it would appear from the discreet note I've received from my bank," her father confirmed.

Jane's mother struggled to regain her composure. "You must do as you see fit, of course, but I wish you would permit me to accompany you. After all, as you have pointed out, Henry is my cousin."

"Under any other circumstances I would agree, but not on this occasion."

Jane looked from one to the other. "What circumstances?" she asked.

"Mr. Vining's visit," her father replied. "I know that

he isn't expected here until Saint Valentine's Eve, but I have no idea how long my business in Bath will oblige me to remain there. Confronting Henry may not take time, but there is the matter of how to deal with him and how to recoup my losses. My bank has only informed me what is on the surface, but Henry may have plunged much deeper than is at present suspected, and I dare not take anything at face value."

Jane's mother looked faint. "Surely you do not suspect him of leaving us destitute?"

"No, my dear, for that would indeed have been obvious before now. I just need to be certain that I retrieve absolutely everything, down to the last farthing. A man does not hold on to his fortune by being casual about the small change, and so I may have to stay for several weeks in Bath, although of course I hope that that will not prove the case."

"But what if Henry has managed to purloin a great deal? Will Jane's match be in jeopardy?" Mrs. Martin asked tremulously.

"Not if I can help it. If worse comes to worst, and dear Henry's fingers are sticky with honey, then I will demand that your Croesus of an uncle makes up the difference. And if the old goat cuts up rough, then I will warn him that his son's misdeeds will be trumpeted the length and breadth of the land. His dread of scandal and odium will be sufficient threat, but I will use such a weapon only as a last resort. At present the matter lies solely between Henry and me."

"But—"

"My dear, it is imperative that I go to Bath, and it is equally imperative that you remain here with Jane to receive Mr. Vining should my return be delayed."

His wife drew a long breath and then nodded. "I will do as you wish," she replied, sniffing a little more and then wiping her eyes.

Mr. Martin went to place an understanding hand on her shoulder. "There, there, my dear, all will be well in the end, you have my word upon it. For the moment, however, I must make arrangements to leave at first light. The sooner I'm in Bath to see what Henry's been up to, the sooner I will return. Ah, the trials inflicted by one's kith and kin. . . ."

As he went out, his wife succumbed to tears, and it was left to Jane to offer what comfort she could. If they had but known it, Mr. Martin's business with the miscreant Cousin Henry was going to take almost two weeks to disentangle, and it would be St. Valentine's Eve itself when he returned.

The rain had stopped at dawn as Jane's father drove out of Priors Court onto the turnpike, and turned south toward the toll bridge over the river. The bridge was a quarter of a mile from the house, and was so ancient a crossing point that it boasted a hostelry that dated from medieval times. This hostelry was called the Barge Inn, and as Mr. Martin drove past there were various stagecoaches, gigs, and wagons drawn up outside, and a line of barges moored along the riverbank, for it was a favorite overnight halt for travelers.

On the day before Mr. Martin's return from Bath, Felix's stylish traveling carriage was going to pull up at the same inn, his departure from London delayed considerably by tiresome but pressing legal matters. As a result he couldn't set out until the twelfth of February, one day before Francis was expected at Priors Court. Such a wait was very vexing, for although he could make sure he didn't arrive at Northwood on St. Valentine's Day itself, his obligation to Francis allowed no such leeway. As it was, he would be able to reach Priors Court only just before Francis was actually expected, which meant that the unfortunate Martin family would already have made all their arrangements. It was impossible to write to them before then, for although he'd tried he hadn't been able to convincingly disguise his writing to look like his friend's awkward sloping scrawl, and there wasn't time to write to Francis, who had long since departed for an unknown address in Bath in single-minded pursuit of Dolly Ainsworth's charms. There was nothing for it but to call at Priors Court as promised.

By the time Felix eventually left London, he was in very sour spirits, and the thought of carrying out Francis's wishes did nothing to help, but at least the weather had relented, and now it was fine and sunny, if still very cold. As the carriage left Faringdon on the turnpike to Oxford, he endeavored to prepare himself for the ordeal of Priors Court, but it wasn't easy, especially on an empty stomach! Seeing the Barge Inn by the bridge ahead, he realized it was gone noon and he hadn't eaten since a very early breakfast of little more than warmed bread rolls and coffee. He knew that it was always a good sign if an inn attracted custom, so if the clutter of vehicles outside the Barge, to say nothing of the sailing barges moored alongside, were anything by which to judge, the landlord's table was to be recommended. Better to pause awhile to eat and assemble the remnants of his manners on a full stomach. He lowered the window and leaned out to instruct his coachman to halt at the inn.

The coachman maneuvered the team of handsome matched bays to a standstill, and Felix alighted. He wore an ankle-length charcoal greatcoat over a wine red coat and cream breeches, and there were spurs on his highly polished top boots. Taking a deep breath, he removed his tall hat to run his fingers through his fair hair, then slammed the carriage door behind him and bowed his head to enter the inn's low doorway. It was very noisy inside. There was a babble of male conversation, a fiddler was scraping out a tune, and pipe smoke hung in the warm air. The talk was mostly of the river and farming, with much grumbling about the recent excessive rain that had left the land waterlogged.

After eating, Felix lounged on a settle by the fire, a tankard of ale in his hand. Ale wasn't his favorite drink by any means, but in the winter when it was ice cold, he found it much more refreshing than anything else. He'd swiftly discovered that his fellow travelers patronized the inn because of the quantities it served rather than the quality, and he'd had a filling if not elegant meal of mutton pie, potatoes, and cabbage. Now it lay somewhat heavily in his stomach, as if throwing down the gauntlet to his digestive system. But indigestion would have set in even if he'd eaten something prepared by Lord Crewe's famous French chef, Monsieur Grillion, for he was loath to carry out his promise to Francis. And then there was Amelia. He glanced resignedly down at his signet ring. He was Foul and Villainous, just as she intended. She had exacted her pound of flesh, and no mistake.

His thoughts moved on to Francis's match, which was surely doomed before it began. He couldn't speak for the lady's character, but he knew Francis only too well. The fellow wasn't capable of keeping faith with just one woman, and he certainly wasn't capable of putting anyone else before himself. Poor Miss Martin. If ever a wife was destined to be neglected, it was she. After Dolly there would be another, and another, and so on until Francis Vining gave up his profligate soul.

"Will there be anything else, sir?"

Felix glanced up at the pert serving girl who'd bobbed a curtsy before him. "No, thank you," he replied, handing her his empty tankard and then getting up.

She smiled flirtatiously at him. "Are you quite sure, sir?" she asked invitingly.

He returned the smile and put his hand briefly to her chin. "Unfortunately, at this moment I'm only too sure," he said.

"Well, if you ever come this way again, just ask for Kate." Her hazel eyes were saucy.

"You're a very forward minx, Kate."

"Only with gentlemen I like."

"I'm flattered. Actually, there is something you can do for me."

"Anything you ask, sir."

He smiled again. "It's a very dull request, I fear. Can you tell me how much farther it is to Priors Court?"

"Priors Court?" She gave him a curious look. "Yes, sir. You're almost there now. The gates are about a quarter of a mile on toward Oxford."

"Thank you." He tossed a coin to her.

She pushed it between plump breasts that were revealed rather obviously by the low cut of her blue woolen dress. Then she studied him speculatively. "So you're the one, are you?" she said suddenly.

"The one?"

"The London swell who's to marry Miss Martin."

Before he had time to reply, the landlord called her away to attend to other customers.

As he retrieved his tall hat and greatcoat from the overloaded hooks in the entrance passage, he thought nothing more about having been taken for Francis, for there was a disturbance in the tap room and the angry landlord emerged holding a young farm laborer by the scruff of the neck.

"Out you go, Jem Randle, and don't come back till you've found your purse and your manners!" he said, shaking the man a little before ejecting him from the inn. Then he stood in the doorway with his hands on his hips. "That's the last I want to hear from you for a while, Jem! No money, no ale!" Wiping his hands on his starched apron, the landlord strode back along the passage into the tap room, leaving the unfortunate Jem to scramble to his feet and dust himself down.

The laborer wasn't blessed with good looks; indeed, he was a gangling young man with a receding chin and lank brown hair. His eyes were set close together above a large nose, and he was astonishingly scruffy, even for someone who worked on the land. And if his looks were no recommendation, neither was his nature, for his mouth twisted unpleasantly as he muttered and gestured after the landlord before tugging on his battered hat and shuffling away across the road to climb over a gate into a plowed field.

Felix watched him for a moment, and then turned up his greatcoat collar against the cold outside before he emerged from the inn, intending to climb back into his waiting carriage and get Francis's business over and done with as quickly as possible. But the Barge Inn's mutton pie had other notions. It still lay like a lead weight, and so he decided to walk it off before going to Priors Court.

He went past the waiting carriage, where the coachman whistled as he polished the Vestey coat-of-arms emblazoned on the gleaming lacquered door. There was a busy stable yard beside the inn, and in the far corner Felix saw a stile over a low wall. Beyond the stile he could see an overgrown path wending its way beside a backwater, where several rowing boats rocked idly on the shimmering water. He quickened his steps toward it and climbed over. As he dropped down the other side, the noise of the inn and yard was left behind and he found himself in a tranquil retreat, where the only sound was the murmur of water and the whisper of a barely discernible breeze through the dry reeds and naked willows. There were water birds, the occasional plop of a fish, and a blackbird that shattered the peacefulness as it suddenly fled noisily at his approach.

He shivered a little, thrusting his hands deep in his pockets and hunching his shoulders as a breath of cold air rippled the surface of the backwater and the feathers of two mute swans that glided past. Walking on beside the water, he became aware of two laughing female voices coming from a little way ahead, where the backwater curved out of sight beyond high reeds. The laughter was friendly and conspiratorial, and told of female plotting at the expense of some unsuspecting male. Felix continued to walk, but more slowly now, and gradually the bend of the backwater brought the women into view.

They were closer than he'd realized, for they stood on a little wooden bridge over the water, and they were leaning on the parapet, gazing down at their reflections as they talked. They were clearly mistress and maid, and the latter was simply dressed in a maroon mantle over a fawn dress. She was brunette, with the healthy glow of a true country girl, and she was so amused about something that she had to put her hand over her mouth to try to stem the laughter. But she wasn't of any interest to Felix—it was her mistress who captured his full attention. He recognized her immediately, for Miss Jane Martin was the image of the miniature Francis had shown him.

She wore a fur-trimmed hooded cloak made of warm golden merino, and a richly embroidered cream gown from beneath which peeped neat brown leather ankle boots. Her hood had fallen back on her head, revealing her face and tumbling russet curls. His gaze was drawn to her eyes. Edged with long, unexpectedly dark lashes, they were memorably large and gray, and so expressive that they seemed to reach deep inside him, even though she had no idea he was there and didn't even glance in his direction.

Transfixed, he could only gaze secretly at her through the swaying reeds that still hid him from view. There was something about her that cast a spell over him, a sweet spell, beguiling and irresistible. He watched her, and suddenly found himself eavesdropping upon the conversation.

Jane was teasing the maid. "Oh, come now, Peg Weston, you can't possibly lose heart now, not after all your stealthy creeping around. It's Saint Valentine's Day the day after tomorrow, and you must carry out your plan."

"But what if he walks straight past? I would die if he did, truly I would," the maid replied, becoming more serious. She drew a long breath. "I know I've been plotting it all for weeks now, but . . ."

"Peg, if a girl can't do something on the fourteenth of February, when can she? You've carried a torch for Jack Johnson for over a year now, and it's time you did something about it. Last Saint Valentine's Day you so lost your nerve that you actually denied having left that knitted scarf on his doorstep as a gift, and I'm determined that this year you don't fudge it all again."

"Yes, but—"

"Peg Weston, do you or do you not love my father's gamekeeper?" Jane interrupted sternly.

The maid lowered her eyes again. "Yes."

"Then you must go through with it." Jane smiled at her. "After all, he hasn't twigged anything yet, has he? He doesn't know you've been getting up at dawn and following him around, does he?"

"No, of course not."

"Which means he has no idea at all that you know he crosses this bridge at ten o'clock every morning, so he will think it really is a coincidence if you and he should encounter each other."

"But Jem Randle knows I'm up to something. He was going home after a night's poaching with his gang of cronies, and he saw me waiting near here. He's been pestering me to tell him ever since, but so far I've managed to put him off. Oh, I do loathe him so, he makes me shudder. I'd like to tell Jack that he's one of the poachers, but I'm afraid to. Jem's a nasty piece of work." The maid shivered and pulled a face.

Jane nodded sympathetically. "I know what you mean."

"He's always chased after me, and no matter how

many times I tell him I'm not interested, he just doesn't listen."

Jane smiled. "Well, when you've snapped Jack up at last, Jem Randle will have no option but to accept defeat. Just keep reminding yourself that a girl is supposed to marry the first man she sees on Saint Valentine's Day, and then see to it that Jack is the one *you* see! Avoid every man in the house, from the kitchen boys up, otherwise you'll break the charm, if charm there is. And for Heaven's sake, avoid Jem! He mustn't be the first man!"

"Oh, don't even joke about such a thing," Peg replied with immeasurable feeling, but then she laughed. "Can you just imagine it? Jem Randle and me? Ugh!"

They both burst into peals of laughter, and since he'd seen Jem Randle for himself, Felix couldn't help agreeing with their sentiments. The fellow was disagreeable in the extreme, and just the type to be involved with a poaching gang.

Felix found himself smiling with the two women as they laughed. They might be mistress and maid, but they were at ease with each other, like old friends. There were many who would have frowned upon such intimacy between a young lady and her servant, but he found it charming.

Their laughter gradually subsided, and Peg gave her mistress a surreptitious glance. "What will you do about Mr. Vining's Valentine gift, Miss Jane?" she asked.

"The wretched handkerchiefs? I still don't know," Jane sighed. "Sometimes I think giving them to him would be an appropriate gesture, and then I think it would be far too forward."

The maid was a little wicked. "What was that you said to me a moment ago? If a girl can't do something on Saint Valentine's Day, when can she?"

"There are times when you get above yourself, Peg Weston," Jane chided, but not unkindly. "Yes, I did say it, didn't I? I suppose you think I should present them to him?"

"Well, he *is* to be your husband."

Jane gazed thoughtfully down at the water. "Oh, Peg, I do wish I at least knew what he looks like. When I sent him that miniature, I was sure he'd respond in the same way, but he didn't, and all I've ever had from him is a polite line or so. It didn't tell me anything at all about him."

Felix raised an eyebrow. That was Francis for you, thoughtless of anything or anyone but himself.

Jane was smiling. "I dream that when he and I come face to face at last, we will fall in love." Then she straightened, a little embarrassed. "How foolish! It's all this talk of Saint Valentine's Day."

"I don't think it's foolish, Miss Jane. I know I wouldn't want an arranged match—" She broke off and went pink, knowing she'd spoken out of turn. "Begging your pardon, miss."

Jane hadn't taken offense. "I've been brought up to expect a husband to be chosen for me, and as an heiress I know that's really the wisest thing, but there are times . . ."

"Maybe you *will* love him, Miss Jane."

"But will he love me? That's the other question. How wretched it will be if we don't like each other at all, or if only one of us falls in love."

Felix drew a long breath. Poor sweet Jane, filled with romantic hopes that were bound to be dashed. Francis wasn't about to offer her any happiness at all. She didn't deserve such a fate, and Francis most certainly didn't deserve such an angel. An angel? Felix gazed at her. She'd affected him from the first moment he'd seen her, and now that he'd watched her for a while and gleaned something of her character, he knew that to him she *was* an angel. She was exquisite, an unspoiled innocent who drew him as surely as a moth is drawn to a flame. Such a creature was wasted upon the Honorable Francis Vining, who wouldn't know perfection if it was labeled and dangled before him on a string. Francis was a fool. In the woman he so insultingly dismissed as Plain Jane, he had a prize worth dying for. But he didn't want her, he wanted Dolly Ainsworth—at least, he wanted the actress now. Who knew who he'd want in a week's time?

Another breath of wind rippled the backwater, and Jane glanced back toward Priors Court. "I think we should go back. It wouldn't do for me to catch a cold now, and be red-nosed and snuffling when Mr. Vining arrives."

She pulled her hood farther forward over her delightfully unruly chestnut curls, and then she and the maid left the bridge. For a moment Felix feared they would walk his way, but to his relief they turned in the other direction.

He feasted his eyes on Jane until he could see her no more. He hadn't been relishing the prospect of calling at Priors Court to lie to her, and now he found it positively distasteful. The thought of hoodwinking her on behalf of a man as base as Francis was almost too much to bear.

He turned to retrace his steps toward the inn, and the farther he went from the bridge, the more savage his thoughts. Suddenly he knew he couldn't do what Francis asked. Obligation or not, he couldn't face Jane Martin and pretend anything for her husband-to-be, for that would mean knowingly condemning her to wretchedness. Such a prospect was something with which he could not live. The only honorable course was to tell her father the truth about the match he'd arranged. Tell the truth, and shame the Devil!

But his good intentions were to fall by the wayside. Indeed, he was soon to be guilty of an even greater deception than that which Francis had demanded of him.

*   *   *

It took only a few minutes for his carriage to drive from the Barge Inn to Priors Court, and it so happened that Jane and her maid arrived back at the house at the very moment his coachman drew the team to a standstill. The maid went on in, but Jane paused beneath the colonnade at the entrance to see who had called, and it was clear to Felix that he would have to speak to her before he had a chance to explain everything to her father first.

He alighted, and his heart both sank and soared as she emerged from the colonnade to speak to him. He was suddenly tongue-tied as he swept her a bow.

She approached. "I'm afraid my father is away from home at the moment, but may I be of some assistance, sir?"

He continued to gaze at her.

She found his silence unsettling. "Sir?"

Swiftly he removed his glove and drew her hand to his lips. "Miss Martin, I believe?" he murmured, trying to collect his scattered wits.

Suddenly she smiled right into his eyes. "Mr. Vining, I presume?" she said.

The smile cut through him like a knife, and he was conscious of her fragrance. Lily-of-the-valley. Yes, that was it. . . . Then he became aware that she thought he was Francis. "Vining? Why do you say that?" he asked, wanting to keep her fingers enclosed in his, but knowing he must release her.

"Because of your signet ring."

He looked swiftly at his hand. *F* and *V*. Felix Vestey. Francis Vining . . .

Her gray gaze was very direct. "I'm honored to make your acquaintance at last, Mr. Vining," she said softly.

"And I yours, Miss Martin," he heard himself replying.

"I–I have wondered so much what you would look like," she said a little hesitantly.

"I trust you are not disappointed," he replied, plunging still further into a morass of untruths and deceit. It was as if he couldn't help himself. Right now he wanted to be Francis Vining, he wanted it more than anything else in the world, and somewhere at the back of his mind he could hear Francis's voice. *The only member of Plain Jane's family I've met is her father, and that was on the day he and my old man deigned to inform me they'd settled my future.* She had just said that her father was away from home at the moment. . . .

She gave him another smile. "Disappointed? Why, no, sir, on the contrary."

"I'm glad," he said truthfully.

"I trust you can say the same of me?"

He gazed into her eyes. "Indeed I can, Miss Martin," he replied softly. He wanted to take her in his arms and kiss those sweet lips. A madness had seized him for he knew that such a deception was doomed to discovery, but still he went on with it. It was worth it if she was his for a while, just for a while.

She lowered her glance, the bloom on her cheeks warming still further. "I have thought so much about this moment, Mr. Vining. I was so afraid you wouldn't like me."

"Not like you? There is no man on earth who wouldn't like you, Miss Martin." Except the real Francis Vining, who was surely solid bone between the ears!

Something suddenly occurred to her. "We weren't expecting you until tomorrow, Mr. Vining. I trust we haven't made a mistake about the dates?"

"I, er, decided to come early. I couldn't wait any longer, I had to meet you."

"I'm glad," she said softly.

The desire to hold her was almost too much for him, and he had to look away. Then he remembered the telltale blue and gold Vestey coat-of-arms on the carriage doors. Francis always wrote on vellum embellished with that of the Vining family, which was red and black. He distracted her attention. "The, er, park is very fine, Miss Martin," he observed, positioning himself properly between her and the carriage door the moment her gaze was diverted.

"My grandfather laid it out."

"He was a man of great taste."

She smiled. "Yes, he was."

"Did you say your father wasn't here at the moment?" he asked, hoping to learn that the gentleman concerned would be away for a long time, time during which he could set about winning Jane's heart.

"Yes. I'm afraid he was called away to Bath and has been delayed there, but my mother is here, and you are still more than welcome."

Of all places, Mr. Martin was in Bath? Heaven help Francis if he was caught, for the match by which his father set such store would crumble into nothing in a moment. "I, er, I'm sorry I won't meet your father again just yet," he murmured.

"Please come inside to meet my mother."

He offered her his arm, and she slipped her hand over his sleeve.

The coachman urged the team into action again, following a beckoning groom who showed him into the stable yard. Soon the carriage was ensconced out of sight in one of the coach houses, and as Felix accompanied Jane toward the colonnade he was relieved that the coat-of-arms hadn't caught her attention. But he knew it couldn't be long before he was exposed as an imposter. His great aunt had accused him of lunacy for breaking off his match with Amelia, but this was real lunacy. He was completely moonstruck, behaving in a way he'd never dreamed possible. To actually pretend to be someone else, and to do so in the full knowledge that a shameful unmasking was the only

possible outcome, was conduct worthy of the most witless inmate of Bedlam itself.

But still he meant to proceed. He intended to be
Francis for as long as he could because he wanted her
for himself; he wanted her more than he'd ever
wanted any woman before. It wasn't mere carnal desire, for he'd looked at her and fallen in love. She and
her maid had talked of St. Valentine's Day, but today
was that day for him. There was magic in the air.
Magic, and hearts, and the scent of lily-of-the-valley.
And a young woman with breathtaking gray eyes and
flame-colored hair.

Mrs. Martin was enjoying a quiet hour at her tambour frame in the great parlor, and was put in quite
a pother by "Mr. Vining's" unexpected arrival a day
early. She had been hoping against hope that her husband would manage to return from Bath in time to
receive him, but that hope was dashed in an instant
when Jane brought Felix into the room and introduced
him.

"Mother, may I present Mr. Vining?"

For a moment Mrs. Martin stared blankly at him,
and then hastily set her tambour frame aside and rose
to her feet in an agitated flurry of olive cashmere.
"Mr. Vining? Oh, forgive me, I—"

Felix took her hand and raised it gallantly to his
lips. "I am the one who should seek forgiveness, Mrs.
Martin, for I have arrived somewhat prematurely. I
trust I have not caused you any inconvenience?" As
he smiled at her, he was again conscious of how out-
rageously he was behaving.

His elegance of manner charmed Jane's mother.
"Inconvenience? Why, no, sir, indeed we are delighted
to receive you. Please take a seat, Mr. Vining." Mrs.
Martin indicated a comfortable chair, and when they
were all seated she asked him if he had had an agreeable journey.

The ensuing conversation was polite but pleasantly informal, and Felix was aware of how easily he fitted in. The real Francis Vining would have adopted such airs and graces that these opening minutes would have been very tense indeed. It was good to be here like this, good to be accepted as Jane's future husband. But it was make-believe, and he was deluding himself that it could ever be anything more. In the meantime, however, oh, in the meantime . . .

After sitting together for nearly an hour in agreeable conversation, Felix was conducted up to his room by the butler, and the moment he'd left the great parlor, Mrs. Martin turned to her daughter.

"My dear, he is utterly charming. And so handsome!"

"Yes."

"Is that all you have to say?"

Jane blushed a little. "Mother, I hardly dare put into words how happy I am. I was so afraid that our meeting would be a disaster, but instead it has been perfect."

Her mother went to hug her. "If you are happy, then so am I. There's just one thing that puzzles me."

"Puzzles you?" Jane looked inquiringly at her.

"Yes. When your father returned from his meeting with Mr. Vining, I am positive he described him as having very dark hair and eyes, but the opposite is the case."

"You must be mistaken about what Father said."

"Yes, indeed I must. Ah, well, of what importance is such a detail? Now, I have much to do, for I must see that an appropriate meal is served at dinner tonight." Gathering her skirts, Mrs. Martin hastened from the room.

Jane went to the window and gazed down over the park toward the river. Elation had seized her, so much so that there were tears in her eyes. She had dreamed of falling in love with Mr. Vining at first sight, and that was surely what had happened. From the moment he'd kissed her hand, she had been lost. And she was sure that the feeling was mutual, for during the past hour she had felt his warm glance resting frequently upon her. She was truly the most fortunate of creatures, for how often did it happen that an arranged match promised such happiness?

The joy continued. Dinner that night was very pleasant indeed, and Jane was conscious of how much she glowed in his company. She wanted to look her best, and she did. With her russet curls swept up on top of her head and wearing a lemon taffeta gown, she knew that she had seldom appeared to better advantage, and she was rewarded by his smiles.

A whirl of excitement coursed constantly through her, and it was so restless a feeling that when they retired at nearly midnight she knew she could never sleep. She lay in her bed gazing up at the canopy, willing the hours to pass swiftly until morning, when she could be with him again.

Felix was similarly beset by sleeplessness, and for the same reason, except that his excitement was tempered with a very guilty conscience. What he was doing was very wrong. He'd found fault with Francis for wanting to deceive her, but that was precisely what he himself was doing now. And doing with complete success.

Still fully dressed in a black velvet coat and white silk knee breeches, he stood by the moonlit window, staring down at the silver park. The clock on the mantelpiece behind him struck one, and he turned to glance at the bed. Sleep? He might as well try to fly to the moon that shone so brilliantly tonight. If he'd been in London he would have solved his sleeplessness by taking a stroll, but that would hardly do here.

Then a thought struck him. Houses like this nearly always had a long gallery on the top floor. Such galleries were intended for strolling in during inclement weather and would serve his purpose now. With sudden decision he left the room and went out into the candlelit passage, where he'd earlier noticed the staircase leading up to the next floor.

He walked quietly, for he didn't want to disturb anyone, and in a short while he discovered that his guess was correct: there was indeed a gallery. It was in darkness, but the curtains weren't drawn and the moonlight filtered in, casting an almost ghostly glow over everything as he began to stroll slowly toward the far end, pausing only to warm his hands briefly at the first of the two fireplaces.

His thoughts were all of Jane and the overwhelming effect she'd had upon him. In the space of a heartbeat she'd taken over his whole life, and nothing would ever be the same again. He didn't just want her to be his, he *needed* her to be his.... He felt about her in a way he'd never felt about Amelia, and he knew it was a feeling that would never leave him. But his very presence here was based on a lie. She believed him to be Francis Vining, and it was Francis she was contracted to marry. A sense of hopelessness washed over him. Did he dare to confess the truth? Could he take the chance? He was sure she was as enamored with him as he was with her, but would she still feel the same way when she learned how he'd deceived her?

He paused, and as chance would have it he was next to the window seat where Jane liked to come. She'd been there earlier that very day, and her book of poetry lay where she'd left it. The moonlight shone on the gilded leather cover, attracting his attention. Curious, he went to pick it up, and as he looked inside he saw Jane's name. He could tell that the volume was much read, and then he turned to the page where she'd placed her bookmark. By the light of the moon he read the very lines that had recently so disturbed her.

Those awful words 'Till death do part'
May well alarm the youthful heart:
No after-thought when once a wife;
The die is cast, and cast for life;

His thoughts winged back to the moment he'd first
seen her on the bridge. It was no coincidence that this
poem was marked, for it had been in her mind when
she'd spoken of Francis. How wistful and uncertain
she'd been, and how different now. Her doubts had
been removed because of the dishonorable lies perpetrated on the spur of the moment by the man she
believed to be Francis Vining. he had to tell her the
truth. His conscience and honor would not allow anything else.

As he read the poem in the gallery, Jane herself
was tossing and turning in her bed, still unsuccessfully
trying to go to sleep. She sat up at last, pushing her
tangled curls back from her face. This was hopeless.
The more she tried the worse it became. Perhaps if
she read for a while. Yes, that was the thing. She
turned to the little table at the bedside, where the
night light glowed softly in its holder. Her book of
poetry wasn't there. For a moment she was puzzled,
but then she remembered. Of course, she'd left it in
the gallery that morning!

Flinging the bed clothes aside, she got up and put
on her warm pink wrap. Then, after lighting a fresh
candle from the fire, she slipped from the room, her
bare feet making no sound as she went up the
staircase.

Felix didn't hear her approaching, but he saw the
swaying light of the candle as she came up toward the
gallery. With the book still in his hand, he moved
several windows farther on and pressed back out of
sight as whoever it was reached the top of the staircase. As he glanced cautiously out, he saw that it was
Jane.

He gazed secretly at her as she hurried unknowingly toward the window seat where she'd left the book. How beautiful she was, with her glorious hair tumbling in profusion over her shoulders. He watched as she reached the window seat and paused with her brows drawn together.

Then he stepped out. "Is this what you seek?" he asked, holding out the book.

At the sound of his voice she whirled around so swiftly that she almost dropped the candle. The flame smoked and threatened to die, but then she shielded it with her hand.

"Mr. Vining?"

"Forgive me, I didn't mean to startle you," he said, going toward her. "I couldn't sleep and guessed there would be a gallery up here."

"I–I couldn't sleep either," she confessed. "I thought reading might help."

He glanced at the book, and then met her eyes in the candlelight. " 'No after-thought when once a wife/ The die is cast, and cast for life,' " he murmured.

She lowered her glance quickly, and even in the soft light he could see the flush that stained her cheeks.

He wanted to touch her but resisted. "I didn't mean to embarrass you, Miss Martin. It's just that I looked at the last page you'd read. It would be difficult not to guess the thoughts such lines would arouse," he said, putting the book down on the seat.

"Past thoughts, sir," she replied, looking at him again. "I admit that I was very nervous indeed about meeting you."

"And now that you have?"

She smiled, her eyes more expressive than ever in the candlelight. "Now that I have, I could not be more happy."

His heart seemed to miss a beat. "Do you really mean it?" he asked softly.

"What point is there in being coy, sir? Yes, I really

mean it. All my fears have been dispelled, because I am sure that you and I will be happy together." Embarrassed at having been so forthright, she looked down again.

The temptation to touch her was suddenly too much, and he reached out to put his hand to her chin, raising her face toward his again. "Miss Martin, Jane ..." Confession hung trembling on his lips, but died as he saw the way her eyes closed with emotion at his touch. He couldn't tell her the truth, not at a moment as tender and close as this. Slowly he bent forward, brushing his lips over hers.

A sigh escaped her as she met the kiss. Electrifying feelings sang through her, awakening her body as never before. Her lips parted beneath his, and she didn't resist as he slipped his arms around her waist and drew her nearer.

He felt how warm and pliant she was, and her perfume filled his nostrils. Lily-of-the-valley, lingering sweetly on her skin and in her hair. Oh, Jane, my dearest Jane ...

She was suddenly conscious of having welcomed an intimacy that had no place in so new an acquaintance. Disconcerted by the speed with which everything was advancing, she drew swiftly back, her breath catching slightly.

He didn't want to release her, but she slipped like gossamer from his embrace and fled back toward the staircase.

"Jane!"

But she'd gone, the fluttering candle casting leaping shadows up the walls after she passed from his sight. He felt as if she were still in his arms, warm, supple, and willing. She was the stuff of his dreams, and now that he'd kissed her, he knew a confession would be even more difficult, if not impossible. How could he admit that he'd so abused her trust as to do what he'd just done? His conduct, already dishonorable, had now sunk into baseness beyond belief.

He closed his eyes wretchedly. Bitter regret seized him, but it was too late now. What was done was done, and no amount of wishing could turn the clocks back. He was an imposter, and he could only imagine how she would despise him when she found out. Unless her love for him was strong enough to withstand such a blow.

His eyes flew open again, and suddenly they were alight with renewed determination. It wasn't Francis Vining she'd fallen for now, it was Felix Vestey. *He* was the one she'd met, the one who'd aroused her feelings so far as to allow him to kiss her. Tomorrow he had to win her completely, he had to convince her of his love, and then, when he braced himself to tell her he wasn't Francis Vining, he had to make certain that she understood and accepted that it was his heart that had moved him to deception, not any casual whim based on mischief or even malice. He hadn't come to Priors Court intent upon deceit and seduction; he'd come to save her from the misery of a match with the real Francis Vining. But she had affected him so much that when opportunity presented itself, he'd cast caution to the four winds. It was the worst predicament of his life, but one from which he was resolved to emerge with the prize that now meant everything to him, Miss Jane Martin's hand in marriage.

He drew a long breath. Tomorrow was St. Valentine's Eve, and he intended to lay his plans as assiduously as the maid had laid hers for the gamekeeper. The imposter's mask would be removed, but beneath it Jane would see the ardent and true lover. He would never willingly surrender her to Francis Vining. Never.

The following morning was dull and overcast, but there was no rain. Low clouds filled the skies, and sound seemed to travel a long way, so that the post horn of the Faringdon–Oxford mail coach could be heard long before it reached the bridge by the Barge Inn. But in spite of the uninviting weather, Felix engineered it at the breakfast table so that Mrs. Martin urged Jane to escort him on a ride.

Breakfast itself hadn't begun very auspiciously, because the moment he entered the dining room he saw from Jane's swiftly averted eyes that she was still hugely embarrassed by what she regarded as her indiscretion the night before. She was toying with her meal rather than eating it, and he guessed that her slice of toast had been on the plate for some time before he came in.

She looked very vulnerable as she sat there in a dove gray dimity gown, her hair swept up beneath a demure lace morning cap. Her face was pale, and he guessed that she, like him, had had very little sleep.

Mrs. Martin, on the other hand, had slept very well indeed, and such was her relief at perceiving the successful outcome of the match arranged for her daughter that she was in excellent spirits. She wore a cherry woolen gown, and there was a warm shawl around her shoulders. There was nothing poor about her appetite, for she was enjoying a generous helping of bacon and scrambled eggs.

She smiled as he entered. "Good morning, Mr. Vining."

"Good morning, Mrs. Martin. Miss Martin." His eyes swung to Jane as he bowed, but although she met his glance for a second, she looked quickly away again as she nodded a response.

"Mr. Vining," she murmured.

Her mother looked curiously at her, and then gave him another smile as he went to the sideboard to select his breakfast. "I trust you slept well, sir?"

"Yes, thank you."

"The bed is a little old, I fear, but it was once slept in by Queen Elizabeth herself, and—"

"The bed is very comfortable," he said, coming to the table and taking his seat opposite Jane.

Mrs. Martin smiled at Jane. "Well, my dear, and what trickery does your minx of a maid have planned for tomorrow?"

"Tomorrow?" Jane was too preoccupied to pay proper attention.

"St. Valentine's Day," her mother prompted. "I take it that she is still intent upon the gamekeeper?"

"Yes, she is."

"And?" Mrs. Martin looked intently at her. "Oh, do tell me, my dear, for I know she's up to something."

Jane collected herself. "Er, yes, she is. She intends to waylay Jack on the little bridge at ten o'clock tomorrow morning. He always crosses it at that time."

"She wants him to be the first man she sees?"

"Yes. She's going to avoid the butler, every footman, and even the kitchen boys."

Mrs. Martin smiled. "Well, I hope she succeeds, for it's long since time Johnson was married. He needs a wife." She turned the smile upon Felix. "And what is your opinion of Saint Valentine's Day, Mr. Vining?"

"I'm all in favor of it, Mrs. Martin," he replied, looking at Jane.

Mrs. Martin's gaze moved almost slyly to her daughter. "There you are, my dear, your quandary is no more," she murmured.

"Mother!" Jane went crimson.

Felix glanced from one to the other. "Is there something I should know?" he asked at last.

"Yes," Mrs. Martin replied

"No," Jane said at the same time.

Her mother raised an arch eyebrow and then looked at Felix. "She has been embroidering you a Valentine gift, Mr. Vining, but has been dithering about giving it to you."

Jane's cheeks were now quite fiery. "Please, Mother . . ."

Felix smiled at her. "I will welcome your gift, Miss Martin, and will be sure to return the compliment."

Their eyes met for a moment.

There was a discreet knock at the door, and a footman came in with a small silver salver upon which lay a letter that had just been delivered by special messenger. Mrs. Martin gave a cry of delight as she recognized the writing.

"Jane, it's from your father!" Breaking the seal, she read the few hastily scribbled lines, then she beamed. "His business in Bath is almost concluded and he will be returning tomorrow evening. No, *this* evening, for this was written yesterday!"

Felix's heart sank. This evening? That didn't give him very long to convince Jane of his complete sincerity, for the moment Mr. Martin returned he'd know a stranger was masquerading as Francis Vining. He glanced outside, where the overcast morning showed no signs of lifting. Somehow he had to be alone with Jane. But how?

Inspiration came from nowhere, and he smiled at her mother. "The park here is very handsome indeed, Mrs. Martin."

"Why, thank you, Mr. Vining."

"I wonder, would it be possible to take one of your saddle horses and go for a ride?"

She nodded. "Of course, sir. The stables are entirely at your disposal."

His glance moved to Jane. "Perhaps you would care to join me, Miss Martin?"

Jane looked up from contemplating her piece of toast. "I–I fear I have much to do today, Mr. Vining."

Her mother frowned. "Much to do? What nonsense. You must abandon all tasks today and take Mr. Vining on a tour of the park."

"But—"

"I insist, my dear. You're looking a little pale, and a ride would bring the roses to your cheeks."

Jane glanced reluctantly toward him. "I will be delighted to show you over the park, Mr. Vining," she murmured.

An hour later they set off, Jane wearing her rose woolen riding habit and veiled black hat, and Felix in the pine green coat and cream cord breeches that were considered virtually essential riding wear for gentlemen of fashion. The Priors Court stables contained many fine horses, and Felix was well pleased with the lively roan stallion he had chosen. Jane rode her favorite mount, a pretty bay mare whose gentle looks disguised a spirited disposition.

Nothing was said as they left the stable yard and rode across the park in the direction of the river, where the sails of several barges could be seen between the willows and reeds. They emerged from the park not far from the bridge over the backwater, and Jane led him across it and then into the meadow through which the main river flowed. Even this far inland the Thames was busy, and upstream at the inn at least half a dozen barges were moored as their crews took a well-earned rest. Jane rode downstream, following the narrow, reed-fringed towpath, which obliged Felix to ride behind her and prevented him from conducting conversation.

He was soon frustrated, for the whole point of being alone with her was in order to speak. As they reached a fork in the path and she began to continue along the river, he deliberately rode along the other path instead.

"Enough of the river, Miss Martin," he called over his shoulder.

Jane reined in. "Mr. Vining!"

But he rode on, knowing that she would have little option but to follow. As soon as he reached a secluded spot, where alders grew around a little clearing of grass beside another of the innumerable backwaters, he reined in and waited for her.

She rode into the clearing and halted her horse. "If we'd followed the river we would soon have entered the park again," she said after a moment, still avoiding his eyes.

"Where you would no doubt have set off at a gallop," he said.

Behind the net veil of her riding habit she colored a little.

"About last night—"

"Please, I would prefer to forget it."

"Forget it? That's the last thing I wish to do. Jane, I want to talk to you, but you are making that feat well nigh impossible."

"Because my conduct was reprehensible, Mr. Vining."

He raised an eyebrow. "*Your* conduct? What of mine? If you recall, *I* was the one to make the move."

"Nevertheless—"

"You did not spurn me, Jane," he pointed out softly.

She looked unhappily at him. "No, but I should have."

"Why? Jane, you feel the same way about me as I do about you, so why was it wrong?"

"Because I hardly know you, Mr. Vining."

"We are to be married."

"I still hardly know you, and my actions last night can only be described as unbecoming. I would be grateful if you would pretend it hadn't happened."

"I can never pretend that, especially as I see no need to."

She glanced up, for it had begun to rain. The drops fell softly at first, but then increased. "We should return to the house," she said quickly.

"Jane, we have to reach a proper understanding—"

"We'll talk at the house," she replied, looking up again as the rain fell still more heavily.

"Do you promise?"

She nodded. "Yes, I promise."

"Very well." He urged his horse forward, following her as she rode swiftly back along the path.

They galloped home, their horses' hooves drumming on the springy grass of the park, but if either of them had looked toward the main gates and the turnpike road, they'd have seen Mr. Martin's traveling carriage arriving from Bath even earlier than he'd hoped. But they didn't look, for they were too concerned with gaining shelter.

The skies were very dark indeed, promising a considerable deluge, and it was with some relief that Felix and Jane reached the yard and dismounted before handing the reins to the grooms who hurried out to meet them. The downpour was now torrential. Water streamed from the roofs and gutters, and gurgled down into water butts and channels in the cobbles. Jane made to run back to the house itself, and Felix followed, but as they passed the open doors of one of the coach houses, he suddenly caught her arm and dragged her inside.

"You promised we would talk," he reminded her.

"At the house—" she began.

"No, here, where we can be completely private." He removed his top hat and gloves, and placed them on the wheel of the nearest carriage. It was his own vehicle, although he was so intent upon Jane that he didn't realize it.

He raised the veil of her riding hat, the better to see her eyes. "Jane, last night I took advantage of the situation, I admit it, but if you only knew how much I wanted to kiss you, how much I want to kiss you again now ..." He put his hand to her wet cheek. "It's Saint Valentine's Eve, and I have to let you know what's in my heart."

There was a window next to where he stood, and on impulse he reached up to write in the dust. I love you.

She stared at the words.

He put his hand to her cheek again. "I do love you, Jane, I loved you at first sight yesterday." Dear God, was it only yesterday? He felt as if he'd loved her forever.

She gazed up into his eyes, trapped by the beguiling feelings his touch aroused, and by the sheer joy his words brought. He loved her?

"Have you nothing to say?" he asked softly, caressing her with his thumb.

"I love you too," she whispered.

"Oh, Jane ..." he breathed, pulling her into his arms and kissing her on the lips. There was nothing hesitant now—he crushed her close, his lips moving richly and passionately over hers, and he was rewarded by the way she pressed against him, her passion meeting his. His fingers curled in the damp hair at the nape of her neck, and the scent of lily-of-the-valley seemed to envelop him. It was an intoxicating fragrance, one he knew he would ever after associate with her.

There were tears of happiness in her eyes as they drew apart at last. "Oh, Francis, I can hardly believe this is happening," she breathed.

Francis. The name washed coldly over him, reminding him of his deception. He moved away slightly, trying to find the right words.

She looked a little anxiously at him. "Is something wrong?"

"Jane, there is something important I have to tell you." He faced her, his courage at last screwed up to the necessary pitch.

"Yes? What is it?"

"I—" He broke off irritably as the rear door of the coach house was suddenly opened and two grooms came in, laughing and chattering together as they went about some task without realizing there was anyone else nearby.

Jane glanced nervously in their direction, aware that anyone seeing her alone with Francis like this would be bound to spread titillating whispers. It wouldn't do, it wouldn't do at all, even if she *was* going to marry Francis.

She looked urgently at Felix. "We mustn't be caught in such a compromising situation. We should go back to the house," she whispered urgently.

"Jane—"

She shook her head. "Please, Francis," she insisted, turning to go outside into the rain. But as she turned her glance fell at last upon the blue and gold coat-of-arms on the carriage door. She stared at it, her eyes a little puzzled. Something wasn't quite right. Her puzzlement increased then as she realized that it wasn't the same coat-of-arms at the top of the letter he'd written.

There was something else too. . . . Slowly she looked at the window. The writing wasn't the same as Francis's either. The words on the glass were upright and firm, totally unlike her future husband's. Suddenly she recalled what her mother had said about her father describing Francis Vining as dark-haired and dark-eyed.

Dismayed, Felix saw each successive thought cross her face, and knew he was found out. Damn the carriage door! And damn Francis for having such distinctive writing!

She began to tremble. "You're not Francis Vining, are you?" she whispered.

"No, I'm not. Jane, I—" He reached out to her.

But she gave a silent gasp of alarm and backed away.

"Please let me explain," he begged, taking a step toward her.

"No! Don't touch me!" she cried, and then gathered her skirts to hurry out into the rain.

For a moment he was too dismayed to do anything,

but then he collected his wits. He had to make her listen. Leaving his hat and gloves on the carriage wheel, he dashed out after her.

In the coach house, the two bemused grooms exchanged curious glances.

Jane was deeply shaken as she ran into the house, but as she reached the foot of the staircase she was halted by the unexpected sound of her father's voice.

"Ah, there you are, Jane!" he called from the other end of the hall, where he'd just removed his greatcoat and hat and was greeting her mother.

Slowly Jane turned to face him. She was so upset that she couldn't say anything, but simply stared at her parents.

Mr. Martin's smile faded and he became concerned. "Jane? What is it, my dear?"

Before she could respond, Felix hurried into the hall behind her. "Jane, please allow me to explain!" he cried, coming to an abrupt standstill as he too saw her father.

Mr. Martin looked at him. "And who are you, sir?" he asked.

Jane's mother was taken aback. "My dear, it's Mr. Vining. Surely you—"

"Remember him? Oh, yes, I remember Mr. Vining very well indeed, and this is certainly not he," Mr. Martin replied.

His wife looked faint. "Not Mr. Vining?" she repeated.

"That is correct." Mr. Martin's gaze hadn't wavered from Felix. "Well, sir?"

Felix drew a long breath, glancing again at Jane's distraught face, and then bowing to her father. "Felix Vestey, your servant, sir," he said, sweeping a bow.

"Well, Mr. Vestey, I am sure you have a glib explanation to hand for your disgraceful masquerade, but I am not interested in hearing it. You are to leave this house immediately."

"Sir—"

"Immediately, sirrah!" Mr. Martin snapped, his face furious. "How dare you perpetrate this deceit upon my wife and daughter!"

"If you will only allow me to explain—" Felix pleaded desperately.

"Do you think you deserve such a concession?" Mr. Martin demanded coldly.

Felix lowered his glance for a moment. "No, sir," he admitted.

"Then on that at least we are agreed. I don't know what you and that scoundrel Vining have concocted between you, but it has not succeeded! Now, sir, I requested you to leave, and that is what I expect you to do."

Jane stared at her father. That *scoundrel* Vining? Why had her father used such a word to describe the real Francis?

Felix noticed the word as well, and hazarded a guess that Francis's presence in Bath had not only been detected, but that Jane's father had actually discovered his prospective son-in-law's liaison with Dolly Ainsworth!

Mr. Martin was impatient. "I await your departure, *Mr.* Vestey!" he snapped.

Felix looked at Jane again. "I meant every word I said. I love you and my intentions are entirely honorable."

"How can I believe anything you say to me, sir? You told me you were Mr. Vining, but that was quite patently untrue."

"Jane, please—"

"I don't want to have anything more to do with you, Mr. Vestey," she cried, and then turned to continue swiftly up the staircase to hide how close she was to bursting into tears. He'd lied to her in the cruelest of ways, luring her into trusting him, and then using that trust to make advances that now, when it was far too late, she wished with all her heart she'd spurned. She was unutterably ashamed of her indiscretions with him, and now wished to hide away from the world.

Reaching the top of the staircase, she fled to her room, where she flung herself tearfully onto the bed, burying her face in her pillows and giving in to the racking sobs that shook her whole body.

In the hall, Mr. Martin's icy fury was directed at Felix. "You heard my daughter, sir, she doesn't wish to have anything more to do with you. Now, if you do not leave immediately, I will have you thrown out."

A nerve flickered angrily at Felix's temple. Under any other circumstances he would not have suffered anyone to speak to him like that, but these circumstances were so very different. He was in the wrong, and Jane's father was justified in treating him like this. For the moment all was lost, and he had to concede temporary defeat. But he wouldn't give up, of that he was certain. He wanted Jane, and he meant to win her back.

He inclined his head to Mr. Martin. "There will be no need to resort to force, sir, for I will go."

"You may wait outside, sir, and I will have your belongings brought out and your carriage prepared."

Felix glanced through a window at the rain, which still fell heavily from leaden skies, but then he bowed to Martin. "As you wish, sir," he murmured.

"And let me warn you of one thing, sir. If I hear a single whisper which is to my daughter's disadvantage—"

"You dishonor me to even hint at such a thing, sir," Felix replied stiffly. Then he turned on his heel and walked out into the rain.

Behind him, Mrs. Martin looked askance at her husband. "My dear . . . ?"

"I will explain directly, as soon as I've attended to

the removal of that imposter from my property," he replied shortly.

"But what of the real Mr. Vining?"

"I called him a scoundrel, and that is precisely what he is!"

His wife stared as he strode across the hall calling for the butler. Then she glanced unhappily up the staircase, thinking of her daughter. Poor Jane. Last night she had been so very happy, but today, on St. Valentine's Eve, she was reduced to a mortifying misery the depth of which could only be guessed.

Tears filled Mrs. Martin's eyes, but she didn't go up to her daughter. All in good time. First she had to find out exactly what had taken place in Bath.

Half an hour later, with the rain still sluicing down over the park, Felix's carriage drove out of Priors Court. He had instructed his coachman to drive on to Northwood, but as he looked back toward the house, he suddenly knew that he couldn't go that far away. He had to stay nearby, and fight for what he wanted.

Lowering the window glass, he leaned out into the rain. "I've changed my mind. Go to the inn instead," he shouted above the weather.

"Sir." The coachman touched his wet hat and then slowed the team to maneuver the carriage around in the road. Then he brought them up to a trot again toward the Barge Inn.

A minute or so earlier, Mrs. Martin had been standing by one of the great parlor windows, watching Felix's carriage as it drove toward the gates, but she turned back toward her husband before the coachman was reinstructed,.

"Mr. Vestey has left now, my dear," she said, "and so I trust you mean to explain what all this is about?"

"About? I have no idea about Vestey, but I can tell you that I wish to God I'd never even *heard* of that reprobate Vining!" he replied, helping himself to a large measure of cognac and then standing with his back to the fire.

Mrs. Martin's hand crept nervously to her throat "Reprobate?" she repeated weakly.

"No less a word will do to describe him. I fear that if it had not been for Cousin Henry's sleight of hand with my money, for which he has apologized profusely and made satisfactory recompense, Jane would have been married to a libertine."

"Oh dear ..." His wife sat down abruptly.

He drew a heavy breath. "It so happened that one evening I chose to attend the theater, to see Miss Ainsworth in *She Stoops to Conquer*." He gave an angry laugh. "And stoop to conquer she did! I noticed young Vining in one of the boxes opposite, although he didn't see me. He didn't take his eyes off her throughout the performance, and it was plain that he found her very much to his liking. Needless to say, I watched him closely, and I saw him give a note to the box man. When Miss Ainsworth next came on stage, I distinctly saw her nod at him. The note was quite plainly for her, and she was indicating her agreement to whatever it said. I made it my business to wait outside the stage door when the evening was ended, and I saw him among the other would-be *beaux* gathered there. He alone was admitted. I stayed, keeping well out of sight until long after the area had cleared, and, sure enough, he came out with her. They were exceeding cozy together! They entered his carriage, and I followed them in mine. They went to the Sydney Hotel, where I learned they enjoyed an even cozier dinner together in a private room. After that they adjourned to the house she has taken in Laura Place. It was very late by then, and I was tired, so I bribed an urchin to inform me exactly when he departed, and the following day I was told he'd left after breakfast!"

"Oh, dear ..."

Jane's father drew another long breath. "To cut a long story short, I found out where he was staying and called upon him. To say that he was startled to see me is an understatement, for he went positively green! I told him all that I'd observed, and that the match with my daughter was at an end. I also informed him that I would tell his father exactly why I had withdrawn from the contract. He actually had the audacity to beg me not to because his allowance would be stopped! The fellow has gall, I'll give him that. My dear, I believe Jane has had a fortunate escape."

"Fortunate indeed," she murmured faintly.

He looked at her. "That is my story concerning the real Vining. I wish to God I knew why he and Vestey contrived their plot, but no satisfactory explanation comes to mind. What did they hope to achieve? It's quite plain that Vestey's imposture would soon be uncovered."

"I don't know."

"We may never learn, but in the meantime I wish to know exactly what has been going on here during my absence, and whether or not this Vestey person has compromised Jane beyond all redemption!"

Mrs. Martin was aghast. "Oh, please don't say that!"

"It has to be faced, my dear. His activities may have brought about her ruin."

His wife stared. "Oh, no, Jane wouldn't . . ."

"You saw the state she was in a few minutes ago, and that was *before* I exposed him as an imposter. If he has attempted to seduce her, or worse, if he has actually succeeded in—"

"Don't say it!" Mrs. Martin begged, her voice almost a squeak.

"Just say what has happened."

She composed herself, and then told him all she knew, from the moment Jane had brought Felix into the great parlor the day before.

Mr. Martin's brow darkened. "So, he spent last night beneath this roof, and he was alone with Jane this morning when they went out riding. And she returned from that ride in a state of some distress."

She bit her lip. "Yes, but—"

"What buts can there be? At the very least the fellow must have attempted to force his attentions upon her!"

"I don't think so, my dear," she replied, her voice suddenly more calm as she thought about it all.

"Thinking and knowing are two different things," he snapped.

"You weren't here, my dear, you didn't see them together. Last night Jane was happier than I've seen her in a long time. She was delighted with the man she believed to be Mr. Vining, and she believed her arranged match was going to be a complete success. I would even go so far as to say that for her it was a case of love at first sight. As for Mr. Vestey, well, imposter he may be, but I believe he is equally attached to Jane," she declared with conviction.

"Vile seducers are always excellent actors, my dear, especially if they are impoverished and pursuing a fortune," he pointed out tersely.

"I don't profess to know why Mr. Vestey behaved as he did, my dear, but I do not believe he is impoverished or that he had dishonorable intentions."

"So it's honorable to masquerade as someone else?"

"No, of course not, but—"

"Your heart has always been far too soft, my dear," he interrupted.

She fixed his gaze then. "Maybe so, my dear, but if I'd listened to others when you were pursuing me, I'd never have married you."

He returned the look for a moment, and then cleared his throat. "That was different."

"Was it? Your amorous reputation, if my family had

known of it, would have been sufficient for them to have put a stop to all thought of our match."

"My reputation was exaggerated in the extreme, and *I* didn't pretend to be someone I wasn't!"

"Possibly not, but nevertheless you *were* misjudged," she replied quietly.

He exhaled. "Where exactly is this leading?" he asked patiently.

"I merely wish you to hear what Jane has to say, and *then* make your judgment." She glanced unhappily toward the window. "It may already be too late, of course, for we have no idea where he has gone, or how to find him."

"You are somewhat premature, my dear, for Jane may yet tell us that he forced himself upon her."

"In front of us he told her that he loved her and that his intentions were entirely honorable. Maybe I'm a poor judge, but I believed him," she replied. "I beg of you, please speak to Jane before you leap to any final conclusion."

"It goes against the grain to be lenient when such a gross deception has been perpetrated."

"I know that Jane has said she doesn't want to see him again, but that was in the heat of the moment. Her whole future happiness may be at stake if the wrong decision is taken now. And it *is* Saint Valentine's Eve," she added.

"My dear—"

"Please," she pleaded. "All I request is that you ask Jane about it all."

"Oh, very well."

"Thank you."

Jane was still weeping into her pillow when her father came to her room. His anger was immense as he saw how distressed she was, but he bore his wife's request in mind and sat gently beside her, putting a comforting hand out to her.

"Jane?"

She tried to quell the sobs and sat up miserably, wiping her tear-reddened eyes. She had discarded her riding hat, and her russet hair had fallen loose from its pins. Several soft curls clung to her hot face.

"Oh, my dear," he said gently, brushing the hair back.

"I'm s-sorry, Father," she whispered, still trying unsuccessfully to compose herself.

"What happened?"

"I-I was fooled, I really be-believed he was Mr. V-Vining ..."

"I know. Jane, forgive me but I have to ask you this, did he, er ... ?"

Her breath caught. "No!"

"I ask your pardon for putting such a dreadful question to you, my dear, but when a man comes to this house, under the guise of being your future husband and carries out that pretense so successfully—"

"He didn't seduce me," she said quickly, but she couldn't quite meet his eyes.

He put his hand to her cheek. "But he did take advantage in some way?"

The touch of his hand reminded her of Felix, and she drew sharply away.

"Did he take advantage in any way at all, Jane?" he repeated.

She was silent.

"I can only presume that he did." Mr. Martin got up angrily. Damn the fellow, damn him to hell and back!

"Father, he didn't do anything I did not welcome."

"Welcome?" He turned swiftly to look at her.

She lowered her eyes guiltily. "He kissed me."

"And that is all?"

"Yes."

He was taken aback by the admission. "You met

him for the first time yesterday, and actually permitted such an intimacy in that short time?"

She nodded. "I–I thought I loved him," she whispered. "When I first saw him yesterday I liked him so very much, and I thought he liked me as well. I believed he was Mr. Vining, right up until—"

"Until the moment I exposed him as an imposter!"

"No, I knew before then."

"Before?" He stared.

She explained how she'd suddenly realized the truth. "That's why I ran into the house as I did, and why he followed me."

"I see. So, if you hadn't put two and two together, he probably wouldn't have confessed?"

"It—it didn't happen quite like that. You see, I think he was about to tell me when I saw the coat-of-arms on his carriage door and realized something was wrong."

"Jane, do you have any idea at all why this Mr. Vestey should do what he did?"

"No. I know nothing whatsoever about him."

"And you are quite adamant that he didn't force himself upon you?"

"Yes."

He drew a long breath. "You were very unwise indeed to permit him to kiss you."

"I know." She looked away, shame suffusing her cheeks. But she couldn't help remembering the sweetness of the embrace in the gallery, and the ecstasy of those few stolen moments in the coach house. . . .

"Am I to take it that this association is now at an end?" He didn't quite know how to word the question. All he knew was that his wife's warnings about Jane's future happiness now rang clearly in his ears.

She nodded. "Yes. I don't ever wish to see him again."

"That is your final word?"

"Yes."

He studied her for a moment, and then accepted what she said. "Very well, the matter is closed."

"You won't mention it again?"

"No."

Fresh tears stung her eyes. "Thank you," she whispered.

His heart ached for her, and he went to drop a kiss on her forehead. Then he left.

As he went down the staircase to the hall, he saw his wife waiting anxiously at the bottom.

"What did she say, my dear?" she asked.

"That she doesn't ever want to see him again," he replied.

"And you believed her?"

"Yes."

Mrs. Martin glanced toward the top of the stairs. Her feminine intuition told her that Jane didn't mean what she said.

Mr. Martin paused when he reached her. "I know that look in your eye, my dear, but she is quite firm. She doesn't want the subject mentioned again, and I gave her my word that it wouldn't be."

Jane's mother glanced up the staircase again, still not convinced, but she didn't say anything more because at that moment someone knocked at the front door.

The butler hastened to answer. It was the son of the landlord at the Barge Inn, and the butler was outraged at his audacity in coming to the front door. "Be off with you, the back entrance is for the likes of you!"

The boy dodged a cuff on the ear. "I got a message for Mr. Martin!" he cried, keeping out of reach in the rain as he waved a note at the butler.

"A message?"

"From the swell at the inn."

The butler hesitated, guessing that the "swell" must be the gentleman who'd just departed so ignominiously. He glanced uncertainly back toward Mr. and Mrs. Martin, not sure what to do.

Mr. Martin was about to tell the boy to take the note back to the inn, when his wife nodded at the butler. "Bring it here," she said.

Her husband frowned. "My dear, I—"

"You may believe Jane when she says she doesn't want to see Mr. Vestey again, but I don't," she replied, taking the note from the butler and handing it to her husband. Dripping wet, the boy waited outside to see if there was a reply.

Mr. Martin unfolded the paper with ill grace, and read the hastily written lines. *Sir, I apologize most sincerely for my deceit, but swear again that my intentions were entirely honorable. I beg you to come to the inn and allow me to try to explain, for if my actions have seemed unworthy, I promise you that the opposite is the case. Your daughter means everything to me, and I crave your indulgence, gentleman to gentleman, to put my case to you. If, at the end, you still wish me to leave, then you have my word upon it. I am, sir, your obedient servant, Felix Vestey.*

His wife read it as well, and then looked earnestly at him. "We must go to him, my dear."

"We? Perhaps I should point out that the note is addressed to me, gentleman to gentleman," he replied.

"I must be there, to hear exactly what he has to say."

"Well, I have no intention of going anywhere, and I forbid you to either."

"If we don't, we may regret it forever." She put a hand on his arm. "For Jane's sake, my dear," she urged.

He sighed and then pocketed the note. "Oh, very well, for I can see you will not leave the matter alone." He nodded at the butler. "Tell the boy that Mrs. Martin and I will come to the inn at seven."

Mrs. Martin shook her head. "We must go now, my dear," she said to her husband.

Mr. Martin refused to be budged. "I have just arrived from Bath, and I intend to change out of these clothes and then eat. After that I intend to write to Sir Horace Vining informing him of his son's disgraceful and unbecoming conduct, and then I mean to rest for a few hours."

"But—"

"If Vestey is so anxious to put his case, he'll wait," he replied, nodding at the butler again. "My message stands."

"Sir." The butler bowed and returned to the boy, who was given a coin and the response to Felix's note.

As the boy hurried away through the rain, Mr. Martin looked firmly at his wife. "That is my last word on the matter for the moment, my dear," he said, before going to the staircase and then halting again. "I trust the cook has something tasty prepared for me?"

Mrs. Martin stared at him. Their daughter's heart was breaking, and he thought only of his stomach? "I, er, believe there is a pigeon pie . . ."

"Excellent." He inclined his head and then proceeded up the staircase.

Mrs. Martin gazed crossly after him, and then turned to look at the long case clock that stood at the other end of the hall. Seven o'clock was hours away yet, and it seemed like a lifetime to a mother impatient to put matters right for her distraught child.

The inn was lamplit and busy. Barges had moored alongside for the night, and two stagecoaches were waiting outside while their passengers snatched the hasty meal they were allowed. The fiddler was playing again, and there was much stamping and clapping as people danced to the strains of "Over the hills and far away."

It had stopped raining and the sky was clear and

starlit as the carriage from Priors Court halted close
by. The coachman had been instructed not to stop
directly at the door, and Mr. Martin wore his greatcoat
collar turned up and his tall hat pulled low over his
forehead, for he did not particularly wish to be observed by all and sundry calling upon the gentleman
who must by now be notorious in the neighborhood
for having been thrown out of Priors Court after pretending to be Jane's husband-to-be. Such goings-on
were bound to have leaked out, and Mr. Martin
wished now that he hadn't given in to his wife's pleas.
A dignified silence would have been far preferable,
but it was too late, and he was committed to hearing
what Felix Vestey had to say.

Jane's mother wore a hooded cloak, and she paused
for a moment to look up at the stars before going
inside. It was a perfect St. Valentine's Eve. At least,
she prayed it soon would be. Every instinct told her
to trust Felix, although why she couldn't say. She
hoped her judgment was to be relied upon, for if she
was wrong, then she had insisted upon giving a rogue
a second chance!

She turned to accept her husband's arm, but as she
did she noticed the scowling figure of Jem Randle
standing outside one of the inn windows, staring in at
the merrymaking from which he had been banned. A
shudder of distaste passed through her, for there was
something about him that made her skin crawl. She
could well understand how Jane's unfortunate maid
loathed being pursued by him.

Mr. Martin didn't observe Jem as he ushered his
wife toward the inn door, but just as they entered,
they encountered someone coming out. It was the
gamekeeper, Jack Johnson, the object of Peg Weston's
Valentine strategem. He was a burly, ruddy-complex-
ioned young man with thick black hair and shining
brown eyes, and was exceedingly youthful to be head
gamekeeper of an estate as large as Priors Court. But

he had learned his craft from his late father, and had been brought up to the life. There were few game-keepers more astute or more dedicated.

Catching a glimpse of Mr. Martin's face in the lamp-light, he halted in surprise. "Sir?"

"Johnson." Jane's father replied reluctantly, annoyed at having been perceived almost immediately.

Jack had heard all about events at Priors Court, for the inn was positively buzzing with the tale, but he gave no sign. "Begging your pardon, sir, but I request the opportunity to speak to you urgently first thing in the morning."

"Urgently?"

Seeing Jem lurking nearby, Jack lowered his voice. "Poachers have been at work in the east wood, sir, and I'm about to lie in wait and see if I can identify them, although I doubt if they'll be out on a night like this. It's too bright, especially with the full moon about to come up. . . ."

"Oh, do get to the point, man!" Mr. Martin snapped impatiently, for he wished to get the business with Felix over and done with.

Glancing back at Jem again, Jack whispered guardedly. "Forgive me, sir, but I have a strong suspicion that Randle is one of them."

Mr. Martin looked toward the silent figure by the window. "What is it exactly that you wish to see me about?" he asked.

"It's just that I must discuss with you how best to deal with the problem. I'm sure there's a good few in the gang, so I'll need organized help if I'm to put a stop to it."

Mr. Martin nodded quickly. "Yes, yes, call in the morning and we'll discuss it in detail."

"Would nine be convenient, sir?"

"Yes. I'm not doing anything in particular tomorrow."

"Thank you, sir." Jack touched his hat and then

hurried on into the night. He hummed to himself as he went, for the poachers weren't his only reason for going to Priors Court the following morning. He had a Valentine gift to leave at Weston's bedroom door, and he meant to get there before the maid was up and about. Maybe she wasn't interested in the likes of him, but he had to at least try.

The landlord himself conducted Mr. and Mrs. Martin discreetly upstairs to Felix. "This is the room, sir," he said, bowing and then hurrying away.

Mr. Martin took a long breath and then knocked.

"Come in."

The room was lit by a fire and a solitary candle, and the draft from the open doorway made the flames flutter for a moment. It was a clean, simply furnished chamber, and Felix was lying on the bed in his shirt and breeches, for it was warm in the room. On seeing who came in, he leapt to his feet and donned his coat to face them.

Mr. Martin closed the door, and as soon as his wife was comfortably seated in a chair by the fire, he turned to Felix. "Well, sir?"

"I'm very grateful to you for allowing me this opportunity to—"

"I don't want any pretty speeches, sirrah. I want an explanation for your disgraceful conduct."

Felix lowered his eyes for a moment. "I realize how my behavior must seem to you both, but I didn't set out to deceive your daughter."

"I find that hard to believe, Mr. Vestey. I suspect collusion between you and Vining."

"No, sir, that isn't so, at least not in the way you believe." Felix searched Mr. Martin's face. "Do I take it from your tone that you encountered Francis in Bath?"

"Yes, sir, you do. And do I take it from your question that you knew all about his, er, liaison?"

"I did know, yes." Felix shifted his position awkwardly. "Francis obliged me to come to Priors Court to make his excuses. I was to tell you he was unwell and regretted being unable to call as planned."

"Obliged you?"

"Yes, sir. I had refused to do it, but he called in a debt of honor."

"Go on."

"Before calling at the house I halted here at this inn to have a midday meal that proved so indigestible that I felt the need to walk for a while afterward. I saw your daughter and her maid on the bridge over the backwater behind the inn."

Mrs. Martin nodded. "Yes, Jane and the maid did go out yesterday at about that time."

Felix glanced at Mr. Martin. "Sir, I'm ashamed to say that I eavesdropped upon them. I knew your daughter because I'd seen the miniature she sent to Francis. I found her utterly charming, enchantingly so, and I thought her far too good for someone like Francis, who hasn't a scrupulous or faithful bone in his body. By the time they left the bridge, I knew I couldn't consign her to the wretchedness of being his wife, and I therefore went to the house with the express intention of informing you about the real nature of the man your daughter was to marry."

"You are very free with your criticisms of a man who obviously regards you as his friend," Mr. Martin observed coolly.

"The fact that he is my friend doesn't blind me to his faults, sir, and he has them by the legion. That doesn't make him unlikable. Francis is selfish and willful, but he has good qualities as well."

"I have failed to unearth a single one, sir. Anyway, proceed with your tale."

"I arrived at Priors Court at the same time that Miss Martin and her maid returned, and Miss Martin mistook me for Francis because she saw my signet ring. Francis and I have the same initials." Felix paused, remembering the moment his deception had commenced. "I didn't even realize I was going to do it," he said softly. "She thought I was Francis, and I found myself confirming it. I couldn't help myself. From the first moment I saw her on the bridge, I knew how I felt about her. I had no right, I admit it, but she is the most exquisite, delightful, perfect creature in the world."

"I fear she does not regard you in a similar light, sir," Mr. Martin replied trenchantly.

"No, I don't suppose she does. I know how badly I've behaved."

"Badly? Sir, your conduct has been monstrous!" Mr. Martin snapped.

Mrs. Martin got up and put a gentle hand on her husband's arm. "It is only monstrous if Mr. Vestey is unworthy, my dear."

"Of course he's unworthy!"

She looked at Felix. "Are you, sir?"

"No, madam, I am the Honorable Felix Vestey, son and heir of Lord Northwood of Northwood Castle. Your servant." Felix bowed.

Mr. Martin was taken aback. "Lord Northwood's son?" he repeated.

"Yes, sir."

Mrs. Martin smiled at her husband. "Do you still regard him as unworthy?" she murmured. She knew the man she'd married only too well. The whole point of the Vining match had been to ally Jane with a titled family. Felix Vestey was evidently an even finer catch.

Mr. Martin cleared his throat. "And you insist that your intentions have been honorable, Mr. Vestey?"

"I do, sir. If I could only have your permission to pay proper court to your daughter—" Felix broke off desperately. "Mr. Martin, I know at the moment she probably despises the very sound of my name, but given a little time, maybe I can win her heart again."

Mr. Martin pursed his lips. "Anything is possible, sir, but right now she considers herself to have been gravely wronged, and I have to say that I agree with her."

But Mrs. Martin smiled a little. "My dear, if you consider this objectively, you will conclude that although Jane was wooed under false pretenses, she was actually wooed for herself. There was no ulterior motive in Mr. Vestey's conduct, no interest in her fortune et cetera. He was simply smitten to the heart. And if she can only be made to see that, and to admit that she welcomed his advances because she is equally smitten, then we will have a very satisfactory conclusion to this tangle. Do you not agree?"

Mr. Martin hesitated. "I know my daughter, and she will *never* agree to meet Mr. Vestey again. She can be very stubborn when she chooses."

"Yes, she takes after you in that respect," Mrs. Martin murmured, and then added more briskly. "Very well, if we accept that she cannot be persuaded by reason, then she must be tricked into it."

"Tricked?" her husband repeated. "How?"

Felix looked at her. "I am open to anything you suggest, Mrs. Martin," he said earnestly.

She smiled. "Excellent, for I believe I have a plan. It concerns a Saint Valentine's Day meeting on a bridge between a maid and a gamekeeper, only the maid must be replaced by her mistress, and the gamekeeper by you, sir. You no doubt recall the meeting to which I refer?"

He nodded. "Yes, it was mentioned at the breakfast table this morning."

Her smile deepened. "If Jane were to think that Peg Weston was going to the bridge to find not Jack Johnson but the odious Jem Randle waiting for her, I am quite convinced she would rush off to warn the maid." She turned to her husband. "You, my dear, must delay your meeting with Jack. He's calling at the house at nine, and the maid intends to be on the bridge at ten. Keep him kicking his heels before you deign to come down. He won't leave until he's spoken to you. I'm sure you can manage that, can't you?" Her glance defied him to argue.

He didn't utter a word.

She returned her attention to Felix. "You are to be on that bridge at ten in the morning, and wait there while I do the rest."

"I will be there," he replied, stepping forward to raise her hand to his lips. "You will never know how grateful I am to you, madam."

She flushed a little. "Don't thank me yet, sir, for there is still the little obstacle of Jane herself, but at least you may rely upon me to do all I can, especially on Saint Valentine's Day. If it is possible to alarm Jane into coming to the bridge to warn Peg, then I will do it. Between now and then I will give the fine details my complete attention."

Mr. Martin sighed. "I can't see this working," he muttered.

His wife nudged him with her elbow. "Don't be so pessimistic, my dear. Even if it doesn't, I won't admit defeat. It will be a case of try, try, and try again until Jane is driven to agreeing to meet Mr. Vestey out of sheer weariness. I'm quite capable."

"I know," he replied with feeling.

She raised an eyebrow. "I don't believe that was a compliment, but I shall ignore it. Now then, we must return to the house and drum the maid into the plot. Come."

When they'd gone, Felix went to the window and drew the curtains aside to stare out at the silver countryside. The moon was bright, and the Thames shone like a metallic ribbon. From here he could just see the bridge where he prayed he would win Jane's heart again. He closed his eyes for a moment. If there was any substance to St. Valentine's Day, then by this time tomorrow Jane would be his.

It was very cold and clear as Jack Johnson crossed the frosty park with a small package in his hand. He was well wrapped against the morning chill, and his breath stood out in clouds as he walked. The package contained his Valentine gift for Peg, a pair of green gloves he'd purchased in Oxford. He knew he ran the risk of being seen as he crept up through the house to leave the package by the her door, and half of him feared being caught in case Peg spurned him completely. But his other half wanted to be discovered, to bring his love out into the open and learn once and for all whether she liked him or not. One thing was certain, he couldn't stand much more of *not* knowing! Over a year it had gone on now, and it was driving him witless.

A flock of rooks rose noisily from the nearby woods, and he paused, his brows drawing together as he watched the disturbed birds wheeling in the icy morning air. Well, whatever had startled them, it wasn't Jem Randle and his crowd, for they'd had a fine old fright last night when he'd shouted out just as they were laying their snares. Talk about rabbits, they'd scattered like they had warrens! He hadn't caught any of them, but he'd seen a few faces, some of them he would never have expected to find out at such work. Next time he lay in wait, he'd hopefully have a gang of Mr. Martin's men to back him, ferrets to catch the rabbits.

He walked on to the house and entered the kitchens, where the early staff, including the cook, were already at their work. The smell of baking hung in the warm air, for Valentine buns were obligatory at breakfast today, and the first of the delicious little currant and carraway seed cakes were cooling on the scrubbed oak table. Everyone greeted the gamekeeper and then went on with their tasks, and no one noticed as he slipped up the back staircase. He made his way quietly through the house toward the attic story, keeping out of sight as a chambermaid emerged from one room to carry a heavy scuttle of coal into the next. As soon as he heard her raking the fire, he hurried on. He knew which room was Peg's because she'd mentioned once that it was in the northwest corner.

There were sounds from some of the other attic rooms as he passed, for it was nearing the time for everyone to be up and about. His heart was pounding as at last he reached Peg's door, but just as he bent to place the package on the floor, the door opened. Startled, he stepped back as he found himself face to face with Peg herself. She was already dressed and ready to go down, and her hair was neat beneath a newly laundered mob cap.

She stared at him. "Jack? What on earth are you—?"

"I, er, brought you this, Peg." He held out the package. His face was as red as beetroot, and he was filled with such a mixture of feelings that he didn't know what to do.

She looked at the package and then smiled slowly, her eyes beginning to shine incredulously. The disappointment she'd felt at having her careful plans appropriated suddenly lifted. "Is it a Valentine gift, Jack?" she breathed.

"Er . . . yes." He pushed it into her hand.

She opened the package, and her lips parted with delight as she saw the gloves. "Oh, they're beautiful!"

"I, er, was afraid to . . ." His voice died away and he shuffled his feet awkwardly. Dear God above, this was harder than trying to trap Jem Randle and his lot! His face felt as if it were on fire, and he was so embarrassed that he wished the floor would open up and swallow him. "I, er, I've got to see Mr. Martin, he's expecting me, so I'll go now," he said, turning to leave.

But Peg caught his hand. "Mr. Martin won't come down to see you for a long time yet. I happen to know what's set to go on this morning."

"Set to go on?"

She nodded. "So in the meantime, I have a Valentine gift for you," she said softly, coming closer to him and linking her arms around his neck. "You're the first man I've seen this morning, and that means you're my sweetheart now."

He stared at her, unable to believe what was happening.

She smiled. "Happy Valentine's Day, Jack Johnson," she whispered, reaching up to kiss him on the lips.

He needed no second bidding. In a moment his arms were around her as he returned the kiss.

A little later Jane was very quiet and withdrawn as she sat before the dressing table. She wore a daffodil wool gown with a white lace collar and cuffs, and Peg was putting the final pins in her hair. The maid's eyes were alight with happiness, and with scheming anticipation, the first because of her success with Jack, the second because she knew what was going to transpire for her mistress over the next hour or so. If all went as planned, this St. Valentine's Day was going to be the most wonderful ever for both of them, although as yet poor Miss Jane had no idea at all of what was afoot.

Outside the sun had risen, and the sky was a crystal blue. The frost lingered only in the shadows, and the air was so clear that it was possible to see Faringdon on its distant escarpment. It was a beautiful day, but Jane's spirits were so low that it might as well have been dismal and raining.

Peg put the comb down. "Will there be anything else, Miss Jane?"

"Mm?"

"Will there be anything else? Only it's a quarter to ten and ..." The maid allowed her voice to die away on the gentle reminder.

Jane roused herself and managed a smile. "And you must soon be at the bridge to waylay Jack Johnson. Of course you may go, Peg. And good luck."

"Thank you, Miss Jane." Bobbing a curtsy, the maid hurried out, but instead of going to her room to collect her outdoor things, as Jane thought, she went down to the kitchens, where Jack waited.

Jane remained where she was. She gazed at her reflection in the mirror. How dreadful she looked. Her eyes were still sore from crying, and there were shadows beneath her eyes, which as a consequence looked larger than ever. What a sight! And all because she'd been gulled by a clever imposter. She wished she were made of sterner stuff, for then she would be able to weather such wretchedness, but stern stuff was the very last thing in her makeup right now.

She was devastated by what had happened, and found it hard to forgive herself for being so utterly taken in. But she'd enjoyed his kisses. They'd brought her to life, awakening feelings she'd never known before, and if he really had been Francis Vining, then everything would have been magically perfect. But he wasn't Francis, he was someone called Felix Vestey.... Why had he done it? Why had he set out so heartlessly to fool her?

She drew a long breath, trying to compose herself for the ordeal of going down and facing everyone. All the servants would know by now; indeed, it must be the talk of the neighborhood. Word like that traveled like wildfire, and had probably even reached Faringdon by now!

Pulling a bitter face at her reflection, she got up and

took her shawl from the back of the fireside chair, where Peg had left it to warm. The maid would be on her way to the bridge now. May she at least find happiness today. Gathering the shawl around her shoulders, she left the room to go down to breakfast.

The smell of Valentine buns drifted through the house, but she didn't find it at all appetizing. The most she intended to have for breakfast was coffee, for the thought of eating made her feel quite ill. As she reached the dining room she braced herself to go in. Her hand trembled as she opened the door and entered.

Mrs. Martin was seated alone at the table. She wore a frilled apricot dimity gown and a particularly lavish lace day cap threaded with ribbons to match the gown. She had already embarked upon the Valentine buns, and was obviously in a sunny mood as she beamed at her daughter.

"Ah, there you are at last, my dear. I was beginning to think I'd have to eat breakfast entirely on my own. Did you sleep well?"

"Not really."

Her mother waited until she was seated. "You mustn't sink into the doldrums, dear, for no man is worth it. Not even your father."

Jane tried to brighten up. "Where is Father?" she asked.

"Oh, he's closeted with the gamekeeper."

Jane looked swiftly at her. "Are you sure?"

"Perfectly sure."

"Jack Johnson is here at the house?"

Mrs. Martin put her bun down. "Yes, that is what I said. Really, Jane, you are laboring the point somewhat. Why is it of such consequence?"

"Because Peg is hoping to waylay him on the bridge. Don't you remember what I told you yesterday at breakfast?"

Mrs. Martin pretended to be confused for a mo-

ment, and then her eyes cleared. "Oh, yes, of course.
I'd quite forgotten."

"Peg's already gone to the bridge, but if Jack Johnson is here it will all be in vain."

Her mother looked a little uncomfortable. "Oh,
dear. I'm afraid she may be in for a rather disagreeable surprise."

"What do you mean?"

"Well, it's just something my maid mentioned this
morning when I was dressing. Her brother is a friend
of that dreadful Jem Randle, and *he* says Jem plans
to be on the bridge this morning to lie in wait for the
girl he wants as his sweetheart."

Jane stared at her in utter horror. "Jem Randle?"
she

"Yes, I fear so."

In a moment Jane was on her feet. "I must go!"

"But your breakfast, my dear—!"

Jane ran to the door. "I must warn Peg, for it will
be too dreadful for words if she finds herself alone
with Jem Randle!"

"Jane—!" Her mother called after her, but Jane was
already fleeing up the stairs to put on her cloak.

Mrs. Martin smiled to herself and then buttered a
fresh bun. Excellent. It could not have gone better. In
a few minutes now Jane would arrive at the bridge
and find Mr. Vestey waiting for her. After that it was
up to him, and if she was any judge, he would win
the day. He certainly had the looks and charm, and
there was no doubt in her heart that he was truly in
love with her daughter.

Felix leaned on the parapet of the bridge in the
very place where he had first seen Jane. He wore his
greatcoat over a sage green coat and cream breeches,
and his head was bare because he was toying idly with
his hat, turning it slowly in his hands as he gazed down

at the shining water below. Set against a flawless blue
sky, his wavering reflection gazed back at him.

He was beset with anxiety, for he could not endure
it if Jane spurned him. What if her mother was wrong,
and the resentment toward him was permanent? He
drew a long breath. It wouldn't do to be defeated
before he commenced. He had to be confident enough
to make her accept that what he felt toward her was
true love; and then he had to make her admit that the
feeling was mutual. When he recalled how she had
returned his kisses, how willingly she'd come into his
arms, he was certain that she loved him. Maybe she
thought she was kissing Francis Vining, but that made
no difference in the end. It was Felix Vestey she'd
kissed, Felix Vestey she'd smiled at and touched. . . .

Suddenly he heard hurrying footsteps, and he
straightened immediately, for the sound came from
the path to the park. Suddenly she was there. She
wore her cloak, and her hood had slipped back from
her head because she'd hurried all the way from the
house. The pins were dislodged in her hair, and her
russet curls bounced freely about her shoulders. Her
cheeks were flushed from running, and for a moment
she didn't realize he was there.

She had actually stepped onto the bridge before she
halted with a gasp. "You!"

"Jane." He said her name softly as he went toward
her.

"Don't come any closer, sirrah!"

He halted. "I must speak to you, Jane."

"I gave you no leave to address me so familiarly,
sir." She glanced around. "Peg?" she called, wondering where the maid was.

"There isn't anyone else here, Jane."

"My maid—"

"Is at the house as far as I know."

"I don't understand."

"You have been sent here in order for me to speak to you."

She stared at him. "That isn't so! My mother told me—"

"A Saint Valentine's Day fib," he interrupted quietly.

She drew back. "This is another of your clever lies, is it not?"

He shook his head. "No, Jane, it isn't a lie. Your mother deliberately sent you."

"No!"

He smiled a little, longing to touch her. "She didn't tell you that Jack Johnson is at the house with your father? Or that Jem Randle would be lying in wait here for your maid?"

Her lips parted. "How do you know that?" she whispered.

"Because your parents came to see me at the Barge last night, and they believed what I had to say."

"That is untrue."

"No, Jane, it's very true indeed."

She was scornful. "Well, I suppose it might be, for you tell a very pretty story, do you not, Mr. Vestey?"

"I told them the truth."

"And now you think to convince me as well?"

"I hope so."

She tossed her head. "I no longer listen to fairy stories, sir!"

"No, you read poems. How do the words go now? Ah, yes, I recall them clearly:

"Those awful words 'Till death do part'
May well alarm the youthful heart:
No after-thought when once a wife;
The die is cast, and cast for life;

"You see? I paid great attention to the page you'd marked. The sentiments expressed in that poem affected me greatly, for they would have applied to you if you'd married Francis Vining. He's very well known to me, and I can tell you categorically that you would have been very unhappy indeed if the match had proceeded."

"You would say that, wouldn't you?" she replied, looking away. She should turn her back on him, stalk away with her nose in the air, and regain at least a little of her lost pride. But she couldn't. Something compelled her to stay.

"He asked me to come to Priors Court, oh, not to impersonate him, I admit, but to offer his excuses so that he could wriggle out of coming himself. He preferred to pursue an actress to Bath, where, you will discover, he was found out by your father."

She stared at him.

He turned to point along the path leading to the inn. "Do you see that bend where the reeds are particularly high?"

"Yes."

"I was standing there the day you and your maid were on this bridge, and I heard everything you said. After that I couldn't do as Francis wished. I came to Priors Court intending to tell your father the truth about Francis, so that you would be released from certain unhappiness. Then you saw my ring and mistook me for Francis, and ..." He hesitated. "And I was already so in love with you that I allowed the mistake to continue."

"You expect me to believe that you fell in love with me at first sight?"

"It is the truth."

"No, sir, it is as false a claim as every other you've made."

"To what purpose?" he demanded.

She shrugged. "No doubt you have need of a fortune," she replied crushingly, determined to have her revenge, verbally at least.

He smiled. "The future Viscount Northwood of Northwood Castle has no need to seek a fortune, Jane," he said softly.

Her eyes flew to his face. "The future—?"

"Viscount Northwood."

She raised her chin defiantly. "Then your deception is even more reprehensible, sir."

"I know my conduct has been despicable, Jane, but my purpose was honorable, I swear."

"Honorable? I find that hard to credit," she replied scathingly.

"Do you? Then perhaps I should point out that I find your present protests equally as hard to fully credit. I don't recall being rebuffed when I kissed you."

Fresh color flooded her cheeks. "I–I believed you were Mr. Vining."

"*I* was the one who came here, the one you smiled at, the one whose kisses you welcomed. It was me, not Francis. Tell me, Jane, if your match had really been with me, would you have complained?"

She didn't reply.

"Have you nothing to say?" he asked softly, moving a little closer.

She didn't back away. "I . . . I can't answer," she said.

"Why? Because you don't know? Or because you know full well but won't admit it?"

"It doesn't make any difference. The fact remains that—"

"That you enjoyed my kisses," he interrupted. He was close enough to touch her, but he held back. "You did enjoy my kisses, Jane, no matter how you may feign the opposite now."

"I don't need to be reminded of my foolishness, sir. You took me in completely, and I thought I was the most fortunate of creatures in finding my arranged match was . . ." She didn't finish.

"Was what, Jane? Set to prove a love match instead?"

She lowered her eyes.

"That *is* what you were going to say, isn't it? You were overjoyed because you believed we would be more than happy together. That's why I made so bold as to kiss you, and why you returned those kisses." He paused. "I was going to tell you who I really was. If it hadn't been for those two damned grooms coming into the coach house—"

"I'd like to think you're being honest now, Mr. Vestey, but I cannot trust you."

He searched her eyes, always so expressive, and saw the deep hurt written there. "I love you, Jane," he whispered, touching her at last.

She flinched and turned away, but he caught her arms and moved close behind her. "I love you, Jane," he said again, breathing in her perfume.

Tears filled her eyes. "Leave me alone, sir, for I want nothing more to do with you."

"I don't believe you," he breathed, bending his head to kiss her neck.

She shivered and closed her eyes. Oh, Felix, Felix . . .

"Do you still deny you love me?" he asked, his lips still moving against her skin.

The tears were wet on her cheeks.

Slowly he turned her to face him. "Jane, this is Saint Valentine's Day, a day for lovers, and we are lovers, whether you admit it or not. I came here to save you from one marriage, but now I want to ensnare you in another. I want you to marry me, to become the future Lady Northwood."

She stared at him, her heart almost stopping within her.

He smiled, brushing the tears from her cheeks. "And in case you suspect me of more deception, let me shout it aloud. Marry me, Jane!" He raised his voice for the last three words.

Two farm workers strolling along one of the paths halted to stare, and some ducks fled from beneath the bridge, wings flapping noisily as they trod the water.

Felix smiled at her. "Shall I shout it again?"

"No."

"Do you believe me?"

Fresh tears shimmered in her eyes, and she nodded.

"Oh, my darling," he breathed, slipping a loving arm around her, then tilting her lips to meet his.

She melted into his embrace, meeting the kiss with an eagerness born of sheer elation. Suddenly all her unhappiness lifted, and the misery of the past hours might never have been. This man had come to her as an imposter, but now he was revealed in his true colors, honorable, loving, ardent, and everything else she could ever have wished.

St. Valentine's Day had worked its spell, reversing the misery and replacing it with unconditional ecstasy. She forgot the men on the path, forgot everything but the rapture of loving and being loved.

By the year 2000, 2 out of 3 Americans could be illiterate.

It's true.

Today, 75 million adults...about one American in three, can't read adequately. And by the year 2000, U.S. News & World Report envisions an America with a literacy rate of only 30%.

Before that America comes to be, you can stop it...by joining the fight against illiteracy today.

Call the Coalition for Literacy at toll-free **1-800-228-8813** and volunteer.

Volunteer Against Illiteracy. The only degree you need is a degree of caring.